PYRRHUS
VENTURE

Randolph Dominic
and
William David Barry

PYRRHUS
VENTURE

An Atlantic Monthly Press Book
Little, Brown and Company   Boston/Toronto

FIRST EDITION

Library of Congress Cataloging in Publication Data

Dominic, Randolph.
  Pyrrhus Venture.
  "An Atlantic Monthly Press book."
  I. Barry, William David. II. Title.
PS3554.O463P9 1983   813'.54   83-9372
ISBN 0-316-18934-0

ATLANTIC–LITTLE, BROWN BOOKS
ARE PUBLISHED BY
LITTLE, BROWN AND COMPANY
IN ASSOCIATION WITH
THE ATLANTIC MONTHLY PRESS

VB

Designed by Dede Cummings

Published simultaneously in Canada
by Little, Brown & Company (Canada) Limited

PRINTED IN THE UNITED STATES OF AMERICA

Respectfully dedicated to Martin Dibner

I

THE BOY

❦❦❦ I ❦❦❦

I CARRIED away from Freetown two things only: my grandson, William, and the heavy smell of rotting vegetation. This last clung to the ship for days after Sierra Leone had dipped below the horizon, so that I welcomed the squalls we encountered off the Cape Verdes, with their cleansing wind and rain. After weeks in the tropics the fresh breeze was doubly grateful, but it soon departed and left behind fog and the lightest of airs.

Fog I would as lief do without, for the dampness gripes my bones, yet there is that about the sight of fog on the ocean which puts me in mind of my home at Portland in the Province of Maine, and my neighbor Billy Hans, who saved the *Phoenix* schooner from being run on the rocks near Portland Head. There was talk afterward that Billy had invented a system of navigation vastly improved over Bowditch, which worked as well in fog as in clear weather. That this should be seemed strange, for Billy was no seaman, nor yet a geometer, but a decayed pensioner of Washington's army, and so fond of the bottle that he could scarce find his way from Marston's tavern home to Spring Street.

Old Joseph McLellan, who owned the schooner and other vessels beside, sent for Billy and offered him a substantial sum to reveal his method. Billy refused, saying that he had use for it himself, whereupon Joseph told him he might navigate to hell if he liked, and would have nothing more to do with him whatever. In the taverns people whispered that the secret had to do with finding Captain Kidd's treasure. Billy drank their rum and kept his own counsel, so that his reputation endured for some time.

In his age the street boys had come to make sport of Billy. He was much afflicted by the pain of his wounds and by what is known down our way as "that tired feeling," for both of which rum is the proper specific. Though no doubloons appeared, Billy eked out his pension by doing odd jobs and with gifts from those of us old enough to remember him in other guise, so that he seldom went without. I employed him as much as any, and he seemed to regard me as his friend. When properly medicated he would talk as long as I would listen, and one night I asked him for the tale.

"Master Venture," said Billy, tapping the side of his nose with a gnarled forefinger, "this was the way of it: there was shoals to starboard and rocks to port, but I conned her through by following the smell of Squire Ilsley's distillery."

When I told the story over dinner, our captain earned himself a laugh by observing that, as with most Yankee inventions, there was nothing to Billy's but vapors. Captain Woolsely having suffered me to sit at his table (albeit below the salt), I thought it unmannerly to mention either Franklin's Gulf Stream, which confounded the English for years, or the quality of his own navigation, which I have good reason to question.

When the captain called for his port, I excused myself and looked in upon William. He was sleeping soundly. Rather than disturb him, I went for a turn on deck.

It having been exceedingly close in the cabin, it was some time before I noted that the air on deck seemed likewise tainted. It was faint enough at first, almost bucolic, although our ship lay some hundreds of leagues from the nearest barnyard. I peered to windward, but there was naught to be seen save the curling mist. Almost had I set it all down to homesickness when the table below adjourned and the diners emerged from the companion.

Meanwhile the odor had increased, so that when the captain came on deck, last as befit his station, he noticed it immediately. He sniffed and looked about him curiously, and bade the watch keep a weather eye. Our late companions had marked it as well. "We are in the lee of a dead whale," quoth one. "No, a floating pigsty," another offered.

"Look sharp, sirs," Captain Woolsely said, smiling the while at his own wit, " 'tis Father Noah and his ark you smell." He looked around amid the laughter and hailed me familiarly.

"Ah, Venture! What a smell! A pity your countryman isn't with us to riddle it out."

At his invitation I joined the group and clustered on the windward rail, but there was little enough to see. We might have been sailing in Limbo. Before and behind the fog seemed to part and then close about the vessel as though enchanted. The jesters fell silent, so that we ghosted along with only the gurgling of the ship's wake in our ears, and all the while the musky smell grew stronger.

The same Providence that had decreed we should meet in the trackless Atlantic preserved us from a collision that must have been fatal, though we passed within yards of the schooner. Clipper-built, she was, with gratings to her hatchways and a brass carronade amidships. Her long black hull was built for speed, and with all sail set to the royals, she ran before the wind as though all the fiends of the Pit pursued her. From her gaff she flaunted the red and gold of Spain.

The nightmare craft hissed past us, forecastle, waist, and quarterdeck, her inhuman stench almost a palpable thing. *"Hijo de puta!"* I shouted at the scowling helmsman. I saw him stiffen with rage just as the fog swallowed the vessel once more.

I straightened up and looked about me. My companions seemed frozen into immobility. I disengaged my aching fingers from the rail and turned to go below.

Captain Woolsely grasped my arm to stay my departure. "What did you say to him?" he asked.

"You speak no Spanish, Captain?" It was not quite a question, my tone not quite polite. I could sense the other passengers watching me intently. "That schooner was a slaver, Captain Woolsely. Bound, no doubt, for Havana, under the terms of the English treaty." I looked him firmly in the eye. "There will be five hundred men and women aboard that schooner. I called him a son of a whore.

"Now, sir, by your leave, I shall go below and look in on my grandson." I glanced significantly at his hand, and it fell from my arm.

William was sleeping so soundly that even my entry into our tiny cabin, not quite six feet square, did not wake him. It was dark, and for some time I lay in the gloom of my berth before rousing myself to light the lantern.

In the uncertain light I looked over at William. His tawny features were calm in repose, but his small hands were balled into loose fists. I reached out and ran my wrinkled hand over his close-cropped head.

"We're going home, William," I murmured. I opened my old sea chest and the smell of camphor filled the cabin. Home! I thought: please God, William, you will know what that word means, though it has taken me a lifetime, and the death of a son, to learn. I looked at the boy again. Suddenly it seemed as though the weight of my years bore down upon me with the knowledge that, approaching as I do the Biblical limit of threescore years and ten, I should not live to see this boy grown to man's estate.

It was a chilling realization, one which I had sought to avoid since setting sail from Casco Bay six months past. William! I thought once more: there is so much to help you learn, and so little time.

I found my hand upon a hard object among my spare linen and withdrew it, thinking to escape my despair in a book. No book this was, but the mahogany lap desk my good wife Sarah had given me on my departure. I sat back on the berth and opened it.

Paper, ink, castor, and a sheaf of quills lay within, each in its own place. Would that life were so simple! It was still unused; I had written Sarah no letters, and there is no one else in the world to whom I would care to write save William, who is some years too young to read. Yet as I sat in the light of the one flickering lantern, it came to me that here was my answer. I took a pen in hand and began to write: this book, this letter, if you will, to my sleeping grandson.

Of my own origins and antecedents I know but little, which has always seemed to me to be one of the most subtly pernicious aspects of the system called slavery: not only is one deprived of his future, but of his past as well. I was born: of that at least I may be certain. It seems likely that the date of this event was 1751 or thereabouts, which would make me five and sixty in this year, but beyond the bare fact of my birth all is conjecture.

I assume that I was born a slave, on the island of Saint Christopher (familiarly called Saint Kitts) in the Leeward Islands of the West Indies. There I lived with my master, Tiberius Fitzgore; his nephew and ward, Frederick, by a year or so my senior; and a few servants, in the house Fitzgore called Lockewood, located on the outskirts of Basseterre, by the road from the anchorage to Saint Peter's church. It has pleased me at times to think otherwise, but in all probability I was originally obtained as a playmate for young Frederick, either by purchase outright or in settlement of some trifling debt owed my master by a neighboring planter. Retiring by nature and a self-styled *philosophe* by inclination, Fitzgore was yet a merchant by trade, and from the sale of English manufacture, French wines, and suchlike luxuries to the agrarian gentry derived an adequate income with a minimum of attention.

My yoke, such as it was, was a mild one. My entire duty was that of being companion to Frederick, and Fitzgore provided for me in the same benevolent but rather absentminded manner. We were clothed alike and fed at the same table, and I was given my own room in the main house, rather than sleeping apart in the servants' quarters. As children will, I accepted my estate without question, and so, in those carefree days, did Frederick. We were in the nominal charge of Atticus the butler, but in general life at Lockewood flowed by us with little notice taken on either side save when we were scolded for the holes we dug in the garden, or for sneaking down to listen to the terrifying stories which the gardener told and which Atticus affected not to believe. Two small boys in a household otherwise entirely populated by adults, we lived like a particolored pair of brothers.

In the year before the French war began, one Abijah Hartshorn, *Artium Baccalaureus*, was engaged as Frederick's tutor. At the time it seemed only natural that Fitzgore should take me for his Emile, designing me, I suppose, a philosopher. In any event I took my seat at Frederick's side and learned my letters from that jilted Bostonian as he did. Or perhaps not exactly as he: honesty compels me to admit that my lessons came more easily to me than ever Frederick's did to him. To Hartshorn's many pointed remarks on this head I attribute the tragic rivalry that, unsought and unbeknownst to me, sprang up between Frederick and myself.

Though our course of study was in some respects haphazard, I took to my lessons with an avidity that gratified my mentor, however frustrated he may have been by Fitzgore's meddling in matters of curriculum. Though I was an active lad with an inquiring mind, there was little system to what I had been taught, and I knew next to nothing of practical value. Almost all I had seen of the world beyond Lockewood's cloistered gardens I had glimpsed on the seldom Sundays when Fitzgore took us to services in Irish-Town, the western section of Basseterre. Fitzgore, himself an Irishman, owned their Popish faith (to which he occasionally relapsed) as well as a catholic curiosity which made him but an indifferent practitioner of any creed, whether secular or divine.

To our own rare appearances and the reports of the few visitors to Lockewood I trace a rumor that crept adderlike into this idyll one afternoon as I sat reading in the spacious flowered parterre before the house. I was perhaps twelve years of age: I assume that the incident occurred after the Treaty of Paris rather than before, because Fitzgore was about to embark on a long-delayed pilgrimage to the Continent. The household was in disorder, Fitzgore rushing about from one task to another in last-minute preparation, and I had taken refuge out of doors.

Two men came to the gate: one the captain with whom my master would sail on the morrow, the other a gentleman of fashion, a wealthy acquaintance come to show him the way. It chanced that when they arrived, Fitzgore was instructing the gardener on the care of the groves in the rear of the property. Atticus admitted the visitors to the study and went to fetch him.

I heard the clink of glasses within through the open French door. Shortly the two men came to stand in the doorway, not twenty feet from me. I gave no indication of knowing they were there, but sat and waited to be noticed. Nor was I long in the waiting.

"That is the boy of whom I spoke," said the nabob. I sat with eager attention so as not to miss a single compliment, though he spoke in normal tones, with no more concern as to whether I heard or no, than if I had been a horse or a hound.

"Eh?" said the captain. "What boy was that?"

"The pickaninny there in the garden. Raised him like a son, he has, along of his own flesh and blood."

"Indeed?" The captain examined me with languid interest.

"Indeed. Though 'tis said that the boy's his own bastard out of a serving-wench at. . . . But hold! here he comes."

"Ah, Fitzgore. Your servant, sir; allow me to present . . ."

I heard no more; at the fatal word "bastard" I had ceased pretending to study and had turned to gape. My master's fortunate arrival had forestalled the discovery of my eavesdropping. I left my book where it had fallen and tearfully sought my bedchamber, where, after the fashion of children regardless of their color or the side of the blanket on which they were born, I cried myself to sleep.

The afternoon was well sped when I awoke. I lay for a while on the soft mattress and stared at the gathering shadows through the net canopy. What, actually, had been said that I should be so upset? Save for the insulting manner in which he had phrased it, the bewigged stranger had but voiced one of my own fantasies.

An English lad watching a nobleman's carriage might dream that he was some misplaced princeling; perhaps a young girl angry at her mother would fancy herself a second Cinderella. For all that he was balding and unhandsome, absent and whimsical, Fitzgore seemed to me the embodiment of all virtue; he and chill Hartshorn, of all knowledge (that they frequently disagreed was no hindrance to my fable). Though I had dared not admit it even to myself, I who had known no father fervently had wished Fitzgore to be he. In the stranger's barbed comment I found the spur I needed to seek the truth of my birth.

I slipped downstairs and made my way to Fitzgore's study. I had the freedom of the house, so there was no need for stealth save that I had no wish to be seen. The door was ajar and I made bold to enter.

Fitzgore stood on a step stool before the shelves that held his rather antithetical library, intent upon a leather-bound volume.

"Please, sir," I said. Fitzgore turned his head and looked down at me. His stockings and the knees of his breeches were stained with sap and soil from the garden, and his sleeves were rolled up past his elbows.

"Ah, Pyrrhus. One moment, my lad, and I'll be with you." He read on to the end of his page. "Yes, I thought so. Here it is indeed." He tucked the book under his arm and climbed down.

"Fascinating subject, don't you know: propagation of pineapples. Practically a state secret on the French islands. I must make sure to leave the gardener his instructions before I leave." He sat down behind his desk and looked at me over his spectacles.

"Now then, my boy, what is it?"

Almost I was afraid to speak, save that he looked so kindly with his watery blue eyes and his frank, homely face red from the sun. I was old enough to know that the subject was an awkward one.

"Please, sir," I said at last, "please, sir, are you my father?"

A look of surprise, followed by one of irritation, crossed his face. "No," he snapped testily. "Of course not. Wherever did you get an idea like that?" He picked up one of the papers that littered the surface of the desk and began to read it. After a few seconds he looked back at me. The hurt that I had felt at his brusque denial must have been plain, for he laid the paper down again and smiled at me crookedly.

"Here, now, Pyrrhus. Do I look like I might be your father? There's a glass on the wall; go and see. I don't know where you may have heard such a thing, but you must put the thought from your mind.

"Father, indeed. What need have you of a father in any case? Do you lack for anything? I think not. I provide for you — have always provided for you — as I do for young Frederick, the son of my own brother. Look at him! His father was of no more use to him than was ours to my brother and me — drunkards and wastrels, the pair of them!

"No, Pyrrhus, father me no fathers. Take it from me, lad, you're best off without one." He bent to his work once more, inking a quill and scratching a few lines beneath what had been written before.

"Please, sir."

Fitzgore looked up.

"Without a father, how am I to know who I am, or what I am, or what I am to be?"

My master raised his left hand to the bridge of his nose and adjusted his spectacles. For a moment he stroked the prominent appendage.

"Proper questions for a philosopher, indeed! Let me essay an answer.

"You are Pyrrhus Fitzgore, my lad, a Christian and a subject of good King George, which is a sufficient start for any man. As for the rest, though I've given you a bit of an education and a good Irish name, I fear that you're a trifle dusky to be an Irishman. In truth, you're as black as a shadow on a summer's afternoon.

"I suppose you might say, for lack of a better pedigree, that you're a shadow in more ways than one — a shadow out of Africa, as it were." He smiled with pleasure at the aptness of the image. "As for the future, you've always been a good companion to Frederick, and I see no reason for that to change. Now run along, my boy. The packet sails in the morning, as you know, and I've letters yet to write after I've made sure of the pineapples."

Obediently I went. Yet, though he sought to cast me as Frederick's shadow, it was old Fitzgore himself whom I admired and wished to emulate. Our relationship remained undefined, for never again did I raise the question of my ancestry, but from the smile that he gave me before I left, I wonder if the conceit had not pleased Fitzgore as much as it had me.

Frederick and I were not permitted to accompany Fitzgore to the quayside next morning, but said our goodbyes at the front gate. Though Frederick seemed a trifle cool, old Fitzgore was as excited as a boy at the prospect of meeting the brother-philosophers with whom he had corresponded over the years. I took some comfort in his delight at the pilgrimage, but I was blinking back tears as Hartshorn ushered Frederick and me to the room that did double duty as his quarters and our school.

"From this morning," our teacher pronounced with evident satisfaction, "you boys are in my sole charge, and I am firmly resolved that when our patron returns he shall be amply rewarded for his confidence. Be you resolved as well, gentlemen, that it will be so.

"Now, as to the curriculum: my esteemed employer and I have often been in disagreement in the past regarding the proper method of instruction and the subjects to which you should apply yourselves. To be frank, I have been much distressed with the manner in which I have been called to alter your instruction almost every time he reads a new book. I confess I sometimes wonder that I have managed to teach you anything at all.

"It was not so in my youth at Boston Latin School, nor yet at Harvard College. It shall not be so here while you are in my charge. I have not time to impart to you all that I was taught in seven years of classical studies, but perhaps I may at least remedy the more shocking gaps in your educations.

"Therefore, from this day, school will commence at six of the clock *ante meridiem* and will continue until eleven; we shall meet again from one o'clock until five in the afternoon. Mornings we shall review Latin grammar — to which you, Master Frederick, had best begin to apply yourself seriously — and the fables of Aesop in Latin, and begin the study of composition with Garretson's *Exercises*. In the afternoons, arithmetic, followed by algebra, French, and geography.

"I fear that in the few months before us I cannot hope to make of you gentlemen senior sophisters, but I may at least instill in you some measure of that respect for scholarship so lacking in these benighted islands.

"For this opportunity, may the good Lord make you truly thankful."

I had not realized before that day that Hartshorn possessed so much passion. I fancy Frederick found our tutor's syllabus and his newly authoritarian manner as surprising as I, but our responses were vastly different. Frederick had fallen in with a group of wealthy young scapegraces, with whom he spent what little free time we had. I must own that I envied him his friends and the adventures they led him into, but under their materialistic influence he soon became a dull and sullen scholar, where before he had merely been undistinguished. He and his friends made it wordlessly evident that I was not welcome to join them, and I turned to my studies to fill my empty hours. Time, hard work, and a consistent course of study proved stimulating and satisfactory, and I made rapid progress, passing from Aesop to Cicero and Virgil and from sums and simple algebra to geometry and trigonometry.

I found myself increasingly in the society of Hartshorn, who, being perhaps almost equally lonely, was far more approachable after hours than he was in the classroom. He was gratified by my thirst for knowledge (which I think he attributed to his own abilities), although he owned himself surprised, as he said, "to find a young Guinea-man should prove so apt a classical scholar." This remark I found somewhat disturbing, as never before, in so many words, had one of the household spoken of me as an inferior. Yet Hartshorn meant no ill by his remark, so I let it pass, and in our leisure hours found him to be a surprising source of knowledge on husbandry, natural philosophy, and the mechanic arts.

Because of this relationship, I found myself on occasion thinking of Fitzgore's return with something like dismay. Under Hartshorn's systematic tutelage I had learned more of value in a few short months than in the years which had gone before. Fond though I was of my master, there seemed a real danger that his ephemeral enthusiasms would result in the interruption of this progress.

During his absence, Fitzgore wrote us from time to time, but the letters were brief and unsatisfying in their sketchy detail. He did inform us of the expected date of his return on the London packet, and when Hartshorn was notified that the vessel had actually been sighted, he declared half-holiday in our studies and sent us on our way. As we left his precincts he added the admonition to use our time well, as we would be expected to recite for the master on the morrow.

I took the schoolmaster's warning very much to heart and passed the afternoon in my chamber, in close colloquy with Publius Vergilius Maro *et alii*. I was hopeful that a good showing the next day would encourage Fitzgore to allow me to continue with Hartshorn's program rather than substitute one of his own. Just as I was settling down with my books, I noticed Frederick slink by my doorway. As best as I was able to discover, he returned only in time for supper; when I saw him at the end of the day he was much disheveled and had a sort of swagger to his gait.

Fortunately, Frederick's dereliction passed unnoticed in the excitement of Fitzgore's return, and the traveler's homecoming meal was a lighthearted affair. Even Frederick was caught up in the holiday mood and listened delightedly as his uncle entertained us with amusing anecdotes of distant scenes, populous cities, and the famous men he had met: Dr. Johnson, the lexicographer; Lord Morton of the Royal Society; Count Buffon, and others. Each, it seemed, had his foibles.

"Rousseau, now," said Fitzgore expansively. He took a sip of port and leaned back in his chair. "Really a most irritating man. Absolutely fascinating, of course, but impossible to get along with! Suspicious as the very devil. Argues all the time! Still, a gentleman of parts: a passionate and persuasive individual.

"You will remember, my dear Hartshorn, the letters he and I exchanged some years ago on the subject of education. He expressed some rather extreme ideas from time to time: no books, he said, and the boys to set their own curriculum."

Hartshorn, perhaps believing himself unobserved, rolled his eyes drolly. "Yes, sir. For some weeks we sat in the garden and caught butterflies, as I recall."

"We may have done."

"And then it seems to me that it was on his advice that we took *Robinson Crusoe* for our text, and tanned the hide of one of the kitchen goats."

"Yes, that is so," said Fitzgore. "The boys seemed quite fond of good Robin, although I must admit that the smell was a trifle distracting when the wind was wrong."

"I confess I found it so, sir."

"Well, that's as may be. Defoe was an Englishman, after all. It may surprise you to hear it, but at one time I held Rousseau in uncommon great esteem."

"Indeed?" Hartshorn's interruption received the brief glare of annoyance it merited before Fitzgore continued.

"The man is quite in disrepute in Paris these days — in the best circles, of course. Been driven from France entirely. Just like the French it is, too. Unstable: not at all like Englishmen."

I thought I heard a choking noise from the opposite end of the table. Perhaps the port was not to Hartshorn's taste.

"I met Monsieur Rousseau at Motiers, near Neuchâtel in Switzerland, and I must admit I find many of his ideas rather unbalanced. I sensed it long ago. He's very bitter about his books: I mentioned that they had been burned, did I not? He spoke of little else. But I can't say I am surprised that he is losing favor. Insults his friends, writes unsettling pamphlets. Hardly even civil to visitors!" He shook his head sadly at this final example of French depravity.

"Well, after I left Motiers, I traveled to a little village near Geneva, where I met the veriest prince of a fellow — a man who is everything that a gentleman philosopher should be. Arouet is his name, although he writes under a pseudonym: calls himself Voltaire.

"A Frenchman, of course, but he might almost be an Englishman. Lived in England for a time, don't you know, and a great admirer of us as a people. Sound judgment — can't abide Rousseau. Not at all well, unfortunately, but he received me very kindly, and gave me a copy of one of his books as a parting gift. A great critic, painfully accurate; a man of perception and ability. I daresay he recognized in me a kindred spirit. I should have liked to have stayed with him longer, but . . ." His glance strayed to the tall clock in the corner of the room.

"I see, my friends, that it is later than I thought." He drained the last of his port and stood up. Hartshorn hastily did the same. "Come, boys, it is time we were in bed. I've a busy day tomorrow, as well you know: first I shall hear your recitations, and then I simply must see how my pineapples have prospered."

Next morning we assembled in the schoolroom. Frederick stumbled through his lessons in a sullen and perfunctory manner, but I made mine so well that Fitzgore clapped his hands with astonishment and delight. Frederick glared at me warningly, but we were quite of a size, and I had no fear of him. What influence he had had on me he had lost when he excluded me from his adventures.

Fitzgore bade Hartshorn give me a bit of Horace to read *ex tempore*, which I did in good style. When I finished with a psalm I had rendered into Latin verse, he rose silently and left the room.

I wondered greatly at his action, but none of us could guess what he was about. We were not kept long in ignorance, for Fitzgore returned shortly with a small book, handsomely bound in calf, which he presented to me. When I examined it, it proved to be the inscribed copy of *Candide* he had been given by Voltaire.

"Pyrrhus, my lad," he said in warm tones, "you have well repaid the interest I have taken in you. There are those not far distant who might well profit from your example.

"Some years ago, my friend Dr. Johnson wrote to me of his Jamaica boy, Frank Barber, who had been raised and taught to read by Colonel Bathurst. As you were but a child, and I had just engaged Hartshorn here to teach Frederick his letters, I put you to study under him as well, that we might determine scientifically if your species is susceptible, as the good doctor speculated, to learning after the manner of civilized men, or whether, as some say, the dark-skinned race is capable of only the simplest of notions. Since that time, Frank has progressed somewhat, but one rose does not make a summer, they say, and he might well have been a sport.

"I congratulate you, Master Hartshorn, on the success of your efforts, and of course, you, too, Pyrrhus. Come, Frederick, shake you his hand as well! As for me, I must prepare a paper to send to Dr. Johnson immediately."

With that he was off. Hartshorn fairly beamed, but when Frederick shook my hand he gave it such a wrench that it hurt me the rest of the day.

I know not what became of the dissertation which Fitzgore sent to London and on which he pinned his hopes for membership in the Royal Society; most likely it was forgotten in his enthusiasm for some new project and cut up into curling-papers by some later resident of his house. A short time after Fitzgore's arrival, Hartshorn announced his intention to return to his native shores. His health had recruited signally in his years with us, and he left for Boston with assurances of continued regard. Frederick took his departure for license to do as he pleased and was every day abroad with his boon companions — wastrels for all that they belonged to some of the best families in Basseterre.

Having nothing else to do, I stayed at home with Fitzgore and read the book he had given me, for which I conceived a great regard. That my opinion was shared is evident in the fact that soon after his return, Fitzgore changed the name of our house to Ferney.

Thus it befell that we found ourselves together more often than not, much as I had shared Hartshorn's society. This I found pleasing, as indeed did he, but my desire to be about something useful and to see more of the world than the house and the church in Irish-Town must have been clear. At last one morning Fitzgore looked up from his desk and asked me how it would suit for me to become a clerk in his establishment in the town.

I replied that it would suit me very well indeed, and that very afternoon he took me to his warehouse in the port.

The walk itself seemed an adventure to rival the travels of Aeneas. The precincts of the harbor, to my naive sight, seemed as fabulous as Cipango, and it was a long time before I found myself able to concentrate on my ledgers and waste-books. The good round hand with which Hartshorn had endowed me stood me in good stead, however, and by application I found that the ledgers themselves told a story as well as any earringed sailor.

It is well that Fitzgore kept a close eye on my progress, for there was much muttering when I entered his service. He began stopping by Liverpool Row at intervals on some pretext or other, where before he had hardly been seen from the end of one year to the next. As I was evidently his favorite, my fellows never had the courage to do more than mutter. Almost imperceptibly, however, Fitzgore's appearance became increasingly regular, so that he took over full control of affairs which had lain in the hands of employees for some time. Before the year was out, he was working the same hours as the rest of us, six days in the week.

I paid the muttering little mind, though in retrospect I believe it increased as Fitzgore took over his delegated powers. Perhaps some of the men had taken advantage of their positions, for the house of Fitzgore thrived despite the competition of the French islands nearby. Their tariff-free ports and cheap sugars, rum, and molasses (for the latter two the French had no domestic market due to their use of wines and brandies) made them more deadly commerical enemies in time of peace than they had been in war. Many planters and merchants, some well known to us, failed in those postwar years. Yet, though times were nowhere near as good on the whole, the rich still prospered. Nabobs still drove to dinners of eighteen courses in varnished carriages.

We lived in no such state, of course, nor would I have found it comfortable to have done so, but I watched the rich with eager eyes when Fitzgore and I were abroad in the town or visiting some favored customer on his plantation. In this manner I passed seven busy years, as happy as any in my life.

2

FITZGORE was not of robust make, there being more whalebone than oak to his frame, but his health was so generally good that I scarcely noticed that he was growing old while I grew to manhood. Thus it came as a shock when, late in the spring of 1771, he pleaded illness and sent me alone on an errand to Saint Mary's Parish, on the far side of the island.

The ague was not sufficient to prevent his seeing me off, though I noticed that he held himself stiffly, as if his back pained him. I felt a sudden guilt that I had not noticed sooner and made a resolve to be more attentive in future.

"May God rot all Jesuits," said Fitzgore peevishly as I led my mule from the stable. "I wish I might come, but this damned bark of theirs has used me harder than the fever ever has. Why, feel my liver! Just like a melon, it is, and my skin has turned as yellow as the Great Cham of Tartary's.

"Well, no mending it now. You've the directions written out? Good. Off you go, then, but mind you don't give Major Meacham that tea until you've his note in your hand. It's always the ones with the money that are slowest to pay. Yes, and don't be bashful about a bite of supper or a bed for the night if the hour is late. He can afford it."

"I'll be home by midnight, sir. And don't worry. I'll be as safe as if I'd taken the packet, and we'll save the fare as well." I checked again to see that my parcel was securely fastened behind the saddle. "But do remember your medicine, sir, and Dr. Parkinson said that you were to rest."

"Ah, doctors! Nothing but dogma and dog-Latin." He smiled wanly. "Be on your way, boy." He swatted Dapple on the rump. "I'll warrant that at my age I can manage without you for a few hours."

I had only a short ride before I left the town for the green of the country. The Carib Indians who once lived on Saint Kitts had styled it "Liamuiga," or the fertile island. Fertile it is, beyond many of its neighbors, but where most of the islands in the West Indies export other commodities as well, sugar is the only article of any account that is produced in Saint Kitts.

No one can travel far on the island without being aware of its dependence upon this one crop. Fitzgore had called my attention to the fact during our travels and noted that, though some small part of each plantation is given over to pasturage, provisions, and cotton, four acres in five are in canes.

"Look well, Pyrrhus," I remember him saying. "Planter or no, if a man would prosper on this island, he must understand that every penny, every half-joe that passes through his hands comes from the cane fields." For this reason, a large proportion of his garden was devoted to experimental stands of cane, and he spoke with authority on matters of manures and the like.

"This island's prosperity," he told me one day, "is rooted in her soil." He waited a moment to see that I got the joke, and then went on. "The best in the world for sugar, it is." Afterward he took me into the garden to see it: a dark gray loam so light and porous as to yield to the slightest application of the hoe. He showed me, too, the way the fires in the boiling-houses make the sky glow at night: from January until April the mills run almost constantly, that the crop may be got in before the spring rains.

Nor did I think that the canes grew and harvested themselves. Numbers proved but a pale reflection of reality, but I knew that the island counted some twenty-two thousand souls, and that of them only one in ten was white. "A plantation," Fitzgore had explained, "ought to yield as many hogsheads of sugar as there are slaves belonging to it.

"I reckon thus: an acre in ripe cane will make two hogsheads of good Muscovado. Mark that only the half of the plantation is cut each year, the remainder being in young shoots. Thus the average may be put at one hogshead, or sixteen hundredweight, per acre, per year.

"More work may be got from less, my lad, but your black cattle die off if not well attended. Allowing for the old and the very young, a man must own as many slaves as he does acres."

I made no doubt that he had it aright, for I had seen strange Negroes by the thousand in town on Sundays. Sunday was their market day, when they did no work, but flocked in from the country dressed in snowy linens or gay checks and calicoes to sell a sucking-pig, some fish, a basket of yams, or a dozen of eggs. Some few also went to church, notably to the Moravians' chapel. The bulk of them seemed to spend their time chaffering for salt beef or other such dainties for their tables, for ornaments for their persons, or in dancing, singing, and the drinking of a sort of beer they call "maubi." It was as good as a play for me to see them meet each other, as formal as dancing-masters with their congés and set phrases, all picked up after their masters like the old cocked hats and cast silk gowns in which they delighted.

Under Fitzgore's tutelage I soon became a very Colonel Martin on the planting of sugar, though to be sure my knowledge was all theoretical. We dealt in no slaves, but I could quote the prices of fresh blacks from the Congo or the Guinea coast as readily as I could grain, salt fish, or barrel staves from the colonies to the northward. Each of these articles was as indispensable to the planters with whom we dealt as was our rum to the captains who carried them thither.

What free time there was I still spent at Ferney, for I had no friend save Fitzgore. For his part, he seemed to solace himself for Frederick's dereliction with my company. Evenings we spent in his study. The long, learned letters he wrote now had to do less with philosophy than with the activities of the Merchants' Society in London and the enactment of duties upon French sugar. These he would read to me, and I, who knew many things but understood, it seems, so little, would nod sagely and accept that noses were made to wear spectacles, and that private misfortunes make up the general good.

Chief among my pleasures, however, was the opportunity to see somewhat of the world at large. At first when we went abroad in the island I found the sights so intoxicating that I neglected to think about what it was that I was seeing. The gangs of half-naked men and women sweating to their unchanging chant of "Work away, body, bo; Work aa, jollaa!" seemed as much a part of the scenery as the cane fields themselves. These apathetic beasts of burden shuffling along the dusty roads were so unlike the gay creatures of Sunday that there seemed to be no connection.

I had taken the muscular black drivers with their two whips, one long and one short, equally for granted until one day when we came upon a field, hard by the road, where a driver was flogging a woman great with child. She shrieked horribly as she sought in vain to avoid his strokes. The rest of the troop looked on dumbly.

"Steady, lad!" Fitzgore cried. He tried to catch me by the arm but missed, and I flung myself from the saddle and proceeded to give the brute a drubbing.

Fitzgore pulled me from the man before I was able to harm him or, as was far more probable, he recovered from his surprise and did me hurt. Fortunately there was no overseer; in the absence of another white man my master carried the day easily.

Me he rebuked for interfering in the planter's business. The driver grinned broadly the while. Then Fitzgore turned to him. He cringed as Fitzgore took him to task for beating a pregnant woman without, as is common practice, protecting the unborn child by allowing the woman to lie over a hole dug in the earth. He concluded with a stern warning to take better care of his master's property in future.

For a time after this incident we had ridden on silently.

"No gentleman," he said at length, "could view such a scene un-moved, my lad. You did no ill to pity the wench.

"But consider this: the planters would not continue to beat their slaves could chastisement be avoided. This has often been tried, but always to no purpose. You are young, Pyrrhus, and you are not as they. Were you better acquainted with the nature of the Negroes, you would see it differently.

"You know me for a humane man. I should hate to see them suffer, did they do so. But it is the suffering of the human mind that constitutes the greatest misery. With them it is merely corporeal. Nature has arranged it that the black man feel no shame or pain beyond that of the present moment."

I have heard this view asserted often, both before and since, and on the highest authority. At the time it seemed unanswerable, for though it accorded ill with how I felt myself, it was true that I had never seen these unfortunates mourn. There was yet that about the idea that made me uneasy, but I could think of no means of expressing that discomfort however long I pondered, and so I held my peace.

This day, however, I did no grailing, but rode along, nodding a bit with the warmth and Dapple's easy gait, and quite resolved to tend my own garden. My copy of *Candide* traveled easily in my pocket, and from time to time I would hale it forth and read a bit. I said no word to the Negroes I met, of whatever station, though I was careful when I saw a white man to salute him politely and yield the way.

In this fashion I reached my destination without incident. I turned off the high road onto a dusty lane lined with cocoa and palmetto trees. It forded a small gut and wound along the stream and through several cane pieces to a low hill. Here, among a profusion of orange trees, limes, and shaddocks, cherries, citron, and pawpaws, was the seat of Major Meacham.

Meacham was an officer in the militia, and esteemed one of the first men on the island. His house was said to be the most splendid in all Saint Kitts after that of the justice, Mr. Hamilton. Certainly it made a grand show; I was met at the door by a slave in wig and livery, and ushered inside with every show of politeness.

It was a house of laughter and looking-glasses and polished mahogany. Somewhere a harpsicord was playing. I followed the manservant past an alcove where a mulatto girl dressed as an infant sultana spoke gravely to a large green parrot. At the end of the passage he knocked softly on a door and opened it that I might enter. I found myself in what was evidently the major's study. A red-faced man in breeches and top boots stood with two others on the far side of the room by the windows.

"Ah!" he said, too heartily for me by half. "You'll be from Fitzgore, I wager. And how is your master, boy? I thought to see him today." I explained Fitzgore's indisposition, and the beefy militiaman nodded. "There's a deal of fever this season. I wish him a quick recovery.

"Now, as to my tea." He turned to the others with a deprecating smile. "You'll excuse me, gentlemen. My lady wife has been vaporish these three days without her tea." He reached for the package.

"Your pardon, sir," I said as politely as I might. "My master particularly requested that I obtain payment of your current balance before I make delivery." I proffered him the slip of paper on which Fitzgore had inscribed the figures.

The major was clearly unaccustomed to being balked. For a moment he seemed as though he might strike me. A deep furrow appeared between his brows, but the mood as quickly passed and he accepted the paper. He nodded to his two companions and left the room.

The other men seemed nearly as embarrassed as I. They ignored me, so I stood back and examined the equestrian portrait of the major, which dominated the room. In a moment I had apparently been forgotten and conversation was resumed.

"So I called on the planter and asked if there be any work, and he said no; but his wife up and said that she saw no reason to waste the occasion and set me to flog her two housemaids. A matter of principle, as you might say, sir.

" 'Spare the whip and spoil 'em, Mr. Jeffries,' she says to me, and rightly, too. These blacks understand nothing better."

The mild tone in which this callous statement was delivered took me rather by surprise. I caught myself just in time for my turn to appear casual.

The speaker was decently dressed in leather breeches, brass-buckled shoes, and cotton stockings, and a coat of bottle-green that looked drab beside that of his brocaded neighbor. He might have been about eight-and-twenty years of age and looked as respectable as a churchwarden.

I could not make out the reply of his companion, whom I took from his dress and complexion to be some planter but newly come from England.

"No, sir," said green-coat with a frown, "I seldom use the cart-whip myself. It's wasteful — cuts the flesh as well as the skin, it does. It's poor economy, your honor, to have a slave laid up for a fortnight. They still eat, even if you can't work 'em. No, sir, take it from me, a dose of the cat's the thing. 'Tis my business, after all, as planting's to be yours."

"Quite so, Mr. Jeffries, I'm sure, but I've one slave to whom your common flogging's but a jest. My own overseer is at his wits' end."

"Ah, sir, he'll be Coromantyn, then, I'll be bound. A stiff-necked people!"

"You mean to say that the breed or whatever of these brutes makes a difference? How curious! I vow they all look alike to me."

"And so you might say, sir, until you've spent as much time with them as I have. But just as some are blacker than others, they've different natures, too. Some pointers and some setters, so to speak, sir, and some pure pit bull.

"Now, I wouldn't give a clipped shilling for a Coromantyn: too warlike; nor yet for an Eboe. Your Eboe's so gloomy he'll up and die for no reason. The Paw-paw makes a good field hand, though, and your Mandingo is like to be a gentle sort, though prone to lies and thieving."

"Indeed!"

"To be sure, sir. But I've said before, and I'll say again, there's none of them but will be better off for a good dusting once in a way." He paused while he drained a cup of punch from the bowl at his elbow.

"It's curious about the Mandingo, sir. I've met some of them as claim that they can read. Not proper English, of course, so's you could catch 'em in a lie, but Arab, they say, they being disciples of Mahound. A queer fancy, I call it, but I suppose they might memorize some of the words — some of 'em are as 'cute as monkeys."

At that moment the major rejoined us and handed me a folded piece of paper. I gave him the box of tea and had begun to withdraw when I chanced to examine the draft he had given me. He was smiling with his guests and reaching for a cup of punch when I broke into the conversation.

"Your pardon, Major Meacham, but you've forgotten to sign this note."

All three men paused and looked at me. I thought for a moment the major might be seized with an apoplexy, so red did his face become. Presently he snorted, seized the document, and signed it at the sideboard. He handed it back to me without a word, though his eyes boded me no good wishes. I bowed slightly from the waist and took my leave.

I waited for no footman, but made my own way out. The turbaned sultana watched me pass in silent alarm. I flung myself on my mule and rode down the lane.

I suppose it must be easier to sustain anger and indignation on a horse than it is on muleback. Prod her as I might, Dapple would proceed no faster than a brisk walk, and even that soon subsided to her customary ambling pace. The major had hurt my pride with his suave attempt to cheat Fitzgore, but before I had gone a mile the mule's swaying gait and the somnolent heat of the late tropic afternoon combined to sap me of the will to be angry.

I awoke to the last gleam of the sun and the sudden realization that I was lost. The night wind had already begun to rustle the leaves over-head, but the coolness of the air was not entirely pleasant to one clothed for the heat of the day. I found my coat and put it on. There was nothing to do but trust to Dapple's sense of direction. I rode on through the gathering darkness.

To this day I have not forgotten the gray pigs seen at night that are enchanted, nor the hideous little wizards who roll about the country-side in calabashes during the dark of the moon, nor any of the other nameless horrors that peopled the spirit world in which Fitzgore's gardener believed so devoutly. Even after the dim landscape had begun to look familiar I dared not look behind me, and it was with a profound sense of relief that I urged Dapple around that last corner and up the hill to Ferney. I saw a light burning in my master's window and realized with a quick rush of guilt that I had not thought of him since leaving Meacham's, and resolved to look in upon him as soon as I was in the house. Still, I did not neglect to whistle three times over my shoulder to drive off the jumbies before I entered the house.

The kitchen was dark, which concerned me until I realized that the cook and gardener had been allowed to take two days' holiday to visit family at Palmetto Point. I struck a light and rummaged about for something to eat. There was little enough but dry bread, but my hunger proved excellent sauce and I washed it down with the last of a bottle of claret. I had just resumed my search for a bit of fruit or a piece of cheese when I heard a step behind me and turned to look.

Atticus the butler stood in the doorway with a pewter chamberstick in his hand. It dripped hot wax on the floor unheeded.

"Thank the Lord you're home," he said. "Come with me, quick. Old Master's took terrible sick."

3

Y master lay in his bed, insensible, with the coverlet pulled up to his chin. He looked drawn and very old. A spot of bright red on either cheekbone served only to accentuate the pallor of the rest of his face. I could see that he had been sweating by the way his fine white hair clung to his scalp.

His lap desk and tin deed box lay beside him on the counterpane. I handed them to Atticus, who placed them on the large chest of drawers against the wall.

"How long has he been like this? Why isn't the doctor here?"

"Not long," said Atticus. "He was took sick after dinner — you know he felt poorly today — 'nen about ten o'clock he seemed better. He told me get his writing things. I looked in on him later, and he had broke out in the sweats. I wanted to get the doctor, but Mr. Frederick, he's been out all night and I was afraid to leave him alone."

I sat down and placed my hand on Fitzgore's brow.

"He's burning with fever, Ad. Get me a cloth and some cool water, and then run and fetch Dr. Parkinson."

Atticus left, returning a few moments later with an ewer and basin and a piece of white linen. I poured water into the bowl and gave it to him to hold. Soaking a strip of cloth in the liquid, I wrung it out and gently placed it across Fitzgore's forehead.

Somewhere downstairs there was the sound of a door opened and shut. Unsteady footsteps were followed by a clatter, the crash of breaking crockery, and hard upon that, muffled curses. Atticus and I exchanged glances and he went out into the hall to investigate, leaving the basin on the nightstand. Soon he came back.

"It's Mr. Frederick," he announced. The relief he felt was evident in his voice. "He says he's coming."

Presently Frederick lurched into the room. His eyes looked red and somewhat glassy. The neck of his shirt was open, and I could see that he had buttoned his waistcoat wrongly, but it was neither the time nor the place to comment on his appearance.

"Thank goodness you've come," I said. "Your uncle is very ill."

Frederick looked from me to Atticus, and then at Fitzgore. He rubbed at his eyes with his hands and shook his head to clear it. To his credit, a look of concern replaced the haggard fuddlement on his face. He went to the nightstand and plunged his head into the basin of water. He emerged gasping for breath but seemingly in much better command of himself.

It was wonderful to be able to turn over to him the responsibility for Fitzgore's welfare. I told Frederick what little I knew while he dried his face with the remaining piece of linen.

"What did you do about the doctor?" he asked when I had finished.

"I was just about to send Atticus, here, to fetch him when you arrived."

I looked at the butler. Between his anxiety over Fitzgore and his fear of the very spirits at which he laughed during the daytime, he might be nearly incoherent by the time he reached the doctor's lodgings. If that were the case, valuable time would be lost before Dr. Parkinson would arrive.

"Now that you're here, Frederick," I volunteered, "why don't I get the doctor? Ad can stay and help you. Unless you'd rather go yourself — it might be that he'd come more readily for you."

It seemed to me that Frederick's eyes rested for an instant on the chest of drawers behind me before he came to a decision. "No," he said, reaching into his waistcoat pocket, "do you go, Pyrrhus." He produced a few coins and handed me a golden guinea. "The doctor will come if you give him this."

Dr. Parkinson lived in an inn not above half a mile from Fitzgore's house, but I was breathless and sweating by the time I arrived. At first the doctor tried to put me off until morning. It may be that he did not even recognize me. At the sight of the gold he became more obliging. I was for starting out on the instant, but the size of his fee may have reminded the good doctor that he was too dignified to dash about on foot. He sent me to seek out the ostler while he dressed and adjusted his periwig.

By the time the doctor appeared at the stable door his horse was ready. I carried his small black valise and trotted at his stirrup, counting the seconds until we arrived back at Ferney and begrudging every one.

Frederick was alone with Fitzgore when I escorted the doctor inside.

He had pulled a chair alongside his uncle's bed and sat sipping coffee with a satisfied air.

The remains of a small fire glowed on the hearth. "Put that out directly if you would have the man live," the doctor told me. "I can see from here that he is having difficulty with his breathing, and small wonder. This room is like an oven." He took his bag and sat down on the bed. "Now let's have a look at him."

I went to put out the fire. It seemed to be mostly twigs and scraps of paper and was nearly burned out, but I splashed water on the embers and stirred them about with the poker. When I turned from the fireplace, I noticed Frederick was watching me narrowly, but presently he looked away.

The doctor was taking Fitzgore's pulse. For some moments there was no sound but the ticking of his pocket watch. I had the uneasy feeling that something was happening, but that I had missed it. Finally Frederick left the room, closing the door behind him.

The doctor shut his watch with a loud click and stowed it away in his waistcoat. "A very rapid pulse," he observed. He said the words in such a pleased fashion that I was quite misled until I realized that it was only his sense of self-importance that made him speak so. He laid his hand across Fitzgore's forehead and then drew the lid of one eye down with a finger. "Yes, rapid pulse, high fever, and a yellowish tinge to the whites of the eyes. Skin considerably jaundiced as well." He spoke without looking at me. "How long has he been in this state, boy?"

"Since the late evening, or so the butler says, sir. I only returned to the house a short time ago. He had been taking the medicines you prescribed, though he complained of a touch of the fever when I left this afternoon."

"He has more than a touch of fever, you may lay to that, Coffee." My worry must have been evident indeed for him to notice it. "There, now, boy, I'll do for your master. Pyrexiae, that is to say, febrile diseases, are a specialty of mine."

Less to me than to himself, he went on. "I should have liked to administer bark of Peru, were the fever less advanced, yet in phlogistic disorders it is often better to abstain." He thought for a moment and then looked up at me. "Think, now; has your master complained of pains in the vicinity of his liver?" I answered affirmatively, and was rewarded with a brilliant smile. "There! 'Tis just as I thought. No tonics, then, nor wine either.

"Just now, all I may do for him is to relieve him of a few ounces of blood. Will you assist me, boy, or are you prone to fainting?" I said I was not, and held his basin.

"That's done, then," he said when he had bandaged the small wound his lancet had made. He stood up, wiping his hands on a bit of rag he carelessly stuffed back into his satchel. "I may as well stay here until morning. If he is fortunate, his fever may break by dawn and a sweating fit begin. Then we shall see. Under the circumstances I should not like to administer any drugs.

"It is not unlikely that he may wake. If he is sensible, he will be thirsty, and you may give him as much water as you may. No aciduous juices, however, and if you value your hide, no wine. As for me, I have a thirst as well, and no prohibition exists. Is there by any chance a decent sherry in the house?"

For a moment the scene wavered before my eyes, and I reached out a hand to the bedpost for support. Often had I looked in at night to find Fitzgore sitting propped up with pillows in this selfsame bed. He would set aside his reading and bid me draw up a chair. That he might never do so again suddenly bore heavily upon me, and I felt tears start from my eyes and run down my cheeks.

There was the pressure of a hand on my shoulder. I shook it off, but the doctor seized it firmly and spun me around to face him. "I asked for wine, Sambo. I applaud your loyalty, but your manners leave much to be desired. Directly your master is well enough I shall suggest that he give you a lesson in deportment."

I clenched my fists involuntarily, but before I could do more the door opened and Atticus entered. The interruption gave me a chance to think; anger would help neither me nor my master. I took a breath and turned back to the physician. "I ask your pardon, Doctor," I said, hating the taste of each word. "I meant no disrespect; I was over-wrought. Atticus will be delighted to serve you. He knows where everything is.

"Atticus, the good doctor would like some refreshment. Kindly show him the parlor, and bring him a bottle of wine and whatever else he may require."

Dr. Parkinson seemed satisfied with the abjectness of my manner and followed the old slave downstairs. When he had gone, I spat in the ashes on the hearth.

The night was wearing on, and I was tired. I made myself as comfortable as I might in the armchair by my master's bed and resolved to watch over him until daylight, but my exertions proved too much for me. I remember thinking that it would not hurt merely to rest my eyes, but that is all.

The candle was guttering when I awoke. It was nearly light, but I rose quickly and lighted a new one with the last of the flame. Fitzgore moved in the bed restlessly and I took his hand in mine. His brow still felt heated, so I wrung out the cloth again and replaced it.

At the cooling touch, the old man's eyelids flickered. He opened them feebly, and his cracked lips parted, but no sound came forth. I poured him a glass of water and supported him while he drank. When I laid him back down he looked up at me and the edges of his mouth twitched as though in an attempt to smile. I bade him rest; then I went to the door and called down the stairwell for the doctor.

However weak he might be, there was no doubt that my master was conscious. His lips moved again, shaping the word "water." I gave him to drink once more. At last he pushed the glass away impatiently.

"Pyrrhus, lad," he whispered.

"I'm here." I put the glass aside and took his hand. "Don't try to talk. Let me go and fetch the doctor. He's just downstairs in the parlor."

His hand tightened on mine and he shook his head. "No," he said. "Must talk." He tried to push himself up on his elbows as if there were something he wanted.

"What is it?" I asked. "Lie back down. I'll get it for you, but you must rest."

He got one elbow under him and tried to point, but he fell back against the pillows. He smiled up at me as though in apology for being so weak. "Box," he said at last. "Papers. Frederick." He looked at me to see if I understood. "Not . . . bad, but needs help. Papers . . . provided for . . ." Before I could ask him what he was trying to tell me, the door burst open and the doctor elbowed me aside. He looked half-asleep and smelled strongly of wine.

"Don't waste your strength, man," he told Fitzgore peremptorily. He rifled through his bag and came up with a small vial. "Half of this in a wineglass full of water," he told me. "You damned idiot, why didn't you call me sooner?"

I stood by while he gave Fitzgore the draft. "A sudorific," he said. "From the look of him, it is imperative to get him to sweating, even at the risk of creating an imbalance of the humors.

"Damn your eyes! Don't just stand there, darky, get the nephew and then come back here. There is risk to the heart, but I may have to prepare a plaster if the salts don't work."

Atticus was waiting anxiously in the hallway. I sent him to wake Frederick and went back into Fitzgore's chamber, but the doctor just snapped at me to stay out of the way. He had poured some brown liquid into a tumbler and was trying to get the old man to swallow it.

Frederick came in, still wearing his rumpled clothes. He held the brandy decanter in one hand and a glass in the other. He poured himself a stiff dram and tossed it back with practiced ease. "Here," he said. "Take these and wait in the hall."

There was an uncomfortable straight wooden chair in the hall. For perhaps an hour I sat there miserably, holding the things Frederick had thrust into my hands. Atticus hovered anxiously in the background, but neither of us had anything to say. Finally the door opened and the doctor emerged.

I stood and faced him. I had no heart to ask him the only question that mattered, and at last it was the doctor who spoke. "Your master has gone away, Coffee," he said. I looked at him dumbly. My tears fell unheeded. Behind me Atticus began to sob. For an instant the doctor seemed moved. He smiled kindly and put his hand on my shoulder. "There was nothing I could do. His heart just gave out. But I promise you, he felt no pain."

Then he noticed that I still held the decanter and Frederick's empty glass. He took them from my unresisting hands. "Brandy!" he said, as if greeting a friend long absent. "Physician, heal thyself!"

4

THE passing of old Fitzgore wrought many changes, both at Ferney and on Liverpool Row. The pace at the warehouse slowed, and it was evident that my master's sharp eye was sorely lacking. Yet not all of the changes proved so ill. By the terms of Fitzgore's will, Atticus was given his manumission and made free; he and the gardener and the cook his wife received small bequests. There was no reference to me, save that "the boy, Pyrrhus, be taught a trade," which was thought queer, but Frederick pointed out that the testament was of twelve years' date. He allowed that perhaps his uncle Tiberius would have done differently had he written it anew, but as he had not, it must stand as it was. To each of us, however, Frederick gave somewhat out of his own pocket, so that the town spoke favorably of his generosity and called him a changed man.

Atticus and the others removed to Palmetto Point after the funeral, whereupon Frederick bought him a comely yellow wench to cook and to clean. What her other duties may have been I shall not speculate, but Esmée was given to putting on airs, and we did not get along.

Whatever her station, Frederick was out late at nights less often, perhaps feeling the responsibility of his position as master of the house and of Fitzgore and Company. About a week after the funeral he came to me and said it was time we had a talk and came to an understanding.

"We have talked of my uncle's will before," he said, "and I think we can agree that you have been taught a trade. Indeed, as his clerk you learned rather more. It was an opportunity I might have had, and did not. Be that as it may, I am in his stead now, and I find I regret my youthful folly.

"I have a whim to travel abroad, but before I do, I must set the House of Fitzgore to rights. Only then may I depart.

"I would be glad if you could be my agent. You would, I am sure, prove an excellent steward, yet there are reasons obvious to both of us why I may not leave affairs in your hands.

"You came here a slave, Pyrrhus, though you were always treated as a member of the family. A slave you are today, but I promise you that you shall not remain a slave in this house for long. I have need of your aid. Help me now, for I promise you that your future is assured."

Thus I undertook to teach Frederick what his uncle had taught me in his turn. To my surprise, it went quickly, for Frederick was no dullard save when it suited him. I enjoyed the labor doubly well: it seemed to me as though I were repaying a debt long owing, and with Frederick's appearance, the sidelong glances and mutterings which had begun again subsided for at least as long as we were in the room.

It was not long before Frederick was able to conduct the firm's affairs with assurance. One afternoon he pushed the papers from him with the appearance of sudden decision and announced that we had labored long enough; he proposed that on the morrow we should hold holiday and ride out into the country.

"I shall have Esmée cook us a chicken and pack it in a hamper," he said, "and we shall have bread and cheese and wine, and such other good things as the kitchen affords that will travel well. What do you say, Pyrrhus? We can ride out to see the apes at Monkey Hill. It is long since we were there together, but you were fond of them once."

I was pleased both by the suggestion and by the fact that he still remembered how as children we had laughed at the antics of the monkeys. They sometimes did damage to fruit trees in the neighborhood when they came down off their hill, but the planters did not much molest them, for they were one of the island's chief diversions. It was said (with much merriment) that they were the descendants of the original French settlers of the island, only that they had better manners.

Accordingly we rose early and went to make our preparations. I saddled Dapple and Frederick's sturdy mare while he saw to Esmée and the food. He came from the kitchen looking flushed and merry with the hamper ready-packed. We rode out in the cool of the morning with the town just beginning to awaken about us. I looked over my shoulder at Ferney as we neared the first bend in the road.

"Come, Pyrrhus," Frederick called. "There's no need to think about affairs in Basseterre now. If the store cannot get on without me, it is better that I find out now. Meanwhile, this day belongs to us: to you, and to me."

The day was fine and hot, and Dapple would not go faster than a walk, so it took us near twenty minutes to reach the ford at Fountain Gut, and over an hour passed before we stood at the foot of the hill, which lay between General Fleming's and the Milliken plantation, opposite Mardenbrough's. Here Frederick proposed that we tie our beasts in the shade and proceed on foot. We climbed the hill along a path until we came to a grove of fruit trees which bore the signs of use by the apes.

"We'll rest here awhile," Frederick announced. "I am weary, and it seems to me that this is a fit spot for monkey-business." He smiled serenely and I grinned back. We sat and ate some fruit and cheese from the basket, washed down with a draught of water from a bottle he had brought, reserving the chicken for later in the day. I soon found myself nodding. Frederick bade me sleep if I would, and said that he would wake me when the monkeys arrived.

I awoke to a gentle kick in the ribs and looked up into a grinning simian face with a red fringe of chin-whiskers. My first thought was that the monkeys had arrived in force, and I started up in fright with Frederick's name on my lips. The gorilla menaced me with a spade.

"Sit you down, little master," said a voice that seemed somehow familiar. I looked past the figure that stood over me and saw a mild sort of man decently dressed. "Yes, lad, Jeffries the jumper it is, at your service; or rather, at your master's." There was something ominous in the words, however soft-spoken.

"Frederick Fitzgore sends you his regrets. He had pressing business at Mr. Justice Hamilton's. A dreary affair; I believe it had to do with a runaway slave. Thief he was, too. Stole a half-dozen silver spoons. The cook saw him, 'tis said, but I don't believe they'll ever be recovered. What do you think, Murphy?" Murphy smiled hugely and shook his head.

"You should be more careful, boy," the jumper went on. "You have a habit of becoming inconvenient. Certainly the major found you embarrassing. You are fortunate not to belong to him! But you have put my good patron, your master, to a deal of trouble as well.

"Not to mention the expense! There were the spoons, of course, but in addition Murphy and I were paid a round sum to ensure that your body was never found." I stared at Jeffries open-mouthed. He seemed to enjoy my surprise and paused to savor it before continuing.

"As best as I can make out, your late master Tiberius had intended that you be freed and share in the estate with his nephew in return for your affection and service. I met Frederick in a tavern, and he took me into his confidence. He had found and destroyed the documents, but feared that awkward duplicates or reference to them might appear — thus we conceived your ungrateful theft and subsequent flight."

Jeffries paused once more. "It is lucky for you that it was me he met, and not Murphy. It came to me afterward that it was not essential that you die for me to fulfill the compact. After all, a healthy young buck such as yourself — though you be not overlarge — is worth full thirty pound in any market in these islands. Murphy, here, is a man of little imagination, but he is the owner of a small shallop and will take us to Antigua. Or if you prefer he can dig you a hole under this tree.

"What say you, little master? Potluck and life in Antigua, or death and a shallow grave on Monkey Hill? If it is of any interest to you, both Murphy and I will be quite vexed if you choose death, for already our purses are too thin, and I fear I cannot promise you that he will be gentle."

In my time there have been many who have echoed the cry to "give me liberty, or give me death," but it is in my mind that few of them have been faced with the necessity of making an instant choice between them. I hesitated only a moment and chose — life; though I knew that it would likely be a short one should I find myself in the cane fields. Jeffries and Murphy exchanged knowing smiles. They bound me hand and foot and we settled down beneath the fruit trees to wait for the coming of darkness.

When evening came Jeffries led us back to the road, but rather than turning left at General Fleming's, we went to the right and followed the road down Gillew's Gut past the mill to the bay. Here Murphy's shallop rode to anchor. At his hail, the deckhand rowed ashore in a jolly boat near half as long as the shallop herself. They tumbled me aboard and he rowed us all back. There was a fitful breeze; Murphy and the seaman got sail on the shallop and we ran before it.

I remember little of the passage to Antigua save the stink of the shallop's bilges. We should have made landfall in a matter of seven or eight hours; that it took us a night and a day of beating about suggests that Murphy was not overanxious to show his face ashore in the sunlight. At length he ran into the harbor and cast his anchor. The seaman hauled the launch alongside and rowed us all ashore.

I looked for an opportunity to make a run for my freedom, but I was closely watched, and there was no slack in the ropes that bound me. My captors led me through dark streets until we stopped before a large stone warehouse. A sign over the door in gilt on black read "H. Gibbs: Dealers in Slaves." The door itself was thick with tattered handbills. I came up short as I should at the door of Hell itself and looked about wildly. I thought for a moment that Murphy would strike me, but Jeffries stayed his hand and drew me aside.

"Here we part company, little master," he said. "Though you think of me as your enemy, I bear you no ill will, and since in a fashion you do me a service, I will give you good advice in return.

"You feel yourself hardly used, but those within will care as little as my friend Murphy. Do not try their patience, or that of the man by whom you are purchased, with your troubles. It will only make things worse for you. You may remain here a few days, or it may be longer before a ship arrives from the coast, but for good or ill, here you will be sold. Tempt not fate, lest you find that there are masters in this world sterner than Murphy or I."

He nodded to the Irishman, who thumped upon the door with his fist until it opened. The doorward who answered led us into a large shadowy room. In one corner a man sat at a desk and wrote by the light of a single candle which smelled more of a tallow than of wax. Our guide led me to one side while Jeffries and Murphy addressed the man behind the desk. He gave me a brief, practiced stare that seemed to penetrate to my very soul, but I could not hear what was said. After a few moments the men seemed to strike a bargain. Coins gleamed in the candlelight and there were smiles and handshakes all around. The Irishman and the jumper left without a backward glance, and the third man, whom I took to be Gibbs himself, resumed his seat. He nodded at the watchman and jerked his thumb toward the rear of the building.

The guard produced the stub of a candle from his pocket and lit it from Gibbs's before proceeding. Bound as I was, I had no choice but to follow him, down a dark corridor with barred arches on either hand. In one of these arches I saw an open wicket. Here we stopped. The watchmen loosed my bonds and thrust me inside. The door slammed shut behind me and I watched the glow of the guard's candle as it receded.

Morning found me asleep on a heap of straw. I woke and looked about me. Though seemingly more fit to receive an animal than a human being, the cell was at least no worse than a decent stable. I burned with shame and anger, but at least my new captors seemed disposed to keep me alive and well. Yet I had been either more or less than human had I not plunged myself into reflection upon the injustice — nay! the infamy — of my treatment by Frederick, who had consigned me, as he thought, to death. I lacked for terms of opprobrium, but it seemed to me Frederick was far worse than the infidel sailor in *Candide,* who, after being pulled from the water by the Anabaptist James, allows him to fall into the water and be drowned. That day I devised many ingenious plans for his requital.

It is difficult to describe and painful to recall the bitterness I felt as I waited to be sold. In my own defense I can only advance that at the time my Christian upbringing had been of the scantiest and most interrupted kind, or I had been more forgiving. Doubtless Frederick has been dust long since, and today I have grace to hope that he has found the same mercy, according to his deserts, to which I myself aspire. In those first days of captivity, my hate was blacker than my skin.

I was fed twice daily while in that cell, upon a sort of gruel of maize, yams, and plantains with once a day the half of a dried salt herring, split lengthwise. Each afternoon the dayguard led me to a large courtyard compassed about with walls some nine feet in height. Here I was bid take my exercise under his watchful eye, which I did, but lost no chance to spy out the opportunity for escape. I had no doubt that there would be broken glass atop the wall, but it seemed to offer a chance. My fate should I fail was plain in the form of a stout post, from which a pair of shackles depended, planted in the center of the yard. The ground about the post was dark with blood.

My plan demanded that there were others in the yard at the moment I made my attempt, that the guard's attention be divided. I resolved to bide my time until a ship should discharge a cargo of fresh sufferers from the Slave Coast.

These "colored Goods," when at last they arrived, were far from prepossessing, being nearly naked and still wet from the wash-deck pump of the vessel that had borne them from their native shore. Many had a sort of white scurf about their skins, not unlike leprosy in appearance, which is said to be but a matter of their having lived too long on salt provision. Some of the men had a fierce and warlike mien: most of these wore heavy irons and the scars of the whip; some were merely yellow-eyed, sullen, and watchful. The women and children were in a pitiable state.

I watched through the windows of my cell as the newcomers were herded and graded. All within the exercise yard was confusion. At once I pitied the terror of the captives and welcomed it, too. Though they feared a darker fate, the worst they needed to apprehend was the prospect of working out their natural lives in the cane, perhaps with the loss of a limb or so, like Voltaire's Negro of Surinam. Given my chance, their uproar would serve to cover my escape.

My own fear seemed more justified and far more real to me than theirs; perhaps my exercise would be postponed until the new slaves were lotted and put in their cells. I waited impatiently for the sound of footsteps in the corridor.

It was somewhat past the accustomed hour when I was let out, but I found myself ignored by the guards when once I had entered the yard. With great hilarity, these had separated the new arrivals by age and sex, shouting and shoving and cracking their great whips in the air. Distraught individuals broke away and tried to join the group in which some child or friend or lover had been placed, only to be beaten back into line. The young women the guards herded into the middle of the arena, where they proceeded to serve them as the Moors had searched captives for diamonds in *Candide*. Many had to be made fast and lay screaming on the ground as this was accomplished, but one, and she I thought to be of such great but quiet beauty as I had never beheld, submitted without a struggle. She stood motionless in the midst of the jeering throng, a huge mud-colored ruffian holding her wrists while silent tears coursed from her large brown eyes and washed the dust from her cheeks.

So affecting was this spectacle that I near forgot to attempt the wall. I looked about and saw that all eyes within the yard were fixed on the figures in the center. I carefully took off my short riding-jacket and privily wrapped it around my hands and lower arms. There was a break in the crowd near to where the male captives were held, and I made for it. I drew a breath and ran; leaped and caught the ledge at the top of the wall. The shards of glass I had expected were there, but hardly scratched through the fabric on my arms. My feet scrabbled against the stonework, and I hooked one elbow over the edge. There was a narrow alleyway before me. In a few seconds I could be over and running for the crowded harbor quarter.

I heaved again, but I felt my legs seized in a powerful grip. I kicked at my assailant as he dragged me down, and held to the wall with all my strength, but it was to no avail. I looked around into his eyes: the triumphant eyes, not of a white man or one of the mulatto guards, but one of the chained slaves. I lost my grip on the ledge and fell to the ground

In an instant I was surrounded by guards and overseers who haled me before the man I had seen when first I had arrived at the warehouse. The yard was in tumult around us, and I struggled vainly, but the men who pinioned my arms were near twice my bulk. Gibbs took no notice of the confusion around us. He stepped forward and forced me to meet his eyes with the butt of a whip beneath my chin.

"I was told you were trained, boy," he hissed. "It would appear I was misinformed. You need a lesson, and thanks to you, so do these others.

"Strip me this," he said to the men that held me. "Strip it and chain it to the post."

My shame at being thus naked in front of others seemed only to be exceeded by my terror of the brutal instrument I had heard Jeffries describe. Neither could compare to the pain I felt when Gibbs struck me. The first stroke of his whip drove the breath from my body, so that I could scarce cry out though each impact wrung a grunt from me. I think it was the sixth that left me unconscious; I could hardly have received more than a dozen in all and not have been permanently maimed. I woke later in some lightless hole in the basement of the warehouse, feeling more than half dead. Someone must have thrown a bucket of salt water over my back to stanch the blood, but I received no other medical care that I can recall, to which I am inclined to attribute my recovery. I think that I may have drifted in and out of consciousness for two or three days before I was well enough to eat the yams that were all my food while I lay in this dungeon.

Twice a day an earthen pan of boiled yams was brought me, together with a water jug of the same ware. In that dark cell I had no other way to mark the passage of time. The pain in my flayed back gradually lessened, and mercifully I escaped infection, but I sank further and further into despair. Escape and freedom faded from my view. After a week, all I wanted was to see the sun again; in a fortnight I had almost ceased to care.

I think that Gibbs was able to calculate this response to a nicety, for when at last I was half-carried from that cellar into the daylight I was as tractable as he could have wished. Despite the chains with which I was now encumbered, a cell with a small window and plenty of dried straw seemed ineffable luxury; even the slave porridge and the daily "one-eyed fish" was almost too rich a diet.

I felt strangely removed from things around me, as though only my will had been sapped while my powers of observation were intact. I noticed that the recently arrived slaves were now fat and sleek, while I had lost flesh. The day after I was brought back from below we were paraded in the yard. I and a few of the oldest slaves were culled from the line and led aside. A close haircut and a little soot from one of the cookpots converted the graybeards into the "decent prime fellows" Gibbs's handbills would doubtless be touting, and they were let back into the line.

My own case was otherwise. The alleged doctor of the auction house poked at my slack muscles and fingered my dull skin and prescribed a draught compounded of a mineral drug I have never heard named, plus rum and red pepper. This he followed at intervals with a dose of gunpowder and lemon juice, which induced a thirst the like of which I have never known. That night, for the only time in my brief residence, the guards brought me all the water I could drink. By morning I felt bloated and feverish, but my limbs were round and firm. One of the menials rubbed me with oil until my skin shone with counterfeit health and led me outside.

The other slaves were already in the yard, standing singly in the case of few prime males, or in small groups. All were more or less naked except for a few I took to be skilled workmen bought from planters in the locality; each had a large numbered placard hung about his neck. A guard shoved me against the wall and put a sign around my neck as well. I looked down and found myself to be number 39.

A few early shoppers were already examining the merchandise. I know not how long or how many times I was myself poked and prodded; how many dirty thumbs were thrust into my mouth, the better to see my teeth; how many times I was thumped upon the breast, before the auctioneer began the sale.

One by one the lots of human merchandise were brought up to view and sold. The auctioneer, a tall, black-whiskered, ill-favored sort of man, was yet a master of his profession, and the bids came fast and high. Soon a guard pushed me forward. I stumbled on the stairs as I climbed to the block, and a laugh ran through the crowd. The auctioneer gave me a warning look and began his chant.

"What am I offered for this prime young specimen? Thirty pounds for him, sirs? Who'll say thirty? Sound as a nut, upon my honor, and an estate item, or he'd not be here. Who'll say thirty, thirty, thirty?"

I looked out on a sea of bored faces as the auctioneer dropped his request to twenty-five pounds, then twenty. A man in the front row nudged his companion and whispered something that had him laughing uncontrollably.

Even at twenty pounds, half the price a healthy slave of my age should have brought, there were no takers. The auctioneer looked across the yard to Gibbs. I saw him nod sharply, and the bid dropped to fifteen. There was an edge to the auctioneer's voice now. The crowd seemed to sense his frustration and a low titter ran through it. Ten pounds were asked without a word of response. Then five. I looked across the arena into the eyes of the dark beauty.

In the grip of a mad fancy I stepped forward. If I was to be sold a slave, at least I would bring a proper price. The auctioneer paused for breath, and I stepped into the breach in his harangue in perfect cadence.

"Come, gentlemen! This will not do." My voice was as near a mimic of the auctioneer's as I could make it. "Look at me! Not five pounds for a young buck in prime condition? Sound of wind and limb, with all his teeth. And mark ye: he can read and write! Yes, and cipher, too; knows French, and geometry, and bookkeeping! Come, sirs; what am I bid?"

The titter had become a roar of laughter. One of the guards stepped forward with a whip to strike me down, but the auctioneer stayed his hand. I stood there breathless as the noise subsided. At last the man in the front row who had first laughed raised his hand. "One . . . one pound," he wheezed, breathless.

For an instant the yard was silent. Then from the shade of the wall a second voice rang clear: "Two!"

I looked across and saw a man with sandy hair step forward from the shadow. The auctioneer glanced back to Gibbs, who nodded once more.

"Two it is," he took up smoothly. "Who'll make it three? And four, sir?

"Yes, and five. Six? Seven, who'll make it seven? And the eight. Eight, eight, and nine. Nine, yes, and ten: Ten once. Eleven?" The man in the front row shook his head and said something about carrying a joke too far. "Ten twice," said the auctioneer. "Going for ten. Going, going, sold for ten pounds to the man at the back, and thank you, sir.

Now the next lot is . . ." but I heard nothing more as the guard pushed me off the block and through the crowd to where Gibbs stood. The man with sandy hair walked over to meet us.

5

"TEN pounds, then," said Gibbs the slave dealer to the sandy-haired man. He was deeply tanned and dressed all in linen, although he carried a blue coat with plain cloth buttons over one arm. "Ten pounds, and a guinea for the irons makes eleven."

Steely blue eyes bored into mine until I had no choice but to look away. The strength had run out of my body with the crash of the auctioneer's gavel. I lacked even the ability to feign defiance. Fitzgore had taught me to think of myself as a human being, but it was all a lie: I was property, and I had been sold.

"No irons," I heard him say.

There was the click of coin upon the table. "Ten pounds it is, sir," said Gibbs at length. "And your name, if you please, for the bill of sale?"

"Ross," was the reply. "Captain William Ross, of the schooner *Pretty Polly*. From Falmouth, in the Province of Maine."

I listened dully. Of Maine I knew next to nothing, except that it lay far to the northward and that it was uninhabited save by Puritans and Indians, each as rude and savage as the other. But whether I was to be bloodily murdered upon my arrival or merely hounded to an early grave, I had ceased to care.

Gibbs came out from behind his table to retrieve my manacles and leg irons. Ross stood by, examining his receipt.

"So your name is Pyrrhus, is it, boy?" he asked.

I stood mute and listless, still staring at my feet.

"Answer your master," snapped Gibbs. He rose from his knees, the chains dangling menacingly from his right hand. "Damn your black hide, answer him, I say!"

I heard the chains cut the air and tensed for the blow I had come to expect. It never landed. I opened my eyes and slowly looked up. Gibbs stood, arms upraised, the irons dangling loose. Between us was Ross, and the slave dealer's eyes were locked on his.

We stood thus for a long moment. Presently Gibbs lowered his arm. His glare burned me for an instant, then he went behind his table and busied himself with his papers. The corded muscles in Ross's shoulders, obvious even beneath his shirt, relaxed, and he turned to face me. I looked at his face and saw for the first time that those steely eyes held a kindly warmth mingled with their intensity, and that they looked out from under high arched brows the color of his hair.

"Pyrrhus, I think, was the name?" His voice was calm, the clash forgotten.

I nodded.

"Come along, then, Pyrrhus," he said, and he turned and walked to the door.

I followed Captain Ross out into the street, and then into a narrow lane which ran downhill toward the waterfront. Just as we got into the lane we were forced up against the wall by a number of pigs pursued by a troop of laughing Negro children, each as naked as the day he was born. Near the end of the lane was a slopshop seemingly much frequented by sailors, and here my new master set about completing my outfit.

My breeches, once as elegant in material and in cut as any in Saint Christopher, were foul and torn, and he bade me exchange them for a new pair of coarse Osnaburg linen. This I did while he selected a checkered shirt made of cotton, a flat straw hat and neat blue woolen coat, and a pair of shoes with steel buckles, hardly worn. The shoes and coat he had done up into a parcel, which the storekeeper gave me to carry.

At the seaward end of the lane was a wharf belonging to a Mr.

Nichols, a Scot and one of the principal merchants in the island. Indeed, I had occasionally dealt with correspondence bearing his crabbed signature in the time, now so remote as to seem unreal, when I had worked at the side of old Fitzgore. From the wharf, Ross hailed a passing boat to row us to his ship.

Like many island craft, the boat was built with a cradle rather than seats or thwarts amidships, being designed to ferry hogsheads of sugar or molasses to waiting vessels. Bow oar was a white man with gray hair and a gold earring. He was talkative enough, after the manner of his kind, although Captain Ross gave him little encouragement. On the after thwart was a muscular Negro, but whether slave or free I know not, as he neither turned nor spoke. Captain Ross sat motionless, lost in thought. I, however, listened eagerly to the cheerful old chatterbox of a waterman and fidgeted on my uncomfortable perch. With the resilience of youth, I was beginning to recover from my depression, and looked about with interest as we threaded our way through the crowded harbor.

The old man shifted his quid and spat expertly over the leeward side. "Rat Island," he said, nodding at a high rocky eminence rising out of the water. "Barracks were built back in fifty-four. Them troops you see landing" — I looked and could make out the buff facings on their red coats, and the silver lace and glittering buttons of the officers — "them's the Fourteenth Foot. Lose a sight of 'em, sure's a gun, before the year's out. Fever takes the fresh'uns quick."

He ran on while I shifted my seat and looked astern. Behind us the low houses of Saint John's, chimneyless but each with its trees and gardens, climbed ivylike up the hill from the jumbled inns and warehouses of the waterfront. Around us the harbor was populous with shipping, from Moses boats like our own and half-decked island shallops to a greyhoundlike frigate, proud with paint and gilt carvings gleaming in the sun.

There seemed to be no end of merchantmen. A few were foreigners — Danes and Dutchmen and some whose flags I did not recognize — but most flew the red ensign of England; sloops and brigs and ships, all neat and businesslike as a Scots factor. Almost I forgot my slavery as I stared at vessel after vessel. Each one, I told myself as we approached, must be the *Pretty Polly*, and I swelled with pride and possessiveness, only to be deflated again as we passed.

We must have rowed near a mile and were on the very edge of the anchorage when the boatmen steered to pass to the leeward of a singularly unimpressive craft, a schooner of about fifty feet in length and without topmasts save a spindly pole at the main. She had seemingly been painted, or rather daubed, with soot, for she had a blotchy, unhealthy look. I turned to Captain Ross for reassurance, but my words stuck in my throat. His frank blue eyes held the look that men reserve for their wives and their homes, and I knew then that to Ross this unsavory hulk was both. This was the *Pretty Polly* of Falmouth.

The captain tossed the old waterman a coin as we came alongside and hauled himself nimbly aboard. Swallowing my apprehensions, I clambered up the low side of the schooner in his wake.

Once on deck, I discovered that the worst of my fears were unfounded. Although affairs on board were evidently not carried out in man-of-war fashion, the topsides were far from slovenly in appearance. With an acute sense of relief I noticed a certain purposeful air about the neatly coiled lines and the well-used deck furniture. The *Pretty Polly* was neither new nor sightly, but there was that about her which said that she would carry her cargo to its destination and bring her men home again.

Captain Ross went aft to the break of the quarterdeck. He stepped up and over the low coaming of the hatch and began to go below. Realizing that I had lagged behind, he turned to where I stood gawking at my unfamiliar surroundings.

"Come along there, you. Step lively." There was a sense of resigned impatience in his voice; he had dealt with green hands before.

I nodded dumbly and began to follow.

The impatience became more evident. "You might as well learn now, you benighted inkblot, that while you are aboard this ship, you'll answer me when I speak to you, and you'll sing out cheerfully at that. Now say, 'Aye, aye, sir!' Say it, blast you, you heathen blackamoor!"

The epithets burned, but though his words were hot there was no fire in the captain's eyes. Already I had learned much about the man who was my new master. "Aye, aye, sir," I said, and was not a little amazed to find that the respect was not all pretended.

Captain Ross turned and clattered down the ladder with me at his heels.

At the foot of the ladder was the door to the captain's quarters. The

Pretty Polly's "great cabin" proved to be great by courtesy only, as it was no more than twelve feet broad and perhaps as many long. There was a small skylight let into the deck overhead, and though far from tall, I found I needed to stoop beneath the low beams. I had not thought — and never did think — of Captain Ross as a small man, yet I noted with surprise that he could stand upright.

Unlike rooms ashore, the cabin was not rectangular, but narrowed toward the stern. The captain's bunk, a tiny desk with a shelf above for books, a green sea chest, and a small table filled the place to capacity. Apparently the chest served as a second seat when the captain entertained a guest.

Captain Ross selected a thin volume from the shelf, and a pen, ink, and a pewter sand-castor from the desk. Seating himself behind the table, he leafed through the book and began to write.

"I'm entering you in the log as the ship's cook, Pyrrhus," he said by way of explanation. "Please God you'll be better than the last. Near poisoned us all before he ran off last week." He looked up with a half-smile on his lips. "Only question was whether I'd murder him myself or the crew'd mutiny first. Bad bargain, that 'un. Best rid of him.

"As I said, Pyrrhus, you'll call me 'sir' or 'Captain.' Anyone else will be 'mister' to you. Understand?"

"Yes, sir," I replied smartly. "Aye, aye" seemed a trifle ostentatious.

"Very well. Do your job and you'll have nothing to fear, either from me or the crew."

"Now, any questions before I show you the fo'c'sle and the galley? Anything you wish to say?" He squinted up at me in a kindly fashion.

"Yes, sir," I said diffidently, although to this day I do not fully understand why. "If you please, Captain, I may be a blackamoor, but I'm not a heathen."

Ross's blue eyes hardened and he started to rise. For just a moment he stood, gripping the edge of the table top. Then he sank back and the smile returned.

"High church or low?" he asked.

I tried not to let my relief show. "Catholic, Captain."

"A Papist, eh?" He snorted. "Well, by God, Pyrrhus, you're a Protestant now, and it'll be up to me to see you're a good one." He winked, slapped the table, and stood up.

"Come along. I'll show you where you're to sleep."

We went back up on deck. Just abaft the massive windlass near the foremast was a small hatch. Captain Ross slipped down through it with the practiced ease of a gymnast. I followed as best I could, and dropped into a tiny space in the fore part of the hold. There was a small stove on a brick hearth, three kettles, a stack of firewood, and what were evidently casks of provisions.

"Galley," said Captain Ross. He indicated a door in the forward bulkhead. "Fo'c'sle. Your berth's the port upper."

Sensing my confusion, he grinned. "Port's the left. Starboard's the right." He peered at me quizzically in the dim light. "I take it that you can tell which is the upper?" He turned and took a step toward the hatch.

"Aye, aye, Captain, sir," I heard myself say and immediately wished I hadn't.

Ross stopped in mid-stride. Then he shook his head and I thought I heard a low chuckle. "Crew won't be back for a couple of hours. You can sleep until then." He pulled himself up through the hatch and was gone.

I was conscious of a slow trickle of cold sweat as I stared up at the patch of sky.

If the *Pretty Polly's* orderly deck and neat cabin had laid some of my fears to rest, they awoke again in the forecastle. It was a cramped and lightless hole made more uncomfortable by the bowsprit and foremast, which took up most of the center of the room. The bed places were crudely built against the hull, two on each side. There was an odor of men, of mildew, and more than a hint of bilgewater. At that, it was better than the cell at Gibbs's.

" 'Optimism,' said Candide, 'is a mania for maintaining that all is well when things are going badly.' " I stretched out on the uncomfortable mattress. For the first time since Fitzgore's death, I fell asleep with a smile on my lips.

6

I AWOKE in Bedlam.

At first I thought I had merely fallen from my bunk, but then the rope around my ankles came taut and I was jerked out of the forecastle and into the galley. There was another heave, and I dangled head-down beneath the hatch. Then cackling madmen seized my legs and pulled me up on deck. I screamed as they carried me to the rail.

Captain Ross's voice cut through the idiot laughter. "What's the meaning of this, you men?" he demanded. The capering lunatics dropped me next to the windlass and stood, wavering.

The largest of the three, a six-footer with a chest like a hogshead, stepped forward. He towered over Ross.

"Just a little fun, Cap'n. Wash some of the dirt off yonder monkey."

" 'Yonder monkey,' as you call him, is the new cook. And from the smell of you, Frost, you need the bath more than he."

The big man paused, brow furled with thought.

"Well," he said at length. He glanced drunkenly at his mates for support. "Well damn my eyes, Cap'n, cook or no, we ain't sleeping with no monkey."

Ross looked up at the burly seaman. The captain seemed to smile. Frost relaxed, and I could see him grin in triumph. He turned his head to leer at the others.

The blow was too fast for my eyes to follow. There was a crack as the captain's fist met Frost's jaw. The big man staggered. His heel caught on the low rail at the ship's side, and he fell. There was a splash as he hit the water.

Ross turned to the others, rubbing his right hand with his left. "Fish the fool out before he drowns," he said. "I'll be in my cabin."

Frost's friends ran to help him and the captain left without so much as a look at me. I scuttled below to the galley.

Supper that day was fortunately no test of my culinary art, being composed of small beer, cheese, and soft bread which the captain had purchased ashore. Though I noticed an occasional curious glance, there was no hostility in my treatment by the crew. Even Frost, nursing a sore jaw as well as a headache, seemed to have accepted my presence. It was clear that my shipmates were far from being a terrible lot once the fumes of strong liquors had cleared from their brains.

Under the captain's watchful eye, the task of completing the schooner for sea was performed in workmanlike fashion. We swept out of Loblollo Bay, as the outer harbor of Saint John's is sometimes called, at nightfall, with the last of the ebb and the first of the land breeze. Though a part of me was apprehensive regarding my future, I was by no means sad at leaving the town which had treated me so ill.

A half-moon had risen above the island, and I could see the bathing house and the weathered bulk of old James Fort as we rounded the point. The surf where it beat on the shore and, indeed, the wake of the *Pretty Polly* herself gleamed softly with phosphorescence. Captain Ross set a course to clear the Sisters and left Frost to handle the tiller.

Two hours later we were free of the land breeze and on the edge of the trades. The captain came on deck again and called all hands to get the schooner before the wind. As "all hands" evidently included the cook, I was handed a rope by one of the seamen and added my own ill-timed efforts to theirs. The *Pretty Polly* squared away with the wind on her starboard quarter and ran with all the grace she could muster.

Although I was no hand as a sailor, there was nothing wrong with my vision, and so I served my first watch at sea as the *Pretty Polly*'s lookout. I stood at the break in the forecastle, grasping the weather foremast shrouds, and gazed earnestly out over the moonlit sea. Occasionally the schooner passed through a shoal of flying fish, and from time to time one or two landed flopping on the deck. I had met with these before at Fitzgore's table and thought to gather up the unfortunate victims when I was relieved. I had no doubt that they would make a more appealing breakfast than the contents of the brine-tub could provide.

I found I had rapidly become accustomed to the vessel's motion. She lay over on her port side, the low rail amidships nearly awash. Each wave sent a shower of spray across the foredeck. I was constantly wetted, yet the night was not so cold as to make me more than slightly uncomfortable. The bow rose as the schooner met the seas, and she rolled slightly in the wind. Then as each wave passed aft, the bows dropped, the stern rose, and the *Pretty Polly* heeled again with the force of the easterly breeze.

Almost as quickly, I had become aware of the sounds the schooner made as she gave under the pressures of wind and wave. The hum of the standing rigging was as comforting as the cradlelike motion of the *Pretty Polly* through the sea. Against this played the creaky melodies of the running rigging, sheets and blocks and halyards, and of the booms against the masts, accented by the counterpoint of the timbers of the ship herself.

I recognized this concert as the sound of life at sea, for to survive, even in such gentle weather, a ship must be supple rather than rigid. That much seamanship I had learned from my tutor.

Among the myriad sounds of the night, only one caused me concern. It was a particularly dead, discordant note, one somehow subtly different even to my untrained ear. It seemed to come from close by, from the foremast itself. Although I told myself repeatedly that there was no cause for alarm, I found myself staring at the mast again and again.

My fear seemingly deafened me to all else, for while I strove in the darkness to see what was the matter with the mast, the captain had come up behind me unnoticed. I jumped in surprise when he spoke.

"Yes, Pyrrhus," he said, "that's a rotten old stick, but she'll hold till we see Falmouth again if we're careful, Lord willing." I must have looked fearful indeed, for he slapped me on the back heartily. "There, there, boy! Nothing to worry about. Call all hands, and we'll take a reef or two if it'll settle your nerves."

I studied the captain intently for a few moments. It was plain enough that he was not planning to shorten sail simply to ease the mind of his landlubber Negro cook.

"Storm coming, Captain?" My attempt at nonchalance was a failure.

"Well, the glass has dropped some," he admitted, "but this old girl has been through heavy weather before, and will again." I saw the flash of his smile in the darkness. "Now get below and wake those sots in the fo'c'sle."

The moon had long since set, and low cloud had obscured the stars before we succeeded in taking two reefs in the main and the foremast staysail. The foresail we brailed up tightly against the mast. I must have been of little assistance on deck, for the captain soon sent me below to boil up ten pounds of pork and dried peas.

When I came on deck again, Captain Ross was on the quarterdeck with Frost, and Bibber and Titcomb, the remaining crewmen, were rigging the lifelines along the deck. These I seized gratefully, for I had yet fully to acquire my sea legs, and the schooner's motion was no longer quite so regular. There was a subtle heaviness to the seas as she met them, and the wind had backed gradually northward and became prone to flaws and gusts. I made my way aft to report the food cooked and the galley fire doused.

The captain received the news with satisfaction. "Let her blow, then," he said. "It may be cold fare, but we'll have more than hard biscuit and rum to eat."

He indicated the lifelines. "How d'you like that, Pyrrhus? Safe as in your mother's arms."

"Very fine, Captain," I replied with a weak grin. "Thank you for your trouble."

The captain flashed me another grin. "No trouble at all, boy. If you go overboard, the *Pretty Polly* loses her cook, and I lose my venture." He looked about searchingly. "Besides, we may all need 'em before this blows itself out."

I judged it best to overlook his last comment and fastened instead upon an unfamiliar expression in the preceding sentence.

"Venture, Captain? What did you mean, you'd lose your venture?"

"You, boy. You." Seeing that I still did not comprehend his meaning, he continued. "That ten pounds I paid Gibbs when I bought you, that was my money. Nearly all there was left after fitting out this vessel. I'd set it aside to buy something special — my wedding present to Polly.

"Well, I ventured it instead, which is to say, I invested it in you. When I sell you in Falmouth — or maybe Boston," he mused, "I could get a better price for you in Boston — I'll make enough of a profit to buy her something really handsome and have money in hand to boot." With a smug look he added. "Besides, a regular cook would've had to be paid."

I was thunderstruck. Already I had come to think of the captain as my master, as though his ownership of me was in some way reciprocal.

Ross at least I could respect. Was I to be sold again to God-knows-who as casually as a barrel of salt mackerel?

Alas, Dr. Pangloss, I thought bitterly, if this is the best of all possible worlds, what are the others?

I might have pressed the captain further regarding his plans for my future, but his mind was evidently on his ship rather than on our conversation. I grasped the lifeline again and began to work my way to the forecastle.

I had reached the main hatch when I heard Ross's bull-like bellow.

"All hands! All hands to reef sail!"

I strove to be of help this time, one hand for myself and one for the ship, while Ross stood at the tiller and Frost, Bibber, and Titcomb put in the third reef. Nor had the captain been beforehand in his decision. No sooner had we complied with his order than the schooner heeled over to a violent gust and a flurry of enormous raindrops clattered on the deck and stung our hides like a charge of birdshot.

The rain squall was brief but violent. The water seemed to hit us in solid walls rather than in separate drops, and then, as abruptly as it had begun, the rain was over. In the wake of the squall the air became furnace-hot. The seas had mounted, and the *Pretty Polly* pitched and rolled drunkenly as she struggled through them. Every few seconds she staggered and took green water over her bows as a particularly large wave surged past.

I had long since ceased trying to move about, and clung desperately to the main shrouds. I could hear Ross shouting orders to the others, but it was all I could do to keep my feet. The wind had continued to back, however, and it was no longer possible for the schooner to hold her original course.

"We must tack ship," I heard Ross bellow. "Frost, get for'ard and handle the stays'l. Bibber, Titcomb, the main sheet!"

Struggling to keep their footing on the deck, the men took their places. Coolly, the captain waited until the next rogue wave had passed before yelling, "Ready, 'bout!"

The captain put the tiller down and with the staysail flapping, the *Pretty Polly* came up into the wind. The momentum of her turn carried her past the wind's eye. Then the staysail filled again, and the schooner was on the port tack.

The storm worsened as the night wore on, and by the end of the morning watch the seas were surging gray mountains. Under the low sky the light of the new day had a sickly cast. The captain rubbed eyes red from lack of sleep and searched the horizon. At last he seemed satisfied, and we hove to with just a scrap of canvas showing aft.

Leaving Bibber and Titcomb on the quarterdeck, Ross made his way to where I stood along the rail.

"We've nigh on two foot of water in the well," he shouted, mouth to my ear. I could hardly hear him for the wind. "A tot of rum and a biscuit all 'round, Pyrrhus, then you're to man the pump. The others have earned a rest."

I made my way around the vessel and managed to serve out the rum without either spilling too much or being swept overboard. Titcomb and Bibber staggered below to collapse in their bunks in the fore-castle, although how either they or their bedding would ever be dry again was beyond me. In view of my awkwardness, the captain gave me a length of line with which I fastened myself to the mainmast, and I threw myself into the arduous job of pumping the bilges.

My back and arms grew tired with the monotonous labor. From time to time I fell when the schooner's rhythmic motion was upset by rogue waves, yet I felt no resentment toward my idle shipmates. Indeed, I was glad to take a share in the common task of survival.

The watch changed at noon. Frost and I choked down a few clammy mouthfuls of cold pork and pease porridge and threw ourselves on our bunks. Drunk with fatigue instead of rum, Frost made no remarks about sleeping with monkeys. For my part, I was too exhausted to care.

The tempest continued to intensify through the afternoon and evening, and the larger of our two anchors came adrift at six bells in the night watch. There must have been some slack in the lashings, and the line had chafed and frayed until at last it let go.

Three hundredweight of iron swung free from the cathead on the weather bow, so that the anchor thundered against the planking like the fist of a giant demanding admittance. The massive oaken cathead had begun to splinter by the time Frost and I had worked ourselves into position to secure the anchor. The impact of the iron against the bow was such that we hesitated momentarily in fascinated horror, although I could see that it was no time for indecision. The captain's voice reached us faintly from the quarterdeck.

"Cut . . . it . . . loose!" he was shouting, the words spaced to carry better into the wind.

I looked around wildly for an ax.

An ax! There was one in the galley. I plunged through the hatch and seized it, ignoring the questions of the sleep-drugged sailors emerging from the forecastle. Fear lent me agility as I regained the deck and made my way forward.

I threw myself at the hawser. Wet and resilient, the hemp resisted my blows, Frost plucked the ax contemptuously from my grasp and pushed me clear. With two mighty strokes, he severed the cable and turned to the remaining lashing at the cathead. This rope was thinner and it parted readily. The anchor vanished as the bow rose to yet another wave.

I heaved a sigh of relief, and Frost and I looked aft. In the faint glow of the binnacle I could see the captain point downward. "Below!" he seemed to say.

This time it was Frost who understood. He disappeared through the galley hatch like a huge cat. I followed at a slower pace, the bravery of terror having left me. I found him in the forecastle with Bibber and Titcomb, bracing a mattress — mine — against the battered planking. Fortunately the damage was not serious, although the forecastle and its contents were wetter and less comfortable than ever. Frost and I made our report to the captain, and he judged it wise to come about and heave to on the opposite tack to minimize further leakage. When we had done this, he bade me issue another tot of rum before I turned in.

As I passed him again with the empty pitcher, the captain clapped his hand on my shoulder.

"Well done, boy," he shouted against the gale. I gave him a tired smile and nodded my thanks.

Wrapped in sodden blankets on the bare boards of my bunk, I wondered, in the moments before weariness overcame me, how just one mug of rum could make a person feel so warm.

7

THE second day of the storm, when at last it dawned, looked much the same as the first to me: the same lowering sky, the same unhealthy yellowish cast to the light. Much of the time, the face of the next wave seemed to form the limit of the universe, but whenever the *Pretty Polly* fought her way to the crest of yet another sea I caught a glimpse of an endless vista of marching mountains.

There was no possibility of determining our position with any pretence at accuracy. Reliable chronometers were new and still fabulously expensive. Ross did his best with a sandglass. Naturally the unbroken layer of cloud prevented the captain from taking a noon sight. At intervals he cast the log from the forecastle and marked the results on a small slate. Afterward he would disappear below and, upon his return, he would hang the slate on the binnacle.

"More than a knot of leeway," he observed to Frost on one such occasion when I was nearby. "Not quite one and a half." He looked up and saw me listening. Our eyes met and then he turned aside to answer a question from the burly man at the helm. I had not heard what Frost had asked him, but the answer was clear.

"No, not yet. As long as the wind stays as it is, we've plenty of sea room under our lee." His voice was almost too hearty. It reminded me of the tone he had used with me before the storm had struck. I looked at him narrowly and might have asked him a question myself had he not turned to me then with his ready smile.

"Since you seem to have time on your hands, Master Pyrrhus, would you be so good as to take a turn at the pumps?"

The elaborate courtesy was not lost on me, and I met his smile with one fully as broad.

"Aye, aye, sir," I said cheerfully, and turned to.

I was not the only one who was beginning to feel the strain. By evening, the captain had been on deck almost continuously for over two days. His face was haggard and worn. His blue eyes looked red and sunken, and his cheeks were stubbly.

"You look like you could use a rest, Captain," I offered, greatly daring. He turned and regarded me wearily. "Couldn't you go below for a while?" Ross hesitated and scanned the horizon, then turned to the helmsman.

"Wake me at need, Frost," he said shortly, and stumped down the ladder to his cabin. As his chin reached the level of the deck, he stopped and looked up at me. He seemed about to speak. Then he shook his head as though to clear it and disappeared below.

I was pleased to find him still asleep when I entered the cabin at dawn the next morning. His eyes opened instantly when I touched his shoulder. I mentioned that the wind seemed to show signs of moderating. His acknowledgment of my news was limited to a brusque "Very well, Pyrrhus," and for a moment I was hurt, but I put it down to the early hour and the lack of hot water for brewing coffee. Ross threw off his blankets, jammed his feet into still-wet shoes, and went on deck without favoring me with another word or glance.

I followed him up the ladder, angry with myself for caring whether he noticed me or not, and watched him as he stood there. His eyes sought the horizon automatically, then darted to some scraps of low cloud flying before the wind. He listened to the wind in the rigging, to the sounds of the *Pretty Polly* herself, with the critical air of a French concert-master. Finally he climbed the heeling deck to the weather rail and gazed at the turbulent sea. Perhaps half a minute had elapsed before he faced me.

I waited eagerly for his pronouncement that the storm would soon be over.

"Four ounces of pork and four of peas for breakfast, Pyrrhus," he said at last. "The same for dinner. Ship's bread for supper. Tot of rum at noon as usual." He started to turn away again, but stopped. My hesitation seemed to infuriate him.

"What are you waiting for, you black belly-robber? Get below!"

For an instant I felt incapable of motion. The captain took a step toward me. "Get below, I say, before I take a rope's end to you!"

I fled before the captain's wrath, but even as I went I began to sense that it was not simple anger that made him speak as he did.

Bibber and Titcomb were asleep in the forecastle when I arrived with their unappetizing breakfasts. "Poor fare, this," said Titcomb between mouthfuls, "but better than that last cook, damn him, and better than we had down to Louisburg. Have I told you about Louisburg?" He paused, but not long enough for me to reply. "Let's see, that was back in fifty-nine — no, fifty-eight —" I stole a glance at Bibber, who was eating in bored silence. He had heard it all before, but evidently a new listener, even a black one, was more than his voluble messmate could resist. Titcomb was still chattering as the pair went on deck to relieve Frost.

I spent my watch below exhausted but sleepless in my bunk, listening to Frost's rasping snores. When we were called topside again at noon, I found the captain still at the taffrail. It appeared to me that he had not moved from the spot since our encounter that morning.

Ross accepted his dinner wordlessly and ate it with an air of preoccupation. I knew it could only be the weather that concerned him so, but I, at least, could see no cause for alarm. Though the waves were as large as ever, the *Pretty Polly* rode them like a duck, and the wind was no wilder than it had been at dawn. It seemed as though perhaps the worst were over, but I suppose that in my ignorance I had grown complacent. Soon I could feel the captain's moodiness creeping over me like the onset of some sinister tropical fever, and I went unbidden to the pumps for solace.

It was nearly nightfall before the god of storms launched his final assault on the schooner.

A sudden squall, nearly double the strength of the parent tempest, roared out of the east to strike the *Pretty Polly* from abeam. Reeling under the blow, the schooner heeled over until her masts were nearly in the sea, her decks almost vertical.

Below in the galley, I was certain that my last hour had come. An avalanche of loose gear buried me as the ship went over on her side. I remember thinking that we must have struck some uncharted rock or reef, and that my only chance was to get on deck before the schooner sank beneath me.

I thrust my head through the hatch in time to watch Bibber slide by, clawing vainly at the planking, his face contorted with a scream I could not hear above the insane shriek of the wind. With nightmare slowness he slipped over the side and vanished.

As if appeased by this sacrifice, the squall was gone, and the wind reverted instantly to its former intensity. With that awful pressure relieved, the schooner rolled forcibly back to starboard. The shifting winds had whipped the sea into mad peaks of violence. The *Pretty Polly's* bow crashed through a wave as high as the topsails of a frigate just as she reached the limit of her roll.

Even above the wind I could hear the tearing crash. I looked up. Six feet from the deck, there was a crazy angle in the foremast. For an instant the mast stood against the gale, still held by its shrouds and stays. Then it began to fall. Great splinters as long as a man's leg leaped out as it fell and embedded themselves in the deck or were snatched away by the wind. I saw the main topmast snap off short at the cap and follow the foremast overboard before I lost my grip on the hatch coaming and dropped to the galley floor below.

I believe now that from the time the squall hit until I stood at last on the deck of the battered schooner was less than the time it would have taken me to climb the forty-odd feet to her main top. It could hardly have been more than a minute. I stood there dazed, and I remember thinking that the broadside of a two-decker could scarcely have wrought more damage. The captain and Titcomb were on the quarterdeck. As far as I could tell they were not much hurt. Frost appeared through the hatch, but I could make no move to assist him. I stared stupidly at the stump of the foremast and the tangle of spars, canvas, and cordage in the water beyond our starboard bow.

The captain's rough voice dragged me from my stupor. "Look alive, there, damn you," he barked as he shoved his way past me to the cluttered forecastle. I came around then, and sought to be of help, but in truth there was little we could do until the storm broke and the sea became calmer. The mess that had been our foremast trailed in the water. It was still attacked to the hull by the starboard shrouds and the forestay. Cutting it adrift entirely would have meant sacrificing the spars we would need in order to construct a jury-rig, and the drag of the wreckage in the water, like that of a sea anchor, would reduce our drift to leeward while the storm lasted. Satisfied that the shrouds would hold, the captain determined to sever the forestay, which, even I could see, imperiled our bowsprit.

Ross looked at me and then at Frost. I could no more have crawled out on the slender spar, more often in the water than above it, than I could have flown home to Ferney. Frost, I sensed, would have gone

had the captain ordered him to do so, and in Ross's momentary hesitation I could see that he knew this as well.

His jaw set in a line of grim determination. "A line, Frost," he
ordered. Frost started to speak, but was silenced by the captain's stern
glance. He stooped and cut off a length of what looked to me like a
part of the foresheet.

Ross bent the end of the line around his waist and gave Frost the
other. The lanyard of his sheath knife went around his wrist. He
straddled the butt of the bowsprit and turned to give us what must
have been intended as a reassuring grin. Wrapping his limbs about the
spar, he began to crawl.

It could hardly have been more than fifteen feet to the hounds
where the forestay was made fast, but it seemed to take the captain an
hour to shin himself close enough to reach the rope with his razor-
sharp gully. Again and again he disappeared into the bowels of a wave,
but each time he emerged, clutching the bowsprit with two legs and
one arm, gasping for breath, but always sawing away at the wrist-
thick cable of tarry hemp.

He must have cut through all but a final slim strand when the forestay finally parted under a sudden strain. Suddenly the lifeline around
Frost's middle was taut and the bowsprit empty against the sea as the
captain was flung from his perch.

We hauled him aboard and stretched him on the foredeck. I remember noticing that his knife still dangled from his wrist. Frost put
it back in its sheath. There was a cut on the captain's head with a
lump around it the size of a hen's egg, and my breath seemed to
catch in my throat as he lay there bloody and unmoving. Frost knelt
by his side and looked up at me helplessly.

Then I saw the captain's eyelids flutter. With a sudden surge of
gladness I ran to the galley hatch and swung myself down. In the
darkness I felt around until I found a tin pannikin and filled it with
rum. This I carried carefully back to the deck.

Ross was up on one elbow, leaning against Frost. There was a rude
bandage about his brow. He gave me a wan smile as I handed him the
rum and drank it off in one draught. The captain tried to get up, but
he was still unsteady and Frost and I had to help him aft to his cabin.
He started to protest as we stowed him in his bunk and then stopped.
"All right, blast you," he said, smiling weakly as I pulled his blankets

around him. "I'll rest awhile, but I'll have the hide from your black carcass if you don't wake me an hour before dawn." He closed his eyes and slept.

"Aye, aye, Captain," I said, and went to join Frost on deck.

❦❦❦ 8 ❦❦❦

THE storm blew itself out during the night. Deprived of the impetus of the wind, the tumultuous sea began rapidly to subside. By dawn only a moderate swell disturbed its surface, and when the bright rim of the newly minted sun showed itself above the eastern horizon, all hands were turned to, preparing for the task of fitting the schooner with a jury formast.

I had awakened the captain according to his instructions and had been relieved to find him alert and well. Despite the news of Bibber's loss, the fortuitous change in the weather had put him in good spirits, and he joked with us as he directed our labors or added his strength to ours. Indeed, I could see little sign of his injury other than the bloodstained strip of linen with which Frost had bound the wound.

At first I found myself wondering at the captain's recuperative powers. Then I reflected that he had for years led the sort of life that either broke men early or tempered body and soul together into the sort of iron constitution that laughed at hurts, hard work, or long exposure to the elements. How different he was from the men I had known in Saint Kitts: rich men, merchants, and planters. How different his life from that drunken luxury to which Frederick and his cronies had aspired, although the wealthy whites of the islands were not known for their longevity. Ross's life was more like that of the fresh blacks from the Guinea coast with whom I had shared the block at Gibbs's. Either the hardship and toil killed them young or they seemed to endure forever. Ross was one who would endure.

However it was, an hour before first light Ross stood on the quarter-deck coordinating our exertions when he was not straining beside us.

"Take those sweeps for'ard," he barked, pointing to a pair of long ashwood oars. "We'll use 'em to fish the new mast to the stump. You, Frost, take the other two and lash 'em together for shear-legs. No, no, the other end!

"Good. Now set those butts firm against the rail, there, and over there. Titcomb, lend a hand! No play in that lashing or she'll give way and we'll have to do it over again. Here, let me show you."

The *Pretty Polly* lay hove-to on the starboard tack, tiller lashed over, as we raced against the coming of the sun. Our spare cordage was laid out, together with what blocks and deadeyes we had salvaged, but our success would depend upon our recovering the spars we needed from the waterlogged mass alongside.

"Never mind that old mast, boys," Ross told us after a few minutes' examination and thought. "The four of us would never get her hoisted up even if she were worth saving. Get the gaff and the boom first, and that topmast."

It was Titcomb, gone aft for a forgotten tool, who first noticed the long line of gray-blue which stretched along the southern horizon.

"Land!" His shout startled us, tugging and hacking intently at the wreckage forward. "Land off the port quarter!"

"How far?" demanded Ross. He picked his way across the littered deck to squint at the distant hills.

"Good ten mile, I make it, Cap'n."

Ross stood on the deck, back to me, and I watched while he pondered this new development.

"Guadeloupe," he muttered at last. He turned and saw Frost and me watching him idly. "Get a move on there, you sluggards!" he snapped. "Plenty of time to get the job done before we drift ashore — or had you planned to wait until afterward?" We leaped to obey.

With land under our lee, we worked like madmen, and the morning was no more than half gone by the time the new foremast was ready to be raised.

From the stump of the old mast, stretched out along the bowsprit, lay what had been the boom of the foresail. Already we had rove new stays to support it fore and aft, and shrouds lay coiled loosely, to be set up taut after the new mast was in place. Frost and I stood ready at the windlass. A line ran from the barrel over the shears to what would soon be the masthead. Titcomb stood ready on the forecastle, with lengths of line already cut and to hand. These he would use to lash the butt of the boom to the stump of the ruined mast once it had become sufficiently upright that the bitts there would no longer secure it from rolling from side to side as the ship did. The captain had stationed himself aft, where he could take up the slack in the backstay and whence he could observe and correct the efforts of the rest of us. It was a tremendously complex procedure, as intricate as the steps of any gavotte poor Hartshorn had endeavored to teach me.

"Handsomely, now, on the winch," Ross said, timing the commands to the pitch and roll of the schooner. Frost and I threw our weight on the handspikes and the slim spar began to rise. By cautious increments we hoisted it to meet the apex of the shears. Titcomb ran loops of line around mast and stump as we worked and tightened them, tourniquet fashion, with another handspike.

" 'Vast hauling, there! Belay that!" the captain bawled at last. I tripped the pawl on the winch and sank back gratefully. But the captain was in no mood for rest.

"Frost, come aft here and lend a hand on this backstay. Titcomb, let Pyrrhus do that. You cast loose the shears and then start setting up those shrouds. Two port and two starboard's good enough for the time being." Hastily we took our new positions.

"Ready? All right, Frost, on the count of three, heave!"

The new mast, deprived of the steadying effort of the shears, swung with the motion of the schooner, and it was not easy for me to restrain it as Ross and Frost pulled it upright. Their skill and timing carried the day. It was not long before Titcomb was tightening down the lanyards threaded through the deadeyes at the ends of the shrouds. The *Pretty Polly* had her new foremast.

This was far from the end of our labors. Although the old gaff would serve as a boom, another gaff had to be fashioned from the main topmast. Neither Frost nor Ross was a proper ship's carpenter, but they made shift to create the necessary fittings with the limited tools and materials we had at hand. Meanwhile, I helped Titcomb, a capable man with needle and sailmaker's palm, to rouse out a set of spare sails and cut them down to fit our makeshift rig. A jib was the first order of business, for with the pressure of a jib forward to balance that of our reefed mainsail aft, we could at least get some way on the vessel and begin to claw, albeit slowly, to windward and away from the threatening lee shore.

Being accounted clever with my hands although inexperienced, I offered to help Titcomb in sewing the boltropes along the edges of the sail. It was slow work, and often painful, as I soon developed a blister where the stiff leather palm rubbed on my own, but I would have enjoyed my task except for Titcomb's interminable storytelling. Had half of what he said been true, Wolfe and Amherst might better have stayed home in England. It seemed to me that he must have fought with his musket in one hand and his breeches in the other; between winning battles on his own and begetting a race of bastards from Cape Breton to Quebec, Lemuel Titcomb could scarcely have had time to dress until the peace treaty was signed in 1763.

He was shaking his head at one particularly lurid episode when Captain Ross asked for assistance in raising the new gaff. I had ceased to care whether the tales were memories or pipedreams by then and welcomed the interruption.

Frost and I hauled away with a will and the gaff rose swiftly. Then one of the sheaves fouled. We could accomplish nothing from the deck. "I'll free it, Captain," I said, and leaped into the rigging as I had seen the others do.

Almost I went over the side, as I had chosen the lee, rather than the windward side of the vessel, but I kept my hold and managed to free the pulley. Before sliding back to the deck, I began to survey the surrounding ocean from my new point of vantage.

An irregularity on the seaward horizon caught my eye. I pointed, and had begun to sing out, "Sail ho!" in true seamanlike fashion, but my one-handed grip gave way and I slid gracelessly to the deck.

I had expected that my discovery would occasion some excitement, but I was doomed to disappointment. Ross took the spyglass up the weather main-shrouds and examined the distant vessel.

"Brig," he said shortly. "Should pass far to the wind'ard of us. Too far off to be of much help anyway." He looked down to where I nursed a new crop of blisters from the rope. "Don't worry, boy, 'tisn't Bloody Morgan, nor Blackbeard either.

"Titcomb!" he shouted, forgetting me. "Isn't that jib ready for hoisting yet? By God, you've had time enough to make a mains'l for a frigate!"

"This minute, Captain!"

We forgot the distant sail in the flurry of getting the new jib set and drawing. Ross took the tiller and put the *Pretty Polly* about on the other tack. Frost and Titcomb set to work on a new foresail while I went below to get the galley back in order and to start cooking our first hot meal since before the storm. Everything was knocked into one great hoorah's-nest below, and it was an hour or more before I could announce that dinner was nearly ready.

When I came on deck, Ross was gazing contemplatively at the approaching brig, now so close that it was in easy view from the deck and hull-up. He received my news with absent-minded satisfaction. As I turned to leave, he said, "Stay on deck, if you please, Pyrrhus. I'll be putting the ship on the other tack. No; on second thought, go down to my cabin and get the ensign from the locker under my bunk. Let's have a look at this fellow's colors."

I went below and came back with our flag, the red British ensign flown by merchantmen. Ross bent it on the halyard and raised it to the maintop.

"There," he said with evident satisfaction. "Let's see what that scares out of the bushes." He reached for the spyglass in its rope beckets on the taffrail and squinted across the narrowing strip of water at the stranger.

"Aha! I thought so!" The exclamation was involuntary, but he noted my puzzlement and added, "Look there, Pyrrhus! A Frenchie!"

I took the proffered telescope and focused on the brig. At her masthead flew a white flag with gold lilies, identifying her as a French man-of-war.

"Good day to you, Mongseer le Frog!" Ross called out gaily. "Nothing to worry about there, Pyrrhus! We're well outside French waters, and there's no fear of impressment. If she'd been English and short-handed, well, there might have been trouble. Still, better safe than sorry." He altered course to leave the Frenchman dead astern. "Call Titcomb to take the tiller, Pyrrhus," he said as the *Pretty Polly* steadied on her new heading. "I'll have my dinner now."

I passed the word to Titcomb on my way to the galley and he went aft to take the helm while Frost continued to stitch at the foresail. When I came on deck again after serving the captain, the Frenchman was visibly nearer.

"Reminds me of a brig we took off Martinique in sixty-one," observed Titcomb as I went aft to the rail for a better look. "I was third lieutenant of the *Fox* privateer out of Boston." He smacked his lips at the memory. "What a cruise that was!"

I took the spyglass from where it hung and examined the brig once more. There was a menacing air to the way she followed in our wake, coming ever closer and closer. It seemed to me, too, that there were more men on her deck than was needful. While I watched, her head-sails began to shiver as she came up into the wind.

I looked down at Ross through the cabin skylight. "If you please, Captain," I said, "I think the Frenchman is up to something." Ross looked up, nodded, and rose from the table.

". . . brig was full of Frenchwomen from Martinique," said Titcomb. "They took off the officers and crew and put on six of us, with me as prize-master. There was this one, a beauty she was, too . . ."

The brig was nearly broadside-to now, and I could see that she mounted six guns a side. Captain Ross appeared in the hatchway as the port-lids came open and the muzzles of the canon began to appear.

"Captain Ross, I began.

". . . couldn't keep her hands off'n me," said Titcomb.

"My God, Captain, they're going to fire on us!"

❧❧❧ 9 ❧❧❧

THE foremost of the brig's guns fired at the precise instant that Ross's feet touched the quarterdeck. I ducked instinctively, but the cannonball pitched into the sea a cable's length in front of the schooner. The shot had been merely the recognized summons for us to halt. Neither Ross nor the others had reacted fearfully. I looked my repentance at the captain.

Ross opened his mouth to speak, but whether he intended to rebuke my evident cowardice or simply to issue the order to heave-to I never learned. He looked over my shoulder at the French brig and his eyes opened wide with alarm. He flung himself flat on the worn planking. "Get down, you fools!" he shouted.

Frost and Titcomb followed the captain's example. For a perceptible instant the only sound was that of the wind and our passage through the water. I had just time enough to take note of the unnatural silence when it was shattered by the Frenchman's broadside.

I stood blinking until a ball staggered me with the closeness of its passing, after which I lay on the deck and trembled like a philosopher. A hole appeared in the mainsail and a portion of the low rail amidships was gone, dissolved in a shower of splinters. Towering waterspouts marked the impact of other shots less well aimed. I heard shouts and the rumble of gun-carriages on the brig's deck as her crew reloaded. Eye-watering clouds of smoke drifted down from the Frenchman and enveloped us.

I felt confused and terrified. The attack seemed senseless — certainly it had been unprovoked — and the world, seen through what poets have called the glorious haze of battle, seemed unreal and suddenly malevolent. It was as though a porcelain spaniel should rise from the hearth to snap at one's throat. My thoughts came in disjointed snatches: that I did not want to die; that the Frenchman had allowed us no time to respond to his challenge before he had opened fire. I told myself that the man must be mad. Alone and in evident distress, the *Pretty Polly* was no threat to his well-armed vessel. It had to be a mistake! Why, England and France were at peace: had been at peace for years. Bafflement and a feeling of helplessness drove me to the edge of tears.

I wiped my eyes on my sleeve and looked about me. Frost was ramming a cartridge down the barrel of a musket. Titcomb was just getting to his knees. "Closest call I've had since sixty-three," he began. I shook my head and tried to marshal my senses.

Captain Ross leaped to his feet. "That's no use, Frost! Titcomb! The tiller, blast you! Frost! Let fly the sheets!" His voice cracked with the strain. "Pyrrhus! Pyrrhus, damn your eyes, strike the colors!" I must have hesitated too long to suit him, for even as I rose to obey he elbowed me out of the way and let loose the halyard. The flag lay on the deck like dirty laundry as the schooner came up into the wind.

A gust carried away the last of the powder smoke to reveal the French vessel hove-to on the same tack as we, perhaps seventy-five yards distant. Gold lace flashed on the quarterdeck and the black muzzles of the cannon showed through the gun-ports. I could hear the high-pitched, excited gabble of the crewmen who peered over the bulwarks.

"Fancy an English crew behaving like Portygee bum-boat men!" snorted Ross. "Steady, lads. Show Mongseer how seamen behave! And leave the talking to me if you want to see Falmouth again!"

I found myself literally tugging at his sleeve. "Please, Captain. What do they want with us? Tell them they'll have to let us go! It's time of peace!"

Ross laughed sourly. "Let us go? Who's to make them let us go? It's probably some mistake or other, but if not, well, you at least needn't fear prison. Like's not they'll just sell you to some planter."

"But, Captain, I can speak their language. Let me try — I can tell them —"

"You can shut your mouth, you damned coward, and let me think!" My own guilt added to the pain I felt at his words and I recoiled as from a blow. In more normal tones the captain added, "For God's sake, Pyrrhus, if you do speak French, don't let on. They'll claim you're a fugitive slave if you do. You'll be cutting sugar cane before you can say Jack Robinson and get the rest of us hanged into the bargain."

Though he must have meant this last as a kindness, I scarcely heard him. I nursed my wounded feelings and stared across the narrow gulf at our pursuer. The brig's cutter had been manned and I watched it as it drew closer. I was able to discern that the figure in the stern sheets wore the blue and gold of an officer, but I had no opportunity to examine the boat's occupants as closely as I would have liked. Ross seized me by the arm and mustered the three of us into line abaft the main hatch. With a hoarse reminder for us to hold our tongues, he turned to await the arrival of the boarding party.

I heard the officer's curt order to stop rowing and glanced nervously about as the boat scraped on the schooner's side. From where I stood all that was visible was the tips of the oars and these disappeared as the oars were stowed in the boat. A hand holding a cutlass appeared on the rail, and the first of six heavily armed sailors vaulted aboard. I stiffened at the sight of drawn swords and cocked pistols, but found myself goggling like an imbecile at the man who followed them. The protest on the captain's lips died stillborn.

I had expected a French officer to be elegant in dress and manner, but in truth there was more corsair than courtier about him. I looked him up and down.

His shoes were of good leather, but ill-fitting and much worn, and the buckles were mere pinchbeck. The kneebands of his breeches were unfastened, so that the stockings hung loosely on his thin shanks. He had on a scarlet waistcoat beneath his coat of faded blue broad-cloth; the waistcoat was stained and the coat, though fashionably cut, had a patch at one elbow. Beneath the tarnished epaulet on his left shoulder a seam in the coat gaped to reveal the shirt within.

I noted with distaste that the fine lace at the man's throat was far from clean. His cheeks were sallow and unshaven; his eyes, bloodshot and pouchy. Yet when he stepped forward to speak he bore himself with an air, as though sublimely unaware of the shabbiness of his present appearance.

"*M'sieu' le capitaine?*" he asked. Ross nodded.

"Allow me to introduce myself. I am Lieutenant André D'Agenais, late of His Most Christian Majesty's Navy, and presently an officer in the Revenue Service." His English was heavily accented, the suavity of his smile somehow at odds with the shrewdness of his glance, but he made Ross a leg in genteel enough fashion, and, doffing his huge cocked hat, swept it in a graceful arc down and across his body. The hat was lavishly trimmed in brassy gold lace, one end of which dangled loose.

"I greatly regret any inconvenience, gentlemen, but your vessel is in French waters." He paused theatrically.

"And you, I fear, are my prisoners."

Ross found his tongue at last. "See here, you frog-eating hedge-gentleman," he began. He took a step forward and raised clenched fists.

A loud metallic click came from under the Frenchman's hat. Ross lowered his hands and stood there warily. His jaw was set hard. A muscle twitched in his cheek.

I looked back at D'Agenais. He had lowered his right hand, still holding that Rodomontine hat, to reveal his left hand and an ugly short-barreled pistol, which was pointed at the captain's belly. His smile was unchanged.

"You will oblige me, monsieur," he said evenly, "by endeavoring to control yourselves in this so-unfortunate situation." He looked down at the pistol as though himself surprised to see it and shrugged in characteristically Gallic fashion. He lowered the hammer to half-cock and placed the weapon back in his pocket.

"Now, where was I? Ah!

"You, gentlemen, are my prisoners, or rather the prisoners of Capitaine Homard of the brig *Moniteur*, under whom I have the honor to serve. You are to be charged with smuggling. . . . Keep silent, if you please, m'sieu'. You are impolite. I will examine your papers later.

"My men and I will take command of this vessel, which we shall sail to Basse-Terre. There you will be taken ashore and given a fair trial, at which time you will have the opportunity to explain your presence in these waters. Afterward . . ." He shrugged again. "Afterward, your ship will be condemned and sold. I am sorry if this distresses you, messieurs, but it is the usual practice. His Excellency the Governor has certain expenses, and I myself am far from wealthy.

"Besides, you will no longer have need of a ship, as you will doubtless be His Excellency's guests for some time. I fear that you will find the accommodations rather Spartan, but perhaps you may come to appreciate the distinction.

"But you must be tired, *mes amis!* I forget my duties as host. You have had a busy morning, and now you should rest. Be so kind as to allow my men to make you comfortable."

At a signal from D'Agenais, a pair of the ruffians sheathed their weapons and came forward. Frost, who could have lifted one of them in each hand and cracked their skulls with ease, looked at Ross. The captain shook his head and nodded at D'Agenais. The Frenchman had silently drawn his pistol and had stepped aside to allow the sailors behind him a clear line of fire. Sullenly Frost allowed the two seamen to tie his hands.

The sailors passed from man to man and finished with me. The bite of the rough hemp as it encircled my wrists emphasized my helplessness, but it also brought me to a realization. I could not fight, and there were no diamonds with which to purchase my freedom. Wit would have to serve.

I glanced down the row at my fellow prisoners. Frost glared at his captors like a caged bear. Titcomb might have been anywhere. Ross seemed lost in self-reproach. I felt myself filling with resentment which ripened into anger. Congratulations, Captain, I said to myself bitterly, your tongue and your courage have served us well! But you have only yourself to blame. You at least were here of your own accord!

My thoughts were angry, but I strove to conceal them, smiling at the sailors. Doubtless they took me for a simpleton. When they had finished, D'Agenais looked at each of us in a calculating manner. I grinned at him hopefully.

"Four is too many," he said at last in French. "Take the big one and that other with the face like a cow's behind" — Frost and Titcomb — "back to the ship. Give my compliments to the captain, and tell him we shall be in port by tomorrow night. You, Jacques, and you, yes, and you: you three will remain here with me. The rest of you, back to the ship."

Ross looked on miserably as the Frenchmen bundled Frost and Titcomb over the side into the longboat. He turned to D'Agenais, but the Frenchman brushed aside his protestations. "Your colleagues will be made welcome, my friend. We are not savages." The look on the captain's face showed how highly he valued French assurances. Almost I pitied him, but I had my own concerns.

"Come, come, Captain!" D'Agenais continued heartily. "You will be reunited with them soon enough.

"And now, perhaps, you will allow this man to escort you below? I must get this vessel under way, and then I have business with your servant. You and I shall have time to get better acquainted later."

One of the Frenchmen took the captain forward while the rest assisted D'Agenais in getting the schooner before the wind. We bore off from the *Moniteur,* and for some time I was ignored. It suited me well enough. I needed time in which to think.

Apparently D'Agenais had taken me at face value. I decided that my best course lay in encouraging him to continue to underestimate my abilities. An ignorant, complaisant slave might be despised, but he would certainly have opportunities that would be denied a man more highly esteemed.

But even an actor needs a role. I chose as my model old Atticus, Fitzgore's aged retainer. Inconspicuous yet always present when needed, even I had taken him for granted. This was what I sought.

There is this much merit in pretense: confusion and anger dwindled as I assumed Ad's placid manner. My mind was clear. I became all winning simplicity without, coldly purposeful within.

D'Agenais went below to the cabin as soon as the schooner was on a course for Basse-Terre. He sent a man to fetch me a few minutes later. I noticed that the sailor's sole weapon was the clasp knife with which he cut me loose. If he saw me smile, he must have assumed that it was out of gratitude.

The lieutenant did not look up when his henchmen thrust me disdainfully through the cabin door. The room bore the marks of a hurried but thorough search, and D'Agenais was examining the ship's books and papers. I watched him carefully, trying to appear timid but eager to please. There was a half-empty bottle of rum at his elbow and his sallow complexion had taken on a tone that might almost have been healthy. At length he looked up.

"Ah! You will be the cook." He squinted down at the crew list. "Pyrrhus?" It sounded more like Peru than anything else.

I nodded.

"*Bien.* You will cook for me? For my men? Good. Then you remain at liberty for now. Should you require a knife, one of my men will assist you. You understand? That is settled, then." I concluded that the interview was at an end, and turned to go.

"Your captain, Pyrrhus, is he rich?" The rapid change of subject startled me, and I hesitated before answering. Yes or no might be equally hazardous replies. D'Agenais looked up from under raised brows.

"There should be hard money aboard. Gold." His eyes narrowed. "Where does your captain keep his gold?"

"Gold, Mongseer? Don't know nothin' 'bout no gold."

"There was but one piece of gold and a little silver in his chest, you dolt. He must have hidden the rest." He rubbed his jaw speculatively. "I could beat it out of you, I suppose."

At that moment I would have betrayed my own parents, had I known them. It showed. Gibbs had taught me fear if nothing else.

"Bah! I waste my time with you, idiot. Summon one of my men, and then you may put this sty of a cabin into order. *Va-t-en!* Go, go!"

I was refolding the captain's clothes and stowing them in his trunk when a sailor pushed him into the cabin. He looked at me sharply, but neither one of us, seemingly, had anything to say.

"Ah! Captain Ross!" D'Agenais's manner had again become mincingly cordial. "I trust your accommodations are to your liking? No?

Quel dommage! A pity, but it cannot be helped for the time being. To business, then.

"First, there is the matter of the smuggling charges. A grave offense, I assure you, monsieur, grave.

"But I have the open mind, like all French gentlemen, and I decide to examine your papers. Just when it seems that perhaps you are indeed the unfortunate trader you claim to be, alas! I find this box." He gestured at a small chest on the desk, opening it with a fingertip. It was Ross's medical kit; the lock had been crudely forced. "You English!" He shook his head with exaggerated sympathy. "I fear it will go hard with you, Captain; the laws against smuggling drugs are most explicit. Unless, of course. . . . But allow me to digress for a moment.

"I have told you, m'sieu', that I was formerly an officer in the navy. During the last war, I was in command of a very jewel of a brig when I had the misfortune to encounter a fleet of warships under the command of Admiral Parker. We were hopelessly outnumbered. For honor's sake I fired one broadside and hauled down my flag. The lives of my men — but you, too, know how it is to command.

"For many months I lived like an animal in one of your prison ships. The war ended at last and I returned home. Home!

"I was brought before a court-martial. My actions had been correct, and so I was exonerated. In time of peace, however, the navy is a small one, and a man who surrendered his vessel with hardly a shot fired. . . .

"There was no ship for me, m'sieu'. I tried at first to find some subordinate position. The answer was always different, but always the same. At last I began to understand." He poured himself another drink from the captain's bottle and tossed it off at a draught.

"I turned to drink, to the gaming tables. I ran into debt. Also, there was a duel.

"Finally, to avoid a scandal that would have ruined the entire family, a kind relative exerted his influence to obtain for me my present position."

He slammed his fist on the desk. "*Et voici!* Look at me! I, André D'Agenais! Lieutenant in a washbasin of a revenue brig with a captain — *sacré cochon!* — incapable of navigating from one end of a horse trough to the other!"

D'Agenais gulped another tot of rum and sat for a moment staring into the glass. When he spoke again his voice was calm.

"I tell you this, *monsieur le capitaine,* so that you will understand that I have no cause to love you English, you who began my misfortunes. I tell you frankly so that you will believe what I am about to say. I wish you to know that I am quite capable of flogging you to death, or worse, if you are obstinate.

"I am convinced, Captain, that you have a quantity of hard money concealed aboard this vessel. Come, m'sieu', do not trouble yourself to deny it. It is the usual practice.

"A moderate sum in gold which, shall we say, escaped the notice of my superiors would be of great service to me at present. As I have told you before, I am not a wealthy man." He gestured to indicate his faded finery. "On the other hand, my friend, I am not ungrateful.

"For your, ah, cooperation, monsieur, I will undertake to place you aboard the first vessel we encounter after the funds are in my hands. I will claim you were killed in an attempt to escape. No one need be the wiser!" He looked at Ross shrewdly.

"Come, Captain! These are favorable terms! Of a surety, you lose your money and your vessel, but these are lost to you in any event. I offer you your life and your freedom!"

I looked at Ross. He was staring at D'Agenais and seemed to be considering what he had said with some favor. Almost I cried out to him, for I had no good opinion of the Frenchman's sincerity. With an effort I reminded myself that I owed the captain nothing and went back to folding the clothing that had been scattered when his sea chest had been searched. It seemed a long while before the captain spoke.

"How do I know I can trust you?"

D'Agenais was genial, expansive. "Oh, monsieur! You would question the word of honor of a French officer? For that I should call you out! It is something no gentleman should allow.

"But see! I am magnanimous. You may trust me, my friend, for the simplest of reasons. After you have shown me the hiding place of the gold, I of course will not want the authorities to question you, lest certain of them who are my enemies — evil-minded men, all of them! — should misinterpret my actions."

I could not believe that Ross would accept such a transparent argument, yet when I looked at him I could detect no hint of suspicion. Very well, Captain Fool, I said to myself. You got us into this, get your own self out. I told myself that it was every man for himself;

that it had to be. I stole another glance at Ross. There was something unsettling about the way he looked at me, and I turned my head away.

"What about Pyrrhus?" I kept my eyes on my work and tried to ignore the captain's voice.

"The black? He is worth little enough. Very well, you may keep him."

Ross mulled the Frenchman's words, but it seemed obvious that D'Agenais had won. "I'll need some time to think, Lieutenant."

"But of course, of course! I am patient as well as magnanimous. You may have until dawn." Ross turned toward the door.

"Captain Ross?" The tone was flat, chilling. "Do not try my patience beyond the sunrise. It is not unlimited. And remember that there remain other ways of extracting information at which I have some small skill."

D'Agenais stared at the closed door for some time after the sailor had led Ross away. Absently he sipped the dregs remaining in his glass.

"Bah! What filth!" He threw the tumbler against the bulkhead, where it shattered. "Is there no wine aboard this floating chamberpot? No brandy?"

"No, Mongseer. We got more rum, though. It's good rum, Mongseer. You just sit back. More rum and a new glass, that's what you need."

D'Agenais lurched irritably to his feet. "Clean up this mess, blackbird. Then get forward and prepare supper. It will be the worse for your backside if it is not ready to eat at sundown."

He slammed the door behind him. I listened to his steps as he climbed the ladder to the quarterdeck. He paced back and forth for several minutes before he addressed the man at the tiller. I could hear his voice clearly through the cabin skylight, but I worked on as though I understood no word of what was being said.

"Is it possible . . . ? No! No, there is money here! I can smell it!" His footsteps traveled the length of the deck and back. "Then why wait until morning? Ah, that fool of an Englishman! Does he think he can outsmart me, the dog?"

The helmsman said something I could not make out. D'Agenais laughed. It was a flat, mirthless sound.

"No, my friend, no bargains! I mean to have it all. And afterward, willing or not, it's all one to me. I do not care to chance His Excellency's hearing of our little transaction. Let the Englishman complain to the fishes.

"But he will tell. He will beg to tell. There are ways, my friend. As a boy in Marseilles — the Algerines! A pitiless people, but adroit, most adroit. The poor wretch we found may have lived for days."

The reply was again indistinct. I caught but one word, "*nègre.*"

"The *moricaud?* He knows nothing, but he is worth a few francs on the block at Basse-Terre. He may join the captain or not. We shall see when the time comes."

I waited for several minutes before I dared show my face on deck, lest my appearance reveal what I understood of D'Agenais's plan.

The galley was a cheerless place despite the sunlight which found its way in through the hatch. I looked in at Captain Ross. Well-trussed with ropes, he had been laid in one of the forecastle bed places. I had assumed he was asleep, so that it came as something of a shock when he spoke. He asked me how I fared. I repeated to him what I had learned.

"Well done, Pyrrhus," he said respectfully, "though I'm damned if I know how it's going to help us. Still, well done.

"I can't say I'm surprised. I confess I never thought he'd go so far. I thought a bribe, perhaps. . . .

"The drugs, of course, were just an excuse for seizing the ship. They'd know that any vessel would have 'em, laudanum and tartar emetic and such.

"D'Agenais must be desperate for money. I've half a mind not to tell him. Yes, he's right, there's specie aboard. Quite a lot of specie, and well hidden. But perhaps he'd force me to tell in the end." He was silent for a while.

I could think of nothing to say, either. At last Ross seemed to come to a decision. "I'll tell him," he said. They are determined to be shut of me in any event. Perhaps they'll let you be if I don't get their blood up first."

I tried to thank him, but he went right on. "There's no way to save the money, or me. But I don't see any reason for you to die, too. Or do you have a plan?" He smiled to show how likely he thought it that I might find a means of escape where he had failed. I started to speak again, but he hushed me. "Someone's coming! Get back to the galley. Quickly, now!"

I was rattling my coppers energetically and stoking the galley fire when one of the sailors, evidently sent to keep an eye on the captain and me, dropped through the hatch. He went into the forecastle with a sidelong look at me and tested Ross's bonds. Finding them secure, he made himself comfortable in one of the vacant bunks and produced a plug of tobacco from the pocket of his jumper.

Much of our provision had been damaged by the storm, but there were a few vegetables left as well as a piece of dried cod. I combined them with salt beef in a stew known in the islands as "pepperpot." The seasonings in such a highly spiced dish would mask any signs of spoilage as well as the deficiencies of my cuisine.

I was no closer to resolving my concerns a half hour later. I stood in the galley, staring into the bubbling stew. My thoughts mirrored the haphazard mess as it simmered.

It seemed I would have to attempt to escape. It was less than an even wager that D'Agenais would allow me to set foot on land.

Against my will I had been touched by the captain's concern for me, and though I resented his status as my owner, Ross was a necessary element in any escape at sea. The *Pretty Polly*'s boat had been destroyed in the storm. That left only the schooner itself, but I could think of no way in which Ross and I could overpower four hearty men and retake her.

"Damn it, man, spit in the kid, not on the deck!" The captain's voice startled me. The offending sailor made no audible reply.

Savory steam drifted up from the kettle. I dipped a spoon into the stew and tasted it idly. I remember thinking that a bit more pepper could do no harm, and reaching for the tin on the shelf. There was perhaps enough to fill a snuffbox left in the canister. I added a pinch to the mixture on the stove and watched as it disappeared.

Then, smiling, I poured in what remained.

THE smile I wore when I entered the forecastle twenty minutes later was not the same. It was deferential when I handed the guard a heaping plate and condescending as I fed Ross his scanty helping. The captain eyed me with suspicion as he ate, but I teased him with each mouthful as one would a backward child. I doubt the Frenchman understood one word in three, but as he ate he chuckled at the mockery in my voice and at Ross's evident discomfiture.

It was dark by the time the two had finished. I had set aside a portion for myself in the galley, but there was time only for a few hasty swallows before the word came for me to fetch the lieutenant's supper aft. Steam still curled from the tray as I set it down, and I had refilled his rum bottle, but when I held the chair for him, D'Agenais swore at me negligently and told me to leave. Spurred on by oaths from the two men on deck, I hastened to feed them. They must have nearly scalded themselves, but they roared with greedy pleasure as they shoveled the spicy concoction into their mouths. I smiled then like any proud cook, and smiled more broadly still when I returned to the galley to find that Ross's guard had eaten the remains of my supper and cleaned out the pot as well.

I returned to the cabin for D'Agenais's plate and found him examining the captain's ledgers with an expression of intense concentration. His uniform coat hung over the back of the chair and the half-empty rum bottle stood at his elbow. He rubbed his face with his right hand and shook his head, mumbling to himself. I poured him another glass of rum before I slipped out of the room with the tray.

There was nothing to do but to turn in when I had cleaned the galley. Sleep was an impossibility, of course, so I watched through lowered lids as each of the sailors took a turn as guard after a shift on deck.

I think it was the one D'Agenais called Jacques who had the night watch. A short time after he arrived in the forecastle, I noticed beads of sweat on his brow. He wrapped the blanket about his body and slumped back in the bed place with every appearance of distress.

I stretched and yawned as though waking and slid out of my bed. The sailor paid me no attention, but Ross was awake and he looked at me curiously. I shook my head minutely and went on deck as though to answer a call of nature.

Despite the lantern that burned in the forecastle, I did not find it much darker on deck than it had been below. It took my eyes only a few moments to pick out the silhouette of the forward lookout. He was bent over the lee rail, retching painfully. I reached out and removed a belaying pin from the fife rail and ducked back through the hatch.

The guard was now actively ill. As I entered he doubled up and vomited. It filled the spit kid and spilled out onto the deck. He looked up at me with glassy eyes. He was too sick to speak, and I felt a spasm of pity. I waited for him to look away before I raised my arm. I can remember wondering how hard I should hit him.

He looked up again just as I started to strike. I tried to stop the blow even as the makeshift club caught him across the bridge of his nose. He fell back, half-stunned, with the blood running down his face. It glistened metallically in the lamplight, and for a few seconds I stood there staring. Then as he struggled I hit him again, hard, and once again.

"Get his knife, for God's sake, and cut me loose." The words seemed to come from far away.

"His knife, Pyrrhus! Get his knife!" I looked around. The captain had struggled to a sitting position and was looking at me oddly. I was breathing in little gasps. I felt sick to my stomach, but turned to obey in mechanical fashion.

The effort of touching the Frenchman was like a plunge into cold water. By the time I had found his clasp knife I had regained some semblance of composure. I went to work on the captain's bonds, and in a few short sentences I explained about the tartar emetic which had been masked by the spices in the pepperpot and the thirty drops of laudanum in D'Agenais's bottle of rum. The look that Ross gave me as I spoke might well have been one of respect, but at the time I scarcely noticed.

I must have been perilously near the end of my strength by the time the captain was free, for I felt only relief when he took charge. He paused briefly over the man in the other berth and then motioned for me to follow him.

The lookout on deck was still making his offering to Neptune. Ross handed me the clasp knife and stepped out of his shoes. The sailor apparently never heard a sound as the captain crept up behind him; I watched as Ross seized the waistband and the ample seat of the seaman's breeches and heaved him over the side.

Only the man at the helm remained on deck. Ross took back the knife and led the way aft.

We paused at the break of the quarterdeck to prepare for the final rush. I could see that the man had a bucket at his feet. As we watched, he doubled over, but there was nothing remaining in his tortured stomach.

"Come on!" Ross whispered urgently. He rose to run. I got on one knee to follow, but the helmsman must have let the schooner's head fall off slightly. She lurched unexpectedly. I lost my balance and fell against the captain's legs.

My eyes met those of the Frenchman at the tiller. For a long moment we stared at each other in fascinated horror.

Even as he opened his mouth to shout the alarm, Ross was on him. The captain grunted savagely as he drove the knife into the man's abdomen and bundled him, still living, over the taffrail and into the sea.

I was kneeling in a pool of vomit. Someone had kicked over the Frenchman's bucket during the brief scuffle, but from the taste in my mouth, some of it was mine. I looked about. The captain was lashing the tiller to keep the *Pretty Polly* on course. I crawled over to the skylight. Had D'Agenais heard the commotion? I listened intently and then smiled up at Ross when he came and stood at my side. The only sound from the cabin was that of heavy breathing. D'Agenais was asleep.

We slipped cautiously into the cabin. I held my breath as Ross searched the pockets of the Frenchman's coat, but he found the little box-lock pistol quickly. He stood back and cocked it and then he nodded to me.

I shook D'Agenais gently by one shoulder, then more forcefully. He pushed my arm away without waking. Ross motioned me out of the way. "Mongseer!" he said sharply. "Wake up, Mongseer!" Then he pushed the chair over with his foot.

D'Agenais woke when he hit the floor.

"*Sacré nom d'une . . . !*" He rubbed his face and sat up. Then he saw the captain. Ross laughed grimly.

"Good evening, Mongseer," he said, with evident relish. "Pray excuse my informality. We English are not so well schooled in politeness as you, but I shall do my best.

"Mongseer, now you are my prisoner."

D'Agenais looked from Ross to me and back again. From one of confusion, his expression changed to consternation, to controlled rage, and back to his habitual courtly urbanity. He offered no resistance when we took him on deck and tied him to the mast. Ross left me on guard while he went below. When he returned, I saw that he had a keg in his arms. From the way he handled it, I could tell it was empty. Ropes were tied around it. He handed it to me and addressed himself to D'Agenais with a bow.

"Please accept my thanks, Mongseer," he said with a wolfish grin, "for your hospitality." D'Agenais smiled and nodded sardonically in return. "I would like to return the favor, but I fear you must be leaving." He handed me the knife and drew and cocked the Frenchman's little pistol. "Cut him loose, Pyrrhus. It is time for us to say goodbye to Mongseer D'Agenais."

I had seen enough death to last me a long time, but after all, the Frenchman deserved no better treatment. I was careful not to step between Ross and D'Agenais as I cut the ropes that bound the prisoner to the mast.

"Free his hands as well," said the captain. I wondered, but I did as I was told. D'Agenais massaged sore wrists and eyed the captain warily. He looked as though he were steeling himself for a leap, and I gripped my knife tighter.

"The tide is on the make, Mongseer," Ross said. D'Agenais and I both started at this seeming irrelevance. The captain smiled again.

"We are less than a mile from shore. Do you swim well?"

D'Agenais's features relaxed into a smile that was genuine. "Indifferently well, m'sieu'."

"I thought as much. We will throw the keg overboard after your departure. It may be of assistance." He gestured with the pistol. "And now, Mongseer, if you will." D'Agenais climbed onto the windward rail and held the main shrouds. "Goodbye, Mongseer. I dare not go any closer. I hope you will not be too greatly inconvenienced."

"Think nothing of it, m'sieu'." The Frenchman's teeth flashed in a last smile. "'*Voir.*" He stepped off and was gone. I flung the cask overboard.

Ross uncocked the pistol and pocketed it once more. "Prepare to come about, Pyrrhus," was all he said as he walked aft to take the helm.

Our new course was northwesterly; once we were safely on our way, the captain sent me below to dispose of the body in the forecastle. When I was done, I reported back on the quarterdeck.

"It's Montserrat for us, my boy," the captain said. "Closest friendly port, I make it — only about half the distance back to Antigua. Rum go all the same with just the two of us. No rest for the weary till we're there. Game?"

"Aye, aye, Captain," I said. My stomach began to growl and I thought longingly for food. I turned to go below for a bite of biscuit.

"Pyrrhus?" The captain's voice had an uncomfortable note to it. I paused.

"Thank you, Pyrrhus. For everything."

"Aye, aye, Captain," I replied smartly. Had I known how, I might almost have saluted.

Thirty sleepless hours later we dropped anchor in Plymouth harbor. I slumped to the deck once the sails were furled, exhausted, but Ross hailed a passing boat and went ashore. He returned later with two hands who had agreed to make the passage to Falmouth and thence to Boston and set them to work before he consented to rest.

We spent only two nights in Montserrat. Certain that the temporary repairs to the *Pretty Polly*'s rigging would hold for the passage back to Falmouth and mindful of the high costs of spars and other gear in the islands, we left as soon as our stores were renewed. Under skies of cloudless blue we sailed across the Caribbean to the Mona Passage and out into the broad Atlantic.

The blue skies had turned a dirty gray when, eight days later, a low hummock appeared on the northwester horizon.

"Mount Agamenticus!" Captain Ross exclaimed jovially. "We're nearly home now. If the wind holds, we could be in Falmouth by noon."

He stared at the mainsail thoughtfully. "I shan't be sorry to be back," he said. "By God, it'll be good to see Polly again. With the profits from this voyage I can ask her for her hand at last and have done with her damned shilly-shallying! No more excuses about having to wait until we can afford to be wed!

"Yes, and I'm to have a share in the gold as well." At the mention of gold, my head snapped around. Ross laughed and rubbed his hand across my close-cropped skull. "Oh, yes, there's gold aboard the *Pretty Polly*, although to look at the old girl you'd hardly think so.

"Old Bryce McLellan arranged it. He's been a second father to me since I went to sea instead of to Harvard as my family intended. More so since my father died and left everything to my brother George.

"Mark you, that was no surprise — he'd been brought up in the business. They'd intended me for a minister." He spat deliberately over the side. "They're a close-knit clan, the McLellans, Bryce and his cousin Hugh in Gorham. Not rich, mind you, but hard-working, and they stick together. Polly is Bryce's sister's girl, and I think he's pleased to think I'll soon be one of the family in earnest.

"Be that as it may, when Hugh began to talk of bringing specie back from the islands, Bryce said that I was to go, and Hugh gave me a bill on his agents at Saint John's. It's not a fortune, but it's all they have, and it's hidden — well hidden." He laughed. "You might say it's as safe as Polly's virtue! The Frogs would never have found it, but I'm glad to be bringing it home.

"It's a rare service you've done me, Pyrrhus. Me and old Bryce and the rest." He put his hand on my shoulder. "I want you to know that it won't be forgotten. There'll be no more talk of selling you in Boston or anywhere else. I'll see you rewarded as you deserve."

There was a lump in my throat as I thanked him. Could freedom indeed be so close as that? I was too overcome with anticipation to speak and looked out at the approaching shore.

For a while Ross, too, was silent. Then he pointed. "Look there, Pyrrhus!" I could just see a steeple among the trees. "That's Wells. Bryce lived there after the Indians burned Falmouth years ago."

The mention of Indians awoke my fear of the savages, and I questioned the captain closely regarding what was to be expected from them. Although the fall of the French near a decade before had ended the danger of attack, Ross took childish pleasure in reciting story after story which, I am sure, lost nothing in the telling.

"Look you there, Pyrrhus," he said as we approached a promontory he called Cape Elizabeth. "There lies Richman's Island, where the treasure is buried!" He proceeded to tell of the piratical "Great Walt" Bagnall, who extorted a fortune from the Indians before they murdered him in the bloodiest fashion. He described Bagnall's death with such relish that I left, lest he tell me more, and took up a vantage on the forecastle.

Presently I noticed a small craft making its way from the mainland toward the island. We passed within pistol shot, and I noticed with a delicious chill of excitement that the occupants were paddling, rather than rowing in civilized fashion. Doubtless this must be a canoeload of Indians bound for their camp on the site of the ancient massacre.

I examined the savages as calmly and carefully as possible, considering my excitement. They were a ragged and unruly lot, as much so as any of the waterfront beggars and ne'er-do-wells I had seen at home. Three fowling-pieces leaned against the center thwart of the craft, and I recalled that Hartshorn had taught me about the tribes' moving to the seashore during the warm weather, to hunt and fish until winter drove them inland once more.

A bottle passed from hand to hand in the canoe, and the trio hooted and waved as we passed. I noticed the captain wave in reply and I followed suit. Though dressed in old clothing which they had probably stolen from their white neighbors, the Indians were evidently friendly.

With studied nonchalance I drifted back to the quarterdeck. "The Indians hereabouts don't seem all that fearsome to me, Captain. Could be that you've been taking some liberties with the truth."

Ross raised his eyebrows in query. "Indians? What Indians?"

"Why the three in that canoe, of course. A dirty lot, and likely drunk as well, but otherwise they might almost have been Christians."

The captain was seized by such a fit of laughing that he steered us off course and we nearly jibed. "Almost Christian!" he sputtered delightedly. "You might say so indeed! Almost Christian! Pyrrhus, you goose, those Indians, as you call 'em, were Deacon Jordan of Spurwink and his two sons. One of them's a student at Harvard! Indians indeed! I'll show you Indians!" And he began to laugh again.

I might have taken offense and gone forward to sulk had the captain not recovered sufficiently to speak once more. "Come, Pyrrhus," he said, "stay here with me and I'll show you the sights." Mollified, I stayed, despite an occasional chuckle I deemed it wiser to ignore.

The captain steered inshore to pass between the granite cliffs at Portland Point and Bang's Island. Here and there along the shore a trail came out from between the trees, and once in a while there was a house, but the country did not seem much settled by the standards to which I was accustomed.

We were abreast of House Island when I spied a cluster of houses grouped around a wharf. A half-dozen vessels, one of them a brig half again as large as the *Pretty Polly*, swung to their moorings offshore.

"There, Captain! Is that Falmouth?"

He smiled and shook his head. "Simonton's Cove. A good deal of the West India trade's done here, though. I've seen it so busy that men'd come down from town to find work here."

We rounded Purpooduck Point and bore away for a hill the captain called Munjoy.

"There," he said, "that's Falmouth!"

The whole mouth of the Fore River was alive with shipping: fishing sloops and shallops, a ferry on its way back from the settlement on the southern shore, rude vessels called gundelows and trim merchantmen, sloops and brigs and schooners and snows, as many as ever I had seen in the islands. Among them were four elephantine ship-rigged vessels with odd-looking high-sided hulls: ships which I later learned were specially constructed to carry on the masting trade that was so important both to Falmouth and to England and her navy.

I was enthralled by the ships, and by the myriad small craft that swarmed about them like so many water bugs, with oars for legs. And it was a goodly town that overlooked this activity, for all that the bare gray boards of most of the structures gave it the look of being unfinished. Even the two large churches were unpainted. Yet there were houses by the score, some quite large and grand, along the three main streets that ran parallel to the shore, and more lined the side streets and lanes. The waterfront was the most crowded and the busiest, I think, I had ever seen, with breastworks and wharves the whole length of Fore Street, from the distillery and King Street on the one end to the brickyard at the foot of Love Lane on the other.

The tide was out, so that many of the lesser wharves did not reach beyond the broad mud flats which were the domain of the numberless quarrelsome gulls. They walked purposefully about, poking into masses of half-rotten seaweed or tearing at dead fish or other refuse, and fighting over the choicest bits, so like the stevedores and mechanics and merchants above them that I was forced to laugh.

Ross brought the schooner up into the wind just beyond the brickyard, near a short wharf which barely reached the water. Above the wharf a wooden stairway crept precariously up the hill to a cottage surrounded by a plain board fence. Though small, the cottage bore a well-weathered coat of reddish paint which attested to the sometime affluence of its owner.

Scarcely had the anchor sunk out of sight in the murky water before the captain was helping us furl the last of the weather-stained sails. After the two hands had helped us launch the new jolly boat we had acquired in Montserrat, Ross gave them leave to go below and prepare for going ashore. Me he took aside.

"Have you ever wondered where the gold was hid, Pyrrhus?" His eye held a mischievous twinkle. Without waiting for my reply, he swung over the side and into the boat. I followed. Ross took the middle thwart and got out the oars, so I lounged in the stern sheets like a captain. He rowed us around to the bow, beneath the figurehead carved in the semblance of a beautiful dark-haired woman, and tied the boat's painter to the bobstay.

"Remember what I said about the gold being as safe as Polly's virtue?" He stood in the bow of the boat and pried with his knife at a bolt-head which formed a brooch at the center of the woman's bodice.

"Carved her myself last winter," Ross remarked as he worked. "Not a bad likeness — there! — of Polly herself at that." The bolt had come free as he spoke, and he handed it to me. Then to my amazement, he slid a portion of the wooden bosom out like a drawer.

The captain reached inside and withdrew a heavy leathern purse. Gratified by my reaction, he chuckled as he replaced the secret compartment. "That part was Bryce's idea," he said. "Here, now, you take the oars. 'Tisn't fitting that the master should work while the man looks on!"

We picked up the two sailors and rowed to the ramshackle wharf. I tied the boat to a ladder on the end and waited while the others ascended. The sailors left in search of a grogshop, while Ross and I strolled the length of the pier, he indulging in the excited small-talk of the homecomer and I at last beginning to believe that my tribulations were coming to an end. I reflected that there was nothing waiting for me at home in the islands. This Falmouth, now, looked like a peaceful enough place. When I became a free man once more, as I had no doubt I soon should, it would be a pleasant place to live.

Just as we approached the foot of the stairs leading up the embank-
ment, a string of wild oaths exploded from the bushes above, followed
by a huge figure with a hatchet in one hand and a blurred yet bloody
shape waving wildly in the other.

The specter threw itself at us, taking the stairs three at a time.
"Indians!" I shrieked, and leaped between the savage and the captain.
How I expected to protect him is still a mystery, but it is no secret that
my last memory was that of receiving a gigantic fist full of bloody
something directly in my face.

I am told that I cartwheeled off the wharf, through a tangle of briers
and sprawled full-length in the mud and rotting rockweed below. I
came to my senses a few seconds later and sat up, spitting ooze from
my mouth and well-nigh blinded, to hear, not the sounds of mortal
combat, but of helpless laughter. When I had cleared my eyes, I saw
Ross above me, embracing our erstwhile assailant. Beside me in the mud
was a headless and half-plucked chicken.

"Father McLellan," said the captain, "this is my man Pyrrhus, who
for the second time in one day has taken one of the pillars of our
community for a savage. Pyrrhus, this is Bryce McLellan, my friend
and benefactor, and constable of the town of Falmouth." Laughing,
the two turned and started up the stairs, leaving me to follow as
best I was able.

II

I SCRAPED the worst of the mud from my face and started after them.
The captain and the old man — I say old, because at this time
Bryce McLellan was near seventy-five years of age, though his frame
and hearty manner were those of a man in the autumn rather than the
winter of life — had paused at the top of the stairs and were closely
engaged in conversation. I was certain that the conversation had to do
with me, for I could feel their eyes upon me though no single word

reached my ears. Once the captain pointed at me and said something that McLellan must have thought heartily funny, for he laughed and slapped his knee.

I did not share their mirth, though I was curious about what had been said, but I had to contain my curiosity, for as I came up with them a third figure strode from the door of the cottage. He was a lean and swarthy man in butternut homespun smock and trousers, belted at waist and knee with gay red sashes.

"I must be off," he announced to McLellan abruptly. Then he must have noticed me on the stairs. I was caked with half-dried mud, very uncomfortable, and had thought myself sufficiently embarrassed even before he began to laugh. There was a difference between his laughter and that of Bryce and the captain, as though he relished my discomfort more than the humor of my plight. I took an instant dislike to him.

"I'll have those goods for you Tuesday week," said McLellan hurriedly. He did not seem particularly anxious to dissuade him from leaving, although he was studiously polite. The stranger stared pointedly at the captain for a moment before McLellan caught the hint. "Oh, yes," he said. "Murch, meet young Will Ross. He's just back from the Indies with the *Pretty Polly* schooner and his man Pyrrhus."

Murch hesitated for a moment before taking the captain's hand. "Ross? Ross, you say? He'd be George's brother, then." He shook my master's hand with a smile, but there was something malicious in it that made me mislike him still more. Even McLellan seemed offended.

"Next Tuesday, then, Murch," he said hastily, and drew aside so that there would be no hindrance to his passing. Murch favored us with a final half-smile and left.

McLellan lost no time in changing the subject. "You'll stay to lunch, of course, Will. I'll have Eliza set another place." This seemed to remind him of something, and he turned to me.

"Well, boy," he said, "where's my chicken?" I started with surprise. Of course the chicken lay in the mud at the bottom of the hill. Before I could protest, he laughed and slapped me on the back. "No harm done, boy. Eliza could never cook a chicken so's it was fit to eat anyhow. You two follow me." He turned and went inside. His voice boomed out of the door in his wake. "Eliza! Eliza, guess who's home!"

I made to follow, but Ross took my arm. He seemed in good spirits at his homecoming. "Well," he said, "here we are. What do you think of our Indians now you've seen a real one?"

"Indians?" I was puzzled. "Surely that old gentleman isn't . . . ?"

"No, you ninny, but Murch is. Half-blooded at least. I've heard of him before this. He's a trader up-country, or so some say, though others say worse.

"But no matter. I wanted to tell you right off, since I've spoken to Bryce and he agrees. I said I'd provide for your future, and I've given it a deal of thought on the voyage." I looked at him expectantly and he gave me a satisfied, benevolent smile. "The best thing for you is to send you to Cousin Hugh McLellan's farm in Gorham. That's what I thought, since you'd be with your own kind, of course. Most of the slaves work at Hugh's: Prince and Romeo and the others. Polly and I could never keep you in town anyway."

I looked at him in disbelief. This was my reward? My first reaction was that I would have been as well off in Antigua or Guadeloupe, but Ross must have taken surprise for pleasure. Certainly he seemed well pleased with himself. From the doorway the voice of Bryce McLellan summoned us into the kitchen. Ross put his hand on my shoulder in a friendly fashion. It came away muddy, and he laughed good-humoredly and wiped it on his breeches. He went inside and I followed him numbly.

Eliza McLellan was setting the long pine table. Flushed with heat and with both hands full, she stopped long enough to give the captain a motherly peck on the cheek. He tried to take the dishes from her, but she weaved artfully and told him to sit down and get out of her way. "If you really want to help," she said, "have your darky fetch me some water."

There was a wooden bucket near the back door. "The well's in the yard," Ross told me. He lowered his voice slightly. "For God's sake, take off those muddy shoes and wash your hands before you bring it in. She's small, but she's a terror on dirt in her kitchen."

When I came back with the water, he handed me some bread and cheese and a mug of rough cider. "Here," he said. "This'll hold you for now. You can eat it on the step."

In the kitchen Eliza was speaking. "You'll stay the evening, I hope, Will? I'm dying to hear what the women are wearing this season in Saint John's."

"Some other time, Goody. After all, I've been away. I'm that anxious to see Polly, and I know she'll be anxious too."

"Anxious?" Eliza broke in sharply. "I guess she's anxious. She married your brother George last week."

Ross stopped in mid-stride. I saw the old man wince, and he buried his face in a mug of beer. Ross looked at Eliza, who returned his gaze defiantly. He turned to Bryce as if he expected to be told that this was some joke, but McLellan merely stared morosely into his beer.

"Damn him," said Ross. "Damn him to hell." He clenched his fists. I could see the color mount to his face. The muscles along his jawline swelled. "Come with me, Pyrrhus," he said curtly and spun on his heel. I took a quick pull at my cider and followed as fast as I could.

It was all I could do to keep up with him, for I was unused to walking barefoot and the road was dusty and filled with stones. We went along Fore Street as far as the brickyard and Deacon Cotton's tannery, and turned up Love Lane to Spring Street. Here Ross cut right across an orchard and then picked up a path through some boggy ground and a meadow. The path came out into Middle Street near a shop that had a saddler's sign hanging above the front door. Ross walked boldly up to a house two doors from the saddler's and let himself in. With many misgivings I followed him, though I noticed that particles of dried mud were falling from my clothes onto the polished floor and the floorcloth, which was painted to resemble a Turkey carpet.

There was a real carpet in the parlor, albeit a small one compared to some I had seen at home in the islands, and a gilt looking-glass on one wall as well. I was so taken by the contrast with the rough-hewn comforts of the McLellan household that I failed to notice when the captain stopped and ran right into his back. Even he seemed impressed.

Over his shoulder I could see the dining room, where a handsome woman stood by a polished mahogany sideboard. She had been decanting a bottle of wine.

The captain's mouth opened and closed twice. "Polly!" he croaked at last.

Polly's left hand had flown to her throat, but mingled with her surprise was the smug contentment of a cream-fed cat. She set the bottle down with what was almost a flourish.

"Lud, but you gave me a turn, Will. Whenever did you get back?"

"Polly, what did . . . by God, if George has hurt you, I'll . . ."

She laughed then. It was a merry sound, but a cold one, like the clink of the crystal prisms on the chandelier. "Hurt me? Why, Will, whatever would make you say a thing like that about your own brother? Come, give your sister-in-law a kiss." She opened her arms to him and took a step forward, turning her head to present one perfect porcelain cheek.

Ross ignored the gesture. "Why damme, Polly, how did George force you to marry him otherwise? Surely Bryce and Eliza didn't."

She looked at him boldly, but she lowered her arms and smoothed the dress over her hips before she spoke. "Force me? La, Will, I wanted to marry him!"

"But you said — " Ross began. He stopped and tried again. "I thought — "

Polly looked up at him. I noticed that her eyes were a startling blue, but as empty and cold as a doll's. "You thought," she said with hurtful emphasis, "you thought, Master Tarpaulin, that I would be content to live like Uncle Bryce and Aunt Eliza, with never a stick of decent furniture and no husband six months in the year. And so did they — indeed, I think it was all their idea from the first, to bring you into the family. Well, I wasn't.

"You said that you wanted me. Wanted me, yes, and loved me! And you never asked me what I wanted. I wanted a nice house, like this one George had from your father. And dishes and furniture and pretty clothes and real wax candles. And I wanted a husband that isn't gone somewhere half the time and that doesn't stink of tar and bilgewater when he's home." She stamped a foot.

"I wanted all of this." She gestured at the room, and something glistened on one cheek. "I wanted it, Will, and I got it."

For a moment Ross stood facing her. Without warning he spun around and pushed me aside so that I could no longer see through the doorway. Events had moved too swiftly for me to react, and I watched him until a shocked exclamation called my attention back to Polly.

She had taken a step after the captain which brought her through the doorway and face to face with me. Her astonishment reminded me that I was in no case to be seen in gentlefolks' parlors. Chunks of dried mud had fallen off my clothes and lay in a circle about my feet. I thought to apologize for my presence, but then the front door slammed, and with one last look at Polly I fled.

I ran clumsily along in the captain's wake and finally caught up with

him in the orchard. He tore a branch the thickness of my thumb from
the first of the trees and belabored the grass with it as we walked.
There was nothing I could say to console him, and it did not seem a
propitious time to ask questions. I followed him down the hill and
along Fore Street to McLellan's wharf. At the end of the wharf he
stopped and pointed down into the boat.

"Get in," he said.

Eliza McLellan appeared at the head of the stairs. "Will!" she called.
I paused on the ladder and looked up at Ross.

"Get in," he repeated. I went down the ladder and took a seat in the
boat. The captain followed me and cast off. He took the oars from
me and drove the little craft viciously through the water.

When we reached the *Pretty Polly*, he tied up to her main chains
and wordlessly climbed aboard. I followed, carrying the tattered apple
branch which he had left in the bottom of the boat.

For some time he paced the quarterdeck with his head down and his
hands laced behind his back. When at last he looked up I started to
speak, but his expression warned me that it would be wiser to hold my
tongue. He snatched the branch from my hand and sat down abruptly
at the break of the deck, pulling out his clasp knife as he did so, and
began to whittle at it. The shavings fell to the deck. At last he stood
up and put the knife away.

"Fetch the carpenter's chest, Pyrrhus," he said. "When you've got
it, bring it up to the bow."

I did as he bid, and found him there beforehand with a strip of stout
canvas and some rope. He rigged these as a bo's'n's chair under the bow
of the schooner. He chose a drawknife from the toolchest, tested its
edge, and handed it to me. I took it and wondered what he had in mind,
but he was not about to enlighten me. "When I ask for that, hand it to
me," was all he said, and swung himself nimbly over the bow rail. In
a moment his hand appeared, and I gave him the drawknife.

I could hear him cutting away, and though I was near consumed
with curiosity I did not look. From time to time he called for a
different tool, and I would give it to him. After a long while he came
back aboard. He told me to put the tools away. When I came back on
deck, I saw he had emptied the paint locker. Brushes and paint pots
were spread out over the narrow expanse of foredeck. He set me to
stirring and mixing and went back over the side. He called for half a

dozen or more colors before he seemed satisfied with whatever it was he was doing and came aboard again. Setting aside the pots of black and white, with two of the smaller brushes, he unshipped the bo's'n's chair and rolled it up under his arm.

"Clean those brushes and clear that truck away," he ordered, and headed aft. I noticed that he rigged the sling over the taffrail and worked briefly at the schooner's transom. When I had finished up forward, he was just about done aft. He passed me the last of the paintbrushes with a satisfied air. "There," he said, "finish these and we'll see how she looks." He smiled grimly.

When I had done, we got into the jolly boat once more and cast off. I rowed down the ship's side to the stern. I wondered what it was I was supposed to see that pleased him so. It looked to me as though he had merely touched up the paint on the stern.

I rounded the transom and started forward. As we came up to the bow, Ross looked up and said, "Well, Pyrrhus, what do you think of our fine lady now?" I gave the oars one last pull and looked.

I gasped. The fresh-painted figurehead gleamed in the late afternoon sunlight. Ross had pared away at the carving so that now it stood brazenly bare-breasted under the bowsprit. There were bright red nipples on each of the breasts, and a mole on the swell of the left one, where the dress had once covered it. Then I looked at her face. Ross had done something to the smile. Where once her expression had seemed demure, there was now a wanton look that was almost frightening.

"Tell me," he said, "now that you've seen her, isn't that Polly to the life?" His voice was cruel, but there was hurt in it as much as hurting. There was nothing to say.

"She's a new name as well," he said. I looked again and saw the quarterboards had likewise been repainted. For a moment I was puzzled, for I read what I had expected. At last I noticed that the second *P* had been altered to an *F*. The schooner's name now read *Pretty Folly*.

"Folly indeed," said Ross. "It seems that money and position are the measure of a man. If that be so, why, I can be rich as well as another." He paused for a moment, considering.

"It would seem, Pyrrhus, that my plans have changed. What would you say to another voyage?"

II

THE SHADOW

12

"ANOTHER of these damned Boston lawyers!" Ross crumpled up the note and threw it into the ashes in the fireplace. "Would that they would stay home! I have no desire to meet one, whoever he may be, but as the deacon bids me come, I suppose I must.

"I shall dine tonight at Deacon Codman's, Pyrrhus. He asks that I send you to him to serve; mind that you obey him in all things, for you know he is ill at ease with darkies. Major Freeman will be there as well, and Brigadier Preble, with some troublemaking attorney whom they wish to impress, though the deacon neglects to name him. Put on your best suit, then, before you go, and tell the good deacon I shall be there at seven."

Captain Ross's fortunes had changed for the better in the three years since first we had met. Within a twelvemonth he had sold the old schooner and caused a better to be built, which he named *Industry*. I can think of no name more fitting. Though the colonies were all in a toss over what some called ministerial oppression, it was still a time in which the industrious might fare well, and my master was nothing if not an industrious man. By the time of the celebrated tea-brewing in Boston Harbor, he had rented him a small house on Meetinghouse Lane, and was counted one of the rising lights of the town. As much his secretary as his servant, I was no worse off, if no better, than I had been before Fitzgore had died.

Deacon Codman, from whom Ross let the cottage, was a man of much influence in Falmouth, known for civic pride and for encouraging what young men of promise the town should produce. By trade he was a merchant; in the years before the Revolution he kept a gambrel-roofed wooden store which stood until the war with the Tripoli pirates at the corner of Middle and Exchange streets. His house was one of the best in the town, with a spacious terraced yard, a stately fence, and a view of the harbor which time would give him reason to regret.

The deacon's kitchen-garden adjoined our own, so, after I had changed my clothes, I let myself out the back door and crossed over to his. Hannah, who cooked and helped keep the house, let me in. Hannah was a Long-creeker, which is to say she came from a section of Falmouth on the far side of Fore River, hard by the road to Scarborough, which was considered somewhat less than respectable. Hannah herself was a hard worker, unlike some of her neighbors, and she was, of course, white; though Deacon Codman could easily have afforded to buy a slave, he would have no blacks in his household.

"Not a minute too soon, either," was Hannah's tart greeting; like most of her tribe, she was not conspicuous for tact. "Do you clean them chickens, boy. I've more than two hands can do, what with freshing the fish and baking these pies and all. There, now! Do I have to tell you twice? Just you get to work, and be quick about it!" I put by my coat and set to.

I had nearly finished the chickens when the deacon came out to the kitchen to check on Hannah's progress. "What in the name of Tophet is he doing in my kitchen?" he demanded. His face went red. I thought him about to have an apoplexy, and made to help him to a chair, but he shook me off. "Get out. Just get out of the kitchen! Go help Mistress Codman with the cleaning, if you will, but stay out of this room. I shall speak to your master about this matter later." I left in confusion and went to seek his wife, though I could think of nothing I might have done to engender such suspicion.

The deacon's wife, who was the youngest of Reverend Smith's daughters, met me on the stairs. "I heard the noise," she said. "You must excuse Mr. Codman; he is overwrought." She beckoned me close and I joined her. In a low voice, she said, "You must be studious to obey my husband while you are in this house, Pyrrhus." I said that I would obey him as I would the captain himself, he being my master's friend.

At this, she smiled and seemed to relax. "I thought that you would. My husband has a great regard for your master, you know; if he is wise, this evening may profit him greatly." She looked me appraisingly in the eye. "My father has owned slaves as long as I can recall," she said at last. "I grew up with them, and I can tell there is no harm in you.

"The deacon mislikes Negroes, as you have noticed, though he strives to treat all men as brothers. Yet he bears you no more ill will than he does your master. If he seems harsh, remember that he has his reasons, and govern yourself accordingly."

There was the sound of a door opening below us, and she put her finger to her lips and went back upstairs. I followed and helped her finish putting the house into order before she left to spend the evening at her father's, but though we were in the same rooms for some time thereafter, she added not another word of explanation.

Afternoon wore into evening in the slow way it often has in summer, but at length Mrs. Codman departed, and presently the guests began to arrive. I was given the task of greeting them at the door and conducting each new arrival into the parlor, where Deacon Codman presided over the punchbowl. Most of them I knew at sight: Brigadier Preble, the father of the famed commodore; Major Freeman, who was also a judge and seemed to hold most of the other important offices in town as well; and his son Samuel. Another was Theophilus Parsons, a student of the law who read with Mr. Bradbury and lodged at Deacon Codman's. When the captain came to the door, I greeted him with elaborate form and ceremony and was rewarded for my levity with a stern glance. I ushered him inside, and the party was now complete, with the exception of the guest of honor, whose name I had not yet heard pronounced.

I was not much longer kept waiting, however, as a knock came upon the door, and I went to open it. A man stood on the doorstep; a man with a pleasant round face, prominent eyebrows, and a cleft chin. He was decently, if rather plainly dressed, yet he had an air about him that belied his unexceptional exterior. I inclined my head and waited for him to introduce himself.

"John Adams, Esquire," he said, "to dine with Deacon Codman. Be so kind as to tell your master I am come." Since his epic defense of Lieutenant Preston in the matter of the Boston Massacre, his was a name with which to conjure. Not a little taken aback by his prominence, I led the way into the best room.

"Your servant, sir," Adams said to Codman. "Judge Freeman, your most obedient; General, good evening; Mr. Freeman, Mr. Parsons. Pleasant to see you." The captain was standing in converse with the younger Mr. Freeman. "Your pardon, sir," said Adams graciously, "I don't believe I have had the honor."

Deacon Codman looked up from the punchbowl. "I was forgetting my duties, sir! Mr. Adams, this is my young friend and neighbor, Captain William Ross, who lives in the next house to mine." He offered Adams a cup of the punch. "Will you take refreshment, sir?"

"With pleasure, Mr. Codman. Your servant once more, sir; this comes most grateful after a long day's pleading." He turned again to address the captain. "The next house? I beg your pardon, but surely our host does not mean the large one next door? I thought that disused from the look of it."

"And so it is," Major Freeman broke in. "That one belongs to that damned Tory hound, Savage, who perjured himself in Boston."

"Now, Major," said Codman soothingly, "we agreed there would be no politics before dinner! To answer your question, Mr. Adams, Captain Ross lives in the house on the lane behind."

Adams nodded to Ross and drained his cup. "Damme for a Frenchman if this isn't as fine a punch as ever I tasted," he said enthusiastically. "Though I daresay it is but in keeping with the surroundings.

"You have a lovely home, sir; when first I entered, what with your servant and all, I thought I had got into the house of a nobleman by mistake." He held out his cup to be refilled, and I stepped forward automatically to take it. Deacon Codman fixed me a warning glance. Before he could speak, the door from the hall opened and Hannah looked in. When the deacon saw her, he seemed to forget me entirely. He nodded at Hannah, who ducked back out of sight, and filled Adam's cup with punch. "There you are, sir," he said brightly as he returned it to his guest. "And when you've done with that, I believe we can go in to dinner."

The deacon waited while Adams drank and then held the door for him. The men filed out, with Captain Ross modestly last. I plucked at his sleeve, and he drew aside.

"What is it ails Deacon Codman?" I whispered. "I know he does not like black people in his house, but though I have done him no wrong, he watches me like a very hawk. Every time I get near food or drink, it is as though he feared I would poison him."

Ross turned pale and hushed me hurriedly. "Watch your tongue, Pyrrhus! If what they say is true, his own father died so years ago in Charlestown, poisoned by three of his domestics."

Fortunately, I had little to do with the actual serving of dinner, as Hannah had placed the dishes on the table herself. The deacon's silver made a brave show, and though the menu was spare by the standards of the Indies, for New England it was a memorable dinner, with fish and sauces, bacon and peas, roast chickens and a savory meat pie. I stood by to change plates when necessary and to pour the wine; by the time the second bottle was emptied, even the deacon had ceased to pay me mind.

Young Parsons alone failed to do justice to the victuals. He ate but a little of the chicken and a bit of what looked a very fine salad, and then pushed his plate away. "What news from the court, Mr. Adams? I fear you'll have heavy going with the King case."

Adams looked thoughtful as he chewed and swallowed. "I should have a deal less, I would think, if Justice Hutchinson would leave off his political jibes in the courtroom. Just the other day he attacked the clergy on the occasion of the recent fast. Justice is on the side of Mr. King, yet the king's justice may well be his ruin. Rancor and self-interest have no place in public office."

Adams paused to take another mouthful. Parsons leaned forward. "But surely, sir, self-interest is not found on the side of government alone? All about us, Whigs sprout like mushrooms in the most unlikely places, and if any hereabouts has suffered by it, then I have not heard."

"I shall not argue on that score, my friend," said Adams. "The patriots who mobbed poor King carried off every movable they came upon. Sometimes I wonder if his crime were not that he is rich, than that he took the side of government on the Stamp Act.

"I blush to say it, but I fear there are as many opposed to the tax on tea because it will cost them money, as those who make it a matter of principle. Nay, Major Freeman, hear me out; why was the tea sent to Boston at all, if not to line the pockets of the East India Company's stockholders?"

Major Freeman could hold his peace no longer. "And who are they, damn their greedy black souls, but the same lords who laid the tax upon us in the first place? They and their friends! Are we men, or are we cows, that we should stand idly while they milk us?"

"Calm yourself, neighbor Freeman," the deacon interposed. "Mr. Adams makes no such suggestion, I am certain! He is well known as a man devoted to the cause of liberty."

"Thank you, Deacon Codman," replied Adams. "No, Major, I for one will not be milked, as you put it. More than ever, now that North has sent General Gage and his troops to close the port of Boston, we must stand firm.

"And not in the matter of tea alone, though that is a start. The government seeks to pour it down our throats, whether we will or no, but they will soon see the hateful beverage universally renounced. I have lately begun to wean myself, you know: in this I am indebted to Mrs. Huston, with whom I am lodged. When first I came to Falmouth, it was late in the afternoon and I had ridden thirty-five miles at least.

" 'Madam,' I said to her, 'is it lawful for a weary traveler to refresh himself with a dish of tea provided it has been honestly smuggled, or paid no duties?'

" 'No, sir,' said she, 'we have renounced all tea in this place. I can't make tea, but I'll make you coffee.' Accordingly I have drunk coffee every afternoon since, and have borne it very well."

The captain looked up at him keenly. "And yet, Mr. Adams, if the mob has its way, I fear we shall have a draught to drink more bitter by far than coffee."

"Well put, sir! These tarrings and featherings, and breaking open houses by rude and insolent rabbles in pursuance of private passions, must be discountenanced absolutely. These private mobs, I do and will detest, as befits a worthy member of society.

"But tell me, Captain Ross: you seem a pleasant, likely young man. How are you disposed toward the cause of liberty?"

The captain thought for a moment before replying. "In many ways, not unlike yourself, sir. I am hearty enough for liberty, I suppose, though I am not at all strong for disorder and violence."

Adams nodded. There was a brief uncomfortable silence. The deacon took a last sip of wine and pushed his plate away. "Don't just stand there, Pyrrhus," he said to me. "Fetch the port. You may clear the table later."

The bottle made its round and the men settled back comfortably once more. At length the deacon addressed Adams again.

"I should find it harder to give up port than I shall tea, I am afraid. I am glad it was not wine the ministry thought to tax so." There was a general murmur of agreement.

"How much longer may we look to have you in Falmouth, Mr. Adams?"

"Not long, I think; perhaps less than a week. I am concerned in only two or three more cases." He shook his head. "Such an eastern circuit I never made. I fear I shall bring home no more than I brought away.

"It is dreadful to be from home as often as I must. For the last eight or ten days I have thought of little else but my family and my farm. I confess, gentlemen, that it is a great source of mortification to me that I must leave so many of the burdens of their care to my dear wife Abigail.

"There is no prospect, however, of my spending much time at home this season. No sooner shall I arrive, than I must be off again, this time to Philadelphia for the Continental Congress. A long journey indeed!" He smiled kindly at my master. "Not, perhaps, as long as those which you essay, but you must know the pain of parting as well as I. Tell me, sir, are you married?"

For a moment the captain seemed lost in a memory. "I, sir?" he said at last. "No, I am not."

"Captain Ross is too modest by half," Parsons interjected. "He is affianced to one of our most attractive young ladies: the sister of Robert Pagan, who keeps on the corner of Fore and India streets, below the customs-house."

"Ah, yes, that would be down the hill from Mrs. Huston's." Adams turned back to Ross. "I give you joy, sir," he said, raising his glass. Ross acknowledged the toast, but it was evident that he was not about to enlarge upon the subject. There was another awkward silence.

Brigadier Preble pulled a watch the size of a turnip from his waistcoat pocket. "Your pardon, gentlemen," he said in his gruff voice. "It is time I was going." He stood up and pushed back his chair, and the deacon escorted him to the door. Samuel Freeman left soon after, and Parsons took the opportunity to excuse himself and went upstairs to his room. My master seemed to take their departures as a hint. Thanking the deacon for his hospitality and bidding Major Freeman and Mr. Adams good evening, he went home as well.

Meanwhile I made shift to clear the table and to spread fresh linen in place of the soiled. As soon as I had done, Deacon Codman led Adams and the major back into the room, calling for clean glasses and another bottle.

For a time I was busy enough, carrying the dishes and what remained of the food out into the kitchen for Hannah to deal with, so I know not what secrets they shared. By the time I returned, they were talking low and relaxed, in the way friends will at the end of a long day, and I paid them as little mind as they did me until I heard the captain's name on their lips.

"This man Ross, now," said Adams, "he puzzles me. Almost I would call him a king's man, had I not met him in this house. And surely I have heard the name of Pagan before this."

"That you have," the major growled. "He is the chiefest of the Tories in this place, and hosted a frolic a week ago Wednesday, to mock the fast for Boston."

"Now, friend Enoch, you must grant that Squire Pagan has ever been a good neighbor before our present troubles, and that he is much beloved by the people."

"Say rather was, Deacon, and I will agree," Freeman said, but with ill grace. "But though Ross shows poor taste in his choice of a brother-in-law, he comes of good stock. His father I knew, and his brother George, they say, is a committeeman himself in Salem."

"That he is; and a Freemason as well, though to be frank I never liked him as I do young William. There was some unpleasantness between them at the time George moved away, Mr. Adams, but I will not repeat old gossip.

"What is certain, is that at present Ross leans more to conciliation than to action, as do many of our leading citizens. You may know, Mr. Adams, that some nineteen or twenty of them sent an address to Governor Hutchinson in opposition to the resolves of the committee. Ross and Pagan, as well as your colleagues Bradbury and David Wyer, were among them. I do not doubt that it made an impression, for all were men of substance, save only the captain, and with his marriage, he bids fair to be."

Adams nodded and took a slow sip of his port. "You have struck upon one of our greatest difficulties in that," he said.

"A notion seems to prevail — and not among Tories alone — that it is politest and genteelest to be on the side of administration, that the better sort, the wiser few, if you will, are on the one side, and that the multitude, the vulgar, on the other. Unless we can shake this belief, gentlemen, we are beaten before we begin. Either we must win over the young men of promise, the moderates, the men who fear the breach more than the oppression, the Captain Rosses among us, or we shall lose them. I fear there will be no room for neutrality a year hence: we shall have to win our point, or go back to drinking tea.

"Meanwhile it is of the greatest importance, my friends, that we do nothing to turn men like Ross away. From what you have told me, the country people roundabout are restless and hasty men. Do what you may to restrain them. Incidents such as occurred with Mr. King cannot even be excused upon any principle which can be entertained by a good citizen.

"I pray it may not, but there may come a time for action. It is not yet. Meanwhile, we all have our duty. I will do mine, though I dread the thought of the Congress's falling short of the expectations of the people of this province, and of the continent at large. Great things are wanted to be done, and I fear only little things can be done." He drained his glass and stood up.

"Enough of that! I will do my duty, as I have said, and leave the event. If I have the approbation of my own mind, whether applauded or censured by the world, I will not be unhappy.

"And now, gentlemen, I bid you good night, and thank you for all you have done. Major Freeman, will you walk with me as far as your house?" Codman rose and saw his guests to the door, and then looked in upon me before retiring.

"You may go, Pyrrhus," he said with a yawn, for the hour was late. "Be sure to snuff the candles ere you leave.

"Yes, and one more thing." I paused politely for him to continue. "Thank your master," he said, "for the loan of your services."

13

THE next morning I told my master what I had heard said of him after he had left Codman's house. Though he listened with a thoughtful expression, he said nothing, and the news did not seem to sway him from his charted course. In those days it still appeared, perhaps, that a man might tend to his own affairs and let the tempest pass him by; besides, there were indications that the captain's new connections were like to be profitable ones.

What had shaped my master's choice of a bride is hidden from me, but Elizabeth Pagan's brother Robert was without question a prosperous man. His store near Preble's wharf kept the best stock of goods of any in town, and he owned an interest in the shipyard next the old fort as well. He, and his charming sister likewise, were handsome of person and had the sort of manners that comes only of gentle breeding; they were known to possess a number of books, and, what is more, to read them.

As near as I can tell, it was the shipyard and not the store that made Pagan's fortune. Most of the vessels he built there were not employed in domestic trade, but were sent laden to Europe, there to be sold with their cargoes. Only on occasion would he build on some other's account.

So many were his concerns that it was rare to see him abroad in the day, so that it was a surprise to me when he hailed the *Industry* from the wharf and bid me fetch him aboard. This I did, and brought him below to where the captain labored in the cabin. After a glass of Madeira and a few polite preliminaries, he came to the point.

"I find myself in something of a press," he said. "It may be that you can help, and be of service to yourself at the same time.

"You know, of course, that my shipyard is engaged with the building of Captain Thomas Coulson's *Minerva*." This, indeed, was common knowledge along the waterfront. Coulson, who had come to Falmouth from Bristol in England at about the time I had arrived, had bespoke a vessel of one thousand tons burthen, to be fitted for the masting trade. The *Minerva* was a source of much gossip and not a little pride, for she was the largest vessel ever laid down in Falmouth; so large, indeed, that she had occupied the whole of the yard and its people for some time. It would be spring before she would be ready to launch, people said, and even then much of her cordage and other gear would have to come from England.

"So busy have I been with Coulson's vessel, Captain, that I have had no time for aught else. Now I have a cargo of dun-fish for Cork, and no bottom of my own in which to convey it. I had thought that perhaps the *Industry* would serve if her captain were willing.

"I do not pretend to presume, sir, upon our expected relation, and will pay you fair charter. Will you not go? You'll not be the poorer for it, I promise."

His request could not, I think, have been plainer put, nor more delicately, and it was the hurricane season in the Indies, so the captain could hardly have found more profit elsewhere. Still, he hesitated before giving his assent, so that I longed to speak for him. It may have been his Yankee nature, which some call shrewd and some merely contrary, but I think he was concerned lest he appear too anxious and so feel obliged to his in-law, which no sane man would relish. Be that as it may, they soon struck a deal, and the captain and I prepared to depart for the coast of Ireland.

We set sail from Falmouth in August, dipping our ensign to a visiting English sloop-of-war we passed in the sound off House Island. We came around under her stern close enough for me to read her name, *Canceaux*, in gold leaf on the transom, and squared away to the eastward before a fresh breeze.

In Cork the folk were friendly, and eager to find out what might be afoot in the colonies. They had heard of the great Continental Congress which was to be holden in Philadelphia, but that was all the news they had, though rumor there was in plenty. Our fish they bought briskly, and at a fair price, but the captain knew no more than they and may have cared less, so that it seemed to me that many went away disappointed with their bargains.

Whatever our case had been in Ireland, we found news and to spare upon our return to Falmouth in October, yet here, too, it was rumor held the whip hand.

"It was Sam Adams's boys did it, if you ask me," I heard Pagan tell the captain. "They are trying to manage the convention as they did the town meetings in Boston.

"No sooner did the delegates arrive in Philadelphia than the alarm went out that Gage had shelled Boston. Half of New England turned out before the truth was known. Fortunately for all of us, the Congress took no hasty action. From all we have heard, most of the delegates are reasonable men: men of substance and responsibility. There are too few like Galloway, of course, but even your friend, that other Adams, though one of the leading Whigs, has withal some respect for property and for law.

"Yet the Congress is but a stone tossed into a millpond: the further from the center, the wider the ripples. Boston, they say, has called upon the colonies to withhold their taxes. In Salem, our representatives" — he said the word as though it left a foul taste on his tongue — "our representatives, I say, must needs go further. Not content with meeting in despite of the governor's edict, they have styled themselves a provincial congress, and now pretend to rule all of Massachusetts in his stead." He smiled grimly at Ross's exclamation of surprise, and took a swallow of wine to moisten his throat.

"You think this savors of treason, my friend? It seems precious close to me. Once men of affairs could be trusted; now, what with their infernal committees and such, they seem determined to sow the wind.

"The fools shall reap the whirlwind yet; I only hope that it does not sweep up the lot of us with them. Already things are getting out of hand. Near a month ago, before they went south, Freeman and the others called a county meeting for Mrs. Greele's tavern. The country people, encouraged by the actions of their betters, rose and came to town: five hundred or more, near one-half of them armed, to dictate their will to the convention." Pagan paused once more.

"What did Major Freeman do?" Ross demanded.

"Do? What could he do? He has as much to lose as any of us. He invited them in, Long-creekers and squatters from Gorham and from Brunswick, and asked them their pleasure.

"I hold as firm as any to my rights, as well you know, friend Ross. Yet if I am to have a despot erected over me, let him at least be a royal despot, and not one of a mob of fatherless sons such as came to town that day! At their behest, Freeman haled forth the best man in Falmouth, even Sheriff Tyng, like a common thief, that he might answer their questions and give surety not to exercise his authority under the late Acts of Parliament.

"The sheriff humbled, the rabble dispersed to their kennels. But the mischief had been done, and where this shall end, I know not, though I have my fears.

"But come, neighbor; perhaps these ripples may find their way back to Philadelphia and teach the Congress caution. Even the major talks more quiet now he has seen that the saber he was wont to rattle slides so easily from its sheath, and might cut friend as well as foe. I would not go to Mrs. Greele's, but there is still a tavern in Falmouth where an honest man may drain a glass to a friend. You'll be wanting to see Elizabeth, I know, but will you not share a bowl of punch with me at Marston's ere you go?"

To this the captain readily agreed, and bid me return home, saying that he would meet me there in the evening. This I did, and busied myself about the house, but the captain came home sooner than I had expected, and looking like anything but a man who has spent a pleasant hour in the company of his intended. In his hand he held a newspaper; when I asked him what was amiss, he bid me read it. I took the sheet in hand: it was newly come from Philadelphia. Full on the front page was the legend, "The Association of the American Congress," followed by column on column of print. There was too much of it to read in an instant, and I looked to the captain.

"What is it they mean to do?" I asked, for it was evident that this was the cause of his alarm.

"They mean," he said, "to ruin us all. They mean to have a war."

14

I MAKE no doubt that there were men in Carpenter's Hall who strove as ardently to lead the colonies into war as some others sought to effect a reconciliation. Doubtless, too, men of both factions were animated by patriotic motives as well as private ones. Yet though the fourteen articles restricting trade with England made peace more precarious, they did not precipitate the immediate ruinous war the captain had predicted. Some averred that the resulting loss in revenue would bring the king to his senses, so that war would be unnecessary. Each day's events made this desirable end more remote, but for a time at least it seemed that life might go on almost as before.

The captain and I made two short coastwise voyages in November, but still we kept busy enough, and there was a constant stream of visitors to the house whenever we were at home to receive them. Elizabeth Pagan and her brother were daily callers. I studied her cautiously but with deep interest; when she became my master's wife she would be a most important figure in my own life. Elizabeth was of a height with Ross, very fair, and scrupulously neat in her person. So far as I could judge, she possessed a lively intellect, although the men spoke only of light and pleasant matters while she was present. The year was nearly spent before I could form any idea of her character or political attachments.

Elizabeth was in high color when she arrived to meet the captain and her brother late one afternoon in mid-December.

"If I have to deal with one more of these dreadful committeemen, I shall scream," she said petulantly to my master, who had come into the hall behind me to greet her. She flung her cloak and hood at me and stormed into the parlor with one errant curl hanging down over her forehead. Ross followed.

"I vow I do not understand how my wedding dress is become a matter of state," Elizabeth was telling the men as I entered. She brushed her hair back impatiently. "Has Sam Adams hung out his sign as a milliner? If so I had not heard of it. But each time I go to Mary Bradbury or Goody Robinson for some ribbon or some lace, they tell me that it is not come, or that it is not expected until this winter, on the *John and Mary* from Bristol, and that I must go to the committee to secure permission for it to be landed.

"I went to the committee, and they looked grave and asked me if that same *John and Mary* is not Captain Coulson's vessel, and if it is not carrying naval stores and cordage, and would I place the boot of ministerial oppression upon our necks forever? As though it were the cordage I wanted after all, that I might hang them and their precious Hancock and their Adamses, and not a yard of ribbon for my gown."

Elizabeth turned down the glass of sherry I offered her. "That Mary

Moody, you know, I think she has ribbon, but she won't sell it to me. No, she won't. She comes to her door and greets me all mealy-mouthed, with her 'Good morning, Mistress Pagan,' but no matter what it is I need, she simply hasn't any, and haven't I tried Mary Bradbury?

"The other day I wanted some lace for the bodice, and I went to her. Oh, no, she had none, but that very day she sold a piece to Dorcas Ilsley. I saw Dorcas with it later, and of course the poor girl knew no better than to tell me. So I went back to the committee of inspection, and I said to Major Freeman, why don't they inspect Mary Moody? That John Waite said that I must expect to be treated so, if I were among the disaffected, but the others hushed him up and said only that she must have found some later."

Her brother looked surprised. "I didn't know you had gone to the committee. You shouldn't have bothered them, my dear."

"No," said Ross. "There's no need to make trouble."

"Trouble? We've trouble already, and not of my making! Haven't you been listening? This business with Mary Moody is but the beginning unless something is done about it. What if that John Waite decides that Ephraim Broad had best not sell me flour or onions?"

"Then we shall buy them of Pote or Oxnard, Elizabeth, as we perhaps should do in any case. We must stick together in such times." Pagan took out a short pipe and began to load it. "I think you are getting far too upset about a bit of ribbon."

"It was lace."

"Lace, then. But you needn't get involved in what doesn't really concern you, my dear; politics is a man's business."

"Oh, is it indeed?" Her tone was now so sharp that the men winced. "Man's business, Robert? And I suppose you agree with him, William. Man's business, when we've committees of this and that, committees of inspection looking into our tea-caddies, as though it was any of their concern if I take a dish of tea now and again; fusty old men with leather strings to their shoes who tell me I mayn't have a yard of this or a bolt of that. How am I to be ready for April? My goodness, Robert, if William hadn't bought me satin when he went to Maryland, I'd have had to be wed in wool, like some Long-creek girl.

"But it's men's business, all the same. When will it get to be a woman's business? When they form a committee to inspect our petticoats?"

"Elizabeth!"

"Elizabeth!" she mocked. "It's come to that, I think, if some snip like Mary Moody can tell me I shan't buy a piece of lace, but Dorcas Ilsley can! And all I want is a proper wedding, with a proper dress." She paused and turned to me.

"Get me my cloak, Pyrrhus. I shall find my own way home." The captain and her brother jumped to their feet, but she shook off their offers of company. "No," she said, "I've said my say; do you have yours in peace. I can still walk home in safety, I think. After all, they've a committee for that too, now." With that last sally her expression softened. "No, really. Enjoy your pipes and bowls. I shall be fine, and the air will do me good." She pulled on her gloves and went into the hall. I went before to open the door, and the two others followed, protesting that they would have her stay. She smiled sweetly then. "No," she said, "I've aplenty to be done at home. I would but trouble you and tire myself were I to remain." With that, she said her good-byes and left.

We went back into the parlor, and Ross called for the brandy. Pagan crossed to the fireplace and bent down for the ember-tongs.

"I'm afraid," he said, puffing at his pipe while he held a coal to the tobacco, "that our Elizabeth tends to be rather outspoken. You might have chosen a quieter woman, William." He returned to his chair and nodded his permission for me to fill his glass with brandy.

"I might," said Ross with a wink. "But I like her spirit, and, what is more, she's not wrong. There are those in Falmouth who do not love you, Robert, nor Sheriff Tyng, nor the Potes, nor the Oxnards."

"Rabble," Pagan sniffed. "Long-creekers and longshoremen."

"Some," admitted Ross. "But the Freemans aren't rabble, and neither is old Brigadier Preble. He is to be ranking general of the provincial forces. Bryce McLellan told me so, and Bryce should know. He and Preble are that close, and then his son Joseph's a member of the committee of safety."

Pagan sucked at his pipe and looked thoughtful.

"I didn't want to alarm Elizabeth, you know, but Bryce told me that things are like to get worse before they're better. The committeemen are bound that no goods will be landed after the deadline. She might have trouble getting those fripperies from the *John and Mary*. It'll be a long while before they'll deny you necessaries, I guess, but Bryce says they've marked you a king's man all right, and that there's talk against you, however popular you were a year ago. Against you, and against others, too. Bryce says there'd been questions about me, too, save for I'm known as a friend of his, and that my brother's a committeeman in Salem. Bryce says —"

"Bryce says," interrupted Pagan. "Oh, I'm sorry, Ross. I mean the old man no disrespect, nor you either. But I'm tired of the tension and the whisperings. Time was, and not so long ago, when Falmouth men minded their own business instead of their neighbors'. We all got on then, yes, and made money, too.

"I wasn't here in those days, being but a 'prentice-boy in Scotland, but well I remember hearing these same committeemen tell how glad they were when Wolfe fought Montcalm for 'em in fifty-nine. They've got shorter memories today, Will.

"They made their fortunes, those that have two coins to rub together, under the English flag, and slept sound o' nights under that same flag. They got rich selling masts for the king's ships that flew the flag and kept the French from their coast. Now they are set to go to war against that same England over a matter of threepence on a pound of tea. I won't have it! I'm not saying that things are perfect: Lord knows they aren't, but the taxes are worse at home in England, and there's many an Englishman has no one to speak for him in the Commons. I — oh, I want too much, I suppose, but the idea that a Hancock or an Adams or a Sam Thompson from Brunswick, or a George Ross, for that matter, and a band of malcontents and ne'er-do-wells should run things makes my very blood to boil." He drew at his pipe once more, but seemingly it had gone out, for he rose and knocked it out against the side of the fireplace. "I'm sorry, Will," he said. "The vapors seem to run in the family today: I'm as bad as Elizabeth. I think I'd best be off home as well."

"Come, Robert," the captain protested, "the hour is yet early. Come with me to Marston's for a glass and a tune."

"I had better not. In my mood I would sour their ale for a twelve-month, and so have no place to drink the king's health this side of Halifax. No, Will, do you go by yourself. I am off for home."

The captain was in a pensive mood after Pagan's departure, for he sat staring into the fire for a time without saying a word. At last he roused himself and looked about.

"I don't know what times are coming to, Pyrrhus my lad. The wind and the current are at odds, though, that is certain, but I am damned if I can tell what course to set.

"You needn't stop for me; get on with your work. It's just that I feel the need to talk, though there be nobody to listen. These are trying days, Pyrrhus. You are fortunate that you need make no decisions. As for me, when I have most need of a friend's advice, I find that all who are close to me are at odds, one with the other, so there is nowhere to turn."

I had gathered the glasses and decanter on a tray and made to take them from the room, but he halted me at the door. "Sit you down a moment, Pyrrhus," he said, indicating the low stool between his chair and the hearth. I set the tray down and did as he asked.

"Ah, I have half a mind to go to Marston's and forget it all," he grumbled. "I thought to ask Robert's advice, but he was in so foul a mood that Bryce's very name would have set him off again.

"It may hap that he is right. For me to undertake to sail to 'Statia on the committee's account might mark me for good and all, and yet I am loath to refuse Bryce aught needful. He and Joseph would take it hard were I to refuse them.

"You see, Pyrrhus? All is shoals and lee shores, with breakers on every hand." He shook his head and stood up.

"Perhaps things will seem plainer in the light of morning. There is nothing for it now but to mind my luff until we see how sets the wind. I am for Marston's, Pyrrhus. I shall not need you again." He paused then, as though struck by a sudden thought. "No, by God, I'll drain a glass at Alice Greele's, I think; 'twill be a change, at least." He reached into his pocket. "Here, Pyrrhus," he said, holding out some coins. "You can finish your work tomorrow as well. Tonight is your own."

I took the coins and watched him leave. There was the tray of glasses, of course, and the things from dinner, to take care of, and for a while I thought of saving the money and doing the washing right away. Facing dirty dishes in the cold dawn is not my favorite task. In the end, however, the idea of a few hours to myself proved irresistible. I banked the fires, put on my coat, and went out.

I went down to Clay Cove, to the King's Head, a low pothouse whose name, once a patriotic gesture, had come of late to have an entirely different connotation. It was frequented by sailors, longshoremen, and travelers, mostly poor, for the Head's only virtue was cheapness. This same cheapness made it the choice of apprentices, bondsmen, Falmouth's few free blacks, and those slaves who could boast a shilling with which to drink their masters' healths, whatever hazard the harsh liquor might prove to their own.

The Head was crowded and noisy as usual, but I saw a small knot of black faces amid the many white, so I bought me a pot of what passed here for ale and took a seat beside Prince McLellan. He seemed well along in drink, which was a failing of his, and he greeted me boisterously.

"God's truth," he chuckled, "here's Pyrrhus Ross, with his book-learning and all. Ceasor, show Pyrrhus your paper, you hear?" Ceasor Hamblen, easily the drunkest of the group, passed me a piece of paper with an impressive notary's seal.

"Mister Hamblen went and freed Ceasor," Prince said. "Ain't that what it say?" I nodded and handed it back. "It all legal and lawyer-fashion." He took a swallow of rum, which he preferred above all else when he could get it, especially sweetened, which I could never stomach. "Come spring, we all going to be free, Pyrrhus! Ain't that grand? Mister Sam Adams, he going to kick the king out of 'Merica, and we all be free, same's white folks."

I had only half listened to his chatter, but this brought my head around. My heart beat faster. "Where did you hear that?" I demanded.

"Around. I hear it all around, all the time. That Captain Thompson from Brunswick, he over there somewhere" — and he pointed vaguely at the other side of the room — "he say Congress pass a law 'gainst slaving, so we all going to be free once they kick out that old king."

"Wish I knew where he live," said Cato Shattuck. "I'd kick him myself and not wait till spring."

"You be quiet, Cato," said Prince. "You know Cap'n mighty particular about that."

This touched off an argument, but I paid them no mind. The non-importation agreement signed in Philadelphia had a clause banning the purchase of slaves from abroad, but Congress had dealt with the issue as a matter of economy only, and as offhandedly as they had prohibited the export of sheep. I had thought the struggle touched me not at all, for a slave had no vote and paid no taxes; the Liberty party cried for an end to taxation without representation, but they had given scant sign of advocating freedom for anyone other than themselves. The drunken maunderings of a few farm workers were hardly proof that I might have a stake in what was to come. Yet one man at least was free. Could the Tories say as much?

A hoarse bellow wrenched me back to the present. "Rum! Landlord! More rum!" Samuel Thompson, himself a Brunswick innkeeper, had emerged from the crowd across the room and was pounding on the bar. Next to him stood the trader Murch. "More rum," Thompson shouted again in a voice like a teamster's, and Murch and the others took up the cry. I noticed that the new-made Captain Thompson affected a uniform of blue wool where a suit of plain gray broadcloth had previously sufficed. He wore a tricorn hat with a white cockade, pushed back to reveal a considerable expanse of forehead down which sweat ran in streams.

The host came to pour for him, but Thompson snatched the bottle away and raised it high. "Confusion to Fat George," he called, "and to all his friends as well." He drank deeply. There was a roar of acclaim, and Thompson disappeared back into the unruly mob.

I had long since lost the thread of the conversation that eddied around me, and I needed time in which to think. I lifted my glass to Ceasor in a last salute, emptied it, and left the tavern.

I walked west along Fore Street to Deering's wharf and stopped to skip a stone across the water. It was a cold night but nearly windless, and the stars showed clear. Off the end of the wharf the *Industry* lay at anchor. As I watched, her head came around to meet the first of the incoming tide.

I realized then that a time would come for the choosing of sides, but I knew that when it came no one would ask my opinion. It would be the master and not the man who did the choosing, and I would fare as he. Yet the issue was far too vital for me to stand idly by. Though the choice would be the captain's, might I not have some influence upon his decision? There was much for me to ponder. Regardless of my hopes, it would not do to choose the losing side.

The loyalists of Falmouth seemed most of them capable men, and the captain had valuable connections among them. With his marriage to Elizabeth Pagan these connections would be more valuable still, provided always that England could hold the colonies. Of this I was no longer certain. There were men of ability on the other side as well, men like John Adams, though there were many like Thompson, who boasted openly of his lack of education. But if it came to open rebellion, could any amount of ability tell against the might of England? Would a Samuel Thompson, or even a John Adams, dare stand and fight a regiment of red-coated regulars? Where would the colonies find the ships, and the guns, and the powder to defy the strongest nation in the world?

I stood up and looked about. The hour was late, and scarce a window in all the town remained lighted. Doubtless the captain had gone to bed long since.

I had turned to go when I heard a shout from down the harbor. I looked. A sloop under full sail was approaching Preble's wharf. Even as the rest of the crew rushed to get in sail, a man lit a lantern and held it aloft.

The hail was repeated. There was an excitement to his voice that drew me irresistibly, and I found myself running along Fore Street to meet him.

A light came on in Brigadier Preble's house, and then another. By the time I reached the wharf, the sloop had come alongside. One of the crew threw a line, and I caught it, but before I could make it fast a man had leaped from the sloop to the dock.

"Paul Revere's took the fort at Portsmouth!" he cried. "Where's Major Freeman? I got to report."

I promised to lead him to Freeman's, but the door to Preble's house opened and the brigadier came out with a coat thrown over his bedgown. "I'm Preble," he said. "You can tell me. Boy, run and fetch the major."

I took a step or two and hung back to hear the news.

"This afternoon it was," the man from New Hampshire said. "The redcoats couldn't keep them out! They took the fort, and the powder, and the guns: sixteen great guns and sixty-odd muskets! Where's Freeman? I got to report to Freeman!"

It had begun so soon! My heart pounding, I turned and raced up the hill.

15

MAJOR Freeman lived on Middle Street, between Fiddle Lane and Reverend Wiswell's English church. I roused him and his household and then raced home to wake the captain.

"You've got to hurry," I told him as he dressed. "The messenger is there now. He says the Liberty Boys have taken William and Mary Castle on the Piscataqua. I think there was a battle! Please do hurry, Captain, or we'll miss all the news."

We made what haste we could, but by the time we arrived before the brigadier's house, the committee was already closeted within. None of the others who waited outside knew any more than that which I had heard. We were on the point of returning home when the door opened and some men came out.

"It looks as though the meeting is breaking up," the captain remarked. "There's Joseph McLellan talking to the brigadier. Wait here when he leaves, and I'll see if he'll tell me what has happened."

When the general had finished, Ross went up to McLellan. I was too far away to hear what was being said, but the committeeman was evidently in a hurry. They had exchanged but a few sentences before he left and the captain motioned for me to join him. He looked disappointed.

"So much for your battle, Pyrrhus," he said. "I fear it's another case of making much of little in a way, though we have not yet heard the last of it, I'll be bound.

"Four hundred Sons of Liberty captured the fort yesterday. That much at least of your story is true. The men came from Portsmouth and the country around Kittery and Pipestave Landing.

"Yet it was hardly a battle. Far from it! Oh, there were cannon enough, and a hundred barrels of powder, but the garrison was just five sick privates and a captain. A brave show!

"But the committee's all atwitter! I don't understand it. It looks to me that the Portsmouth Sons were loaded for bear. Joseph here tells me they want him to fetch the nine-pounder out of that old French War fort in Windham to put into the fort at the foot of King Street.

"Fort, hell! Any pimply-faced midshipman in the king's navy could take Fort Loyall with a longboat's crew and a brace of pistols. Even that little eight-gun corvette that put in here last fall would blow it clear into Back Cove! And what happens to Falmouth then? What of the people? Don't they realize we've got to live here?

"They act like they've beaten England! They, and the other committees they write letters to, and these damned Sons of Liberty! They haven't beaten England! They could never beat England, not unless every man in the country was with 'em, and they aren't. All they beat was six sick men in a tiny little fort. I ask you, Pyrrhus, what does that prove?"

He looked at me then, a bit breathless from his outburst, and stood with his hands on his hips.

"I think it proves a lot, Captain. It proves that they're not just talk and no action. They've made a start. It's a small enough one, but that's more than has been done around here for years.

"Maybe not everyone feels the way they do, not yet. Maybe they haven't beaten England. But England's a long way off, and this is a big country. In God's name, Captain, if with all her strength England can't hold one little fort in Portsmouth, New Hampshire, how in hell can she expect to hold a continent?"

My voice had risen unseemly, and when I met the captain's eyes at the end of my speech I saw the familiar warning light in them. He opened his mouth to answer, but as he did his look became thoughtful. He rubbed his jaw with one hand and the storm was past.

We walked home in silence. He was so deep in thought that I hardly knew if I should bid him good night, and when I did he answered in an absent tone.

He was unwontedly quiet again next morning, though he seemed more purposeful in his movements, and he left early with only a curt notice that he would be back at noon. I wondered at such odd behavior, but there was enough for me to do about the house that I soon resolved to wait for his explanation. Nor was it long in coming. It was scarcely eleven o'clock when my master returned.

"Get dinner cooking, Pyrrhus," he called cheerfully from the hall.

"Best make it a good one: it's salt beef and biscuit for us again. I'll be upstairs packing."

"Packing, Captain?"

"Yes, packing! Packing my green chest! You had better pack your seabag while the food cooks. And pack warm! We're off for Quebec on the morning tide."

"Quebec!"

"Yes, Quebec! Now get a move on, you wool-headed slowcoach! Elizabeth was furious when I told her, of course, but I promised we'd fetch her back some dress goods, and I will if I can get them past the committee. That shut her up!" His face disappeared from the doorway but swiftly returned. "One more thing: after we eat I'll need to go down to the waterfront to sign a crew and see to our stores. Major Freeman should be coming by with some money to cover our expenses for the voyage."

"Major Freeman?" I was puzzled. "What have we to do with Major Freeman?"

"Can't you guess? It was your idea, in a way."

I shook my head.

"We're going to Quebec to buy drugs for Dr. Lowther. On the committee's account."

For an instant I was speechless, and before I recovered my tongue he had gone. I followed him and caught him on the stairs.

"Captain Ross!" I said. He paused and looked down. "Does this mean that you've changed sides, Captain? Gone over to the committee?"

"Changed sides? Damn it, Pyrrhus, I haven't changed sides. I haven't taken sides at all. Hell and damnation, that's what's wrong with this town, yes, and the country as well. Everybody's taking sides against each other!

"Look what they did to poor Savage. He was their neighbor, and a good one, too. Minded his own business and paid what he owed. Six years he lived here. They ran him out of town, though, didn't they? Well, they'll not do that to me! I've more to concern me than three-pence a pound tax on tea. I don't even like tea!

"But I got to thinking about what happened last night: about what you said. And I realized that it wouldn't do to burn any bridges, not just now. What if the Liberty Boys were to win?

"So then I remembered that Dr. Lowther, who lives across from Pagan's, was low on drugs. The committee was worried, what with winter coming on, so I went to see 'em.

"Elizabeth didn't see it that way, but I figured it would be hard to hold it against a man for buying medicine, whatever was to happen. It's not as if it was arms or powder. But Elizabeth will get over her mad a lot sooner than the committeemen will forget who helped and who didn't, if it ever comes to war." He gave me a shrug and a wry grin. "It struck me that in times like these that a gentleman of property needs all the friends he can get.

"But we'll have plenty of time to talk once we've put to sea. Right now there's much to do if we're to catch the tide in the morning."

I nodded and began to make my way back down the stairs, but the captain stopped me before I had gone more than a step or two.

"I almost forgot," he said with an enigmatic smile. "There was more news this morning from the southward." He paused dramatically.

"Had you heard? It wasn't just Portsmouth. Yesterday the Sons of Liberty took the fort at Providence in Rhode Island as well."

16

THE *Industry* sailed from Falmouth on a day so mild as to be almost springlike, but she rounded Cape Breton in a prodigious storm, and by the time Quebec hove into view the weather had become uniformly foul and cold. We anchored in the shadow of the citadel Wolfe had taken from the French when I was a boy and went ashore in the lower city near the place where Montgomery was to fall a twelvemonth later.

I confess I would have been glad enough of a chance to see the city, but Captain Ross said that there was no time. The season was sufficiently advanced that there was great danger of ice in the Saint Lawrence, and he was anxious for the safety of his vessel. As it happened, we

completed our business there and came away again without having to
spend a single night in the place.

Captain Ross passed the word to keep a sharp lookout for British
cruisers, but we fell in with the schooner *Hallifax* off Fundy and were
forced to come under her lee. Our papers were in order and the officer
who came aboard used us politely, yet I should have known that my
master would be tense. Before he left, Lieutenant Nunn remarked that
Vice Admiral Graves had sent the *Canceaux* and the *Scarborough*
frigate from Boston to Piscataqua in time to prevent the people there
from removing the largest of the cannon from the fort. I started to ask
him for further news when Ross gave me such a look that I found it
convenient to spend the next several hours out of sight in the galley.

Fortunately I found him in a better humor when I came on deck
again. He was standing at the tiller, watching the luff of the mainsail.
From time to time as I approached I saw him glance aft over his
shoulder.

"Your dinner is ready, Captain," I said, though I own I felt some
misgivings. Dinner was a new receipt he had had from Elizabeth; I had
made it to please him, but it had not come out the way I thought it
should.

"Have a look astern, Pyrrhus," he said. "We are walking right away
from her, and weathering on her as well." I looked and saw a tall brig
with her yards braced up sharp for a long beat to windward. From the
cut of her sails she was a man-of-war, and so could only be British,
though she was too far away for me to see her colors.

"It's not to be wondered," I said, gauging the wind as best I could.
"We're lying near a point closer than she is." I looked from Ross to
the brig. "In time of war she'd make your fortune, Captain. The
Industry could sail rings around her. With a few guns and some more
men, you could take her easily."

"*Industry*'s too sharp-built for fighting, Pyrrhus," the captain said.
"Cannon would only make her crank: she'd never carry the metal. And
there's little profit in fighting cruisers. All you get is hard knocks." I
saw the flash of a smile, but it was a grim one. "I still have hopes that
there will be no war, but if war should come, we'll put our faith in
flight. Unless, of course, you've grown homesick for a simpler life in
the Indies." He smiled again, tightly. "There would be a ready market
there for captured slaves."

Before I could think of a proper reply, I saw a cloud of smoke erupt from the brig's bow. "Look there," I said in surprise. "They have opened fire!"

The captain's head whipped around in time to see the last of the smoke before it was whirled away by the wind. "I think not," he said. "It was just a warning. They would have to yaw to hit us, and they have not altered course." He looked about him carefully. Apparently he was satisfied with what he saw, for he called one of the seamen aft to replace him at the tiller.

"I think you said that my dinner was ready," he remarked calmly. "I may as well eat it now."

I went to the galley and brought his meal to him in the cabin. He had taken but one tentative mouthful when the man at the helm shouted down through the open skylight.

"Brig's opened fire, sir," he said. "I saw the fall of the shot."

"Very well," Ross told him. "I'll come." He wiped his mouth and stood up. "Don't look so disapproving, Pyrrhus," he chided. "I'll finish my meal later." He picked a fragment of food from his teeth. "This won't be going anywhere while we have a look at her."

I followed Ross up the companion ladder. He took the brass telescope from the binnacle and mounted easily into the ratlines. I watched him train the glass on our pursuer. The brig seemed to have lost ground. In a minute or so it veered again and I saw the smoke of the gun.

"He knows he can't catch us now," Ross said without removing his eye from the lens. "He must be hoping for a lucky hit." There was a distant splash as the ball fell short. The brig's captain must have been waiting for that, for even as the water fell back into the sea, the shapes of her sails began to change.

"She's hauled her wind," he said, closing the spyglass. "We've seen the last of her. At least now we've a story to tell when we get home. Elizabeth will —" He came to a full stop and smote himself on the brow.

"What's the matter, sir?" I asked him.

"Elizabeth's the matter. Or she will be. Damn my eyes! I clear forgot that I'd promised her some dress goods from Quebec. Well, there's no mending it now. There won't be a yard of cloth to suit her this side of New York."

"That's true," I agreed. "But it's after the first of the year, Captain.

The *John and Mary* may have arrived by now — she was due over a month ago. And it seems to me that I recall your good lady saying that she expected some lace or such among her cargo."

"You're right, Pyrrhus. I think she did at that." He looked up at the sails and then back at the British man-of-war, by now a mere speck on the horizon. "One way or another," he said, "we'll know by noon tomorrow. If this wind holds, we'll be in Falmouth in time for dinner."

"Speaking of dinner, Captain, you haven't finished yours."

"I know," he said. "Very well; you take the tiller for a spell, and one of the hands can get his at the same time." He went forward and opened the companionway door. "Did you really make that from Elizabeth's receipt?" he asked. I nodded and he shook his head sadly. "I shall have to hire a real cook once she and I are wed." With a grimace he added, "Lord knows what that mess will taste like cold. It was bad enough when it was hot."

When the captain came on deck again, he was nibbling at a piece of biscuit, so I expect that the ship's cat dined well that day. Ross altered our course slightly to conform to the run of the shore, which required us to tack several times during the course of the afternoon. When night came we shortened sail and made a long board to seaward, so that sunrise found us out of sight of land. The captain said we were between Townsend and Brunswick, and put the helm over again.

We came abreast of Clapboard Island at the northeast limit of Falmouth Harbor well before the sun had reached its zenith. The tide was just turning, and it was a simple matter to drop down inside Hog Island, tack around the ledges, and run for the mouth of the Fore River. I could see only a few vessels in the inner harbor, mostly sloops and schooners.

Ross had his telescope out and was scanning the anchorage. "No sign of the *John and Mary*," he said. "Not that I can see."

"Perhaps she's come and gone," I suggested.

He gave me a curt nod in acknowledgment, and raised the glass once more. "Make for Preble's wharf," he ordered. "We can lie there for now and make for our usual mooring later.

"It will be easier so," he explained. "Dr. Lowther's house and shop are both handy by, and we won't have to carry the things we bought him so far."

"Besides," I said with a smile, "it is closer to Pagan's that way."

Now that we were in the harbor, Ross was in high good spirits. "Yes," he agreed. "It is that."

It was a crisp day rather than cold, and though it was well into the month of January, the ground was bare. We passed Jordan's Point and the wharf near Colonel Waite's house where Ilsley distilled rum from West India molasses. I could smell its sweet odor on the wind.

For a few hundred yards we held to our course and there was nothing to do but wait for the captain's next command. I took advantage of the lull to catch a glimpse of the town.

Captain Coulson's *Minerva*, as big as a frigate, dominated the lower end of King Street. During our absence the shipwrights had planked her hull. Men swarmed over her, and I heard clearly the ringing of the caulkers' mallets as they filled her seams with oakum. At that rate, it would not be long before she was launched and tied up at Pote's wharf to be masted and rigged.

"If Coulson's sloop has come, it would not be too early," I observed. "They must have every ship-carpenter in the county at work in the yard."

Ross scanned the waterfront and nodded. "Captain Coulson's politics have not made him a popular man of late," he said, "but the people seem to like his money well enough. They've made good progress even so. I had not thought to see her so nearly finished. But look there: I'll wager the committee wishes Joseph had done as well with their fort. He must have had damnable luck getting workmen. All I can see is a bit of fresh-turned earth and a new flagpole."

Indeed, Fort Loyall, perched on its low rocky mound overlooking the harbor, appeared much the same as it had when we had left. Someone had cut the brush away from the earthworks, but I could see no cannon in the embrasures along the walls.

Evidently the seaman next to me had been following our conversation. He stopped what he was doing and straightened up to stare at the fort. This was too much for the captain.

"Get your eyes inboard," he snapped irritably. "This is no seminary for young ladies — you can moon all you like once you're ashore. There's work to be done. Get for'ard and take in the foresail when I give you the word. Jump to it! We've far too much way on." The sailor trotted to join his mate. "Now!" Ross bellowed, and they doused the sail and furled it expertly.

"Stand by the sheets!" Ross marked our progress with a practiced eye. "Ready with that anchor on the fo'c'sle!" He waited another moment before letting the sheets run and brought the schooner up into the wind. Our canvas flapped idly. "Let go the anchor!" he shouted.

There were sails to be got in and lines to belay, but these tasks took only a few minutes. Even so, by the time we had launched the longboat I noticed that a knot of people had gathered on the pier to watch. Among them was the old brigadier, leaning on his silver-headed cane. Ross left the sailors on board and I rowed him in.

Preble greeted the captain warmly. "The committee will also be glad you're safely home," he added. "They are meeting even now in the library chamber. Shall I send a boy with the news, or will you stop there yourself?"

"Thank you, no," said Ross. "I'll be going presently."

The onlookers made way for him and I followed swiftly, lest they close in again behind. Once we were through, Robert Pagan detached himself from the fringe of the crowd and joined us.

"It's good to have you back, Will," he said. He might have meant anything. "I trust that your voyage was profitable."

Ross eyed him carefully. "Not exactly profitable, I wouldn't say. You might say I did it for friendship rather than money."

"I should see to it that I didn't make the wrong sort of friends if I were you, Captain. It could work to your disadvantage."

Ross rounded on him. "Meaning what, Robert?"

"Meaning nothing at all, Will. Nothing at all. It's just, well, there's been talk about town since you agreed to go to Quebec for the committee. You know the sort. It wouldn't do to give people the wrong idea, now, would it?

"But enough of this. I really didn't mean to go on so. Elizabeth and I will be expecting you for dinner, of course."

"I'll be there." They came to a stop outside Enoch Freeman's impressive house on Middle Street. The major's many offices, which included that of librarian, had made it virtually a public building.

The captain turned to Pagan. "Tell me, Robert," he said earnestly, "What the devil is going on around here? The committee is still running the town, or so it would seem. Yet from some of the things you've said, I half-expect to find royal commissioners in there instead of Freeman and his friends. People seem edgy — even you. Why, except for yourself and the brigadier, no one has even said hello. They just mumble, or pretend they haven't seen us.

"And while we're at it, what happened to the grand plans they had for the fort? To hear Joe McLellan, there was going to be a citadel to match Quebec's by the time I got back. From what I saw coming in, they've done damned little."

Pagan glanced about and took Ross by the arm. "I'll tell you," he said in a confidential tone. "What has happened is that people hereabouts have realized that Boston isn't as far away as they had thought. It's made some of them kind of nervous.

"When the news came from Portsmouth that the country people had taken Piscataqua fort, a lot of folk, and I mean no offense by it, felt that that was the end of it. Your friend McLellan was ready to mount a couple of squirrel-guns in the fort and bid General Gage to go back to his knitting. An old woman they called him, and worse. That other trouble in Rhode Island helped not a bit.

"Well," he said triumphantly, "they soon found out that the old woman had one hell of a reach. Before they could get any of the big guns out of the fort, Gage had Barkley there in the *Scarborough*, and young Mowatt as well. You haven't met Henry Mowatt, though, have you? It seems to me that you were off for Ireland last year when he arrived.

"Anyway, the two of them have sealed up Portsmouth as neat as a cork in a bottle. The country people have gone home, of course, and those who live there are stuck with it.

"Well, that gave Falmouth something to think about, I tell you. Since then the committee has walked a good bit softer. Joseph may have had a few of the slaves brought in from Gorham to dig around the fort and fix up the old stone guard-room, but there has been precious little else done.

"I must say, though, you don't seem as surprised as you might be, Will. I had thought to catch you out with the news about Piscataqua."

Ross smiled and shook his head. "I had that story of Lieutenant Nunn yesterday. They are making no secret of it. And I can tell you this, since it will be all over town as soon's I let the committee know: there's a brig been cruising between Townsend and Penobscot. I was chased by her, and when I wouldn't heave to, she fired two shot at me. This time Gage means business."

Pagan whistled. "This is news! And to my mind, Will, it couldn't come at a better time. Now if Coulson's damned sloop would just come in so we can finish the *Minerva*, I'd say we were out of the woods."

"There's still no sign of her, then? Worse luck for me! I had hoped that she was come and gone again. But look, Robert, you don't think that Freeman would let you unload a cargo from England without an argument, do you?"

"Perhaps not without an argument, Will, but how is he to stop us? The way he's pussyfooting about right now, I think we could get the goods ashore. That's the main thing, after all.

"And I don't mind telling you, I'll be glad when *Minerva*'s done and in the water. I've entirely too much tied up in her not to finish her now, and the workmen have gone nearly as far as they can without the gear Coulson had sent from Bristol. That sloop's got her ironwork, canvas, cordage — the lot!

"You saw her coming in, of course. She's big, Will. Big enough to make or break half a dozen of us. Oh, I'd manage, I suppose, though I shouldn't like to have to prove it. But Coulson himself, he would go under for certain. He's even got a cargo of masts laid by against her first voyage!

"Look, I should get back to the yard. Some of the men slack off if I'm not there to watch 'em. You know how it is. Take care of your business with the committee, and then stop by the house. Elizabeth's there, I think. I'll try to finish up and join you when I can."

He left us then and Ross and I went up the steps to Freeman's house. There was a man inside who asked our business and then bid us enter.

"Right this way, Captain," he said, and stepped across the hall to a closed door. "Your boy can wait in the kitchen if you want." My master nodded his permission.

The man opened the door for the captain and closed it behind him. For a moment he stood by the door as though in thought. He seemed very pleased with himself for some reason, though I could not see that he had done much of import. Suddenly he must have remembered that he was not alone. He looked at me with the expression of a man who has found something on the bottom of his shoe. Disdainfully, he jerked a thumb toward the rear of the house. "The kitchen is back there, boy," he said.

I walked down the hall past the ornately carved staircase and around to where the thick Turkish carpet gave way to floor cloths of painted canvas. There was another door near the back stairs. I opened it and looked inside. A woman in a plain wool dress and a mob cap knelt before the fireplace, surrounded by kettles and a tin roaster. Her back was toward me.

"Mr. Fulton?" she said. I took it that she had heard me at the door and thought I was the dour individual from the hallway. "I'd be grateful, Mr. Fulton, would you go and tell Major Freeman that his dinner's 'most ready."

Not knowing what I should say, I cleared my throat softly. She rose and began to turn her body before looking in my direction. When she did I saw that she had skin the color of strong coffee with a hint of cream, high cheekbones, and snapping brown eyes. When her eyes met mine, a warm smile spread across her face. "Why," she said, "you ain't Mr. Fulton!"

"No," I agreed, and found that I was smiling just as broadly. "No, I guess I'm not."

17

Sarah Darling was her name; she was perhaps two-and-twenty years of age, slender but pleasantly rounded. Her ruffled cap came to my chin, and when she took it off and looked up at me, I saw that she had glossy black curls that framed her face and made her eyes look very wide and vulnerable. After a moment my throat commenced to feel peculiar and lumpish, and then Sarah laughed and shook her head so that her curls danced. She crossed the room to a long pine table. While she fixed my food, she told me that she had been born in Falmouth, and that although she cooked for Major Freeman she still lived with her family at Long Creek.

"White house up the hill from Davis's ferry," she told me. "At least the front is: white, I mean. And there are flowers in the yard in springtime. I plant 'em myself."

"How do you find time for that?" I asked around a mouthful of cornbread and butter. "Cooking in a house like this must keep you busy enough as it is."

"Woman's always got time for pretty." Her mouth was prim. "Besides, I get Sabbaths to myself. Mostly I go to morning services and spend the afternoons at home. 'Less we have visitors, I use that time to make the house look nice." She gave me a glance that was almost shy. "We don't get many visitors, so I have plenty of time for flowers. Daddy don't have much truck with folks thereabouts."

Abruptly the door swung inward. I looked up and saw the captain. His eyes were grim. He nodded at me and I rose to follow him. At the door I remembered my manners and turned to bid Sarah goodbye. "Thank you for the cider and cornbread," I added. "The way things look I'm afraid I'm going to miss my dinner."

"Can't do nothing 'bout that today," she said. "This's Friday. You just hurry along and do the best you can. You keep the captain waiting, he make you work Sunday too, and I wouldn't like that." I stared at her for a heartbeat or two, scarcely daring to draw breath. She put her hands on her hips. "Go now, Pyrrhus Ross, you know I can't plant no flowers in January. But you best get there by one o'clock, or you won't get fed on Sunday either. Daddy's some particular 'bout me serving his dinner on time."

I could not have stood there more than a few seconds before hurrying out to catch up with the captain, but the picture of Sarah standing in Major Freeman's kitchen remains graven in my memory to this day. The pair of us must have been a sight, with me so gay and the captain somber. Somehow we caught Fulton by surprise, and it was all I could do to keep from laughing at the look of dismay on his face when he realized that there was no way for him to reach the door in time. I opened it for my master with a bit of a flourish. He strode past oblivious to the byplay, though I was near to bursting from sheer high spirits.

Ross had nothing to say as we walked along Middle Street and down King to the docks. I confess I was just as glad, for I kept seeing Sarah's face and hearing her voice. At the bottom of the hill he stopped abruptly, and I saw that he was watching an old black man who was sweeping out the guard-house. Apparently he was all the garrison Fort Loyall could boast. Beyond him the aging earthworks seemed to crouch beneath the keel of Coulson's monumental mast ship. Perched on a spidery framework of scaffolding, the workmen stood out in stark silhouette against the fresh-cut planks of her hull. The captain stood there for a time, hands clasped behind him. At last he shook his head and moved on.

I knew by now that he was sorely concerned. Not until we were at the boat did he speak, and even then he merely told me to row back out to the schooner. "I'll be along in a while," he said. "First I want to see Elizabeth. But the doctor will be coming for his medicines, and you should be on board to receive him. Tell the men that I said they were to help. Can you manage that?" I assured him that I could, though I knew as well as he that the men preferred getting their orders directly.

As it turned out, I had no difficulty with either the crew or the doctor. When he had left, I went below and began to prepare for going ashore.

Captain Ross returned while I was stripping the bedding from his bunk in the *Industry*'s cabin. I looked up in time to see him slam the door behind him.

"Lay off that damned nonsense and pour me a drink," he said. "Rum." He threw his hat on the disordered bed and sat down hard in his painted armchair. "You may as well leave the blankets. We'll be sleeping on board tonight anyway."

I poured an inch of rum into a tumbler and offered it to him. "On board, Captain? Here in Falmouth? Why, is there something wrong?"

"Wrong?" Ross reached out and took the bottle from me. He took a long drink and laughed. "Whatever could be wrong?" He drank again.

"No, Pyrrhus, everything's fine. Just fine. Except that everyone in Falmouth save you and me has gone stark mad.

"You may as well sit down," he told me. "I've got to talk to somebody, and Elizabeth's no help at all. She's as bad as the others. She believes anything her brother says. All she cares about is her damned ribbons and the devil with everything else."

He gestured with the hand that held the bottle. "That's the problem, you know. Nobody gives a damn about anything but what they want. It's going to end up like Portsmouth, or maybe worse. Freeman says he'll see Coulson in hell before he lets him unload the *John and Mary*.

Coulson claims he's a ruined man if he doesn't, and says he'll have the stores to finish the *Minerva* whether the committee will or no. And here sit the rest of us, squarely in the middle. This town could blow up as soon as that sloop is hull-up on the horizon."

"Surely it can't be as bad as that," I protested. "You don't mean to say they'd really come to blows over it."

The captain eyed me impatiently. "You think not? Where have you been these last months? Boston shut up over a few chests of tea, and Portsmouth now as well. You have lived in Falmouth long enough by now to know we are not so different from the people in Portsmouth or Boston. There were men at the meeting at Coulson's house who are willing to force the issue, and there are those on the committee who would call out the militia to stop them." He gave a triumphant look and punctuated his answer with a pull at the bottle.

"But they can't all be like that, Captain. They know what could happen. Surely some of them would rather talk than fight.

"What about Mr. Pagan? He has always seemed a sensible man. What about Bryce McLellan? What about the sheriff, for that matter? Keeping the peace is his job."

The captain shook his head. "Bryce hasn't the influence in a matter like this. He might perhaps sway Joseph and one or two others, but not the whole of the committee. And Sheriff Tyng would never stand against them. Not since last fall. He'd be mobbed for certain, and he's a family to consider.

"As for Robert, why, you heard him yourself. He's just like the rest. He says the time has come to end this business of tyranny by committee, that a show of force is all that's needed. You should have heard him a few minutes ago! The committee's finished, he said. It has been ever since Gage sent the *Scarborough* to Portsmouth, only nobody has had the courage to stand up and prove it. He's been telling Coulson and the others that if they act together now, Freeman will back down and let the cargo land."

"If he thinks that, he doesn't know Major Freeman."

"Exactly what I tried to tell him. The thing is that he is right up to a point." He held up his hand for quiet. "I'm as tired of this committee business as the next man, and I'd be glad to see it end. But they're going about it the wrong way. They ought to let it die of its own weight.

"If Coulson brings in his cargo unopposed, the committee is dead in Falmouth. So Freeman can't let it come ashore. He has to stop it. Even if he didn't want to, he knows we'd have Sons of Liberty here from all over the country inside of two days. They won't know Whig from Tory, and what's more, they won't care. They'd have the town down about our ears."

"There must be someone in town who feels the way you do," I said. "Deacon Codman might help. I'm sure he'd listen. He's always thought well of you, or so his wife told me once."

"His wife?" The captain's face became thoughtful. He took a sip of rum. "Perhaps the deacon could do something at that. Or the parson: old Reverend Smith, I meant, not that hothead Deane. Even Major Freeman would have to listen to him.

"But there's no time for that just now. The *John and Mary* could sail in at any moment, and I want this ship out of harm's way when she does." He rose wearily and went to the door.

"Come bear a hand once you get that rum locked away," he told me. "I'll go roust out the others. You can take 'em ashore afterward, and if there's anything you need in town you can get it then. Mind that you're back within the hour, though. I'm to dine with the Pagans tonight, if Elizabeth will leave off complaining long enough for me to chew and swallow." He gave me a bleak smile. What Ross had said was sufficiently disturbing that I must have been alone for some time before I noticed he was gone. When I came to myself again, it was with the uncomfortable sensation that something in the cabin had been altered.

I looked about carefully, noting each familiar object. The captain was a straightforward man. His needs were simple, his comforts Spartan: a bed, a chest, a desk and chair, a roll of charts, and a few books on navigation. At this remove I am not certain whether or not there was a Bible, though if there was, Ross would have classed it as but another ephemeris.

The tally was short, however, and everything was in its appointed place. The room was the same as it had always been. It was the captain himself who was changing. The easy confidence I had come to expect of him was overlaid with his own inner knowledge that here was a situation he could not dominate as he might an unhandy ship or a rebellious crew. Ross was out of his element; he knew it, and he was afraid.

Never before had I seen him show fear, not even when the foremast had gone by the boards off Guadeloupe, but my respect for him was not diminished by the realization. Indeed, I think I liked him all the more for the humanness of it, and because I too was afraid: afraid for myself and for him, and now for Sarah, and for the rest of Falmouth as well. For the first time I became aware of the terrifying complexity of the times. It was no longer a simple matter of choosing the winning side. Whatever we might do, we would be in danger, and it might well be that those we held to be friends would prove a greater threat than our enemies. I closed my eyes as though to shut it all out. Sarah's face came to mind once more, but this time it seemed a mere mockery of all my hopes.

The whole ship trembled then, as the anchor cable came taut, and I heard Ross call my name. "Coming, Captain," I answered. "I'm coming." I looked at the glass of rum in my hand, the one I had poured for my master, then I drank the spirit down and went out.

We anchored at the edge of the fairway, a hundred feet or so from Deering's wharf. "Plenty of water under the keel, whatever the tide," Captain Ross observed with satisfaction. "And we're a good quarter-mile from the foot of King Street. That's where the trouble will be if it comes."

He had been speaking as though to himself alone, but now he addressed me directly. "I may as well go ashore with the men if you've no objection, Pyrrhus. It will save time, and from the look of the sun I'll not be early at Pagan's: not that I'd mind, of course. Keep an eye on the ship, but you needn't wait up for me." There was no chance for me to speak with him as I would have liked, for the men were there and they were impatient to get ashore to the rum at the King's Head and the other dubious delights of the waterfront. I told myself there would be plenty of time to speak of Sunday on the morrow.

As it happened there was not. My master was in a bilious temper and went ashore with scarcely a word. Morning became afternoon, and the sun was low in the sky when at last he returned.

"Captain Ross!" I said joyfully as he swung over the rail. "I thought you would never get back."

"Whatever you want, it will have to wait," he told me. "I've been running around Falmouth all day seeing people, and I just came aboard so that I could clean up and change my clothes. Elizabeth and I are invited to Deacon Codman's for the evening."

I put out a hand to stop him. "If you please, Captain," I pressed, "I'm afraid this can't wait." His brows came together and still I plunged on. "I'm to dine ashore tomorrow myself, and I'll be wanting the afternoon free."

To be fair, my timing was poor. For an instant I thought Ross would explode, but he mastered himself with an effort and spoke reasonably. "You'll have to go another time," he said. "I'm not going to be aboard tomorrow either, and I won't leave the *Industry* unwatched, not just now.

"Look, Pyrrhus, I'm in a hurry. We can talk about this later." He fished a copper from his pocket. "Here," he said. "Take this. Maybe you can get one of the boys from the waterfront to take a note." He tore himself away and went below.

I idled about the boat for a few minutes after Ross went ashore, watching him as he walked along the waterfront toward Clay Cove. As soon as he was out of sight, I climbed the dock ladder and raced off to Major Freeman's house, up Fish Street hill, and right on Middle. I arrived at the back door with my heart beating trebly fast from exertion, anticipation, and the guilty knowledge that I had disobeyed the captain's orders. I caught my breath and then knocked on the back door. When no one answered, I rapped more firmly. Soon I heard footsteps. There was a pause while the person within fumbled with the latch.

It was Fulton. "You!" he said when he saw my face in the gleam of his candle. It took me a moment to gather my wits sufficiently to answer.

"If you please, Mr. Fulton," I said as humbly as I might, "may I speak with Sarah Darling?"

"No," was his reply, and he started to shut the door. Impetuously, I put my hand out and stopped him. "Please, sir. It's important. If she's busy, may I send a message?"

He looked at my hand on the door with unmistakable significance. I let it fall. "You're too late," he said with evident enjoyment. "Sally's gone for the day, and won't be back until Monday." His casual use of her name hurt. He looked at me narrowly. "Does your master know you're about, bothering honest citizens?" My startled expression must have told him he had hit the mark. "I thought not. Well, be off with you, then, and don't let me see that black face of yours again lest I tell him more than you'd like him to know!" He slammed the door and left me standing in the dark.

There was no question of my taking the ferry to Long Creek, which was my first desperate thought. I went back to the *Industry*, made a cold supper of biscuit and hard cheese, and tried to sleep.

Unfortunately, sleep proved elusive. Around midnight I rose and walked the deck, noting with surprise that the captain was not yet come, and turned in once again. It must have been well into the early hours when at last I fell into an uneasy doze.

I woke in the gray dawn, sleepily wondering what had roused me, until I heard low voices aft and the hollow thump of a boat butting against the side of the schooner. I slipped into my jacket and shoes and went to see what was afoot. I moved silently to the galley hatch and raised myself just enough to see over the low coaming. A man had boarded the schooner. He was walking away from me, in the direction of the captain's cabin, and taking obvious pains not to be heard. Just as I was about to challenge him, he cocked his head as though he had heard a noise, and I saw that it was only Ross. He looked as though he might have dressed hurriedly and in the dark, and the way that his hair escaped from beneath his hat in little tufts made me suspect that wherever he and Elizabeth had begun their evening, it had not ended in the deacon's parlor. He was clearly hoping not to be seen, and though I longed to speak to him about Sarah, it was no time for a confrontation. With a mixture of annoyance and envy I dropped from the hatch and went back to bed.

Through some ill fortune I fell asleep and slept soundly until late morning, when I woke suddenly with a cold chill upon me. I heard a laugh and opened my eyes. There stood my master, with my blankets in one hand and a pannikin in the other. "Show a leg, you slugabed," he chided. "Show a leg, or I shall baptize you in ice water. It's time we were up and about. What will people think of me if you let me sleep the clock around?" I sat up and rubbed my eyes, sensing that he was watching me carefully as I did so. When I made no mention of his late arrival, he seemed to relax.

"You must have been tired," he said. "Sleep well?"

"Like the dead, Captain," I assured him.

"Good. Come on, then. I've just time to wash and shave before I go ashore." He handed me the pan of water. "Heat this on the stove and bring it to me in the cabin. There's no time for breakfast, I'm afraid, but you've yourself to blame for that. I'll see that you have money enough for a meal at the King's Head before you come back." He stepped out into the galley.

"Just a moment, Captain," I said. "Yesterday I mentioned that I had been asked to dine with a family ashore. Might I not go there instead?"

"I told you then that I need you on board," he snapped, and for a moment I feared that I had pressed the matter too far. Then his expression softened. "Why not?" he said. "After all, they must live along the waterfront somewhere, and it will take you no longer."

I should have left well enough alone. "They live in Long Creek," I told him. His smile became a frown, and I hastened to continue. "Please, Captain, I'll hurry back, and I'll pay the ferryman myself."

My earnestness seemed to disarm him, and I think that he might have relented had not the church bell rung, signifying the end of the morning service. "There," he said, "that settles that, I'm afraid. I had no idea how late it was. There's no way now that I can spare you in time to catch the noon ferry, and heaven only knows when you would get back. Be gone the whole afternoon, most likely. No, Pyrrhus, for today at least it is out of the question. I want you here. You'll find aplenty to keep you busy on board were you to put your mind to it."

Evidently I let my feelings show. My sulky mood seemed to goad him beyond enduring. "Damn your black hide, Pyrrhus!" he exclaimed. "What in hell do you expect of me? This schooner is the only thing I own in this world, save your own worthless carcass, and I daren't take any chances with her, not with affairs as they are. By damn, you've got things pretty soft around here, too! Do you think that you'd be more tenderly treated back in Antigua? If you do, by God, there's a simple enough remedy!" He spun around and left me staring.

His outburst took me by surprise, and the water was near to boiling before I had recovered sufficiently to react to it. The thought of Sarah waiting for me in her father's house in Long Creek made me both sad and angry. Perhaps she would think that I scorned her hospitality, or that I simply did not care. I went to bring the pan aft, and it helped not at all to see the streets of Falmouth full of people dressed in their best clothes, walking leisurely home from church. But for the color of their skins, the scene reminded me sharply of Sabbaths in Saint Kitts, and such was my vagrant humor that I could not forbear from recalling that there, at least on Sunday, even a slave might go where he listed.

Captain Ross had hung his shaving mirror close to the cabin window and looked absently from one to the other while he lathered his face. I saw him dart a glance at me when he exchanged the brush for his razor. He tilted his head and began to shave the left side of his neck. I stood by with water and his towel. From time to time it seemed that he was watching me in the mirror, but I could not be sure. In any case I was determined that it would not be I who spoke first.

Finally Ross put the razor by. He gave me a crooked smile. "I suppose you think you're being ill used," he said. He paused as if he expected me to protest, and when I did not he smiled again, but more kindly this time. "All right," he said. "Tell me about her. It's that pretty young cook over at Freeman's, isn't it?" I stared at him in astonishment, and he shook his head. "I knew there had to be a woman in it somewhere. What's her name?"

"Sarah," I told him. "Sarah Darling."

He nodded. "Look," he said, "I am concerned about leaving the ship unwatched, and I'll be busy for the next two hours at least. Would it suit you if I could have someone here to relieve you at, say, three o'clock? I'd want you back by dark."

"Thank you, Captain," I began, but he waved my thanks aside.

"Don't thank me," he said. "I did it as much for my own reasons as any. As soon as I knew there was a woman in it I knew I hadn't a chance. Elizabeth's in such a pet over her dry goods that if she were to hear I'd stood in the way of your romance as well I'd never hear the end of it."

❧❧❧ 18 ❧❧❧

To my dismay the ferry to Long Creek proved a crazy skiff, so old and weather-beaten that it might almost have been used by that same Isaac Davis who first petitioned the General Court for the right to carry passengers near a century before. The old man who rowed it was fully as bad. He lived in a hut by the water's edge, and when he came close to me he stank of tobacco, rum, and accumulated filth to the point that I began to suspect that he had inherited his smallclothes along with the boat.

"What'll 'ee want, then?" he asked in a high-pitched, querulous voice. I said I wished passage across the river, although indeed it seemed to me that it should have been plain enough. Once he assured himself that I possessed the necessary fare, the old ferryman bade me board and then took his own seat at the oars. Thereafter he addressed no single word to me directly while maintaining a constant commentary on his aching joints and the smallness of his custom since the new bridge had been built at Stroudwater.

At another time I might have listened with more interest, hoping to hear some useful fact or rumor, for even the poorest of duff will have its raisins, however thinly they may be spread. Today I was in no mood to be patient, and when he paused for breath I broke in and asked for directions to Darling's house.

"Straight up the hill on the right it be," he said. "But it's why 'ee are askin' that I'm wondering." He eyed me shrewdly and gave out with a shrill laugh. "O' course, Lije, you old dotard: look at him! He'll be courtin' Darling's Sarah, he will!" With that he fell to cackling again. I felt my cheeks grow hot and left him to his laughter. When I was halfway up the hill, I heard his voice again. "Luck to 'ee, lad," he called out. "Luck to 'ee!" I turned to look, and he flung me a cheerful wave.

As I climbed to the crest, I turned the old man's words over in my mind. I had not thought of courting Sarah. This was a visit and no more. I looked down at myself for some sign he might have read and saw nothing. I was dressed in my best clothes, to be sure, yet any Sunday visitor would want to look as well as he might. I turned into the dooryard telling myself that the man was a humbug, and I a fool for heeding him. He knew nothing of me or the slightness of my acquaintance with Sarah. Courting her? I did not cut such a poor figure that the idea was laughable. I knocked at the front door. Courting Sarah? Why not, indeed? Finally the door opened. Sarah stood in the hall, looking up at me. In a climax of happiness and despair I understood why I had come, and yet why I must be a visitor and not a suitor.

"Pyrrhus!" Sarah exclaimed. She bit her lip and added softly, "I'd thought you weren't coming."

I started to reach out to comfort her but controlled the movement just in time. "I'm sorry I'm late," I said. The words sounded more brusque than I had intended. "I had to work and couldn't get word to you."

Puzzlement showed on Sarah's face. There was more that I needed to say, but the doorway seemed the wrong place, and under the circumstances I didn't want to go inside. She parted her lips to speak, but I cut in. "Look," I said, "we can't talk like this. Can't you come outside for a moment?" She nodded, wiped her hands on her apron, and ducked out of sight. When she came back into the hallway, she had a cloak thrown over her shoulders and was tying the straps of a bonnet beneath her chin.

"Come on," she said. There was a hint of fierceness in her voice.

She walked to the side of the house, amid the brown fallow beds of what must have been a beautiful garden in season. The yard looked out over the roofs of the cabins and shanties which formed the rest of the settlement. I followed and stood beside her. Her arms were folded across her breasts.

"I was born in that house," she said in a tightly controlled voice. "Me, and my brother Nat and Daddy before us. It may not be very grand, but we try to keep it nice, and it's clean. As clean as any sea-captain's house in Falmouth. This land it's built on, the selectmen gave to my grandfather for killing an Indian in Queen Anne's War. Reverend Smith been there, and deacons, and the major, too. Drank tea in the parlor, they did, when people still drank tea hereabouts, and it was good enough for any of them. I never thought to see the day my daddy's house wasn't good enough for a nigger."

I winced at the word, and when I looked back at Sarah, her eyes were bright with anger. She seemed to be waiting for me to say something, but no words came. After a long moment she turned and started to leave.

Without willing it, I found my hand on her shoulder. "Please wait," I heard myself say. "It's not that." Sarah raised her eyes to mine and I could see where the tears had coursed down her cheeks. "Oh, Sarah," I told her, "I never should have come." I could tell that she didn't understand, and yet I could think of no easy way to explain.

"Damn it, Sarah," I blurted. "Can't you see? It isn't the house that's not good enough. It's me. Sarah, I don't work for Captain Ross: he owns me. I'm nothing but a damned slave!"

The shock on Sarah's face was painful to see, but there was nothing for it. I was a slave, and she was free. Nothing I could say would alter that. I thrust my hands deep into my coat pockets and walked despondently down the hill.

I heard her call my name, but I dared not stop. There was the sound of running footsteps, and she was there beside me. I felt her touch my sleeve. I stopped then, and she flung her arms about me. Her cheek was pressed close to my chest. "Pyrrhus," she whispered. "Oh, Pyrrhus, I didn't know." I took my hands out of my pockets and held her.

After a time I took her by the hand and walked with her down to the shore. I spoke of my life in the islands with Fitzgore and all that he had taught me. Sarah made me recite bits of Latin and laughed at the foreign sounds. "It must be wonderful to do all that reading," she said wistfully. "You're just as good as Reverend Smith. Me, it's all I can do to spell out a verse in the Scriptures." Then her eyes went soft and sad.

"I hope you aren't mad at me for not knowing 'bout the captain," she said. "I never dreamed, never once, that you weren't, well, better off than me. All I knew was I liked you, and you looking so fine and talking so pretty. All the slaves I ever met was farm hands, and I could see you weren't no farm hand.

"Anyway," she said, "I still like you." She gave my hand a little squeeze. "I hear over Major Freeman's, there's a war coming, and pretty soon there won't be no more slavin'. Suppose," she said archly, smiling up wide-eyed, as she had at our first meeting, "just suppose you was free right this minute, what would you want to do?"

I showed her.

❦❦❦ 19 ❦❦❦

TACITUS writes of Dead Sea fruit which crumbles to ashes. The joy that I had found in Sarah's arms bore scrutiny no better than it. It melted away even as I sought to savor it, and I was left choking on the bitter realization that I had been a fool to allow things to go so far.

More than a fool. Sarah and I had parted on the road to the water, and the implications of what I had done rose up to impeach me almost before the warmth of her kisses was gone from my lips. So overwhelming were they that I rode back across the river to Falmouth without once looking back to see if she were still standing on the hill above the ferry.

I did not have far to walk, but by the time I reached the schooner I was weak and shaking. Fortunately, the captain took no notice. He bade me good evening, and I watched from the rail as he rowed himself ashore.

I suppose I should have eaten, but somehow I had no appetite. I went to my berth in the forecastle and lay down. Sleep eluded me. After a time my bit of candle guttered and went out.

The words we had whispered in the moment of passion came back to me as clearly as if I had spoken them again there in the darkness. But surely they were more than mere words, or nothing in this world had meaning. The memory of them racked my soul. By what right had I, who could not call the very flesh in which I stood my own, thought to pledge myself to another? I had gone to Long Creek not daring so much as to frame the thought in my mind. That Sarah had pressed me to speak it was no extenuation, and we had gone far beyond speaking.

I had told her that I was no freeman. Still, she had been willing. Surely Sarah was a woman grown and must bear responsibility for her own actions. Ross would have counseled me to put it from my mind. Either I loved the lady, or I did not. He might well say so, for he was at liberty to do as he wished. I was not.

Freedom had seldom seemed more desirable, or so far from my grasp. It was painfully clear that Sarah would never have acted as she had if she understood the extent of the gulf that lay between us. When I would have spoken, she passed it off with scarcely a word, and I had made no objection. She had cradled me against the softness of her bosom, and I had held my tongue for fear the moment would end. But what could a slave do who loved a free woman?

The shelf on which I lay suddenly seemed too confining for the thoughts that warred in my brain. I cast the blankets aside and sat on the edge of my berth.

To continue as we were would soon bring about Sarah's ruin if she were not wed. I was certain there were other men who would have been willing whatever the circumstances, but I could not endure the idea of forcing Sarah to choose between a loveless marriage and a life of lonely shame. Too, there was the danger that my part in the matter might be exposed. I should not care for myself, of course, and the captain would likely laugh it off and call for a brimmer all 'round, but there was a chance that her father could have him cast in damages like the owner of a wayward boar. A pretty picture, that. Would it be the sheriff who would bring the summons, or the hog-reeve?

To seize my freedom, then, as Frederick had stolen it from me. Sarah and I might run away and be married, although that course had flaws as well. It seemed a poor enough way of repaying what obligation I owed Ross, whom I had to admit I liked and respected and who had, after all, preserved me from a worse fate. Where could we go that he could not find us if he would? Not to the Indies, surely. We would not be safe there without papers. And it was not far enough, in any case. China would hardly be far enough. There was no place on earth that ships would sail where I might not someday meet a man who knew Ross and his runaway slave. If I should seek employment with some merchant, which was the only trade I knew, the chances of such a meeting were very good indeed. I had been with him long enough to know that my captain was a passionate man. If he heard of me, he might easily decide to hunt down such a valuable piece of errant property. It would not be the first time that kindness ill used returned the favor, and the law would deal harshly with Sarah as my accomplice. No, it would not serve.

Perhaps I should simply be patient. War was brewing between the colonies and England. Sarah herself had spoken of it as though it were only weeks in the future, and in the major's household she was well placed to know what was afoot. Was it not wise counsel to be patient and wait until I too should be free?

Free. Inadvertently I had spoken the word as I rolled it over in my mind, and I jumped at the hollow sound of my voice in the empty forecastle. Free. It was hard to believe that there had been a time in my life when it had been just a word among others. Would it ever seem that way again?

Suppose I did ask Sarah to wait. I could not quite repress a mocking laugh. Waiting apparently was not one of the things that she and I did best, nor was I certain that it would be a fair request to make. But assuming she agreed, and did not simply laugh in her turn and pull me close instead —

War would not necessarily bring victory, nor victory freedom. Even now there might be no war, whatever the major and his fellows had said. Belike the powerful men who called the tune would settle for an end to the taxes they found disagreeable rather than hazard their all on a single turn of the wheel. They would find it impossible to do otherwise, for they were merchants and planters every one, men of business. There would be zealots among them, of course, who would be wroth, and men such as Freeman and Captain Thompson, who had made themselves odious to the Crown, might fight, but though wars may be fought with zeal alone they are seldom won so.

Beyond was only the hope that someday I might purchase my freedom should my master be willing to sell. That day was too remote to bear thinking of, for moon-calf that I was, I would not suffer it to come on any but my own terms.

One might well ask why I was so particular. Indeed, at this remove I am hard put to explain. Call it pride. If pride is a sin, at least it is a human failing, and a slave cannot cleave too strongly to the humanity all the world seems intent upon denying. I only knew that I could not broach the topic until I might pay Ross fair value for my freedom, and that in my own coin. I would not trade on my master's charity.

Perchance he would offer to sell at the price he had paid, but I could not hold myself so cheap. Even at the time it had rankled. Nor could I allow Sarah, or any other, to pay a part of it lest I should not be truly free, but have effected merely a change of owners. I would feel more a concubine than a husband.

If it came to that, I could not in honor ask Sarah to wait, which brought me to my last alternative. I could leave her, or rather, bid her to leave me. Could I? There was a sort of melancholy pleasure in contemplating how it might be done. When I was a boy, I had read a poem by one of the cavaliers which had made me weep with its poignant beauty. I could almost hear myself speaking the lines the long-dead son of Ben had written, yet in my heart I knew that I had not the courage to carry out such a plan. I wanted no part of leaving Sarah, and Sarah would not understand. She would not have heard of Lovelace, or any other poet since King Solomon. There would probably be a painful scene. Sarah would think that I had played her false; she would believe me one of that contemptible tribe of lovers who are ardent only until their desires are gratified. That I knew I could not abide.

I spat out a short, vicious curse and began to pace. What was to be done?

Hours later I climbed wearily to the deck above for a breath of air. In the east the sky was becoming light. I had wrestled with love and conscience all night, like Jacob with the angel, and in the end I was no nearer to a resolution than I had been the day before. I could not do more. For obvious reasons I could not speak of the matter to the captain, and I had no other friend but Sarah.

A line of brilliant gold appeared on the horizon. I chose to take it for an omen. There was nothing for it but to lay it all at Sarah's feet and pray that somehow, unbelievably, she would understand. I took a last look at the rising sun and went below. This time when I stretched myself upon my berth, I closed my eyes and slept.

Almost at once, or so it seemed, I was awakened by the clatter of footsteps aloft and my master's voice calling my name. I sat up and groped blearily for my shoes. While I was pulling them on, Ross bounded in, looking far too cheerful for my taste at such an early hour.

"Baltimore," he told me. "We're for Baltimore."

"Baltimore?" I repeated. "When?"

"Wednesday," he said. "We sail on the morning tide. We're to buy corn on Deacon Codman's account. It's an opportunity, by God, Pyrrhus: I'm to have a full share for the *Industry*'s hire. Up with you, man, up! I've a crew aboard already. In half an hour I want to be tied up at the deacon's wharf. You'll have to look sharp if you want breakfast. Get a move on. I'll be in my cabin getting our papers in order. I could do with a cup of coffee myself. Hot and strong, mind you!" He winked and struck me lightly on the shoulder. "Damn my eyes, Pyrrhus, but there's money to be made. I can smell it. I feel it in my bones. I'm a made man. Look you: grain is short already. By the time we get back there'll be scarcely a bushel left in town. We'll be able to sell at our own price." Ross gave me another grin and went out through the galley. I saw him dance a jig-step before he hauled himself up the ladder.

I ran one hand through my hair and looked down at the water sourly. "Coffee it is, sir, hot and strong," I muttered. The next two days would be busy ones. I would be hard put to find time to be with Sarah before we sailed.

As things fell out, I did not see her at all. The committee was not pleased to give any vessel leave to depart from Falmouth unladen, so that we were forced to take with us on deck a cargo of cordwood, part of Falmouth's contribution for the relief of Boston.

This circumstance suited the captain ill; that afternoon when I besought him for permission to see Sarah before she should depart for home he fairly chased me from his cabin.

"The devil take you and your Sarah," he roared. "Haven't I work enough without your traipsing off to see some colored wench? No, by God! You shall see her when you return: she'll be all the better for the wait. From this hour not I nor any man of this crew goes ashore for any but the ship's business. You can tell the others that for me." He bent to his work again to show that our interview was terminated. I thought better of making reply and left.

The men were far from cheerful at the news, but Ross kept us all at our work nearly around the clock rather than miss his chosen tide. When at last we were ready to cast off from Codman's wharf, we were haggard from work and lack of sleep. The captain had driven us mercilessly, himself not the least. And he had proved as good as his word. Even Elizabeth had had to come on board to see him off.

"Nay, my love," I overheard him reply when she had taxed him with being an inattentive wooer. "How would you have me do what I had forbid my men?" When she would have answered him back, he interrupted. "Come," he said. "Give's a kiss before we go." She gave him an impatient look but suffered him to put his arm around her shoulder and they passed from my hearing. Still, I found the interchange to be curiously comforting and went back to my labors in better stomach than before.

Presently Elizabeth's brother came to take her ashore, and my master turned away with what seemed like relief. "Come, my lads," he sang out cheerfully when they had gone. "That will do. What we've not cured must be endured. The tide's in ebb and waits no man's pleasure."

"That it don't, Cap'n," agreed a bewhiskered old seaman by the name of Grizzell, who stood at his left hand. He made a show of looking after Elizabeth. "Nor woman's either," he added, and earned a hearty laugh from all hands.

Once we were clear of the harbor the wind was fair for the southward, so that we made Salem in fine style. There we discharged our cargo, Boston still being shut up by the British in recompense for the loss of the East India Company's tea. That done, we bent our course for Baltimore with all the captain and the crew save one in good fettle.

The lading of the cordwood with my other duties had kept me too busy to give my problem much thought before our departure. A man staggering from work and lack of sleep has scant regard for aught save the matter at hand. Still, there was time and to spare for thinking during the lonely watches between Cape Cod and the Chesapeake, and the question was ever in the forefront of my mind. Even had I wanted to forget it, I could not have done so in the face of the captain's constant references to his approaching wedding. Going off with matters between us thus unsettled, I found especially troublous at the start, but by the time the *Industry* had rounded the Delaware capes I had nearly convinced myself that it was better so for us both.

It would have been well for me had I been able to throw myself into some arduous task upon our arrival in Baltimore. But as things fell out there was little for any of us to do except wait while the captain attempted to put together a cargo. To do nothing at all is a sailor's chiefest delight, and as the food was plentiful and good we would gladly have made rope-yarn Sunday of it had not Ross set us to rereeve the running rigging. Even so, the work was light and we had plenty of time for skylarking. It should have been a happy time, and would have, save for a chance remark or two and my own cursed inability to forget.

The willow's seed was planted one afternoon while Jack Tukey and I were making splices under the tutelage of old Grizzell, whose skill in such matters made him a sort of Dutch boatswain. Tukey was a likable lout, more remarkable for his good humor than anything else, who had hardly been beyond lobster soundings and was eager to see more of the world. He was singing of nut-brown maidens while fitting out a pair of pulleys. Of a sudden he stopped.

"Nut-brown maidens!" he said. "I hear the islands is full on 'em, Mr. Grizzell. Shameless, they be, same's hoors, on'y you can pay 'em beads and such. I never been there yet, but I will. Cap'n Ross said he'll sign me on next trip." His voice dropped to a hoarse whisper. "I even heerd they be built different from women hereabout, Pyrrhus. Be that so?"

The captain had been ashore, but he must have come back on board unnoticed, for here he broke in. "Nay, Jack," he told him, "That you'll have to discover for yourself. Our Pyrrhus is a dull dog, I fear: he has but one sweetheart and tells no tales. Isn't that right, you rascal?"

The captain's voice was slurred. Drunk or sober, it was not a conversation I relished. I nodded and continued my work, but Tukey was made bold by the captain's jibe and gave out with a laugh. "Ah," he cried, "here's a shy one, then! Out with it, man! We'll have her name at the least." He leaned over and elbowed Grizzell lightly. "Who knows? Maybe we be acquainted wi' the lady ourselves!"

I saw on the instant that Jack meant no real harm and would have let it go, but Ross plowed on heedlessly. "Her name? Why, 'tis Sally, Jack: Sally Darling, who cooks for Major Freeman."

At that Grizzell's head shot up. I thought that I saw him glance at me from the corner of his eye, but the outburst that followed came so quickly that I could not be certain. "Damn it, Jack," he bellowed, "that aren't no way to strap a fiddle-block! And you calls yourself a seaman!" Grizzell snatched the block from Tukey, who sat with his mouth hanging open while he fished fruitlessly for a rejoinder.

"Your pardon, Cap'n Ross," said Grizzell, "but if you want this lot finished by suppertime, I'll have to ask you not to set our Jack to thinking on what he can't have." He looked up at the captain, who nodded and turned away.

As for me, I kept my own counsel until that evening, when Grizzell chanced to pass through the galley while Jack was still on deck. I stood aside to let him into the forecastle. He went by without speaking. I watched him while he rummaged about in his seabag. At length he gave a satisfied grunt and withdrew a pigtail twist of tobacco, but when he made to leave I moved to block the door. The old man regarded me mildly through watery blue eyes.

"A word with you, if you please, Mr. Grizzell," I said. Taking his silence for assent, I continued, "I am indebted to you for this afternoon. You're a friend, or I'm much mistaken. But I saw how you looked at me when the captain said Sarah's name, and I think there's more to it than that. So tell me, what did you mean by it?"

"Mean? Why nothing: nothing at all. It was only that I know the family, in a manner of speaking." I waited and after a time he went on. "Don't take on so, friend," he cautioned. "I just thought the least said, the soonest mended, if you get my drift. Young Jack's tongue has always been longer than his wit can reach. I was feared he might hear too much, or say some'at as you'd both be regretting."

This was either too much or too little. Grizzell seemed to realize the fact as soon as the words had been spoken, for he gave a little shrug and sat down on the edge of the nearest berth. From his coat pocket he produced a stubby pipe and clamped it in his jaws. Breaking off a piece of tobacco, he rubbed it methodically between his palms until it was reduced to fragments. When he was satisfied with the result he charged the pipe, tamping the tobacco with a scarred thumb.

"I'd be obliged to you for a light," he said at last. I took a spill of paper and lit it at the galley stove. Grizzell puffed his pipe aglow and leaned back.

"It's not so very much," he said, "though there are those who would be glad to hear ill of Sarah Darling. Meaning no harm, mind, they'd make much of your name and hers together, the more so after that other business." He drew again on the pipe and sent a stream of smoke toward the ceiling. He watched it as it molded itself about the beams.

"Man and boy," he said slowly, "man and boy, I've lived at Long Creek full fifty year, and knowed Josh Darling longer than he nor I can remember. Good friends we been, too. I mind when we . . . but look'ee, you don't care about that.

"Some folks seem to like to believe the worst of people," he said.

"There's fools that talk, and fools that listen, and others as repeat what they've heard without thinkin'. Now your Sarah, she's a good girl, though time was she had a taste for finery, as young girls will, and Joshua would buy her what she wanted. I told him no good would come of his spoiling her the way he did, but he didn't want to hear it. Hasn't spoke to me since." He seemed to meditate upon the injustice.

" 'Satins and laces!' I told him. 'Linen and woolen's best for the likes of you and me!' Seems as how I was right.

"This was before you was brung to town, o' course. Sarah must have been rising sixteen and just about that pretty, with all the young men hanging around same's they was bears and she honey, and it must have rubbed some people the wrong way, her dressing above her station an' all. May be they took it for uppity. Anyhow, folks started to talk: mean talk, with not an ounce of truth behind it, and it near broke her heart. Joshua's, too." He took the pipe from his mouth and leveled it at me as if it had been a pistol. "That's why I said what I did about you and her. Like's not it's none of my business, but I'd hate to see her hurt that way again. Not a word against Sarah, mark you, and nothing against yourself, but the time was she could have done better."

I sat there for perhaps as long as five minutes after he had gone. It was a tangled skein, but Grizzell had given me a thread to follow. The further I followed it, the more convinced I became that I should have no more to do with Sarah, both for her sake and my own.

Thereafter I kept to the *Industry* and to myself both. It seemed a long time before our cargo was brought aboard and the last hatch battened down, and in truth we had been longer than we had expected. I had come to long for the freshness of the seawind to blow the fumes of morbidity from my brain, but here even the weather played me false. Having sailed from Baltimore in the middle of February, we were windbound in the mouth of the bay for nigh upon a week with a succession of storms that followed close on each other's heels.

These were miserable days, cold and wet, with the schooner lying uneasy at her anchor. Her motion was quick and skittish, all jerks and starts, but the captain refused to move to a more protected berth.

"Not on your life," he told me when I suggested it. "I'm as uncomfortable as you, but I wouldn't move her now for all the hot food and dry clothes in Falmouth; nay, nor in Baltimore, neither. We'll bide here awhile yet. It's no millpond, but let the wind come fair for half an hour and we'll run ahead of this blow clear to Georges Bank!"

There was nothing to do but wait, though our food was only just warmed through and dry clothes were a thing that could only be remembered. Even our bedding was wetted through, so that I at least found sleep impossible.

Of course, at last the wind did veer, and we escaped from the confines of the bay into the open ocean. The relief I felt was enormous. With the gale on her quarter the *Industry* showed a fine turn of speed; each day at noon the captain pricked off the miles she had run, and speculated on how long it would be before he held Elizabeth in his arms once more.

So exhilarating was our progress that even this did not spoil my newfound good humor. When I found that I could think of Sarah without brooding, almost without regret, I flattered myself that I had finally cleansed my system of the bile which had for so long oppressed me. Though the ending of the affair might be unpleasant, I would feel the better for its being resolved.

So it was that I welcomed the sight of the stern face of Cape Elizabeth, granite-gray under the slaty sky. From the looks of the coast, the storm we had weathered to the southward had brought snow to Maine, but even so it had been moderate, and we might look with confidence to an early spring. I began to feel a little of the old excitement that I had felt when first I had come from the islands. Perhaps spring would bring with it more than just buttercups and daisies. Evidently I was not alone in my elation. Captain Ross called for a song, and Grizzell broke out a squeaky old fiddle. The *Industry* rounded into Falmouth harbor in man-of-war style, with Grizzell on the foredeck sawing away at "A Fig for Care," and Tukey and I setting to partners in the waist.

20

IT soon appeared that our carefree air was ill chosen. There was a great congregation of people on the wharves at the foot of King Street, opposite a small sloop showing English merchant colors and nettings at her rail. Jack Tukey saw them first, and stopped to stare in the midst of one of our figures, but presently we could hear their angry shouts even over Grizzell's music. The fiddle died off into a last mournful wail as the old man turned to see what had captured our attention, so that at last only the rush of the water and the creak of the rigging accompanied the sound of the people's voices.

The captain recovered first from his surprise, rapping out a series of orders as he brought the helm over. We passed well clear of the vessel, but not so far that I could not see the name, *John and Mary*, picked out in gold leaf across her transom. I went aft to inform the captain, but the expression he wore told me that he had no need of my information.

"Coulson's ship at last," he said in a taut voice. "We'll anchor at Codman's. That should be safe enough for the time being. You and I will go ashore. Tell the others I want them to stay aboard until we come back, and that no one is to get on board without my leave. I want to find out what is going on and make sure that Elizabeth is all right."

"Aye, Captain," I said. "Shall I serve out a couple of the muskets for them to use while we're gone? That crowd could turn nasty."

"For God's sake, no! No muskets! That would be all they'd need. Pistols will do — a pair apiece, and tell 'em I'll have their skins if they let the things be seen. No, by God, I'll tell 'em myself. This has nothing to do with us, and I'll keep it that way until they'll have it different. Now get back to your place, but as soon as the anchor's down, I want you to take care of the guns." He paused for a moment. "Best load one for me as well. That small French one, just in case."

At Pagan's house Elizabeth answered the door. Initially she opened it just an inch or two, but when she saw Ross she drew back to let us enter. She looked composed if a trifle pale, but whether this was from concern or surprise I could hardly judge. Ross took her in his arms and kissed her roundly. Presently, but not by any means immediately, she made a sound of protest and pushed him away.

"William, really," she said in a disapproving tone. "Must you act so much like a, well, like a sailor? Suppose someone had seen us!" She smoothed her dress and patted her hair.

The captain smiled. "I don't see anybody," he told her. "Besides, I'm in a hurry. I wanted to see that you were all right, of course, but now I need to see Deacon Codman, to tell him I am back and to find out what in hell is going on. Then I'll go and speak with Robert, if you know where he is."

"Oh, William," she said. "Of course I'm safe. Those people out there would never hurt us. We're their neighbors, after all. And Robert would never have left me alone if he had thought, even for a moment, that I were in any real danger." She pursed her lips prettily. "Though I must say that he is nearly as bad as you are, William. He told me I was to keep the doors locked and then went off with his friends."

"I hope you're right," said Ross. Seeing her brow wrinkle, he added, "I'm sure you're right. I'll just leave Pyrrhus here while I run over to the deacon's house. We might be separated in the crowd if I were to take him along." He gave Elizabeth another kiss, a decorous one this time. She endured it for a moment before disengaging herself. She indicated that I was to follow her and walked to the door of the sitting room. As I brushed past the captain, he grasped my arm and I felt him slide something weighty into my pocket. It was the pocket pistol we had taken from the Frenchman off Guadeloupe. I looked at him sharply, but he put his finger to his lips for silence, a gesture he converted to running his hand over his head when Elizabeth turned to us in annoyance. "Come along, now, Pyrrhus," she told me. "If I'm to have you here, I won't have you hanging about. There are ever so many things that need doing. You may as well get started right away." To Ross she added, "When you find my brother, William, tell him that I shan't hold dinner for him again tonight. Since you'll be staying, that goes for you as well."

I went with her into the room, which for my taste was as genteel as any in the city. Elizabeth sat down by one of the windows in a lolling chair of sky-blue brocade, very handsome. From a mahogany stand next to the chair she picked up a small book bound in morocco; she opened it and began leafing through to find her place. I stood by respectfully for a few moments and then, in as delicate a manner as I could manage, cleared my throat.

Elizabeth looked up. "Well," she said coldly, "can't you see I'm reading?"

"Yes, ma'am," I replied. "But you had spoken of something you wished me to do for you."

"Yes. Yes, well, let me see, then. What is it that you are good for?" She closed the book, marking the page with a finger.

"Ah! I have it. William tells me that you write a tolerable round hand. Then you shall copy out the invitations for the reception after our wedding." She raised her exquisitely molded arm and pointed to a desk on the far side of the room. "Everything that you will need is over there. I've done one or two of them myself: you may copy those for the wording. See that you get it right, and don't waste any of the paper. It's the very best London vellum, and I don't know when we will see any more like it. There's a list there somewhere, I should think. You can tick off the names if you like so as not to miss one." She opened the book again. "When you've done that," she said, running a finger down the page, "I'll try to find something else to keep you busy."

The list was such as would have made interesting reading in the library chamber, but for the fact that any committeeman with wit enough to have read it could have written another just as well. It included the Reverend Mr. Wiswell and all his flock: the Potes, the Oxnards, Sheriff Tyng, Waldos, and several Wyers; old Madam Ross, the widow of Alexander and only distantly related to the captain; Captain Coulson; Mr. Lyde, who worked for the customs; Joshua Eldridge; and others whose names time has taken from me, many of whom were to leave Falmouth forever in the months to come. There were also those whose names the committee would not have found objectionable, who were invited because of their position in the town or because, like the elder McLellan and Deacon Codman, they were particular friends of my master.

Several times during the course of the afternoon I rose to place another log on the fire, or to thrust farther back one that had fallen forward and threatened to send a shower of sparks upon the fine carpet of Scottish ingrain. When at last the light began to fail, I kindled a pine splint at the hearth and carried it over to light the candle at Elizabeth's elbow.

To my surprise she acknowledged the kindness with a nod and a slender smile, so that I was made bold enough to ask her what she was reading with such absorption.

"A novel, I'm afraid," she said ruefully. "French, but I should call it a pretty little conceit for all that, though my brother Robert doesn't approve. He says he has no time for frivolity of this nature." She held it up for me to examine. "Here, perhaps you may have heard of it. I am told that it is quite famous in its way. It's called *Candide*, by a gentleman named Voltaire."

"Indeed I have," I told her. "When I was a child my master gave me a copy which he had had from the author himself. It is a book I have always greatly admired."

"No!" Elizabeth exclaimed. "But that is wonderful! You must tell me what he thought of it. Come, bring your chair here by mine. Truth to tell, it has been rather dreary, reading the thing and knowing all the time that I should have no one with whom to discuss it." She gave a silvery little laugh. "I doubt that either Robert or William has ever read anything save musty old log-books and ledgers."

I had no need of being asked twice. "In truth, madam," I said to her as I set my hard chair by her soft one, "that is a feeling I have often had myself."

"Yes. Yes, of course." There was the merest suggestion of a pause before her voice became brisk once more. "I believe that you said that your former master was an acquaintance of Monsieur Voltaire?"

I told her as briefly as I might of my childhood and old Fitzgore, but she soon made it evident that she was as little interested in my history as her brother was in that of young Candide. She was sitting with her book in her lap. I could see that her fingers were toying with it impatiently. They were very slender fingers, long and well kept. I must have let my voice trail off as I watched her although I became aware of it only when she looked up at me.

"I'm sorry, madam," I said hastily. "You were about to tell me your opinion of the book."

"Oh, yes; *Candide*." Clearly she had not attended to a word that I had said.

Elizabeth leaned forward slightly as she began to speak. Her hands

were clasped firmly about the slender volume in her lap and from time
to time she would lift it ever so slightly and then bring it down again
much the way Reverend Smith thumped the Bible upon his pulpit
whenever he considered that he had made a particularly telling point
in his Sunday sermon. Though I had served her at table and in other
ways on a number of occasions, it seemed to me that I had never seen
her so animated, nor so beautiful.

I do not recall that the sentiments Elizabeth expressed were very
remarkable, but she held forth so gaily earnest that I did not presume
to interrupt. No one had spoken to me of scholarly matters in years,
and evidently she found her audience a treat equally rare. The freedom
with which she spoke put me at ease. I relaxed and began to smile with
unfeigned enjoyment; when I did her manner grew still more warm and
confidential, so that at last an onlooker must have supposed us to be
old friends.

The studied grace with which she moved and spoke was totally unlike that of any woman I had ever known. I watched her with a growing sense of admiration and desire, furtively at first, but more boldly
as it appeared that she was too much absorbed in her discourse to
notice.

I remember thinking that I must have been blind never before to
have seen how classic was her beauty: how I had dismissed hair that
was golden as being merely yellow. Too, there was a hint of a rosy
flush on her skin, skin which had always seemed to be pale, as bluely
translucent as porcelain. This suffusion of color was further set off by
the white gauze fichu she wore gathered about her neck and tucked
modestly into the low neckline of her caraco. I should like to believe
that it was this pleasing contrast which repeatedly drew my gaze
thither, and not the fact that the kerchief was of a stuff so finely woven
as almost to render the upper curves of her breasts more visible than
to conceal them.

Her gown was a dove-gray silk: the jacket I have mentioned and
matching petticoats, all cut in the latest mode. The fabric was of a hue
which harmonized exactly with her eyes, and was picked out all over
with broidered flowers and hummingbirds in a silvery shade. It molded
itself to the curves of her arms and upper body without a fold or
wrinkle. It seemed to me that I could almost feel the suppleness of her
flesh beneath the fabric. Desperately I thrust that thought from me, but

not before I had felt the beginnings of a stirring within myself. My chest felt tight. I found that I had to struggle to retain my composure.

When Elizabeth's book tumbled from her lap to the floor, it seemed a heaven-sent interruption. I bent down for it, yet not quite swiftly enough. Elizabeth's hand was there before mine.

It must have been that I knocked the book from her fingers, though it did not seem that my hand had brushed her forearm hard enough for that to happen. Be that as it may, the book dropped to the floor once more. This time she made no attempt to reach it. I picked it up and placed it in her hand.

For an instant nothing happened. The book was a bridge between us, her delicate white hand on the one end and my black one on the other. I raised my eyes to meet hers.

I usually thought of Elizabeth's eyes as being cold and distant, although they could flash with anger on occasion as well. Now there was an appraising look in them. I would almost have said a look of invitation, save that the idea is still too much for me to credit. And yet I did not imagine what I saw. The feral gleam was real, as were the lips, moist and ever so slightly parted, the labored rise and fall of her breasts. Suddenly I was aware of the scent of perfume rising from hidden zones of her body.

I have no idea how long the moment endured, or might have endured. It was endless, yet there seemed to be no time for thought. My mind recoiled from the impossible and raced from one fragmentary notion to another. And was there at last something of triumph in Elizabeth's gaze, and something of mockery as well?

So intent were we that we gave a guilty start at the sound of the front door being opened. There were footsteps in the hall, and voices: my master's and Mr. Pagan's. Elizabeth sat back and hurriedly composed her features. When she looked at me again, her eyes were the color of shadows on snow. "Thank you, Pyrrhus," she said. "That will be all for now."

I rose and took station against the wall just as Pagan and Ross entered. I did my best to assume an attitude of respectful attention, but neither spared me so much as a glance. Pagan blew upon his chilled hands and went to warm them at the fire. The captain crossed to Elizabeth's side. She smiled up at him and presented her cheek to be kissed.

Pagan chafed his hands and glared into the flames. "I do think you're wrong about the committee, Will," he said, evidently in response to a remark Ross had made earlier. "I admit that they stood up to Lieutenant Hunter last month, when those deserters from the *Gaspée* got ashore. That was different. Freeman knew that Hunter couldn't take direct action without authority from Admiral Graves in Boston, and the common folk would have had his tripes if he had handed three men over to be hanged. Still, the mob has a short memory. You've seen that for yourself. As soon as it's clear that the excitement is done they go home and forget everything. But Admiral Graves doesn't forget, and Freeman knows that, too. That's why tomorrow the committee will meet, and with a great show of reluctance they will let Coulson's goods be landed. Hell, man, it's a simple matter of money. It's not in anyone's interest to let the *Minerva* rot here. Too many people have a stake in her."

Ross seemed to be considering what Pagan had said. "I hope you're right, Robert," he told him, but the way that he said it indicated that he was unconvinced. Then he turned to Elizabeth. "But what of you, my dear? I trust that Pyrrhus has been helpful?"

I hearkened anxiously to her reply. "Yes. As a matter of fact I found him most diverting." She nodded in my direction as though to acknowledge my services, and I was horrified to note the minute flutter of an eyelid. Had anyone else seen it? Elizabeth went on smoothly: "I had no idea of the range of his interests. Can you imagine? He has actually read Voltaire. Why didn't you tell me?" The pause was almost non-existent. "Well, perhaps you did. It is of no account in any case.

"Now perhaps you two would like a bowl of punch. You look as though you might, and I confess I should be the better for a glass of Madeira myself. I so enjoyed my little chat, but literature is such a dry topic, don't you agree?" She looked at me without a sign of emotion. "See to it, Pyrrhus, if you please." I was grateful for the chance to get out of the room. Glancing at the men for confirmation, I bowed and went to fetch the tray.

When I returned, I felt slightly more calm, though my smallclothes still clung wetly to my body. The captain had moved to the chair I had but recently occupied. Elizabeth's brother was holding forth from his spot by the fire. I looked to see if he meant to prepare the punch himself. With an airy wave he signified that I might continue.

"It's quite a farce, really," he was saying. "That fellow Freeman should be in Drury Lane. First he set guards, you know, as though Thomas could have landed anything with that great unruly crowd on the pier, and then he sent to inquire what was the sloop's cargo." He laughed and then looked across the room to make sure Elizabeth had taken his point. "By George," he said, "everybody in town has known these three months past that Tom Coulson had a deal of ship's stores and rigging overdue."

"What of the other things he had looked for?" Elizabeth wanted to know. "The yard goods and the millinery? Did he say anything of those?"

Her brother was impatient to go on. "In God's name, Elizabeth," he said, "what would I know of those? Anyway, Coulson comes down with his Captain Hughes, and tells him what everyone knows.

"Well," he asked sarcastically, "and wouldn't you think that would be enough? He has the owner, and the master, and the sloop's papers in the bargain. And what does he do? I mean, either he intends to uphold the association, or he does not, and if he does it hardly seems to me to matter what the *John and Mary* is carrying.

"No, I tell you that the goods will land — at least those for Coulson's vessel. Oh, he might order something sent back, or else sold at auction like they do, for the so-called suffering people of Boston, but mark my words, it will be a bale of fripperies for Elizabeth, or some such trifle." He turned to where I had knelt to heat a poker in the grate. "Damn my soul," he said, "haven't you got that punch ready yet?"

"This minute, sir," I replied. I withdrew the iron from the embers and thrust it into the pitcher. "There, sir," I said as it hissed and burbled. I essayed what I hoped was a deferential smile. "Will you pour, then, sir, or shall I?"

Dinner itself was still more unsettling. Elizabeth seemed to delight in keeping me close by, so that by the time they had finished eating my mind and body were in a state of ferment. I was infinitely relieved when the captain got up to leave directly afterward.

We walked back through the darkness slowly. I was anxious enough on my own account, but even so it was plain that my master was preoccupied as well. Coulson's ship had not been mentioned again, but it seemed logical that it would be the cause, and I asked Ross if that were so.

"Yes, I am concerned," he replied to my inquiry. "Robert is far too optimistic, of that I am sure. I'd like to know what Freeman has in mind, but I suppose we'll have to wait until the committee meets again in the morning to find out." We had reached the end of Codman's wharf. The captain halted with his hands on the ladder to which we had made our boat fast. He shook his head. "In the meantime," he said, "I've five thousand bushels of corn to land. Pray God nothing they do interferes." He gave me an apologetic smile. "The next couple of days are likely to be busy ones," he said. "I guess you're busting to see that girl of yours, but you'll just have to wait until we're done here."

The tide was in, and we roused out Grizzell and Tukey to warp the *Industry* in and tied her up so as to be able to begin unloading at first light. Mercifully, when I went to bed I slept, and though the work went smoothly the next day we were all entirely too busy to give much thought to other matters. It might have been noon when Greenfield Pote came on board, very excited. He hurried up to the captain and took him by the arm.

"You got to come with me," he blurted. Captain Ross shook himself free as the men on the tackle let a net full of grain sacks fall on the deck.

"I said handsomely, there, you sons of Frenchmen! Don't you know what handsomely means? By God, if you burst those sacks I'll have you picking up the kernels on your knees!" He turned to Pote.

"Now, damn it, Greenfield, what's all this? Can't you see I'm busy?"

"The committee's voted to send the *John and Mary* back," he told him. "Pagan sent me to fetch you. There's a meeting at Coulson's right now. The committee's sitting again at three and they want to decide what to do ahead of time. Coulson's told 'em he can't sent the *John and Mary* back. Says it needs repairs, and can't be fixed unless he lands the cargo so's he can work on her bottom. But they want to know what folks will do if Freeman turns him down."

"Do? I know what I plan to do," the captain said. "Just what I'm doing. I'm going to get my schooner unloaded and get this corn under cover before the weather goes bad on me or something. Tell Robert I'm sorry about the committee. I hope they can sttraighten it out. I know it's important to him. But this schooner and this cargo is important to me, and I don't intend to go gallivanting around like Wolfe at Quebec and lose her. No: you tell Robert that I'll be glad to talk to Joe McLellan for him, or anybody else I know that can do some good. Meantime, whatever the committee does, folks'll need to eat."

"But, Will, look," Pote began. The captain whirled on him.

"Look yourself," he said. "If the committee won't let Coulson land his cargo, they won't, and that's that. Maybe he can appeal to the General Court: I don't know. What I do know is that no meeting at Coulson's house is going to change their minds. How close was the vote anyway?"

"Fourteen to five."

"Fourteen to five. Christ, then that's settled. They'll not change anything now. What do they want to do, unload the *John and Mary* at gunpoint?"

Pote looked pained. "That's supposed to be a secret," he whispered urgently. Ross laughed.

"A secret? Why, damn it, that's the one thing that Freeman would be on his guard against. No, Greenfield, I've no desire to shoot one of my neighbors, or to be shot by one of them either, as seems more likely. Do you know how many men Freeman could call in if he needed them?" Pote appeared unmoved, and the captain shrugged.

"Well," Pote said. "I really didn't think that we could count on you, now that you've got so friendly with the likes of Codman and them anyway."

Ross looked at him with one eye asquint. "What do you mean by that?"

"Oh, nothing. Only that you never know who your friends are until you need 'em."

My master smiled. "I'm your friend, Greenfield," he said. "No, don't laugh. I am. I'm so friendly that I'm going to let you walk off this deck on your own instead of pitching you over the side as I should." Pote looked at him stupidly, but the captain had seemingly lost interest in the conversation. I waited to see what would happen; the Potes were said to be a tempery lot. Eventually the fact that Ross had meant exactly what he had said must have penetrated to Greenfield's brain. He turned on his heel and walked down the gangway. As he came even with us on the wharf, Captain Ross addressed him once again. "Greenfield?" he said, never looking up from his tally sheet. Pote stopped. "When you see Robert, kindly tell him I'll see him at his house tonight for dinner."

Pote huffed and strode off. I watched him go. When he had passed out of earshot, Ross looked up at me. "Well," he said impatiently, "and what do you think you're gawping at? Get back to what you were doing, damn it!" He glared about the vessel. "That goes for the rest of you as well," he snapped. "I'll have you to remember that this is a working schooner, not King George's bloody pleasure barge!"

In point of fact we were not the only ones who were having difficulty in keeping our minds on our work. The *Gaspée* put in on the sixth and left with Freeman's apologies. All that day and into the next the waterfront teemed with idlers, so that at last one could hardly move about the docks for the jostling. Most looked to be apprentices who had left their benches in search of excitement, but I noticed an increasing admixture of countrymen among the townsfolk. Many of these were older: hard-looking men. They tended to stay to themselves. Some wore sprigs in their hatbands; when I pointed them out to the captain, he nodded glumly.

"Thompson's men," he said. "Joe told me they'd be here. In town for the county congress, they say, but if there's trouble it will start with them." He straightened up and scanned the waterfront as though searching the horizon for sign of a squall. "Keep your eyes open," he admonished. "If anything happens I want to cut the lines and haul out into the river."

It was late Tuesday afternoon that Elizabeth's brother came hustling down the dock. I was on deck, sweeping up the last of the chaff and spilled grain, and leaned on my broom to watch him. He looked pleased. "Will," he called. "Where are you, Will?" When he was close enough to address in normal tones, I told him that the captain was in his cabin, but when he went to open the companion door, Ross was already on the way up.

"They'll have heard you clear to Simonton's Cove," he laughed. "What's all this about?"

Pagan rubbed his hands together. "Freeman's backing down," he said. "I knew he would after he crawled to Hunter." My master gave him a skeptical look. "All right," he said. "Not all at once, but he will. I'm certain of it." He went on to explain that what had actually been announced was that the *John and Mary* was to be allowed a week's time in port to make repairs. "But it's a blind, Will," Pagan told him. "Surely you can see that." He looked about anxiously, and I made a show of being busy lest he take the captain below out of hearing.

"The way I make it," he went on, "Freeman's stalling for time. He can't give in with the town full of Sons of Liberty. The sloop's in fine shape. She was docked and breamed ere ever she left Bristol. Sure, she's made a winter passage. She could use a lick of paint and the like, but Tom Coulson could have her at sea tomorrow if need be." He gestured at a knot of men hanging about in front of the King's Head. "Look at 'em," he sniffed. "Not a one of 'em owns more than what he stands up in, and today Falmouth belongs to them. Well, next week it will be different. Only not a word, mind; not to anyone. If Thompson gets wind of it, there'll be hell to pay for certain."

I fell to sweeping with renewed diligence as he brushed past me. When I glanced up, Ross was staring after him with a wry look on his face.

"Well," he mused, "and what do you make of that?" The question took me by surprise. Ross cut off my protestations with a laugh. "Don't try to fool me," he chided. "You heard every word. It's all right, though: you've a good head, and it saves explanations. Just keep quiet."

He placed his hands in the small of his back and stretched. "I guess that's it," he said at last. "It looks pretty good around here. I want you to know I appreciate it." There was a short pause and when he continued I thought I detected a note of embarrassment in his voice. "I saw your young lady on the street this morning," he told me. "I guess she's not any too pleased with either of us, what with the way we went off so quick. I told her that it was mostly my fault." He seemed to be having a hard time choosing his words.

"I'm keeping Tukey and Grizzell on for a while. The weather's all right, and I'd like to get at the bottom while I've got a chance. Jack will be living on board until the work's done as sort of a caretaker, starting tonight. You can keep an eye on the house." He hesitated again.

"I hear," he said, elaborately casual, "that Major Freeman is entertaining tonight. I won't be going, of course: it's for committeemen and others who have come from out of town for the county congress. Apt to last quite late; he's asked his servants to stay, but they weren't happy about it. Every bed in town is full because of the meeting. Don't know what they'll do.

"By the way," he said, "you needn't wait up for me. I'm dining at the Pagans' again, and Robert says they will put me up there." He started to leave, then stopped. "Oh, yes. You'll be wanting some money. There won't be a thing in the pantry." He put a few coins in my hand.

"Now go on with you. I'll expect you to be at Elizabeth's by seven in the morning. Bring me a change of linen when you come. I'll tell their cook to see that you get breakfast." He gave me a pat on the shoulder to start me on my way.

I left the schooner walking like a man moon-struck. Sarah! Since the interlude with Elizabeth I had found my feelings so confused that I had blocked out all thought of her. Now that I felt the need to think, I found that I could not. Whatever could I say to her?

A burly man with a bit of spruce in his hat came out of the King's Head and cannoned into me, so that I narrowly missed being propelled into the water. He left, trailing a stream of curses and the odors of rum and sweat.

There was an eating house nearby. I went in and sat down, as much to stay from underfoot as anything else. The portion I was served was small and swimming in grease. I pushed it away and stared into the congealing fat, but it held no augury.

After a time the host nudged me roughly. "Eat up and get out," he said. "Can't you see we're busy?" This was no more than the truth. I stood up and made my way to the door.

Night was fast approaching, but the waterfront was as busy as before. I kept to the side streets and reached my master's house without incident. Inside, it was dark and cold. I sat down in the kitchen and waited. It may have been close to midnight when I heard her at the door. Fumbling a little in the darkness, I lit a candle. Sarah knocked again and I opened the door.

The light from my candle fell full on her face. It looked tense and careworn. I could tell that she was trying not to let her feelings show.

I opened my mouth to speak, but the words would not come. I lowered my eyes to the ground. When I could look at her again it seemed that her expression had softened.

"Pyrrhus," she whispered. "Oh, Pyrrhus, it's been so long." Then at last she smiled. "Well," she said, "aren't you going to ask me in?"

21

GRIZZELL leaned out over the edge of the staging and spat into the mud and seaweed below. "Fifty year," he muttered, "fifty year I lived in Falmouth, man and boy, nor ever I see a March the like of this one." I smiled at him sympathetically from my end of the plank. The old man had stripped to the waist, but perspiration was pouring from his ropy torso in streams. He wiped a further trickle from his eyes and went back to work, attacking the long-necked barnacles on the *Industry*'s bottom vindictively. "If this be March," he said between strokes of the iron, "God help us come August."

I chuckled inwardly. "If we're still at this job come August," I answered, "then God help us indeed!"

In truth, the weather was unusually warm. Never in memory had there been a winter so mild, or a spring so forward. The frost had been out of the ground for a week, so that already the farmers roundabout were congratulating themselves with thoughts of a fine harvest in the fall.

Grizzell bit off a fresh bit of leaf and took a quick look at the roadstead where the *John and Mary* lay anchored. "There's some in town don't mind the heat," he observed. "They've been soldiering around doing nothing this week past. What about them repairs they was supposed to be making? Committee wanted them done and gone by now."

"You're right there," I told him, "though there were those who thought otherwise. Captain Coulson claims she can't leave until she's been unloaded and hove down, the same as us, on account of a sprung plank in her run."

The gray-haired sailor snorted. "Then why ain't they shown some sign of a leak? They ain't pumped more'n a gill of water that I've seen; no, nor trimmed her to bring that side up in the water either. Coulson's lying, if you ask me."

"But nobody did, you old buzzard," Captain Ross rasped from the rail above us. Both Grizzell and I started guiltily and began working on the hull with renewed vigor. "Until they do, I'd be obliged if the two of you would keep to the task at hand." For a space all I could hear was the sound of our working. I stole a surreptitious glance upward and saw the captain staring out at the sloop from Bristol.

"It may interest you to know," he said, "that a deputation of ship-carpenters and masters of vessels waited upon the committee last night with a deposition to the effect that the *John and Mary* would be in great peril if she were to be sent to sea as she is. Freeman's to announce the committee's decision this afternoon."

"What do you think it will be?" I asked.

"Hell," he said, "I don't know. Elizabeth's brother's bound that the deposition was the excuse Freeman needed." He took a last look at the quiescent merchantman. "I expect we'll find out soon enough." He craned his neck over the side to watch Grizzell, who was swearing under his breath as he pried and scraped. "In the meantime, get those barnacles off my schooner. If the major should send for you, I'll see you get the message."

My master and I were at the Pagans' house when the committee's answer was made public. A man came bearing a note from Captain Coulson; Pagan threw it down and called for the decanter with an oath. "Look at that," he said, having drained his glass at a swallow. "Coulson's to send the *John and Mary* back to Bristol immediately, they say!" He held out his hand for more port. "Damn their weaseling hearts! Listen to this: 'if the said vessel is unsafe for the voyage, then if Captain Coulson will reship the aforesaid goods in some other vessel, and send them back immediately, without breaking any of the packages, it will be satisfactory to this Committee.' Wait, there's more. They've offered him a vessel to carry them to Halifax gratis! To Halifax, mind, or Newfoundland, whichever he should prefer. What a favor! And him with a thousand ton of mast ship that's been waiting on the stocks since last fall.

"Well, William, I guess that tears it. Coulson's called a meeting for tonight. He'll want to unload come what may, and to tell you the truth I can't think what else to tell him."

The missive lay open on the table. Ross took it in hand and stared at it morosely.

Pagan swirled the last of his brandy around in his mouth and then swallowed it. "Will you be standing with us, William? I mean, I know how you feel, but your schooner's in the yard, and if there's trouble she could burn as easily as the *Minerva*. Comes to that, they'll make no distinctions." He moved his chair back and made to stand up.

"If you please, sir," I said, "there may be another way after all." Pagan could not have looked more astonished if I'd announced that I had come from the moon. "Captain Ross mentioned it himself, sir." I looked to my master for permission to continue.

"Go on," he said impatiently. "If you've something to say, then out with it."

"It was last week, Captain. You were talking to Mr. Pote, and suggested sending to the General Court to overrule the committee. The court will be sitting in Concord next week: Sarah told me that young Mr. Freeman will be leaving on Saturday."

"Freeman won't make a very good case for us," grumbled Pagan. "What do you think, Will; should one of us go as well? Damn it, we'll need all the men we have if there's trouble."

"There will be no trouble while the court's in session," my master told him. His voice gained conviction as he spoke. "Not unless you start it. Freeman wouldn't want that. I'd go myself if it would keep the Potes and the Liberty Boys from tearing the town apart, but it would have to wait until I get the *Industry* back in the water."

I had been thinking as they talked. "Maybe it needn't come to that, Captain," I said slowly. "There was that gentleman you met at the deacon's house last year: Mr. Adams, his name was. He seemed to like you, and he's an important man. One of the most important if all we've heard is true. You could write him a letter. A petition."

"By George, Will," Pagan boomed, "I think you've got something! Write to him, by all means! I'm off for Coulson's to tell them not to do anything hasty." He started for the door and then stopped. "Damn my eyes!" he said. "John Waite shall write as well: he's a member of our parish, and an honest man at heart, for all that he is on their damned committee. And he's a selectman into the bargain!" With the door open he came to a halt once again.

"Bid Elizabeth good night for me," he told the captain. "I shall probably not return until late. But before you forget, write that letter!"

The captain drank off the rest of his brandy and went in to Elizabeth in the parlor. I followed reluctantly, for I found her presence disquieting in many ways of late, despite the fact that her attitude had been studiously correct since that one evening.

Elizabeth had disposed herself prettily in the blue armchair by the window. Tonight she had affected spectacles for her reading. When the captain entered, she took them off and listened attentively to his explanation of what had occurred.

"By all means write Robert his letter, William. It will be the work of but a moment, and Pyrrhus may carry it to him at Captain Coulson's. I shall be content to finish my chapter in the meantime."

Ross nodded in deference to her patience. He crossed the room and sat down at the desk, throwing open the inkwell and biting the end of the quill as he began composing his petition. I looked at Elizabeth, who met my gaze with every appearance of ingenuousness, but I noticed with a poignant impulse that she had contrived to hold the book in such a way that I could not help but see the title. It was, of course, *Candide*. With a faintly catlike smile she put her spectacles back on and resumed her place. I moved over to stand by the captain's side.

"I think this will serve," he said to me with his head half turned. I glanced at it quickly. There were scarcely a dozen lines: he had stated the particulars of the case briefly and without seeming to make Coulson's interest his own. I could not have done better myself. At the bottom of the page he signed it: "Your answer will very much oblige, Sir, your humble (&c.) Willm Ross." He cast sand over the surface and blew it onto the floor. "I shan't seal it now," he explained. "Likely they'll want to read the thing before it's sent off." He inspected the ink, and finding it dry, folded the sheet and creased it. "Here," he said, "off you go then, and unless there's a reply you can go straight home after." He winked and added, "That's if you've nothing better to do with your time. Is that lass of yours in town this evening?"

"No, sir," I said somewhat stiffly, deeply conscious that we were not alone. "Tomorrow's the annual fast ordered by the congress, and she was to have gone home early on."

Elizabeth had put by her book while we spoke. "I've been meaning to ask you, dear," she said in the sweetest of tones, "do you suppose the major could be persuaded to part with the girl? Robert would be quite lost without Janet, you know, so we will be needing one of our own after the wedding. As for the cost, why, I shall be coming into some money of my own when we are married, so we can afford to be fair."

Ross shot me a warning glance and said hurriedly, "Actually, that would be up to Sarah, my dear. You see, she works for the major, just as your Janet does for you."

"Indeed? Well, that's a bother then, isn't it? It seemed so, well, so convenient, but I suppose it doesn't matter. You needn't put yourself out; I'm sure we'll find another wench soon enough." She shook her head minutely as if in regret and went back to her book. I took the letter from the captain and left.

I walked rapidly up the hill to Coulson's house. I was furious with Elizabeth, of course, but equally so with myself. She seemed instinctively to have come to know how to reach me in a vulnerable spot without doing anything patently cruel, and she had said no single word to which I could have taken exception. Even if she had, I should be powerless. With each passing day my feelings increasingly demanded an outlet, and yet I was finding the relief I needed ever more difficult to secure. Indeed, there was only Sarah to whom I might speak, and even with her it was not possible to be completely open.

The thought of the paper I held in my hand made me feel more pleased with myself. That had been a good piece of work, for the captain had come close to throwing his lot in with Pagan's tonight in order to protect the schooner. The hazards to which we would both be exposed should he choose that course were only too obvious. On the other hand, it could hardly do any harm to renew my master's connection with a man as influential as Adams had become. Though Ross had written to him on behalf of a man in the opposing camp, what I knew of the Bostonian told me that it would not be taken amiss. Adams himself had done as much, and more. No, it had been a good stroke.

The most important thing was to preserve the captain's freedom of action. Events were far from certain. It looked as though anything might be possible. Parliament and the ministers could be brought to heel by the weight of popular disapproval at home, or dissent in the colonies could erode the influence of the Sons and their supporters. Or perhaps not. Perhaps things had already gone too far for a retreat from the abyss. With the General Court sitting in Concord a week hence, and the other provincial assemblies as well, it would soon be evident. In the meantime, the longer that Ross could be stayed from committing himself, the better for both of us.

The reaction of the committee to the news that Coulson had

decided to take his case to the higher authority was hardly a joyous one. Sarah told me that Freeman had bellowed like a bull when he heard, yet he and the others apparently were content for the nonce merely to grumble. Being themselves men of property, they would weigh carefully before inciting the people to violence. Mobs have a way of getting out of hand, and patriot homes and shops would burn as brightly as Tory ones. As a consequence I was not at all surprised when young Freeman consented to carry both letters with him when he set off southward.

The strength of the major's position became clear at the town meeting, which was held on the twenty-second of March. I remember the date because it coincided with the opening of the provincial assembly in Concord. I had entertained hopes of being able to stay, on the excuse of attending to my master's needs, but when he saw the crush of people at the hall, Ross sent me home.

The meeting was a long one. Afterward the captain stopped in, with Mr. Pagan, to tell me that he would be at Marston's tavern and would not want supper.

"Come, Robert," he said to Pagan, who in truth looked very disheartened, "cheer up. 'Tis but fortunes of war." He turned to me and said, "Pyrrhus! Fetch the rum!"

"Fortunes of war, indeed," Pagan muttered as I handed him a tumbler. "It will soon come to that, I think. Imagine: not a voice in the town for any of us, the most considerable merchants and shipowners in Falmouth. In the Province, for that matter. Freeman, Mussey, Owen, Brackett, and Merrill for selectmen! Even John Waite turned out! I tell you, William, this is a black day for us." He drank off his rum and shuddered. "There!" he said, and gave me back the glass. "Well, off to Marston's to lick our wounds. I wonder what Tom Coulson and the Oxnards will have to say about this."

"Yes," the captain added, "and the Potes, for that matter." He finished his drink and set the tumbler on the tray. "I should stay home if I were you, Pyrrhus. The streets will be no place to be tonight. Better yet: grab yourself a bite and a sup and run you down to the schooner. You can keep Grizzell company, and if there should be trouble, you can come fetch me from the tavern."

In point of fact the streets were no place for an honest man that night, being full of a laughing, jeering throng that had apparently drunk too deeply at the wellspring of liberty. Yet their leaders must have seen no need to signalize their victory with excesses, for the old man and I passed the night without incident. When morning came, the revelers had gone, with only trash and broken bottles about to prove they had ever existed. Yet one more thing there was, too: a new sense of wariness, of expectation, as Falmouth waited to hear what was the result of the General Court's deliberations.

I have already related how, for a variety of reasons, I found it impossible to confide in Sarah. Her unflagging optimism in the face of the tension and guilt which I felt but could not explain was a constant source of irritation, until even the patience with which she endured my outbursts became the source of further asperity.

Finally one night she snapped back at me. "Lord have mercy, Pyrrhus," she said as she sat up, "I know you ain't got it easy, your master being a Tory and all, but coming down on me like that ain't going to make things any better. Let's talk about something else for a change, like do you know what happened to that Captain Coulson?"

"Captain Ross is no Tory," I said automatically. "He's no Son of Liberty, but he's no Tory either. But what do you mean, what happened to Coulson?"

"Same thing as," she retorted, "he's marrying one, ain't he? Anyhow, don't try to tell me you didn't know he'd left town."

"Who'd left town? Ross? He's been here right along."

"No, that Captain Coulson, you ninnyhammer. Leastways, nobody seems to know for sure where he is. I heard old Mr. Freeman was looking to talk to him 'bout that sloop of his, and couldn't find him nowhere. Nobody at his house, they say, but his wife, old Dr. Coffin's daughter that'd be, and the servants. Mr. Freeman, he's fit to be tied."

I must have looked doubtful, for she continued more forcefully still. "All right," she asked, "if he ain't left town, then where is he? And if he has, how come he left that old Bristol sloop of his? You mark my words, Pyrrhus Ross, he's up to something."

Sarah had a point, and the next morning while the captain was shaving, I mentioned what she had said. He listened thoughtfully and then wiped the last of the lather from his face.

"Let's go," he said, throwing me the towel, "fetch me a clean shirt. You can forget about making breakfast; I'll get something at Marston's. Robert should be taking his morning coffee there about now, and if I hurry I can just catch him before he goes down to the yard."

Pagan seemed totally at ease. "No secret there, Will," he told the captain. "Here, sit down and I'll tell you all about it. Pyrrhus, see if you can't get another pot and a cup for your master."

Ross waved me on. "Go ahead," he said, "and have them bring some food as well. Anything will do, except that damned porridge. A steak, maybe, or a couple of chops. They'll give you something to eat in the kitchen if you ask."

They did, and I found out why the captain had referred to Marston's mush as "that damned porridge." It had substance, though little else. When I had eaten all of it I could, I went back into the common room to find the captain. He was sitting by himself. As I approached, he pushed a crust of bread around in the grease on his plate and popped it into his mouth.

"Nothing simpler," he told me on the way out. "Your Sarah, or perhaps Elder Freeman, has begun to see things under the bed. Coulson had Greenfield Pote set him down as far as Salem in his shallop, so as to go to Concord and press his suit himself. I guess that with the town meeting going the way it had, and not hearing anything this week past, he must have been concerned. Can't say as I blame him, either."

"Then what about what Sarah said, that Mr. Freeman had been to the house and hadn't been able to find out where he had gone?"

"I asked Robert," the captain replied. "He said it sounded fishy to him. Most likely Sarah's got it wrong, or Freeman asked one of the servants instead of talking to Dorcas herself."

He fell silent then, and we made the best of our way down muddy Middle Street without another word on either side. As we neared King Street, there came a sudden rattle of drums and the sound of fifes and of shouting. "There's something afoot," he said to me in surprise. He broke into a trot. "Come on! I want to see!"

22

W HAT I had eaten sat discomfortably within me, so that I quickly fell behind and lost the captain in the press. The best that I could tell, King Street was packed full from ten rods above Fore Street clear to Goodwin's wharf. I heard the fifes and drums again. Whatever was causing the stir could only be down by the old fort.

The ground on the far side of King Street was boggy at the driest of seasons. So I cut across the back lots toward Clay Cove and crossed Fore Street between Pagan's house and Moses Plummer's, the same who was called "Old Way" because he preferred to take country pay instead of cash. I was careful to give the brigadier's cow a wide berth and so came scatheless to the alley below Butler's store. Prince McLellan was there, lounging against the bricks. He grinned hugely and nudged a bulging haversack with his foot.

"Better'n splittin' out shooks!" he crowed. "Glorious days, Pyrrhus, just glorious! Captain Joe, he come out to Gorham last night to tell Masta William they's a muster this mornin', and Masta fetch me along to carry he firelock when he come. Be here all mornin', look like, and then walk back this afternoon! Walkin' beats workin' all hollow!"

I had heard of no muster, and said so. Prince shook his head. "Wasn't supposed to. Captain Joe, he say they was to turn out, quiet's a cat, and nobody but them was to know. They's some folks here from down 'round Plymouth way, come to see how good they can march." His eyes grew round and white. "My, my! You should see them Plymouth boys go at it: all quick-like, back an' forth like the insides of Masta William's clock 'fore Plato try to fix it." In a confidential voice, he added, "The thing I like best is the hats they got. I'd join up myself, was they to give me one of those."

There was a gap in the crowd then, and I took the opportunity to move forward into the street. It took some time for me to cross. In the end I could not go directly, but was forced round by Jeremiah Pote's house, whence I got into his shipyard and onto the pile of timbers remaining from the *Minerva*'s scaffolding. From there I could see pretty well. Daniel Ilsley's company was drawn up on the little parade ground that fronted on the street near to the guard-house. Opposite them was a line of men very smartly turned out with black leather accoutrements on wide cross-belts and extraordinary caps knit of bright red wool. A man I took for an officer began to shout, all quite military but hard to understand, and Ilsley's men followed the others through a manual of arms. I thought they looked pretty well. By and by a boy stepped forward from the front row of the crowd and piped away at the tune they call "Yankee Doodle," which was suddenly become very popular. The militia shouldered firelocks like the king's troops I had seen in the Indies and marched off amid cheers and applause from their neighbors. The people closed in around them and the whole moved ponderously up the hill.

I went on down to the schooner, where I found Grizzell, merry as a grig, preparing to pay the new-cleaned hull with a mixture of tallow, pitch, and brimstone. When I asked him what he thought of the display, he whistled. "Never seen the beat of it," he declared, "not in fifty year. O'course marchin' be'n't fighting, but they'll do: they'll do!" He handed me a dripping bucket and a stiff brush. "Up you go, now. Yonder comes the captain. He's Mr. Pagan with him, wearing a face to curdle new milk. Likely they'll be more interested in getting this vessel into the water than in hearing my opinion of aught else."

I clambered up on the staging and got to work. Presently the captain arrived with Elizabeth's brother, and as Grizzell had observed, the merchant looked ill pleased with the morning's entertainment.

"I tell you, Will," he was saying, " 'tis worse than ever. That Thompson and his Brunswickers were bad enough without a troop of troublemakers from Plymouth to stir things up as well. I stopped by Pote's just before I saw you, and they are all for forming a company of our own. We've as much right to drill as anyone."

"For God's sake, Robert, don't let them do that. Every loafer on the waterfront would turn out to watch, and with Greenfield's temper it wouldn't be long before we had a massacre all to ourselves."

"About time, too," Pagan grumbled. "No, I know you're right. We'd be asking for trouble as things are right now. But look: Greenfield brought away a copy of the Providence *Gazette* when he came from Salem. It says the king's ship in Narragansett Bay has been landing arms for loyalists around Newport. We've few enough ourselves, and less powder, and nobody will sell us more. We were supposed to have some of Thomas Smith in January, but it came in on the fourth, after the association was put in, and the committee voted against it. The next cruiser that comes in, I'm going to ask her master for that at least. Yes, and a keg of flints and one of ball if he'll part with 'em."

The captain shook his head at that. "I hadn't heard," he said without enthusiasm. "Only that the *Lively* had took a schooner lately in from Dominica at Cape Ann. We'll have a frigate here next." He turned to Grizzell, who I made no doubt had taken in all that had been said, just as I. As it was, he had heard nothing out of turn, but it would do no harm to caution Ross about it. "How do we fare?" he asked him. "I shan't rest easy until the job is done."

Grizzel gave him a gap-toothed grin. "Well enough," he replied. "She'll float by morning, or my name ain't Jonadab Grizzell."

"That's good," Ross told him. "Carry on, then. With luck we can have her alongside Deering's wharf later to take on her ballast and all." He glanced up at where I was working. "But tell me," he said, "where in hell is Tukey?"

The old man shook his head. "Haven't seen him since the muster began, Cap'n. Belike he run off up to Alice Greele's with the rest on 'em. Seems to me I saw his brother Ben about some'er's. But don't you take on about him, Cap'n. He be no workman nohow. You just leave her to Pyrrhus an' me. We'll finish her in time without him."

Grizzell and I did finish the *Industry* in time, but only just. The next day was Saturday; at noontide she was tied up at the pier, showing a wide streak of tallow which gradually disappeared as we carried aboard the ton upon ton of rocks that gave her stability. Sunday, of course, we did no work. I went with Sarah to hear Mr. Smith preach the morning. Captain Ross had need of me later in the day, and so I walked with her back to the ferry at noon. By then the sun was gone in; Sarah shivered as we walked, and drew closer.

"This will do for the early flowers," she said sadly. "I had such hopes of mine, but it seems we are to have winter in April." She stared up at the sky, which had grown quite threatening. "I had thought to go the long way round, but now I don't know. What do you think, Pyrrhus? If we did, you could come sit with me at the house for a spell."

I weighed my words carefully. "I really can't be away that long," I reminded her gently. "Besides, I don't think your father likes it when I come."

"I can deal with my father," she said. "But I suppose you're right, after all." She looked at the sky once more. "You know," she said, "if this weren't April, I'd say it was going to snow."

Three days later, it did snow, and the ground's being half-frozen once more put an end to predictions of an early and bountiful harvest, upon which both town and country folk had placed great hopes. To the gloom thus engendered was added the latest intelligence from England, in which came news that Parliament had authorized four regiments of troops and fourteen frigates for American service.

The *Industry* was still tied up at Deering's wharf, but nearly complete. It running close to noon, Ross took me with him when he went to bring the tidings to Elizabeth's brother. We found him tending store. When my master told him what he had heard, Pagan seemed surprisingly unmoved. "Actually, William," he said, sitting with pen poised over his ledger, " 'tis no more than I had expected. North means to teach those runagate friends of yours a lesson." He waved the tip of the quill at my master like an accusing finger. "You'd be well advised to stay clear of 'em, lest you be tarred with their brush. I must say that they've brought it on themselves, what with their committees and congresses." The ink on his nib had dried as he had spoken. He made a disapproving noise and dipped it afresh. "I can't pretend I'm pleased in one respect," he observed as he wrote. "It certainly won't do much for business." He came to the end of his line and looked up. "If it gets much worse, I shall be coming to you next, for a berth on your schooner." At this they both laughed.

Still, Ross took Pagan's warning seriously enough, and when we had returned to the *Industry* he decided to move it to an anchorage out in the stream, away from trouble. It was as well that he did, for the days and nights that followed were marked by incidents of violence and disorder. These were not restricted to members of the lower classes, and one in particular, much misrepresented in after years, I shall trouble to record here.

On the afternoon of the eighth of April my master sent me ashore to see if Mr. Pote could supply him with a block to replace one aboard the *Industry* which had cracked. As I walked down Fore Street and crossed King, I passed close aboard Brigadier Preble, who stood talking to the high sheriff, Mr. Tyng.

"It is said there will be a mob tonight," the brigadier was saying. Why he should have chosen to warn the sheriff, who was a high Tory, I cannot say, unless it was because they had been good friends before the troubles. He may have wished to warn him that he would be wise to become indisposed. In any event, I pricked up my ears at the word. The captain was much oppressed with the idea that a mob should harm the schooner before we could haul her off into the harbor. I went over and sat on the front stairs at Mr. Weeks's house, as though to soak up what there was of sunlight.

At that juncture, Thomas Oxnard came down the street. The year before, he had wed Preble's daughter Martha, and the sheriff greeted him boisterously. "Ho, Thomas," he cried, so that folk turned their heads at the sound of his voice. "Your father-in-law tells me we shall have a mob tonight!"

The brigadier must have regretted his kindly impulse, for he grew very red about the face and denied that he had said any such thing. Tyng laughed at this, and called him an old fool. Preble gave him the lie again, whereupon the sheriff became hot as well.

"I should chastise you for that," he cried, "were you not an old man!" He laughed spitefully and added, "Perhaps I should, at that. You were not too old to get Sarah Smith a child, though in truth that is now twelve years gone."

With that Preble went deadly pale. Raising his silver-headed cane, he bellowed, "You villain! Repeat those words, sir, and I shall knock you down!" Sheriff Tyng, who was a proud man, drew his sword, and said he would run Preble through before he suffered him that.

I could scarcely credit such behavior in two of the most dignified and well-considered men in the town, and from the look on Oxnard's face he must have felt the same. He tried to interpose himself between them, but when the sheriff brandished his sword, the brigadier gave a cry and leaped forward to seize him by the collar.

The sight of a man in his seventies shaking one half his age as a terrier will a rat would have been laughable if they had not been in earnest. Oxnard had been pushed aside by the fury of the old man's onset, but now called out for help and with no little difficulty the combatants were separated.

Some two dozen or more people had gathered, with several grouped closely about Preble and a like number with the sheriff. Oxnard flitted solicitously between them, and presently they parted to reveal the pair, sweating and disheveled. Tyng had put aside his sword. He mopped at his face with his handkerchief and stepped forward. "I crave your pardon, sir," he said, though it was plain he liked saying it not at all. "I spoke in a manner no gentleman should employ."

"Granted," said the general gruffly, and made as if to depart. There were angry mutterings from the crowd; the same tensions which had led Tyng to quarrel with the brigadier had made him, as the instrument of the Crown, very unpopular with the populace. Someone inquired of the general if he were satisfied, adding that, were he not, he should have all the further satisfaction that he desired. Preble turned then, and looked back at his friend the sheriff, who had now been twice humbled in the streets of his own town.

"No," he said, and there was nothing of triumph in his voice: merely sadness. "No, nothing more; let him go."

I sought out Mr. Pagan and returned to the schooner, where I advised the captain of the brigadier's warning, with the result that he slept in the cabin that night while Tukey, Grizzell, and I watched by turns on deck. For whatever reason, there was no mob that night. Still, I think my master did not sleep well, for in the morning he looked tired and ill.

"It's nothing," he snapped irritably when I inquired after his health. "Only I feel like when a musket flashes in the pan: for a time you wonder whether the charge has been wetted, and must be drawn, or if she has but hung fire, and is apt to go off any second. I just wish I knew which."

We were still waiting to find out on the tenth, when the committee of inspection saw fit to prime the lock anew. On that day, Enoch Freeman published a resolution which formally named Thomas Coulson a violator of the articles of the Continental Association, and called upon their fellow citizens to have no further dealings with him. This solemn measure, being Puritan New England's equivalent of Papist excommunication and not lightly laid or taken, was deprived of fully half its dignity by the fact that Freeman could not find Coulson in order to serve the writ upon his person. The result was that while he had aroused great indignation among the friends of the said captain, there were also those who found Freeman's discomfiture amusing.

Sarah told me that evening that Freeman had grown exceedingly wroth at the idea that his fellow citizens should make sport at his expense. "They were shut up in the front chamber as usual," she said, "him and the rest of the committee, though they might as well have been in the kitchen with me for all the good it did. When they told him what people were saying, I could hear him rushing about the room like a madman, crying, 'Where is Coulson? Where is Coulson? Oh, thou Amalekite! Would that I had you here now!' "

I confess that what Sarah had said caused me to laugh immoderately, for I was suddenly minded of a tale from my earliest childhood. It is the only such that has come back to me, the one in which the gaffer wishes the fairy's pudding onto the end of his goodwife's nose. When I had stopped laughing, I told it her, and Sarah agreed it was a very pretty story. She kissed me good night then, and went on her way still smiling, but one might say that the cream of the jest did not rise until the following day.

Tuesday morning one of the boys who had gone to pasture their cows beyond the stone wall on Munjoy's Hill came pelting back into town shouting that there was "a great ship" in the offing beyond the islands. His report immediately caused a stir along the waterfront; any person old enough to tell a ship from a brig would know that a three-masted vessel was almost necessarily an English man-of-war.

Freeman came blustering down to Preble's wharf and sent a small sloop to speak the stranger under the guise of offering pilotage. It took some time for her to work out to where the stranger lay. Mr. Pagan sent one of his riggers to the *Minerva*'s main top with a spyglass, which gave as good vantage as any spot in the town save Old Jerusalem's steeple. Thus we in the yard knew even while the committee was being informed that the sloop had rounded to in the newcomer's lee instead of returning independently. His suspicions thus confirmed, the judge went back to his house to await developments.

I should think it safe to say that little useful work was done in Falmouth that forenoon. They closed the shipyard early on, one of the carpenters having cut himself on the shin with his adz. Mr. Pagan swore when they came to tell him. "Good workmen are too hard to find," he said to the foreman, "to have them injure themselves through inattention. Send 'em home."

The captain went to luncheon with Elizabeth and her brother, but neither of the men did more than pick at their food. Elizabeth was so vexed that they kept losing track of her account of the progress of the wedding preparations that she left in a huff with her own plate half-full. Ross let her go. For a time he and Pagan sat over a bottle of what must have been an indifferent port, but finally my master pushed his chair back and stood up.

"Damme for a Frenchman," he swore, "but I cannot sit here one instant more. I am going down to watch her come in."

Pagan looked relieved, I thought, and was on his feet in a trice. "Wait while I fetch my stick and my hat," he said, "and I shall go too."

I tried to maintain an air of indifference, but I confess that I was very glad when they said that I was to accompany them. We walked down to the end of Pote's wharf, where we found Jeremiah Pote and his elder brother, Greenfield. "It's young Mowatt's ship," Greenfield called out as we approached. "Another half-hour and she'll be hull up from the dock. I thought she was gone to Halifax by now: the talk was she had injured herself when the pilot grounded her at Piscataqua in January."

"She seems sound enough now," Jeremiah added. "I had a look at her myself from the masthead not ten minutes ago. Smartly handled she is, too. Her master knows his business. The wind can be dead fluky amongst the islands. I wonder what he's wanting here in Falmouth."

"I think we can guess," was Pagan's cryptic reply. "Though I'll wager a guinea to a pine-tree shilling that there's them not far distant who would give a round sum to know." He pointed at the fort, and the wharves and shipping beyond. Wherever a prominence promised an early view, men had congregated, even to hanging out of upstairs windows in some of the houses.

"I can tell you now," he said, turning to Ross, "that the *Canceaux* is not unlooked-for. I was sorry not to be able to tell you before, but there were only the three of us in town who knew, and we were pledged to silence. If I am not much mistaken, Tom Coulson will be aboard that ship. When Greenfield took him to Salem it was not to go to Concord, but to see Admiral Graves in Boston. We hoped he might send us a vessel to ensure that there would be no trouble while we got the *John and Mary*'s cargo ashore and the *Minerva* rigged and laden. We dared not take any chances until we knew, of course, lest the committee act before we were able." He smiled apologetically. "I should have liked to have told you sooner, but we had agreed to keep it to ourselves. Even Dorcas his wife did not know the truth."

Greenfield nodded enthusiastically. "I don't think Jeremiah would have told me if they hadn't wanted my shallop to take him to Salem in. But I wish I could hear old Freeman when they tell him!"

Sarah did hear, and what he said in reply does not bear repeating. Coulson went in to see him as soon as the *Canceaux* had anchored, and people say that the judge had had to be restrained, else he might have struck him.

The next day the *John and Mary* was moored up against the *Minerva*, with all her people engaged in transferring the stores she carried to the larger vessel. The *Canceaux* lay nearby, her guns, as I heard, having been loaded but not run out. Word was that the crew had slept at their stations as for battle, which was likely true, for every time I saw her there seemed to be a score at least of men upon the deck, which is to say, half her complement. Doubtless Mowatt thought to forestall trouble by establishing from the outset that he meant business. This point was driven home by the news that he had pressed three men from the pilot sloop; thus had he and his admiral evened the score with Falmouth for sheltering the deserters from the *Gaspée*.

By this time, Elizabeth had recovered from her pet of the day preceding and had sent a note aboard the *Canceaux* to bid Lieutenant Mowatt to dinner. He accepted with alacrity, and made a call in advance to pay her his compliments.

The gathering itself took place on the Friday, which would have been April 14. Naturally I was wanted to serve; the party included my master, Mowatt, Elizabeth and her brother, and Jeremiah Pote's daughter Miriam, whom Robert married later that year. There was another young lady present, a cousin, I believe, of Mistress Pote's, to partner the lieutenant, though I do not recall that he seemed to be much taken with her. Certainly the bulk of his attention was given to his hostess, who was at her most scintillating. I would have said that the party was a great success had the captain spoken other than when addressed, and then in monosyllables.

"I hope, my dear sir," Elizabeth said to Mowatt toward the end of the meal, "that we may look forward to your presence here for some time to come? It is so infrequently that a man of your parts visits Falmouth." She simpered coquettishly at his handsome if rather ponderous acknowledgment, and went on. "You know, of course, Captain, that Mr. Ross and I are to be married yesterday week; I should be very glad indeed if you could come. You must see, my dear," she said seriously to my master, "that Captain Mowatt receives an invitation."

"I shall be very glad to attend such a happy affair," Mowatt said gallantly, "although it would be hard to imagine one more pleasurable than the present." He pulled his watch from his waistcoat pocket, adding as he did so, "Always assuming, of course, that the exigencies of the service permit." He checked the time and put his watch away. "Sadly, my duties do not allow me to prolong this delightful occasion further. I trust you will excuse me if I must go back to my ship? Madam? Sir, my felicitations; Mr. Pagan, a most charming entertainment. Ladies." He rose and bowed in courtly fashion.

Elizabeth got to her feet. "Pyrrhus," she said quickly, "the captain's hat and cloak." As I hurried out the door, I heard her address him once more. "Oh, dear," she was saying, "and I had so hoped to entice you to stay for a rubber of whist. Surely all the king's gentlemen are fond of play."

It was rather later that the captain and I left, though from what I saw he was inclined to be sulky all evening. We went by way of Fore Street, it being my master's intention to see that all was well on board the *Industry* before retiring, though we were sleeping in the house ashore. We had gone by Moose Alley and were nearing Pearson's Lane when there was a great hue and cry raised back along King Street. "Elizabeth!" Ross cried, and was off through the darkness like a deer. He had the advantage of me at the start, but my legs being the longer, I arrived at Pagan's before him. All up and down the town there were shouts of "Turn out, turn out," and I thought that I heard one pistol shot from down by Goodwin's wharf. Half-dressed men, some looking like soldiers' ghosts with muskets and nightshirts, began collecting in the cross-roads and drifting toward the fort.

"I'm going inside," Ross told me breathlessly. "See if you can find out what is happening."

This took me some time to do; the men were milling about with no obvious leader, and no one to whom I spoke could tell me anything. I went down to the waterfront and simply tried to keep from underfoot. There was a spot by the rainbarrel at the corner of the brigadier's house. I stopped there, reasoning that when the truth was known he would be among the first to be told.

Presently old Preble came out, fully dressed, save that he still wore his bed-cap. He hailed one of the men in the street, who, it turned out, was a member of the watch, and so I was able to hear.

It seemed that Mowatt had waited until most of the town was asleep and sent a party ashore by one of his boats. Their aim was the taking of one Yorke, who with two others had succeeded in deserting from the *Gaspée* in February, a fourth man, John Lutey, being mortally wounded in the attempt.

With a midshipman in command, the boat's crew had blacked their faces and muffled their oars before rowing from the ship to Goodwin's wharf. "Must have left from the far side of the ship, damn their souls," said the watchman emphatically. "I was down that way not more'n twenty minutes before they come, and saw nor heard nothing."

Apparently the sentry at the guard-house, whose name may have been either Woodman or Gookin, had fallen asleep; in any case, he was overpowered before he could raise the alarm. Then they went up the hill into town, where their intelligence had reported the deserter to be housed. Someone had discovered them, and before they had obtained their object; of that the speaker was profanely certain, and they had been compelled to retreat, taking with them the unfortunate sentry, who being pressed into the navy thus paid a high price for his slumbers. No, said the watchman in response to a question, to the best of his knowledge no one had been wounded in the affray.

"They want men, it seems, not just the deserters," the brigadier observed. "And well they might. They've no crew to speak of and that great ark of a *Minerva* to man. Coulson won't want to sail with less than a dozen on board, and all prime seamen at that. Have to get them from Mowatt, most likely, and hope to fill his ship out with whatever they can get in return. We won't see that one again, no, nor the three from the pilot sloop either. Well, they are still short, according to my reckoning. We shall have to be on our guard henceforth."

By now some of the other principal men of the town were arriving. Jabez Jones, who was a committeeman as well as one of the captains of militia, tried to marshal the men into some sort of order while the others conferred with the brigadier. There had been an angry outcry raised as news of Gookin's fate had spread. As a result the committee-men had their heads close together and I could not tell what was being said. Along the water, torches and fists were brandished at the *Canceaux*, but with her crew alert she was probably safe. I never heard that anyone attempted anything against her. I decided that I had seen enough.

There was a watchful air about the entire waterfront after that. Indeed, when I went the next day to deliver Lieutenant Mowatt's wedding invitation aboard the *Canceaux*, I noticed that there were several men lounging in front of the guard-house and two more standing at Goodwin's wharf with their eyes constantly bent upon the ship and those who had business with her. They looked at me narrowly both going and coming, but though it made me feel very uneasy I was not molested in any way. In point of fact, the midshipman who received me on deck was considerably more bothersome.

Two sailors parted the boarding nettings for me while I climbed through, and the young martinet dispatched one of them below with my note. When I began to look about curiously at the polished fittings and holystoned decks, he must have taken me for a spy. "You there!" he snapped. "Stand to attention." In my surprise I obeyed instinctively. He poked at my ribs with a tentative finger, and I must own that with what old Preble had said in mind, I was in a very unhappy state.

The midshipman's next remark did nothing to comfort me. "Here, Crawford," he said to a crony who was standing nearby. "Have a look at this." Crawford did, while I prayed they would not detect the layer of callus on my palms; any hint that I might be a seaman and my fate was sealed. I fought back the urge to run. I could not have hoped to get away, and they would have been on me like a pair of stoats. I began to sweat.

"Poor stuff," said Crawford at last. There was a sneer in his voice. "Still, all's grist that comes to the miller, what?" He winked at his companion. "Here, boy, let's have a look at your hands."

I clenched my fists without conscious volition, but even this gesture was enough to give me away. The two midshipmen exchanged knowing glances. Oh, God, I said to myself as they closed in upon me, no power on earth can save me now.

Actually, there was one. At that moment Lieutenant Mowatt appeared at the after companion. "None of that, now," he said sharply. "He's not to be hindered."

The men around me sprang to attention. The midshipman of the watch took a step forward and saluted. "If the captain please, sir," he said urgently, "this boy's a seaman."

"I don't give a damn if he's the bloody grand admiral of Timbuctoo! He belongs to a friend of the government, who happens to be a personal friend of mine as well. He's come aboard with an invitation to me from his mistress, and I won't see him mistreated." He fixed the midshipman with a stony glare. "I've my eye on you, Trevor, and no mistake. Your handling of the shore party was far from brilliant. If you wish to improve my opinion of your all too modest abilities, you will have to do much better from now on." He came forward and handed me a note.

"Take this to Mistress Pagan with my compliments," he told me. "I shall be very glad to attend. I'm sorry that you were frightened, but you may go now." He turned back to Trevor. "Help this boy down into his boat," he told him, "and see that he has a shilling for his trouble."

23

THE few days remaining before the wedding were busy ones. The captain and I spent much of our time helping Elizabeth, who seemed to be everywhere at once, laughing and ordering people about. At the same time she was always at her most charming, so that even while I hastened to obey her last command I found myself admiring her against my will. There was so much to be done: there were the last details of the ceremony, of course, and of the reception, which would be held at Marston's tavern. There was also something else, something that occasionally required my master to be elsewhere, and about which he was cheerfully mysterious, saying nothing to anyone, not even me.

Life did not cease about us, but at times it might almost have done so without our noticing. I think it was Saturday that the newly promoted Colonel Thompson passed through Falmouth with a commission from the provincial congress to hinder the activities of one Edward

Parry, the masting agent for the Crown in those parts, and not long after, the major's son and his party returned as well. Then on the seventeenth Andrew Titcomb went fishing and spoke a schooner from Newburyport. Her master told him that a vessel had arrived from England the day before with news that the Intolerable Acts were repealed. This being so contrary to the last we had heard, I do not know that many responsible people credited it. With all there was to do I found scant time to consider the matter at all.

Things were at their most tumultuous on Wednesday morning when I answered the door and found Lieutenant Mowatt on the front step. Attending him were a pair of husky seamen, one of whom wheeled a barrow. "Good morning," he said to me pleasantly. "Would your mistress be at home?"

Elizabeth's voice came from the hall behind. "Pyrrhus? Pyrrhus, who is it?" There was a rustle of skirts, and then she was at my elbow. "Oh," she said, "Henry Mowatt! Don't just stand there, you goose, let the gentleman in!"

Mowatt bowed deeply. "My apologies, ma'am, for the interruption. I know you're busy, but I had hoped that you might do me the honor of accepting a small token of my esteem and heartfelt good wishes." He indicated two crates in the wheelbarrow. "Only a dozen of port, and another of sherry, I am afraid, but the lazarette of an eight-gun sloop-of-war affords little else you might find suitable."

"How wonderful, Henry! With this dreadful association, it may be the last we'll see for some time." She turned to me. "Pyrrhus, show these men where to put it." She took the lieutenant by the arm. "Come," she said, "you must take some refreshment before you go. No matter how busy I am, I shall always find time for the gallant gentlemen of the navy."

I left the sailors in Janet's care and returned to the drawing room as quickly as I might to see if there were anything Elizabeth required. She and the Englishman were seated close together on a settee. Her head was thrown back, and she was laughing gaily. "Go on, Henry," she urged when at last she had stopped. "What happened then?"

"Well," he said, "there I was, I and my steward and those two men, landing the crates of wine, when this poxy little beggar comes up to me. 'Here,' he says, same's he was the First Sea-lord, 'what's all this, then? You can't land goods here! It's against the Continental Association!' Then he starts waving papers under my nose. 'No British goods,' he says, 'nor wines from Madeira or the western islands.' "

Elizabeth laughed again at his imitation of the local accent. Encouraged, he went on. "Of course I listened to him very attentively, and when he had done telling me about this association of his, I asked him when it had taken effect. He tells me, and I say, 'Oh, well, then, this wine is all right. It was imported into New York last year.'

"At that he pulls a long face, and says that if it's so, then they can be landed, but that he would have to have proof.

" 'Then you shall have it, sir,' I say. 'Here, steward, take this gentleman out to the ship and have the purser show him my books.' The Yankee looks a little doubtful at this, and so I take him aside. 'I'd go with you myself,' I tell him, 'but you know how it is. I daren't leave these three here by themselves, not for a minute. I give you my word, as between gentlemen, that this wine will go no further until this matter is settled.' The fellow puffs out his chest, then, my having taken him into my confidence, and gets down into the boat, and they row him out to the ship."

"The matter must be all settled then, because here you are with the wine."

Mowatt drank his wine and smiled. "I make no doubt, madam, that the matter is settled. To my satisfaction, if not to his. By now, one of two things has occurred. Either I must find me a first lieutenant who knows his business, or Mr. Andrew Fulton has enlisted in the navy, and your Major Freeman is in need of a clerk!"

The two of them must have sat and talked for most of an hour, when the captain came to fetch me home. Elizabeth rose hastily when he entered the room, calling his attention to what was, after all, a handsome gift. If my master was not overeffusive in his thanks, perhaps it was merely that he was thinking of something else. The lieutenant found it a convenient time to take his leave, promising as he did so to see them both on the morrow.

The captain had little to say until we reached the little cottage on Meetinghouse Lane. When we got there, he threw the door open wide and stood in the hall for a moment with his hands on his hips. When he swung round to face me, he looked pleased with himself.

"Well, Pyrrhus," he said, "tomorrow's the day! I may still smell of tar and bilgewater, but it's a long way I've come since first we met."

He went over to the sideboard and poured two glasses brimful of wine. Handing one of them to me, he said, "Will you drink with me to my good fortune? These are dubious times, but I swear there's more where that came from."

When we had drunk, he took the glasses and set them down. "Now," he told me, "I want you to go upstairs to my chamber and pack my clothes."

"Aye, aye, Captain, and which clothes will you be wanting?"

"Why, all of them, of course! All of them, save only those that are wanted for the wedding. And pack your own as well."

I looked at him curiously. "If you please, sir, are we going on a journey?" There had been no mention of any such plans. Ross grinned at my perplexity.

"It's a bit of a surprise for Elizabeth. You'll find out tomorrow. Go on, now; you should be able to get a good half of the bags packed before it's time to cook supper."

Directly the captain was dressed next morning, I went to Mr. Brackett's for the horse and chaise he had hired for the occasion. As an indifferent driver, I was dismayed to find the animal rather restive. I was even more so when it became evident that I would have to stay outside the church to gentle him while the ceremony was being performed. The captain's wedding touched my own life almost as much as it did his, and I would have been glad to watch, be it only from the loft. It was lonely on Middle Street with only the horses for company, though indeed there were a round dozen of them. At a time when there were no more than twenty chaises in all of Falmouth, the procession would make a goodly show.

This in itself caused me some ill ease. Saint Paul's was but three doors away from the Freeman house, and many of the people who came and went made unfriendly comments as they passed me, they considering that such luxury was contrary to the eighth article of the Continental Association. Thus for many reasons I was glad when the last anthem began. The doors of the church opened and the people started to come out. I got out of the chaise and held the horse's headstalls with both hands.

Presently the captain and his new wife emerged amid the cheers and applause of the entire party. They came down the stairs to the chaise with a rush, so that the horse shied and tried to rear, but I held him fast.

"Happy is the bride the sun shines on," the captain observed as he helped her up into the carriage. I looked up. The sun had indeed peeped from behind the clouds.

"Yes," she replied, "though if we are to find our happiness in rhymes and old wives' tales, I wish that I had remembered 'Thursday for losses,' and set the date for yesterday instead."

Ross kissed her lightly. "Never mind," he told her, "we shall write our own." He got into the chaise, and I stood aside as he took the whip and reins. "Off to Marston's," he said, flourishing the lash. The horse leaped forward like a hunter, and the chaise was gone in a cloud of dust and a whirl of varnished spokes. Those who had conveyances followed on their heels, the rest walking, and I, with another servant or two, bringing up the rear.

All of Marston's people had been turned out to cook or to serve the dinner, which, notwithstanding the fact that no fresh green stuff or other garden sauce was yet to be had, was fully the equal of that Deacon Codman had served his guests the previous July. The onions had all gone by in March, but there were parsnips and good cabbages from store, with squashes and dried peas as well.

I can remember numerous pies and pasties, beef and mutton mostly, but also mincemeat, and one at least of pigeons, the half of which survived to come back again to the kitchen, whereof we lesser folk made good cheer in our turn. There was a roast of beef, and fowls both boiled and roasted, some dressed with oysters and some without, and a calf's head done turtle-fashion with forcemeat balls. The desserts were likewise plentiful, with a great cake, and when the last crumb was eaten and the toasts had been drunk, we cleared away the tables for the dancing to begin.

All the music that we had was simple, the most notable being fiddles played by old Grizzell and a mad half-Irishman who called himself Lane. While the center of the floor was given over to reels and figures, I made myself useful by carrying around mugs of flip. In a brief lull between dances, I brought one to Grizzell, who was trussed like a turkey for roasting in a sprigged waistcoat and stock. He seized the tankard from me, tilted it upside down, and emptied the pint in a single long swallow.

"Thank'ee kindly, Pyrrhus," he said as he handed it back. "You've saved a poor old man from an untimely death." He whipped his handkerchief from his sleeve and plied it industriously. "A proper do," he observed. "Best I've seen in fifty year, though it's not long that you could dance in Falmouth at all." He searched the crowd quickly. "You see that gent over there? Mr. Wyer, the king's attorney? Not ten years ago he tried Mr. Bradbury on a charge of public dancing at old Josh Freeman's tavern." I must have looked skeptical, for he poked me in the chest with his finger. "Did so," he insisted. "I don't guess you'll find Bradbury here, but John Waite and his wife were there, and most of the others would remember: your master, too, though he'd ha' been just a lad. Made quite a splash, it did. 'Course Bradbury and Wyer being the only green-baggers in town at the time, they was mostly at each other's throats anyway. I recall they got off on an excuse that the room being hired for the purpose, 'twa'n't public at all. Just since then, though, that it's been worth the time to go to a weddin'."

Several of the younger ladies in the party came up then to plead for another tune, and he suffered them to draw him off with no more than a token show of reluctance. With the first strains of music, the couples took the floor and formed their lines. I stood back out of the way to watch.

In truth it was the goodliest company that ever I had seen assembled in Falmouth, or was to see for many years thereafter. More than half of what would be considered the quality folk in town had attended. Most were Tories, either high or low, but there were perhaps as many as eight or ten of the opposition as well. Mr. Tyng stood talking amiably with the brigadier, their recent quarrel seemingly erased from memory. The Freemans of course were conspicuously absent, but the Waites were there, and Deacon Codman, and all three of the ministers, though Mr. Deane had looked a trifle sour when he was introduced to Lieutenant Mowatt. Joseph McLellan, who had stood up with my master during the service, had come with his father; Bryce had begun to show signs of his age but held forth merrily enough from his chair in the corner.

I was not a little surprised at first to find the republican faction so well represented, especially in the light of the animosity I had encountered while I had been waiting before the church. I watched as the people laughed and danced together, and they might not have had a care in the world. Perhaps it had only seemed odd to me because I had been born an outsider. When I reflected that these people had known each other all the days of their lives, had worked and worshiped together, had invested in the same enterprises and suffered the same losses, feared the same French and the same painted Indians, fretted at the same mud in springtime and the same snow in winter, and lived out their spans in every expectation of being buried under the same weather-stricken pine, it seemed that it should be this way rather than otherwise.

With a start I realized that I had stood idle longer than was proper, and went back to work. Even this was not without compensation, for it gave me a chance to observe the costumes of the frolickers at close hand. Sarah would insist on hearing what the women had worn. I watched them when I could, though I could not help thinking how out of place she would look in one of their fashionable gowns of apple green, lilac, or lemon. Elizabeth glided by, everything that a gentleman's lady should be, in palest blue satin. Earlier there had been a white cloak and hood, but she had put them off when she reached the inn. She danced with effortless grace and precision.

Though my master was little skilled in the art, he had partnered her at the start with evident enjoyment on both sides. Thereafter he discharged his duty toward the other ladies in the party quite properly, if with no especial show of enthusiasm. Elizabeth, on the other hand, was an ardent worshiper of Terpsichore and predictably much sought after. Lieutenant Mowatt, too, though built somewhat on the full model, surprised me by proving singularly apt on the floor. When the two of them danced together they were admired by all.

I think that Elizabeth might have enjoyed learning some of the new steps the lieutenant was so willing to teach her, but she never had the opportunity. As soon as the music stopped, the captain would be at Mowatt's side with a fresh drink or some friend who had not yet heard how he had diddled the major's secretary. Since Ross had never seemed to have much use for the Englishman before this, I was worried to see them so inseparable. By eight in the evening my master must have known the story by heart, but he was still listening with devoted attention.

"Young Freeman came aboard that night," Mowatt was saying. I exchanged his empty tankard for a full one. "In a devilish great hurry, he was, too, and very angry. That one will perish of an apoplexy if his physician isn't careful: he needs to be bled some, or to go for a long sea voyage." He raised the mug to his lips and winked at the others over the rim. "Had he looked more like a topman I would have asked him to stay and take a cure." He took a long drink that left him a trifle breathless. After a pause he continued.

"The infernal popinjay starts to order me about, and in my own cabin," he said. "Threatened me with writs of this and that. Got 'em from his father, I gather. Demanded that I produce this Fulton of his, and others whom he alleged that I had passed from Falmouth against their will. I listened while he had his say, of course. There's naught to be gained by antagonizing his sort. Pretended to read his writs, too, though devil a word could I understand of 'em. After all, I wear the king's coat and not a bag-wig! I'll warrant his father's no navigator, however: each to his own, say I." The listeners smiled at the jest, and Mowatt went on.

"Finally he stopped; ran out of breath, most likely, and so I showed him the ship's books. He gaped like a fish out of water, and well he might, for all five of the men had volunteered for the service. Volunteered, mind you, and in writing too. 'You're welcome to talk with any of them,' I told him. 'Any except your Mr. Fulton, that is, he being indisposed at present.'

"That brought him up short. 'Indisposed?' he said. 'I don't believe it! He was well enough this morning.'" Mowatt licked his lips in pleasure at the way his audience hung on his every word. "'Why, yes,' I say, looking straight at him. 'The others had a touch of it too. My surgeon tells me it is a species of claps got in kissing the gunner's daughter.'" There was a laugh at this, and Mowatt smiled. I looked at Ross blankly.

"Kissing the gunner's daughter," he explained in an undertone. "In the navy that means being tied to a gun and flogged." He turned back to Mowatt. "Tell them why Mr. Baillie says it must be a sort of claps, Captain," he urged.

Mowatt smiled still more broadly. "Why, gentlemen," he said, "there's nothing simpler: after the beggars are beaten, the master-at-arms claps them in irons!"

This sent the Tories off again. I was not sorry to see the last of Fulton, but having nearly shared his fate, I could find no humor in the situation. I looked at the captain with a profound sense of disappointment. He was laughing along with the rest, but eventually I noticed that there was no trace of merriment in his eyes. They had a hunted look about them I could not fathom. Just then there was a break in the music; Lieutenant Mowatt's attention turned instantly to the dance floor. There in the middle of the room stood Elizabeth, glancing about her even as she bid an absent farewell to her latest partner.

Mowatt handed me his half-empty tankard. "I hope that you will excuse me, sir," he said to Ross, "but the evening wears on, and I am pledged to dance at least one more dance with your charming lady."

The captain took his arm hurriedly. "Don't go just yet," he said. He was searching the room as he spoke. "Look," he told Mowatt, "there is Sheriff Tyng standing by the door. A loyal subject, my dear Captain, and one who will appreciate such wit as yours. He of all people must hear the story from your own lips." Mowatt was obviously reluctant, but could think of no excuse, and when he looked back at Elizabeth, she had been claimed by another. He gave her a last despairing glance as the music began and then let Ross tow him off to meet the sheriff. The true meaning of my master's sudden fondness for the Englishman was now made clear. I smiled and went on with my work.

Bryce McLellan signaled to me from his chair. I went to see what he wanted, noticing as I did that Joseph had joined a group talking nearby.

Bryce handed me a large glass. "Flip," he said in a low voice. "Flip, or rum toddy."

Joseph turned and looked at him sternly. "Flip for me," he said, "but small beer for my father."

"Small beer," Bryce muttered disgustedly. "A fine thing it is when a son sides against his own father. I tell you, Joe, that young Dr. Coffin will be the death of me, him and his small beer. He's not a patch on his own dad, he's not. There was a man that understood: who knew what's what." Bryce shook his head sadly. "Small beer," he repeated. "Beer's all right for breakfast, and for children and invalids, but a man needs rum to keep his inwards going." He smacked his lips and looked at me hopefully. "Rum, with a little molasses in it, and maybe some butter and cinnamon. Now that's a sociable drink."

Joseph gave me a meaningful stare. "Small beer," he said firmly. I shrugged. Small beer it would have to be.

From the road in front of the tavern came the sound of approaching hoofbeats. Their tempo was rapid: far too rapid for the mud and the darkness. McLellan swung around sharply as the staccato came to an abrupt halt. I heard a startled whinny and the clash of harness. The horseman must have seen the sign outside and reined in.

There was a loud bang from the hall as the front door of the tavern was flung back on its hinges. Conversation faltered and died as people turned to listen to the footsteps that rang in the corridor. They came closer and closer. As they reached the door the music stopped, leaving the dancers in the exaggerated poses of mid-figure. The hall door opened and a man came in. He was mud-caked and reeling with fatigue. He put out a hand to steady himself.

"The regulars are out," he croaked. "They fought with the militia at Lexington yesterday. Folks say they burned Concord. It's war now, war with England." For a moment no one spoke. The courier closed his eyes and shook his head as though to clear it. When he opened them again, he was staring straight at Lieutenant Mowatt. His face fell as he recognized the uniform. "Oh, Jesus," he said. "Ain't this Greele's Tavern?" He turned to run.

Mowatt leaped after him. "Gentlemen!" he cried. "Gentlemen, in the king's name!"

✺⋙⋙ 24 ⋘⋘✺

LIEUTENANT MOWATT got a handful of the messenger's coat and the two of them fell forward into the hall. The men nearest the door were Tories. They rushed forward to help, knocking my master out of their way. Some of the more active among them must have made it through the portal before the crowd pressed forward and blocked it. Fifty clamorous voices shouted curses, advice, and encouragement; with so many talking at once I could scarcely hear the scuffle in the hallway.

The McLellans had not moved. As I turned to them, I realized that the three of us had been left virtually alone. For the moment at least all eyes would be focused on the other end of the ballroom. That was all to the good.

Joseph and his father were staring at each other in shock and dismay. I took the committeeman by the arm. There would only be a few moments left. "Come on," I told him. "We've got to get you out of here." Joseph looked at me stupidly. "Don't you see," I said. "They have him now: it's up to you to spread the news."

My glance fell on a door in the rear of the chamber which led out through the kitchen. I pulled at Joseph's sleeve, but he resisted. "My father!" he said. "I can't leave without my father!"

Apparently the fight was over. People were moving back from the door to let the others in. Soon it would be too late. I looked at Bryce desperately.

"I'll be all right," he said. "Go on. Everything will be fine once they know the word is out."

Mowatt's voice came from the hallway. "Nobody leaves!" he was saying. "Back in the room, damn you! Nobody leaves!"

Joseph was thinking now. He bolted for the door. I risked a glimpse over my shoulder as I followed him and saw the courier being dragged back inside. There was blood on his face. One of the women screamed when she saw it. Someone caught her as she fell into a swoon.

Joseph had the door open. He stepped through it and started to say something to me, but there was no time. I shut the door and tried to look as though I had just come in.

I was none too soon. The stranger had been secured and a solid phalanx of loyalists was forming in front of the door. Several more were headed in my direction. Greenfield Pote was among them, and the younger Oxnard, and the two Pagan brothers from the Penobscot, William and Thomas, who had traveled a hundred miles to be at their sister's wedding. One of them had torn his coat.

Mowatt was shouting again. "No one leaves!" he repeated. "Mr. Tyng, I shall hold you responsible!" The crowd was starting to disperse into smaller groups. A number of the women had gone to the aid of their fainting sisters with fans and smelling-bottles. The men had mostly split into two camps. Perhaps a score who had taken the king's part in the troubles clustered around the lieutenant and blocked the entry. Robert Pagan was there, and Captain Coulson. The few Whigs who had stayed through the evening had come together in the center of what had been the dance floor. Between the two groups and a little to one side stood the captain and Elizabeth. I hastened to join them. As I did, I noticed that Joseph's father had gotten to his feet. Slowly and painfully he made his way to the middle of the room to join the others. Brigadier Preble reached out his hand to help and welcome him with a smile before turning to face the sheriff. "Well, Mr. Tyng," he said, "is it your intention to hold us all here against our will? I warn you, sir, it will go hard with you afterward if you do."

Mr. Tyng's wig had been knocked awry, and in the excitement he had apparently not noticed. It gave him the look of a dissolute official from a Hogarth engraving. He surveyed the determined faces opposite and looked nervously to Mowatt for counsel.

"You must do your duty, Mr. Tyng," the lieutenant told him sternly. "I shall need fifteen minutes at the least to secure this man on board the *Canceaux* and to alert my people."

Reverend Deane stepped to the forefront of the Liberty party. "By God, sir," he swore, "you shall not hinder my passage! No, not were there a hundred of you instead of twenty. Look to yourselves!"

Mr. Deane has often been criticized for want of doctrine, but never for lacking spirit; as he was a well-made man and then at the height of his powers, this was no idle threat. There was a shuffling as the nearest Tories prepared to receive him.

I heard a commotion from the back of the room and looked to see what it was. The door had come half-open; Greenfield Pote was seeking to shut it again. He said something to the unseen person on the other side.

"No, Mr. Pote," was the answer, "I shall come in! This is my inn, after all!" Marston's high-pitched voice was clearly recognizable. An instant later he himself appeared.

"See here!" he piped. "I won't have you gentlemen fighting in my house! What if you should break a window?" He shrugged Greenfield aside and came forward.

"What's all this about? Do I have to call the sheriff? My stars, Reverend, what on earth are you thinking of? Fancy, a man of the cloth brawling in a tavern. First Joe McLellan comes aharing through my kitchen like the devil himself is after him, and now this! And you, too, Mr. Tyng? What is Falmouth coming to?"

Lieutenant Mowatt stepped up and interrupted him. "What did you say about someone running through your kitchen?" He turned to the sheriff. "Was that man in this room when the courier arrived?"

Sheriff Tyng opened his mouth and closed it again. He cast about him for support, but there was none. Finally he made as if to speak, but before he uttered a word there was the sound of the bell ringing from the steeple of Old Jerusalem. The first note was weak, as though the ringer had not got a good pull on the bell-rope, but then it rang out clear and strong.

Old Bryce McLellan started to laugh. "A fig for your secret now, Mr. Lieutenant!" he told Mowatt. "That's my Joe, that is, and he's heard it all!" His laugh changed into a spasm of coughing, and the brigadier and Mr. Deane had to help him to a chair. Mowatt and Sheriff Tyng exchanged glances.

Bryce was breathing again. Preble looked up from where he stood at his side. "Well, Mr. Tyng?" he said. "There will be a company of men formed and ready to march in ten minutes."

"He's right, Captain Mowatt," Coulson put in. "If we don't hurry we won't make it back to our ships at all." He turned to Marston. "Quick, man," he said. "I've a hat and stick here someplace!"

"Right away," Marston replied. He ran to the door and yelled for the girl. "I'll have her get yours, too, shall I, Lieutenant?"

Mowatt settled his coat on his shoulder and followed him. "Yes, do," he said. Tyng looked at him helplessly.

"What do I do with your prisoner, Lieutenant?" he asked.

"Bother the damned prisoner," Mowatt told him impatiently. "You can do what you like with the bastard: hang him, or let him go, but whatever you do, straighten that bloody wig of yours first!" With that he was gone.

Others of both parties followed. Robert and his brothers came to speak with Elizabeth and the captain. "I'll bid you goodbye now," Robert said. "We're meeting at Pote's house in fifteen minutes. I'll answer for you, of course, but the others will understand if you don't come. It's your wedding night, after all." He bent to kiss his sister, but she did not respond. I saw that she was crying.

"Go ahead, William," she said. "Why don't you go with the rest of them? This blasted war is all you men have been able to talk about as long as I can remember. Well, you've got it now! I just hope that you're happy with it!"

Elizabeth fell to sobbing. Ross gave her his handkerchief. She buried her face in it and turned away. When he would have comforted her, she tore herself free and ran to the far end of the room. She stood there in the corner with one hand on the back of a chair and cried. My master watched his new wife unhappily for a few moments before turning back to her brothers. The two from Penobscot seemed extremely uncomfortable with their sister's sudden display of emotion.

"I think that the three of you had best go on without me," Ross said. He glanced at Elizabeth again, and I could see that a deep furrow of sadness had formed between his brows. "This couldn't have happened at a worse time."

Robert gave the other two a meaningful stare and jerked his head at the door. They went to wait in the hall. My impression was that they were just as glad to be going.

"I'm sorry about Elizabeth, of course," Pagan said. He put his hand on Ross's shoulder. "She and I have always been close: much closer than with either of the others. I think I know how she feels. She's been waiting for this day for a long time."

My master nodded abruptly. "She'll get over it," he said. "What else can she do?" There was shouting in the street outside the tavern, and I saw the fleeting reflection of candlelight on polished metal as someone ran by close to the window.

Ross was silent for a time, and then at last he shook his head.

"You know, Robert," he said, "I guess that I never really believed that it would come to this. Not here in Falmouth. Boston always seemed so far away.

"We've had our differences, of course. We always have. Bryce McLellan was my father's friend, but they didn't speak for weeks one year because they disagreed about putting the bell in the church tower. We lived well off the Neck, then; my father said it was a waste of money because we wouldn't be able to hear it. It was terrible. Then the war with the French came, and nobody gave it another thought.

"Then it was Bryce took me in when my father and I fought about Harvard. I didn't have anywhere else to go. William and Joe, they're like my brothers or uncles; took me on my first voyages, they did, and kept me out of trouble in the islands when we got there. They're more like family to me than George ever was. Maybe it's different for you, Robert. You weren't brought up here. Somehow I can't think of the

McLellans as enemies, any more than I do you. When you come right down to it, I've known them longer, even if it was your sister I married instead of Polly. So tell me, Robert, what the hell do I do?"

There was no answer. Ross and I turned to look for Pagan, but he had gone. He must have slipped away while the captain was talking, although neither of us had heard him go.

The captain thought for a space before speaking. "Look, Pyrrhus," he said at length, "this is what I want you to do: run and see the hostler and have him put the horse to the chaise. I want time to talk with Elizabeth anyway. Then go to the house and get the candles lit and the fires started." He stretched out a hand to restrain me. "No, wait," he said. "Listen to me. It's not the old house, the one on Meetinghouse Lane. I've bought a new one. That's why I had you pack all our things. There will have been a wagoner take our boxes down this afternoon. I meant it for a surprise for Elizabeth, but from the way things look now, I'm afraid it won't matter much." He turned his head in her direction and I did the same. Elizabeth was sitting in the chair now. The captain's handkerchief was still in her hand, but she had stopped crying. She seemed to be staring at the opposite wall. Ross continued to watch her as he spoke.

"The house is on Jones Lane," he told me. "The second on the left after Wheeler Riggs's. You know: the small one next to the Widow Clark's. I've laid the fires myself. You'll find a tinderbox on the mantel in the front room if Marston won't lend you a lantern."

A ruffle of drums sounded right outside the inn. Ross went to the window and peered out. "They're forming a company right in the road," he said. "They must mean to hold the jailhouse, unless they plan to march the length of the town. I think Elizabeth and I will wait until they have gone, but you had best go out the back way, just in case." There was another drumroll, and somebody with a fife started in on "The Irish Washerwoman."

"My God," Ross said, looking at the militiamen through the window. "My God! Where will it go from here?"

🌸🌸🌸 25 🌸🌸🌸

THE scene outside was one of great confusion. All the roads that I could see were filled with men: men in every state of dress and undress, men with arms and without; marching men, running men, men riding horses, all traveling in every conceivable direction, but all apparently seized with an urgent need to be someplace else as quickly as possible. It looked to be much the wisest course to stay clear of their path, so when I left the back door of the tavern I went to our house by way of the orchard above the tanyard and the wide hay-field beyond.

From the quiet shelter of the apple trees the commotion in the streets of Falmouth seemed still more senseless and unreal by reason of the contrast. I made the best of my way down the hill through the rank wet grass with one eye on the ground and one on the spectacle. What with one thing and another there was light enough about that the people might have been players and I standing in the stalls.

Nor was sight the only sense to be so occupied, for the night was clamorous with sounds. There were the churchbells, of course, which even now tolled at intervals, the fifes and the drums, men's shouts, the barking of dogs, the neighing of horses. In the large house across from Savage's a baby was crying; at the back door there was a cart into which the family's principal possessions were being loaded in order to carry them into the country. As I passed by they were carrying out a handsome clock in a dark wood case, of which there were only a few in town at the time.

I had no difficulty in finding the house the captain had purchased as it was the only one on Jones Lane that was not showing some kind of illumination. I let myself in and went about the rooms getting candles lit and fires burning. When I had done with the upstairs, I went back down for the captain's bags. There were some others with them that I did not know; these I took to be Elizabeth's, and carried them up as well.

Shortly thereafter my master and Elizabeth arrived. I held the door for them and went out to see to the horse. I wanted him well secured before he was left alone. I returned to find my master waiting alone in the parlor. I remember that he looked very tired.

"You've done well, Pyrrhus," he said, "and I want you to know that I appreciate it. I realize that it has been a long day for you, but I want you to take the chaise back to Brackett's now before you turn in. The boy will be waiting. At least he was supposed to be."

"That's all right," I assured him. "I can manage to get him bedded down by myself if I have to."

"Good. By the way, you've a room to yourself here. It's in the back next to the buttery. It's not much, but there's a bed and a chair, and the window's glass, not oiled paper."

I was pleased, and told him so. He smiled. "You've earned it," he told me. He fought back a yawn. "Bah," he said. "I've had a long day, too. It's sneaked up on me, I guess. Elizabeth won't be very happy about it, but I don't propose to call it a night without knowing that the *Industry* is safe and sound. No telling where Jack Tukey has got without someone to keep an eye on him."

"Look, Captain Ross," I told him. "Why don't I go down to the schooner once I've returned the horse and carriage? If you don't mind my saying so, I think you should stay here." I could tell that he was wavering as I spoke. "Go on," I said. "Mistress Ross needs you."

I have no doubt that it was a difficult choice in a way, but in the end Elizabeth won out. "Thank you," Ross said. "I won't be forgetting. Be careful with that horse, and be sure to send for me at the first sign of trouble. Try and get some sleep while you can, too, or tomorrow you'll wish you had."

The horse proved to be skittish, although I was able to miss the worst of the traffic by going to the bottom of Jones Lane to Fore Street and up Love Lane instead of taking him back by way of Middle Street. He gave me little real trouble until we got to Back Street, where a party of militia had built a bonfire across from the hay scales. The shadows the flames cast nearly sent him off, and if a man had not come out to help me hold him in, he might be running yet.

"Who's that in the chaise?" he said, even before I had time to thank him for his assistance. "Ain't this Brackett's rig?" He peered into the carriage, and I recognized him as Jack Tukey's brother, Benjamin.

"Christ," he said, "it's Will Ross's boy, Pyrrhus. What the hell you doin' in Joshua Brackett's chaise?"

When I explained that I was bringing it back to the owner's stable, Tukey turned to one of the others. "That sound right, Abner?" I looked and saw Abner Dow, who went for a sergeant in Colonel Phinney's regiment.

"Hell," Dow said. "It sounds all right to me. Cap'n just said not to let any Tories out of town tonight, but I guess you could ride along with him if you was minded."

"Not me," said Tukey. "It's too damned cold once you get away from that fire." He stared up at me. "Look, boy," he said, "I'm going to let you go, but mind you come back here right smart when you're done, else I'll make your hide into a cartridge-box."

I did as I was told, and when I came back Tukey bid me warm myself by their fire to show there were no hard feelings. I stopped just long enough to ask if he had seen his brother.

"No," he said. "I ain't seen the jeesly little bastard all day. Ain't he workin' for that cap'n of yours any more? I'll tell you what, though, do you see him, you tell him that I want them two shillin' he owes me by tomorrow. Hard money, mind. You got that?" He gave me an overfamiliar cuff on the head to speed me on my way.

Back Street runs along the most elevated part of the Neck, so that I had a tolerable view of the lower part of the town. My eyes were still a little dazzled by the fire, but my impression was that most of the houses and all of the public buildings were well lit. The main thoroughfares were still crowded with people and conveyances. When I got to Deering's wharf, I found that the *Industry*'s boat was gone. No other was at hand, so I cupped my palms about my mouth and hailed the schooner to see who was aboard.

"Hallo, yourself," came Jack's voice over the water. "Who's there?"

"It's Pyrrhus, Jack," I said. "Come and fetch me, will you?"

"I know it's Pyrrhus," he answered. "Who in hell sounds like that except you? I meant, is there anybody with you?"

"Of course not," I told him. "Now, will you come or won't you?"

"I don't know if I can. Mr. Grizzell, he said not to let anybody on board."

"I didn't mean Pyrrhus nor the captain, you cheese-paring nincompoop!" I confess I was glad to hear Grizzell's voice. "On'y strangers.

Honest to God, boy, sometimes I wonder if that's a head on your shoulders, or a sixty-eight-pound shot with eyes!" I heard some clumsy-sounding noises, as if metal on wood. "For God's sake, Jack," Grizzell said then, "give me that musket before you do yourself an injury! You won't see no redcoats in the boat."

In a matter of a few minutes I was aboard. Grizzell gave Tukey his musket and set him watching from the forecastle.

"Sometimes I wonder about that boy," he said softly when Jack had gone. "I figured it wa'n't such a good idea to leave him be with all the excitement ashore, so I come down as soon as I could get out of Marston's." Grizzell shook his head in wonder. "Had all the arms broke out, he did: six muskets and four brace of pistols, an' all loaded with buck and ball. He was plumb disappointed I wasn't somebody he could shoot."

I nodded. "How's things look?"

"See for yourself. Waterfront's damn near the quietest spot in town. Shipyard seems to be all lit up, and the *John and Mary*, too, but I ain't seen so much's a spark from the *Canceaux*. Guess Mowatt don't want to give nobody no targets. Folks ashore look to feel the same way. There's hell's own amount of 'em comin' and goin' on the streets, but near's I can tell they're staying clear of the wharves.

"You reckon it's true?" he asked. "I mean, burning the town and all?"

"I don't know," I told him. "Englishmen don't do that kind of thing, do they?" When he didn't answer, I asked again.

"Mobs do," he said. "An army ain't but a mob in fancy coats." Ashore fife and drums struck up a military air. He smiled lopsidedly. "Fancy coats," he said. "Ours ain't even got that."

For a while neither of us had anything to add. Finally I yawned. Grizzell laughed and punched me lightly on the arm. "Well," he said, "we ain't neither of us getting no smarter standing here. You look as if you could use some sleep. You want me to tell Jack to run you ashore, or were you planning to bunk down here?"

I thought longingly of the soft new bed that awaited me in the house on Jones Lane, and of my familiar berth in the *Industry*'s snug forecastle. Indeed I was tired, but the old familiar signs told me that I would not sleep. "You go ahead," I told him. "You and Jack have been up as long as I have. I'll wake you when I'm ready."

Grizzell shrugged and left. I heard him say something to Tukey, and then a clatter as they went below. What became of the musket Jack had I neither knew nor cared. Perhaps he slept with it so as to be ready.

When they had gone, I walked up to the foredeck and leaned on the starboard cathead. On the Neck all was as it had been. Anything could have been happening, though from what I saw the people might just as well have been running in place. I never heard that all their efforts amounted to a clipped shilling. I wonder if mine had been any more significant.

I tried until the dawn to imagine what might have happened in Lexington and in Concord, and what might come to pass as a result. At last I gave up and just watched the commotion on the shore. All my thoughts kept getting tangled around the memory of a slender figure in blue satin, as desired and unattainable as freedom itself. When the sun came up over the islands I found myself wondering if Sarah had heard the news, and whether the new day would bring a more authentic account of Wednesday's events.

I shouted down the hatchway to Tukey and had him row me back to Deering's so that I might have a fire ready to prepare breakfast when the captain and his bride awoke. Later he and I went down to the schooner together. He stayed only long enough to be certain that all was as it should be. When we returned to the shore, we found Joseph McLellan waiting.

I had not told Ross how McLellan had happened to escape the night before. Joseph seemed to take it for granted that I had helped him on my master's instructions, and I was glad when the captain made no attempt to disabuse him of the notion.

"Had the devil's own time finding you," McLellan said after his preliminary greeting. "Didn't know you had moved. Finally found the house, and Elizabeth said you'd come down here. How's married life treating you?"

Ross said it was fine so far.

"Well," said Joseph, "the redcoats didn't give you much of a leg up, did they? The reason I come by, I wanted you to know that another express arrived early this morning. News is all over town by now, most likely, but I figured you might not have heard it yet, you being so busy and all." He grinned, and Ross blushed. Then McLellan's face became serious.

"Best we can tell," he continued, "there was about a thousand regulars, sent from Boston to capture John Hancock and Sam Adams before they went to the Congress in Philadelphia.

"A thousand men, Will, just to catch two! Gage must want 'em perishing bad. Anyway, someone got wind of it, and warned them, so they got away safe. We're sure of that, but afterward it's not so clear.

"It seems that Hancock was staying with the minister in Lexington. Word is when the lobsters come and found him and Adams gone they fired into the meetinghouse and killed three of the people inside. I guess they went on to Concord then. Both of the riders say they did, so it must be, but whether they burned the whole of it or not is anybody's guess. The one came this mornin' was considerable het up about it: says they burned the houses with people still in 'em. Thirteen in one house, he says, including children. Children, Will! I don't know, but I hear they bayonetted one old man who was in bed with a broken thigh. A deacon, he was, by God! and another man who was confined to a chair. What he said about the women don't bear repeating." He grimaced at the thought.

"I never heard the like of it, Will. Worse'n what they used to tell about Father Rale and his Indians when I was a nipper! I don't say it's all true, mind: the fellows that come seem pretty confused. The committee's sent one of the Musseys express to Salem to try and find out what is and what isn't.

"One thing about it, though: we won't have to listen to folks laughing about the militia no more. The country's all roused up, Will! There was four, maybe five thousand militia turned out to chase the redcoats back to Boston. Killed a pack of 'em, too, I shouldn't wonder! They're still coming, too: coming from Connecticut, even. Word is they're going into Boston and pitch Gage and all his damned soldiers right out into the harbor. That's what the courier says, and there's more'n a few right here in Falmouth that hope he's right. Matter of fact, that's what I wanted to see you about. Some of the boys from town here have volunteered to go down and give 'em a hand. Probably be about sixty, seventy men. I got the job of finding transport for 'em, and I was wondering could we count on you and the *Industry* as far as Salem."

At this the captain hesitated. "God, Joe," he said, "I don't know. It isn't what you'd call good timing. When were they planning to go, first of the week sometime?"

"Today," McLellan told him. "Soon's they can. I guess maybe the major'll go with 'em. But that's all right. I don't really need her anyhow, and to tell you the truth, I think you did enough last night. No tellin' what would have happened if Mowatt had had a free hand. I really just come by to give you a chance to get in on it before everything's over and done. Kind of put a stop to the talk that had been going around about you and Coulson's crowd. You know how it is." He took a sheaf of papers from his coat pocket. "Look," he said, making a mark on one of them with a stubby pencil, "here's what I'll do: I'll put you down as a 'maybe,' now. It'll look better. Then if you decide you want to go, you come and see me." He put the papers away and clapped Ross on the back.

"I've got to be going," he told him. "You take care of yourself, and give my regards to that pretty new wife of yours, will you?" He smiled again. "Hell," he said, "anybody with eyes can see that you didn't marry her for her politics!" He was still chuckling when he turned the corner onto Fore Street and was gone.

It took Ross some time to recover his composure. "Well," he said at last, "it seems that I've become some sort of a conspirator myself now. What's all this that I did for my friend Joseph and the committee last night?" He listened impassively while I recounted what had occurred.

"It was all I could think of at the time," I told him. "There we were, and there was Mowatt. He might have tried to haul all of them down to the *Canceaux* in another minute. I knew you wouldn't want that, nor to have your wedding supper turned into a battle. I thought it was my duty to help. After all, the McLellans were your guests."

Ross thought it over. "Yes," he said, "they were, and they were friends before that. Not that I would expect to have a king's officer treat peaceable Englishmen that way, but after what you told me, who knows what to believe anymore?"

"After yesterday," I said, "committeemen won't be 'peaceable Englishmen' anymore. Not to Mowatt, they won't."

"Most of that's not true," Ross reminded me sternly. "Even Joe said it wasn't. I don't want you spreading rumors. Most likely word will come tomorrow that it was all blown out of shape like the other alarms we've had. I certainly hope so, anyway. But to get back to this other thing, I think you were right. Someone might have been hurt, else, and there were women in the room. Next time, though, I'd be obliged if you'd take the time to let me know before you get involved. It isn't you the king'll hang if things get out of hand.

"For now, let's try to keep things quiet, all right? Not a word of this to Elizabeth. She's upset enough as it is. She wants me to drop everything and take her brothers back to their place up the Penobscot. I'll do it if I have to, I guess; the last thing I need is trouble with her family. I can't see it doing me much good with the rest of the town. Christ! I'm damned either way. I just hope that Joe has enough sense to keep his mouth shut about how much help I've been."

If Joseph did not, then Pagan never heard of it, or else he found other things to worry about. All through Saturday and into Sunday the country people poured into town, clamoring for passage to Newburyport or Salem to join the army, or seeking to buy up provision against harder times to come. By Sunday noon Falmouth resembled an armed camp. The reports that had been sent out Friday had lost nothing in the repeating, so that the farther the people had come, the worse the stories they told. To add to the confusion, one of the vessels that had been sent away to the southward returned that day with a fresh crop of rumors which quickly made the rounds. I think that it was only the fear of the *Canceaux* that held the people in check at the last; when Elizabeth's brother came by the house, it was mostly to rail against Mowatt for not making some show of force.

"He's missing his chance," Pagan told my master. "Every day that goes by, there's more militia drifting into town, and the damned committeemen cart more of their things off to Gorham or Windham where they'll be safe no matter what. By the time he does do something there won't be one of 'em who has half-a-joe's-worth of goods left where he could get at 'em. All there'll be is what belongs to those of us who are still loyal. And what if Thompson or somebody shows up and starts trouble? We'll be the only ones with anything to lose."

"Now that's not quite true, Robert," Ross said. "It's not, and you know it. They'll still have their homes and shops to consider. They can't move them. What's more, I'm just as glad that Mowatt hasn't started anything. No, hear me out! What's he got on that ship of his, anyway? Eight guns: probably nine-pounders, and forty, maybe fifty men. No more than that. Not enough to protect you from the committee and the others, but plenty enough to make 'em mad."

Pagan waved aside his objections. "All the more reason for acting now," he said. "The sooner the better, while Freeman's lot still has as much as possible to lose. The more they get out of here, the braver they'll get. You notice they don't let us take any of our things out. They've got the militia watching the roads to make certain. Why doesn't he do the same thing?" When Ross started to answer, Pagan raised a hand again and went on talking. "I know, Will, I know. Tom Coulson and I have been over all of it. If he put a party ashore they'd be captured for certain. The road's too far from the water for him to cover them. All right; but there must be something he can do. I tell you, Will, he's missing his chance, and what's more, he's missing ours as well."

The captain shook his head glumly. "I don't know, Robert. Maybe he's waiting for orders. Maybe he expects to get help. It could be anything. I'll say it again, though: I'm glad he's taking things slow instead of doing whatever comes to mind and then sailing away if it goes wrong. I hope it never comes to that, but if it does, folks like you and Tom Coulson'll be the lucky ones. You can pack up and go somewhere else, and all you've lost is a house and some furniture. Maybe not even that. Sell the house, maybe, and load the furniture on board the *Minerva*. Mowatt could protect you long enough for that.

"What happens then, Robert? To the rest of us here in Falmouth when Mowatt's gone to Halifax and you're at Penobscot with your brothers?"

"There would be room for you at Penobscot," Pagan reminded him gently. "After all, you're family now as well."

Ross's face grew thoughtful. "Thank you," he said. "I mean it. I suppose I should have expected you to say as much. The fact of the matter is that I don't really want to leave. I wouldn't have bought a house if I had. I was born in Falmouth, Robert: it's my home. I guess it's as simple as that."

"Nothing's that simple any more, Will. People won't let it be. You're hoping that you won't have to make a choice. That you can go right along, doing business as usual. You're going to have to choose. As far as leaving Falmouth is concerned, I don't believe it will come to that. It may be a little ugly while people get this Lexington thing out of their systems, but they can't reasonably expect that their ragtag militia can hold out against England. You wait: in a week or so that army they talk about will have gone home for the spring planting. Then what? The governor makes a few arrests, hangs one or two of the worst, and ships the rest off to England. By summer it will all be over and done. But the day will come sooner and there will be less trouble for all of us if men in positions of authority — our Lieutenant Mowatt, for example — would give these sunshine soldiers a reminder of what it means to take up arms against your rightful sovereign. Not thirty years ago the old king gave Scotland such a one at Culloden as will not soon be forgotten.

"You are fortunate in America, Will, to have no Young Pretender. There is no reason I can see for things to go so far. I, like you, have every intention of living out the rest of my days in Falmouth. If needs must, however, there is Penobscot, and I want you to know that the offer is still open."

The house on Jones Lane, like the one on Meetinghouse Lane before it, faced west. Pagan looked about as if noticing for the first time the long shadows cast by the afternoon sun. "My God, Will," he said, getting hastily to his feet. "I had no idea it was so late. They'll be looking for me at Coulson's by now." He shook his head. "I hope these troubles are soon ended. Getting so I'm worse than an old woman once I start talking.

"Look, Will, why don't you come down with me? We shouldn't be long, but it's pretty important; we want to be ready for the town meeting tomorrow. It affects you as much as anyone, you know, and frankly it wouldn't hurt if people were to see you there. Besides, if we decide to send a deputation aboard the *Canceaux* like Tom wants, well, it might be worth something to have you along. You seemed to hit it off pretty well with young Mowatt the other day."

Ross was looking the other way when he answered, but it seemed to me that his voice sounded a trifle strained. "No," he said, "no, I really can't. Come by afterward for supper, if you feel like it. Elizabeth would be glad to have you, of course: she's feeling much better today, and when she's gone to bed you can tell me what went on at the meeting."

Pagan nodded. "How is Elizabeth, anyway? Here she's my own sister, and I've been too wrapped up in this other business to ask."

"Fine, I think," the captain said. "She's just tired, if you ask me. I guess none of us realized how hard she had been working on the

wedding. A little more rest and she'll be right as rain." He went with
Robert to the door. When he came back he slumped down in his chair
and poured himself another drink. I waited to see if he wanted to talk,
but he just sat there, silent and rather thoughtful-looking. Well and
good, I said to myself; from what I had heard of the conversation he
had just had, my master had plenty of things to think about. I went
about my business then, and left him to his thoughts.

✳✳✳ 26 ✳✳✳

OF course there was no way in which I might have attended, but
from what I have heard from those who did, the town meeting
was as hotly contested as any debate in the Congress or Parliament. In
the end it was rumor and not oratory that carried the day for the
Liberty party, and all manner of warlike measures were taken. Moneys
were voted in order to pay the militia to exercise for two hours a day
three or four days in the week, according to whether the men in
question lived off the Neck or on it, and to pay bounties of twenty-
four shillings to any such who would answer the call to march out of
the county when required. Funds were needed for the purchase of
provisions, again in alarmingly short supply, and the selectmen received
authorization to borrow "instantly" one hundred thirteen pounds, six
shillings, and eightpence, that powder might be bought for the
magazine.

All these things we lacked, but rumors there were in plenty. Could
the Liberty Boys have filled their haversacks and cartouche-boxes with
rumors, great deeds might have been done, but as it was the people
must have sat through the meeting with one ear cocked to hear the
sound of British cannon. We were told that all of Massachusetts from
Beverly to Newbury had been put to the sword, and I have learned
since that no fewer than seven express riders had come to Portsmouth
in New Hampshire with orders for the militia to march, each in a

different direction. Falmouth in turn had had word from York that Portsmouth itself was in flames, the work of Barkley and his *Scarborough* frigate. Mowatt having come to Falmouth from the Piscataqua, where he had been under Barkley's command, it seemed only too likely that we would be the next unwilling recipients of his superior's attentions.

It is less than surprising, then, that panic was the result that evening when two vessels were sighted coming in between the islands of the outer harbor. It started among the country people and spread; the roads were soon choked, and it is a miracle that very few of those seeking to leave the town were injured.

Elizabeth would not suffer the captain to leave the house, so again it was I who went down to the *Industry*, where I found that the exodus seemed ill founded. The two were sloops, not ship-rigged like the *Scarborough* and the *Canceaux*, and given the quarter in which the wind was lying, Grizzell and I agreed that they could hardly have come from Portsmouth, which was fifty miles and more to the southward.

This in fact proved to be the case. The two were tenders which had been sent by the admiral in Boston to dismantle the Province fort at the narrows of the Penobscot. They had left some two weeks before, performed their mission, and, all-unknowing of the battle or skirmish that had taken place but five days earlier, were returning with the fort's cannon and powder stowed in their holds. When the truth became known, the people seemingly felt so ashamed by their groundless fears that I understand it was only through the greatest exertions that they could be restrained from mounting an immediate attack on Mowatt and these others.

The tenders were already gone when the captain and I went on business the next morning. Apart from the fact that George Lyde, the collector of the customs, with his deputy, Dornett, had been driven to shelter aboard the *Canceaux*, very little seemed to have been accomplished on either side. Some of the people were claiming that his retreat was a victory of sorts, but for his part Lyde refused to issue any clearance until he should be allowed to do so at the customs-house without let or hindrance from the committees, so that it appeared to me that it was a drawn battle.

Pagan himself was in a remarkably good mood. When Ross entered he put off his spectacles and put on his coat, leaving the store to his clerk and ushering us into the inner office.

" 'Tis an ill wind indeed that has no good in it," he said when he had closed the door. "I had no idea how much hard money there was left in this section. Simply no idea. Guineas and shillings, Spanish dollars, joes and half-joes from Portugal, louis d'or: of course I've had to take a lot of paper, too, but some of that's bound to be made good, and it's all the de'il of a lot easier to take with me than the goods on the shelf." I noticed that his speech had lapsed slightly, harking more of his birth in Glasgow than he had wont to let show.

"Take with you?" Ross asked, accepting the glass of wine Pagan gave him. "Are you decided, then, upon leaving?"

"Not at all," was the reply, "though it's no' been far from my mind since I heard about Lyde and Dornett." He put down his own drink to look for something amid the papers on his desk. "Here," he said, "have you seen this? It came in from Boston this morning, and it's supposed to be authentic: damn my eyes, what have I done with it? Well, no matter, the gist of it is that the casualties in last week's battle were as many as two hundred of the regulars to fifty provincials! I found it difficult to credit until I read that the militia, so far from fighting honorably, hid behind the fences and walls which lined the lanes, and so were able to kill and maim without receiving any injury in return. When Lord Percy came out with a small train of cannon, they ran: ran like rabbits!

"Bother the damned thing anyway! Well, William, what of that? It's not exactly the same story you had of your friends in the committee of correspondence, is it?"

"No, Robert," Ross admitted. "It's not. But it sounds sensible as hell."

Pagan was swallowing when he heard this, and nearly choked. "Honestly, Will," he said when he could talk once more, "you've got to be more careful of what you're saying."

Ross regarded his brother-in-law curiously. "A moment ago," he reminded him, "you were talking about leaving yourself."

"Was I? Oh, I suppose so, but you mustn't take all that seriously. If I did, it would only be until things hereabout had a chance to calm down a little. You know, William and Thomas were very persuasive when they were here about my joining them up on the Penobscot. Now that the fort has been razed and the truck-house closed, there will be a deal more business to be done up there; a smart man could make money. Think of it! Masts from the interior, the Indian trade! If the war lasted long enough, you could make it into another Halifax, Will, and the four of us would own it all! You'd be captain of a mast ship, like the *Minerva*, instead of that piddling little schooner."

"The *Industry*'s hardly piddling," Ross told him a bit stiffly. "She's near seventy ton, and as well-found as any her size in Falmouth."

"I didn't mean anything by that, Will, for goodness' sake, only she's not quite the same, now, is she? Anyway, think it over."

"I have, Robert, and though I thank you for the offer, my answer's what it has been: Falmouth's my home, and I've no intention of leaving. But I did notice one thing: you spoke of a war a moment ago. Yes, you did. You know it will go no further, but I can't help thinking there must have been something more that came from Boston this morning. What's happened down there that makes you call one battle a war?"

Pagan took him by the arm and drew him close. "I don't know how much of this the bunch in the library knows," he said. "The communications between them and what passes for a government in Concord don't seem to be very reliable. In any case, I want to do what business I can before they do hear. You can't tell what that bastard Freeman will do when he does." He walked over to stare bleakly out the window. When he spoke his words came out low and toneless as though he were trying to minimize their importance.

"The word from Boston is that there are twenty thousand militia camped outside the city."

"Twenty thousand!" Pagan winced as the captain spoke, and Ross lowered his voice before continuing. "Twenty thousand! My God, Robert, that's an army! Gage himself can't have more than five!"

"Four," Pagan confirmed. "Perhaps less with the casualties, I don't know. Of course, Boston's nearly an island, and there's the navy to help: thank God for that, at least. Otherwise they might take it into their heads to try something foolish, and then either way there would be no stopping this without ruining the whole country and everyone in it. You have to try to put it into perspective. Some of them will be old men, and some still boys. I've heard there are Negroes, even, and Indians! You can't begin to imagine that a rabble like that could stand up to the king's troops, Will. Not for a minute."

"But twenty thousand men, Robert! I can hardly believe it. That's three times what Wolfe had to take Quebec with: maybe the largest army this country's ever seen! And even with your old men and boys and all, there will be three parts of them able to fight. Hell, Robert, Pyrrhus there could carry a musket if he had to, and probably be no worse at it than some raw Irishman in a red coat. With odds like four or five to one, anything could happen. Good Lord, last week it very nearly did!"

Pagan swung around to face him. "What the devil's getting into you, Will? You're beginning to sound like one of them yourself."

"Maybe that's because I am. No, listen! I don't mean that way. But it bothers me to hear all the time how New Englanders can't do anything as well as Englishmen born someplace else. I don't like it, Robert! I don't like it because it isn't true. There isn't a shipyard in England that could turn out a schooner the likes of the *Industry*, no, nor any fat lieutenant in a blue coat that could sail here as well as me!"

"That's not the point, Will," Elizabeth's brother said. "It isn't men like you in that army."

"You think not? Joe McLellan would have gone himself if he weren't needed here, and his brother, too. Between them and their father they taught me near all I know. Joe showed me the list, Robert: there's others just as good. Not all of 'em, but enough to fight if they're led. That's what it all comes down to, you know. Navy or no, Gage is in trouble if they've a general worthy of the name. Have you heard who's in command?"

"Nothing certain. They seem to be milling around down there like so many cattle. Thank God for that, at least!" Pagan sighed and shook his head.

"The hell of it is, Will, that you're right. Up to a point at least. I haven't wanted to admit it, but this thing seems to be getting out of hand. I guess that's why I'm blowing hot and cold all the time. It's the same old story: half-measures, always too little and too late. From a few street-brawlers throwing snowballs to a few dozen apprentices dressed like Indians throwing some chests of tea into Boston Harbor. What does the government do? Nothing. Now there are twenty thousand of them camped on Gage's doorstep, and he doesn't have half the men he should have.

"I'm worried. But it doesn't do any good to say so, does it? That just makes things worse. So I do what any prudent man, any loyal subject, would do, Will. I put up a bold front and make money while

I can. Meanwhile I'm writing letters to General Gage and to everyone I know at home, trying to get them to take this damned thing seriously. Seriously enough to send Gage the troops he needs to end it once and for all. You can say what you want about your New England militia, Will, but I've seen enough of them to know what they're like: every fifth man a general, and more colonels than privates. It might just take them longer to decide who they want to lead them than it will for Parliament to ship Gage an army to beat 'em with." He picked up his glass again and drank. "You know," he said when he had done, "maybe things aren't so bad after all. Twenty thousand men, that's four thousand generals by my count. By the time they've finished fighting each other, maybe Gage won't have to."

The captain swirled the last of his wine in the bottom of the glass and watched it thoughtfully. "Twenty thousand men," he said. "I wonder what old Freeman will make of it when he hears."

I had listened to all of this and had said nothing, but made shift to see Sarah that evening. From her I learned that in fact the major had known before any of us, word having come express from Watertown, where the Provincial Congress had moved to be closer to the army. General Artemas Ward had left his sickbed at Shrewsbury, she said, and was come to take command, but soon there might be no army at all. Although men had marched from towns all over New England to harry the redcoats back to Boston, the force of which Pagan and Ross had spoken was melting away at an alarming rate.

"But why?" I demanded. "Where are they going?"

Sarah shook her head. "Home, I guess. Some of the men from Falmouth are back already. They said it was all over before they got there, so they came home." She laid her head on my shoulder and held me close. "Oh, Pyrrhus," she said, "I'm so confused! I was happy when I heard about the fight at Lexington. I mean, I was sorry for the men who were killed and the families who lost their houses, but I thought that if there was a battle then there would be a war, and then we could be together! Now as soon as the men get there, they leave and come home. Major Freeman was very angry, but there was nothing he could do and so he let them go. If that's all that happens, why was he so happy about the enlistment papers that came this morning?"

"Enlistment papers?" I said, only half listening. "What enlistment papers?"

"The ones that came from Watertown. The men are supposed to

serve until the end of the year, but what difference does it make? Won't they just come home when they've a mind to, like these others?"

"I don't think so," I said. "Mostly they just turn out, sign the muster book, and go, don't they? I think this is something different; and the way Major Freeman acted tends to prove it. What did the orders say? Did you see them? Damn! I forgot. You can't read. Did you hear anything about them?"

She screwed up her face to think. "A lot of nonsense at first," she said. "All about how many men to a company, and how many companies to a regiment, that kind of thing. Then there was some sort of oath, and a note that some of the Falmouth men in camp had taken it, but I forget how many. One of the people who had come to see the major said he thought he could raise a company from Spurwink and Purpooduck Parish, and ran off to get cracking."

I nodded. "I was right, then. I think so, at least. It's hard to tell without seeing the oath. But it sounds to me as though they mean to have a regular army, and that can only mean one thing." I gave her a quick hug and stood up. "I've got to go," I said. "The captain should hear about this, and I need to figure out how much I can tell him without bringing you into it."

As it happened, I needn't have worried, for when you give an officer beating orders to raise men, the word soon spreads. I stopped at the King's Head before going back to the house and found it all common knowledge. There was more to hear as well, for Captain Greenleaf was newly in from Salem with copies of the *Gazette* not two days old. The landlord had put one on the wall with the other notices. It had two lines of black coffins at the top of the page and wide black borders. In letters I could have seen from across the room save for the crowd and the smoke it read, "A BLOODY BUTCHERY, BY THE BRITISH TROOPS: OR, THE RUNAWAY FIGHT OF THE REGULARS." Seemingly every man there who could read had read it, and those who could not had had it read to them. The talk was all of war, and of how long it would be before the British were beaten. I sat and listened. If it was only talk, it was heady stuff. To listen to them there should not have been a man left in town at the end of a month. Some spoke of going for soldiers, while others among them were in favor of persuading this captain or that to fit out a privateer.

"That's the idea, shipmates," one ill-favored fellow insisted. "War's war, I say, on'y why walk when you can ride? 'Sides, my old man went soldierin' in the French wars, and never a penny o' prize money did he make. If on'y he'd 'a' gone privateerin', why, I'd own this tavern 'stead of t'other way round. On'y take my advice, shipmates, an' bide your time! Your chance'll come soon enough."

He had risen from his seat to speak, but belike he had taken aboard more rum than was wise for him, for he slipped in sitting down again so that the rest laughed and went on with their talk about the great deeds they would do as soon as they were in sight of an Englishman. Still, they must have found their own reasons for waiting, as the week came to an end with the *Canceaux* still lying unmolested in the harbor. Sunday her captain came ashore for divine services as was his habit, and went for a walk upon Munjoy's Hill. Any person who has spent much time on shipboard knows the pleasure he must have had in so doing, but I own I thought it an odd sort of war indeed in which an enemy officer might walk abroad unchallenged. I did not know what to make of it, but found myself wondering whether all that we heard were not of a piece with the hysterical report of Indians, which had lately come in from Royalston, fifteen miles or so to the eastward. A woman there claimed to have seen fifty of them at the least, all armed and painted, but when the men turned out they could not find so much as a feather.

In truth I do not think that anyone in Falmouth knew what to believe and what not to believe, with the result that tempers became mercurial in the extreme. At one moment the Whigs in town were rejoicing at word that the people in New York had risen against the garrison, there, but the next day they were nearly unmanned by hearing that General Carleton was supposed to be en route with an army from Canada. Elizabeth's brother, when we saw him, alternated between crowing over this last and cursing Colonel Thompson for a barbarian, for Lieutenant Mowatt had told him of a letter from Brunswick or Long Reach wherein Thompson had been accused of burying alive the mast-agent Parry and four other Tories. Fortunately this tale was soon disproved. Parry and some others had indeed been taken, but they were treated no worse than could be expected. What was undoubtedly true, however, was that the carpenters and laborers who were finishing the work on the *Minerva* had largely been induced to stay away, so that her completion had been delayed. Nor had Captain

Coulson been able to procure seamen to man her, offer in wages what he would. Of course he and his faction blamed Freeman and the others for this circumstance, and not without cause. There was no question but that the committee had done everything short of actual violence to hinder him. In the end Coulson had sent the *John and Mary* to Marblehead and to Salem in hopes of finding a crew. As April ended we looked to see her daily; though no one could know what success she might have had, her going had been but one more reason that each faction had to resent the other.

May 2 was the day that the estrangement between their positions finally became too great to admit of any other. I remember the day very clearly; we had just heard from Boston that the people there had been compelled by General Gage to surrender all their arms. Just after noon Joseph McLellan came to the door of the house on Jones Lane and asked to see my master.

The captain was at his meat, but I could see from McLellan's manner that this was no idle call. I let him into the parlor and told Ross that it was he who had come. The captain rose with his napkin still in his hand and, making his excuses to Elizabeth, went to see what was the matter.

In the few moments I had been out of the room, McLellan had risen from the chair in which he had seated himself and begun to pace the floor. When I opened the door, he looked up. I stood back so the captain could enter.

"I thought I should come myself, Will," Joseph said without preamble. "I didn't want you to get the wrong idea."

"The wrong idea about what, Joe? Look, how about a glass of wine or something? Pyrrhus, see what Mr. McLellan will have to drink."

I started forward, but Joseph waved me back. "Nothing for me, thank you, Will," he said. "Anyway, I'll just be a minute and then you can go back to your dinner.

"What I came about is this: the committee has decided that everyone in town must appear before it and declare their sentiments in public. I said everyone, Will; this doesn't mean that you're under suspicion, regardless of who your wife is related to. I've seen to that this far, and I'll keep on doing it. What I thought was that it might look a good deal better if you came on your own, before they sent someone to fetch you, and just sort of set the record straight. I've known you long enough, but there's others on the committee who don't hardly know you at all. They're apt to judge on appearances, if you take my meaning, and they're determined that life around here is going to be, shall we say uncomfortable, for those who are not shown to be well disposed to the cause of liberty. Why don't you think it over for an hour or so and then go on up? What do you say?"

My master took a breath and expelled it slowly through pursed lips. "I'm obliged to you for coming, Joe," he said. "I can think of some I'd have pitched out into the street if they'd brought me a summons like that in the name of liberty. But I know you've come as a friend, so I'm speaking plainly. I don't like it, Joe. I've helped the committee when I could, and all I've asked of them was to be left alone to sail my damned schooner and try to make an honest living. I don't like taxes any more than any man among 'em. When they passed the association, I went along, even though it cost me money. Now I've a wife to support, and I can't even get a clearance to leave Falmouth because they've driven the customs people on board the *Canceaux*. I don't need to tell you what that means, Joe. You're a seaman, too. But just how in hell am I supposed to live if I can't sail for fear of being taken for a smuggler by the first cruiser I meet?

"You know who's making money in Falmouth right now? I'll tell you: Elizabeth's brother is. It's coming in faster than he can count it. The Oxnards are making money, Joe: so are the Potes, and all the rest of the Tories, because they had the biggest stocks of goods in town when all this started. I guess Tom Coulson's not making any money right now, but as soon as that ship of his is finished he'll make it faster than anybody, because if there is a war the navy will need all the masts he can cram on board of her.

"There are a few other people that are doing all right, too, Joe, only I don't guess they'd like to hear that I've figured it out. Some of 'em will be there in the library chamber when I go up there this afternoon. Don't look so shocked, Joe. I haven't heard that the major or his father have lost any weight recently, have you? Don't worry, though; I won't say anything stupid when I'm there. All I want from them in return is just to be left alone."

There was an uneasy silence. Finally it was Ross himself who broke it. "Oh, hell," he said. "Here you come to try to do me a favor, and what do I do? Let's have a drink and forget it, all right?" He nodded, and I brought over the tray with a case-bottle of brandy from the French islands. He poured a tot into two of the glasses and held one out to McLellan. "I'll be a good boy, Joe. Here, let's see: what shall we drink to?"

McLellan took the glass and held it up against the light. "Not to liberty, I guess," he said with a sudden wintry smile. "How about 'old friends' instead?"

🙧🙥🙧🙥 27 🙣🙡🙣🙡

OTHERS among the committeemen passed word to their friends in the town as well. These in turn acted according to the dictates of their several consciences, with the result that while most of the citizens of Falmouth gave the required assurances, some twenty, more or less, of the most prominent Tories repaired on board the *Canceaux* for protection.

Sarah had told me that the committee was furious when they were told of this, and Major Freeman still more than the rest, so that he raved against the Tories, saying with John the Baptist, " 'O generation of vipers, who hath warned you to flee from the wrath to come?' " In the end most of them returned to their homes, but the Reverend Mr. Wiswell, whose holy orders in the Church of England had included an oath of loyalty to the Crown, said that he could not. He came on shore afterward on at least two occasions, but his announced purpose was to sail with Lieutenant Mowatt when at last the completion of the *Minerva* should make it possible.

That Mowatt should have to leave was inevitable, and the fact occasioned great uneasiness among those in town who supported the king's government. Elizabeth's brother had joined with the others in a petition to Gage and Admiral Graves for continued protection; on Wednesday, which would have been the third of the month, he and Edward Oxnard brought it to the house.

At first Elizabeth seemed delighted to see them, but when she found that they had come on business she professed herself to be fatigued, and retired to her room. The men seated themselves again. Ross read the petition through and handed it back.

"I'm sorry, Robert," he said. "You know that I can't sign this. It would be like setting stuns'ls when there's a squall coming: a good seaman knows when to heave to and let it pass him by."

Pagan folded the brief and put it back into his pocket. "What about the *Industry*?" he asked. "She's the only decked vessel in Falmouth that's in any case to sail."

"That's right," Oxnard put in. "And you needn't worry about clearances, either. Lieutenant Mowatt's promised us a safe-conduct for the bearer."

My master shook his head. "I don't see how I can just now," he told them. "That lower gudgeon on the rudder's badly worn. I really should have replaced it when I had her out of the water before, but I was in too much of a hurry. Besides, if you ask me, half the trouble we've had in Falmouth comes from having that ship here. Why don't you just let her go? No matter what you do, she can't stay forever, and Joe McLellan tells me he's certain the committee will listen to reason if you will. Go see 'em, Robert. Talk to 'em while you're still in a position to. They'll let you be if that's what it takes to get Mowatt out of town."

Elizabeth's brother signaled for me to bring his hat and stood up "Come on, Edward," he said. "We seem to be wasting the captain's time." They went out together, but no sooner were they through the door than Pagan left his companion standing in the lane and came back inside on the pretext of looking for a lost snuffbox. He made but the merest show of searching and then took Ross by the arm.

"You want to watch yourself," Pagan said. His speech had broadened again. "You're playing with fire, Will; when folk do that they have a way of getting burned." He looked to the captain for a reply, but when Ross said nothing, he threw up his hands.

"All right," Pagan told him. "I wouldn't ha' said anything but for Elizabeth's sake. From now on, if you want my help, then say so. Otherwise you go to hell whatever way you like. I won't be stopping you." He left then, and slammed the front door behind him.

The next day Sheriff Tyng was not to be found in the town. Around midday it became known that he and one of the officers from the *Canceaux* had taken a boat and were gone to Boston to deliver the Tories' petition. A number of the more inflammatory people took up arms and went down to the docks, where they were seen by the officer on duty aboard Mowatt's ship, who caused a few turns to be taken upon the spring to her cable. This brought her guns to bear, already loaded and run out as they had been for some days, so that prudence prevailed once more and the crowd retired to a less exposed position. Still, there were many in the town that were heard to complain that the committee was too cautious by half, and that something should have been done to teach the lieutenant a lesson. Thereafter the crew of the *Canceaux* stayed at their quarters day and night, and though the people on shore were under arms as well, they were apparently content to watch and to complain.

How much Elizabeth had heard of her brother's argument with my master I have no way of knowing, but she was so sorely stricken with the vapors that she kept to her room through the first of the next week. The captain blamed her ill health on the weather, which was uncommonly backward for the season, and bid me bring her her meals on a tray. This I would not have minded save for one thing. The room was kept closed, with a fire burning at all hours to drive off the dampness and the chill, my master holding these to be prejudicial to so delicate a constitution as hers. In consequence Elizabeth seldom wore a bed-gown over her chemise or shift, and I noticed that she was decidedly careless about drawstrings and the like. Indeed, it was as though she noticed my presence not at all, the result being that I was rather more aware of hers than was proper for a man to be. With Sarah on Sunday I was ill tempered and churlish for reasons I found impossible to explain.

Late on Monday afternoon Joseph McLellan stopped to pass the time of day; he brought with him news enough, though he admitted that little of it was deemed reliable. When he was getting ready to go, he asked after Elizabeth's health. The captain shrugged.

"A little out of sorts, I am afraid, Joe: probably just some female complaint, or perhaps a slight derangement of the digestion. She says she will have no doctor, so there's nothing to do but wait. I'm certain it will pass of its own once spring is truly upon us."

McLellan meditated on this for a time. "You know, Will," he offered, "it may be that what she needs is a tonic. The south side of Munjoy's Hill is fair alive with greens among the grasses: we boiled a mess for my father on Saturday, and it did him the world of good."

My master was delighted with this suggestion, and said that it would do none of us any harm. "Not even Pyrrhus," he added with a smile. "You've been acting colicky yourself these few days past." There was naught that I could say to this, for there was more than a grain of truth in it, although I would have traced the cause somewhat further than my stomach. In any event it was decided, and so I went the next morning to the hill and filled a hand-basket with greens for our dinners. For a wonder the day broke clear with a pleasant fresh breeze and abundant sunshine. When I had dug enough to feed us, it was still so early that it seemed a shame to go directly home. Instead I walked to the summit of the hill, thinking to stroll around Neck Pond and to enjoy the view from thence, which was esteemed much the finest to be had in the neighborhood.

I should have thought this occupation sufficiently innocent to occasion no predicament worth mentioning, but such was not the case. When I chanced to pass close by a clump of brush that grew along the shore, a number of coarsely dressed men sprang forth and seized me. They tied my arms behind me with a length of line. I was sorely affrighted, they being a rough lot and heavily armed beside, so that they looked more like pirates than even the Frenchman D'Agenais and his rascal crew. Each wore a spruce twig in his hat. One whom I took to be the leader had a white cockade in addition, although he seemed no different than the rest. My suspicion was confirmed when one of my captors turned to him and spoke.

"What do we want with this'un, Cap'n?" he asked. "He ain't but a nigger: he can't do nothin'."

"He can talk, can't he?" he snarled. "You can do that, can't you, Coffee?" My tongue clove to the roof of my mouth when I tried to answer so that all I could do was croak. I was disgusted with myself, but the man just shrugged. "Well," he said, "he talks a little anyhow, and he knows that we're here. Now shut up while I figure what to do with him."

"He looks like a Tory to me," one of them said with an unpleasant laugh. "A Tory in a coat of fresh tar. What say we get us some feathers and finish the job? If they don't stick we can tar 'im again."

"I said shut up, Soule," the captain roared. "Look, you two, take him down to camp and see what the colonel wants to do with him. That's best. But by God, Soule, you be careful while you're about, because if you're seen, I promise you you'll both get a coat to match his, and with the feathers!"

They took me down to Back Cove, to a place called Sandy Point where there was a thick grove of pines not far from the water. In the clearing in the middle there was a sort of tent made of sailcloth and some whaleboats which had been brought ashore and turned on their sides as shelters. The men haled me before the tent and stood me next to a spruce pole with the lower branches hewn off, which evidently served them as a standard. One put his head inside the door of the tent. "Where the devil has the colonel got to?" I heard him say.

"Right here," came a voice from behind me. It was a voice that I had heard often enough at the King's Head. I turned, and there was Samuel Thompson of Brunswick. He looked from Soule to me and back again. "What the hell is this?" he demanded. "I send you men to catch Mowatt, and you come back with some scared nigger. By God, Soule, Henry Mowatt may be a pox-ridden ministerial tool, but I never heard tell he was a blackamoor into the bargain!"

There was a general laugh at this. When it had subsided, Thompson turned to me. "What's your name, boy?" he demanded. "How did you know we were here?"

"Pyrrhus Ross," I told him, "and honest, Colonel Thompson, I didn't know: I was picking spring greens when these men grabbed me."

"That's right, Colonel," Soule said. "He had this basket when we took 'im. You want to watch our for 'im, though: he tried to make the cap'n think he was a dummy so's we'd let him go." Thompson took the basket in one hand and rubbed his stubbly chin with the other.

"It's plain we can't do that," he said thoughtfully. "He may not've known we was here before, but he sure's hell does now. He knows why, as well, or my name's King George, and that tent's Saint James's. Somebody tie the poxy beggar to a tree, and keep an eye on him." He looked about. "Where the hell's my cook?" he asked. "Anybody seen my damned cook?" A man came forward, and Thompson thrust the basket at him irritably.

"Boil these up with some pork for my dinner," he told him. "There looks to be just enough. And be careful about smoke when you light the fire. I'll send word when I want 'em. Right now what I want is rum: a good stiff tot. I've got my letters to write, damn them, and I never could write anything fit to read without some'at to steady my hand. Helps me think, too." He raised his voice to carry across the clearing. "By God," he said, "let's have rum all 'round. What do you say to that, you men?" They gave him a ragged cheer, and he smiled at them benevolently and disappeared into the tent with every evidence of satisfaction.

Soule and the other sat me at the base of one of the pines and lined up to receive their drams with the others. I thought briefly of escaping, but dismissed the notion. For one thing the men were too many, and I could see no reason to chance a ball in the back for the likes of the captain of the *Canceaux*. Beyond that, if I were successful I should have to tell someone what was afoot, and this could rebound upon the captain and myself in any number of ways. No, there were too many hazards, even when I considered the risk that the ship might bombard the town in retaliation. At least no one would single out a prisoner for punishment. I was safest where I was.

There was no reliable way to gauge the passing of time, for the thick growth above me shut out the light of the sun, but it must have been about an hour *post meridiem* when they brought Mowatt into the camp. The *Canceaux*'s surgeon, a thirsty-looking Scot named Baillie, was with him, and poor Mr. Wiswell, too. They seemed to have little to say, but Mowatt was raging. By contrast Colonel Thompson seemed almost urbane.

"By my faith, sir," Mowatt was saying, "unless you give orders for my release this instant I'll see this town in ashes! What! Do you dare to laugh at me? By God, I assure you, sir, I mean what I say! Tell these knaves to unhand me at once!"

Thompson stopped laughing then, and with a sweeping bow that fairly dripped with sarcasm, he introduced himself. After that Mowatt held his tongue for the most part, no doubt mindful of what he had heard about the five men the colonel was said to have buried alive, but his face was red and his eyes bulged with suppressed anger. In the end it was the parson who asked Colonel Thompson what he intended.

"As to that, Mr. Wiswell," he said with a smirk, "the half of what I had intended I have already carried into execution. You men are my prisoners according to the laws of war, a state of which exists between these colonies and England, and has since the barbarous murders of our brethren in Lexington. The balance lies with the same Providence which has delivered you into my hands. It may be that I will have to take you to Watertown to learn the pleasure of the Provincial Congress concerning your final disposition; for now, I shall simply hold you here. I don't suppose, Captain," he said mockingly, "that you would care to give me your parole that you will not attempt to escape? No? Ah, what a pity! You may come to find those bonds tiresome." He seemed to find that funny, and then in a voice that had lost all of its assumed polish he called for the guards to take them away. "Downwind," he added offensively. "I don't want to smell them. And not a word to anyone. Not if you value your pox-ridden hides!" He laughed again as he watched them led away and then he turned to where I lay sprawled against my tree. "Here, boy," he said, and when I was awkward at getting to my feet because of the ropes he swore at me. "Come on, God damn you, boy, I can't be waiting all afternoon." He took a letter, ready folded and sealed, from the bosom of his coat. "For God's sake," he bellowed, "won't somebody cut the beggar loose?" Soule produced a clasp knife and did as he had bid. When he had done, Thompson gave me the letter.

"Do you know where old Judge Freeman lives? Good. You take this letter to his house as fast as you can, and you give it into his hands, mind, and nobody's else's." When I waited to see if there was any more, he lost his temper. "I don't believe you ain't there yet," he said. "Didn't you hear me say hurry? Now run, you poxy little bastard, else I'll see you get some'at to haste you!"

I ran.

I dodged through the trees and came out in the open a few rods from the cove. I ran along the shore until I was well out of musket-shot and then cut up across what we called the Back Fields toward town. Here I could not run, for there were many stumps hidden in the long grass, and whatever the colonel said I had no desire to break my neck in falling over one. I made up for the delay by crossing behind Greele's Tavern to get to Fiddle Lane instead of going around by the street, and then put on a last spurt that brought me breathless to Freeman's door.

The major's face darkened as he read Thompson's letter. "By the great Jehovah!" he swore. "Colonel or no, the man can't address me like this! I won't have it!" He crumpled the paper in his hand. "You, boy: Paris, or whatever your heathen name is, you're certain that Mowatt was taken? You saw him yourself?"

"Yes, sir," I said. "And Mr. Wiswell and the doctor, too."

"The fool," Freeman said in a low voice. "He'll be the ruin of all of us." There was a murmur of agreement from the other committee-men around him, but what happened next brought it to an abrupt end.

There was a sound that shook the house, a sound as of rolling thunder, and before it had died away the front door burst open and one of the militia officers burst into the hall.

"It's the *Canceaux*," he said excitedly. "Two guns. They say that Mowatt's been took, and Lieutenant Hogg says to tell you that if you don't get him back, the next guns'll have shot in them!"

28

BELIKE it was the guns that had brought Sarah from out of the kitchen. Her mouth flew open when she saw me, and a swift little cry of mingled surprise and fear escaped. Small wonder it was, for I must have looked like something that had clawed itself out of a shallow grave. I smiled to let her know I was unharmed, but that was all, for by then Major Freeman had Hogg's letter open before him and was reading it aloud.

The letter was not a long one, and barely civil in tone and tenor. The lieutenant stated only that he had been apprised of his commander's capture: that he chose to hold the town responsible, and that if Mowatt and the others were not returned safe on board the *Canceaux* by six o'clock, he would open fire upon us, nor stop until Falmouth were laid in ashes. At the end was nothing more than the bald notation, "Jno. Hogg, Lieut., RN."

Freeman snorted at the insult. There was a moment's silence while the men around us digested what Hogg had written, and then they were all talking at once. I made to go and look for Sarah, but the major seized me by the arm. "Not yet," he said. "Not until you've told me everything. Is this all? Is Thompson finished, now he's got Mowatt, or is there more?"

The hostile glances directed upon me were hardly encouraging, but somehow I found wit and wind to reply. "I don't think he's done yet," I told the committee. "I think he means to burn the *Canceaux* as well."

As I spoke, Freeman's face went cold with anger. "The scoundrel!" he hissed. "And not four days ago he wrote that we need fear nothing!" He gave no further explanation, but composed his expression, and with more courtesy than he was wont to show, he thanked me and said that I should return to my master's house. From the way he spoke it was obvious that he meant immediately. I took the hint and left.

The major had seemed more wrathful than affrighted, so that I never learned whether he believed that Hogg would carry out his threat. As soon as I stepped out of doors I could see that the townspeople at large were not disposed to question the ultimatum, for the lieutenant's guns had touched off the third panic in as many weeks.

I had thought the cautious and the fearful were all safely gone beyond either shot or sound of English cannon, but clearly I was mistaken. The men were mostly from home at this hour, and so as I ran up Middle Street to Jones Lane it seemed that Falmouth must be completely populated by women. Every one of these women had, moreover, run out into the street before her house, and was in tears, or praying, or screaming; some of them hurriedly throwing bales of goods to a passing cart, and never asking the driver's name though he were a stranger, and others carrying their children safely out of the town. For many this seemed to be the fields around about Joshua Brackett's house and barns. I could see a crowd of them there, well out of gunshot but able to see what befell their homes. I believe that among them were several persons bedridden or but lately delivered of children who were removed in haste, some with no small danger to their lives. Of one at least I may be certain, for her family carried her forth bed and all, and came near to trampling me in their going.

I arrived at the captain's house to find it deserted. This argued that all were safe, though it vexed me not to know where they had gone.

Since there was no mending things I closed the door behind me and went on down the hill to the waterfront.

The wharves I found as quiet as the town behind me was tumultuous. The *Industry* rode calmly at her mooring, breasting the ebb tide. I went to the end of the pier and hailed her. There was no response. She might have been as empty as the house had been, save that close under her bows the jolly boat danced at the end of an uncommon short painter. From the boat I might assume that there was someone aboard; from their silence, that all was not well. I looked about for a boat to borrow. There was none in the water, but in a shed nearby I found an ancient canoe that looked sound enough to bear me as far as the schooner.

That sound it was, but only just. The canoe began to leak as soon as I was sat down within it. By the time I reached the *Industry* there was near as much of the river inside as otherwise, so that it sank beneath me even as I grasped the main chains of the schooner to haul myself on board. Wetted to the waist, I stood on the *Industry*'s deck and congratulated myself for having escaped so easily.

Behind me the companion door opened on protesting hinges. I was half turned around and ready to leap at the prowler when I saw it was the captain. "Get down!" he snapped at me. "Quick, before they see you!" I used my momentum to drop and roll against the rail.

Ross motioned for me to join him. "You can't just lie there," he said. "And for God's sake, keep low! I don't know what's gone wrong, but from the look of it Mowatt's started taking hostages."

"Not Mowatt," I told him. "It's Lieutenant Hogg. Colonel Thompson's come down from Brunswick, and Mowatt's his prisoner."

"Mowatt's took? Good God, no wonder they're hopping! Come on then, and be quick about it: you don't want to be seen." Ross risked a glance around the side of the doghouse as I came up with him, and I asked what he was afraid of. "*Canceaux*'s cutter," he said. "Why in hell did you think there was nobody on deck? Hogg got it in the water right after he fired those shots, Grizzell says. Ten oars, she pulls, and fast! When folks came down to see their vessels safe, they got snatched up. They've caught three boats we know of, and taken the people on board the *Canceaux*. I'm lucky to have got here myself."

The captain led the way down the narrow ladder to his cabin, where Grizzell and Tukey kept watch by the stern windows. When I asked my master if he thought there was much chance that the cutter would come after us, he shrugged. "I don't know," he admitted. "So far they've kept pretty close to the ship. I just can't see any sense in tempting the bastards."

Jack Tukey patted the stock of his musket affectionately. "Let 'em come, Cap'n," he said. "We're ready for 'em!" Grizzell rolled his eyes at the planking above him and told Jack to shut his fool's mouth. Ross ignored them both and told me to make myself comfortable. My hinder parts were still dripping, so I sat on his sea chest in order to preserve his bedding. My master let himself down into his chair and looked me over. Suddenly he laughed.

"You look worse than the first day you came here," he said. "Remember? You jumped off Bryce's wharf into the mud: you and a half-plucked chicken." The memory set him off again. It didn't last long. He stopped and regarded me sternly.

"By God," he said, "I near forgot! You should've been back hours ago! Where in hell have you been?"

I told him what had befallen me on the hill. I hadn't really thought about it before, but in retrospect I found I was angry: angry at Thompson for what his men had put me through, and not a little angry at the captain for his hearty laughter when I spoke of being afraid of a load of birdshot in the breeches as I ran.

"I guess that's all right then," he said, wiping away the tears. "Though you gave us quite a turn. You should've heard Elizabeth! She had conniptions when you didn't show up by noontime. Held the meal up near an hour. And I was looking forward to the greens. We were just finishing when the shooting started."

"The house was empty when I got there," I pointed out. "That was just a few minutes ago."

"I should hope so," he told me. "I bundled Elizabeth and the cook on up to Joe McLellan's for safekeeping. Elizabeth raised cain at first, of course. She was bound she'd stay home while I came here, and then nothing would do but she had to go stay at her brother's place. Her brother's, of all places! It's right in the line of fire! She tried to tell me that didn't matter; Lieutenant Hogg being a king's officer, she said, he would only shoot at the rebels' houses. I didn't waste time to argue the point. I saw that she went to Joe's, by God, and damned quick.

"Frankly, though, Elizabeth's the least of my worries. I'm much more concerned about this deadline business. I don't like the sound of that, Pyrrhus. Hogg's the sort that would sooner burn the town than eat his dinner. I only met him once, but that was enough. What's worse is that he won't stop with the town if it comes to burning. He's a seaman, and he'll plan to burn the shipping as well. He might even fire the ships first, so as to show the folk ashore he means what he says." Ross shook his head morosely at the prospect. He turned toward me and studied my face thoughtfully, and then looked from me to the others.

"Get a rest while you can," he told them. "Won't nothing happen for a while, and you may as well be fresh when it does. Go on up forward there and stretch out. I'll send Pyrrhus to wake you before it gets dark."

They left, and I went aft to sit by the windows. I could see the *Canceaux* and the cutter pretty well and the waterfront as far as Preble's wharf. The sky was beginning to cloud up. It looked like the night would be cold enough that a fire would be welcome. I found myself wondering if Lieutenant Hogg felt the same.

The captain rose from his seat and began to pace the length of the cabin. "It's Thompson who's to blame for this," he said at last. "Why couldn't he have let Mowatt be? There will be war and to spare down to Boston for them as want it. We didn't need it in Falmouth as well." He came and stood beside me, stooping a little so as to be able to see the *Canceaux* for himself.

"So there she sits. The terrier at the rathole. But for Colonel Thompson she'd have gone to her kennel inside of a fortnight, and no harm done. There was even talk of opening the customs-house again. Small chance of that now." He made a hopeless little gesture with his hand. "I feel I should be doing something," he said. "Not just sitting here waiting for Hogg to make his move. The problem is, I'm caught between the wind and the water. Run for the bay, and the *Canceaux* is there with her guns. Tate's Landing would be safer, but the cutter'd be on us before we could loose a sail, and then the tide's dead foul. The last of the ebb is at dusk. By then it could be too late."

The captain's words hung in the air between us. I studied his face carefully. It was on a level with mine, but his eyes were fixed impassively on a point somewhere down the bay. He might almost have believed himself to be alone.

" 'More haste, less speed,' " I quoted. Ross grunted and straightened his back. He fell to pacing again. I resisted the temptation to stare at him and watched the *Canceaux* while I waited for some answer. It seemed very long in coming. Finally the captain threw himself down on his bed and pulled the blanket over him. "Wake me at slack water," he said, and that was all.

I looked at him in wonderment and annoyance. If Ross could sleep with the world all of a flux around us, there was nothing that was further from my mind; yet when I tried to think, I found that Colonel Thompson, and Mowatt, and Hogg, and freedom all kept whirling round in my thoughts so that I sat and watched the tide inch down the pilings of Deering's wharf until I might as well have spent the afternoon in Dr. Mesmer's temple, where they say folk sit for hours staring at their own reflections, and in the end are no wiser than they were when they began.

When night came we buoyed and slipped the cable, and brought the *Industry* to a new anchorage in the wide part of the Fore River beyond the ferry to Long Creek, out of sight of the *Canceaux* and thus safe. Ross and I then made ready to go on shore, but Tukey alleged that he had business in Falmouth that would not wait and we took him as well. The boat we took back around the point and drew up on the shore some fifty or so rods shy of Bryce McLellan's where there were bushes in which to hide it. At the foot of Jones Lane we parted company, Jack shambling off down Fore Street with his musket askew over one shoulder.

The house was so obviously empty that we passed it by and went on up the hill to fetch Elizabeth home. McLellan's place was on the main road out of town, near as far as Brackett's, and so Middle Street was the most direct route. As this would entail passing by Marston's tavern, I suggested that the captain might wish to stop there for a bite and a sup and to hear the news, but my master only laughed and said that if I hungered I would do better to save my breath for walking, that we might get to Joseph's the sooner.

It happened that we stopped at Marston's after all, though not by either my design or the captain's. There was a body of armed men drawn up in two long ranks in the road outside, and when we sought to go by, they barred our way.

29

Tʜᴏᴍᴘsᴏɴ's man Soule came at me then from out of the darkness, and another they called Sergeant Cavanah, a rawboned,
profane sort of man I remembered from the camp, on the captain's
side. I had no stomach for falling once more into the hands of the
Brunswickers, so that I came near to running regardless of their
muskets. Later I learned that it was well that I had not, for the colonel
had caused his men to load with the lead balls cut into quarters, and I
make no doubt but what I would have been stone-dead ere I had gone
ten yards.

This Cavanah seemed particularly anxious that my master and I
should have a good view of the bore of his piece, to which end he
flourished the muzzle back and forth beneath our noses while he waited
for the rest of the sentries to come up with us. I gave it my entire
attention, and thus I failed at first to notice that there were other men
than Thompson's among them. The captain, however, cast his eyes
about and spied Ensign Little of the Company of Cadets. Ross called
out to him and said that he would have leave to pass as far as Joseph
McLellan's house on the high road.

"No call to go all that way," the youth replied. "Captain McLellan's
yonder in the tavern." He gave the sergeant such a look as made it plain
that there was scant love between them and bid him lower his firelock
and stand aside. This Cavanah did, but slowly and with ill grace, and I
held my breath until we were well past him.

The guard at Marston's door was a Falmouth man who saluted Little
self-consciously, as men will when they have known an officer long
enough to remember him before he was breeched. The ensign nodded
gravely and touched his hat, saying that the captain would find Mr.
McLellan in the large room on the left: a grand council was under way
which involved Colonel Thompson and his officers and representatives
of the town's several committees.

The room was the same in which the captain and Elizabeth had held their wedding feast, though this night the tables were drawn together in the middle of the floor. We could only just squeeze ourselves in along the back, for the room was full, but I could see Thompson and the rest wrangling together, and Lieutenant Mowatt sitting red-faced between a pair of bumpkins armed with espontoons. One of the committeemen called upon the colonel to yield up his prisoners to the town if he would not release them himself, and adduced Hogg's letter as sufficient reason. Thompson laughed contemptuously.

"Damme for a Quaker, you cowardly pack of rascals, they are my prisoners, after all. I only consented to this council as a courtesy in the first place, for by my lights I'm the only man here with a right to say what's to be done with 'em, and I say they should go to the Congress at Watertown. As for Mr. Hogg and that pox-ridden ship you're all so wheyfaced about, why, the hell with it! If you supported me as you ought, I would take it as well, but look ye, even so: I say tell Hogg to fire away, sir! Fire and be damned! And for every ball that he sends into the town, I should carve me a joint from his captain's carcass!"

"That is well enough for you to say," old Freeman answered. "Your home and family are not here to receive the cannonade, and by God, sir, it is not meet that you should call us cowards, who do not share our hazard in the same degree." At this point, Colonel Thompson made a rude noise through his lips, or it may be that the greens he had eaten had worked powerfully upon his digestion. However it happened, the timing was unfortunate. The blood came into Freeman's face then, and his voice became louder by half. "It is not meet," he repeated, and added, "Moreover, Mr. Thompson, if we be cowards and rascals, then you, sir, are all of that, and a liar into the bargain. Your design endangers our women and children, yet when we heard of it and wrote to you, you returned to say that you had abandoned it."

The colonel grew exceeding wroth at this denunciation, until I thought that he must call Mr. Freeman out if he did not saber him where he sat, but he mastered himself with an effort. "The plan was secret," he said coolly. "It could not succeed else." He paused. "After all, there is policy in war." Thompson contrived to give his voice a sneering note that our people took very ill. He knew that he lacked the strength to move against the *Canceaux* unless he had local reinforcement, and now that the town was openly ranged against him it was obvious that he could not carry the issue of the prisoners either. After he spoke he subsided sullenly into his chair and let the discussion go where it listed. Still, there was no sign that the meeting was about to end, and after a time the captain leaned over to me and whispered that we might as well leave and wait for Joseph at his home.

I had flattered myself with the thought that my master would remember to see that I got something to eat at McLellan's, but when we arrived Elizabeth was in a pet over something that someone had said, so that we could not come away again fast enough to suit her. The captain sent me on ahead to kindle the fires and light the candles. Even then I had no leisure to get myself a supper, for as soon as Elizabeth was through the door she set me to heat a brick and wrap it in flannel so as to drive the chill from her bed. When she began to disrobe, I popped the brick between the sheets and fled down the stairs to the kitchen, but I came too late even so; the cook had served up to Ross all that was fit for man to eat, and then gobbled his leavings before letting herself out. The only crumb the bulimious old woman had overlooked was a bit of dry rind from a Holland cheese. It seemed to me mortal hard that I go hungry to my bed after the day I had spent, and in the end I waited until it was quiet upstairs and slipped off with what was left of the household money to try potluck at the King's Head.

I know I have said that the landlord's staple trade was in spirits, selling something like rum so cheap that any man might get feloniously drunk for a few coppers, but I may have failed to mention that for those that wished it there was food as well. There was a slate by the bar on which was noted the proffered fare; this night they had pork and wheat-flour dumplings. I called for a plate and found me a seat in a dim-lit corner not far from the door.

The taverner's wife brought my food and stood over me while I ate so as to be certain of her spoon. She was a largish woman, none too clean, and soft and pasty-looking withal, like something served beforetime from her own kitchen. She had bad teeth and worse breath, the which are overcommon in New England, especially among the lower orders, and clearly reflected in their native cookery, for they are much addicted to the use of molasses in every sort of dish, no doubt from an instinctual desire to sweeten their unwholesome exhalations. I never learned to relish my victuals thus, my own mouth being sound enough that I have no need for artifice, but on this occasion I was sharp-set and did not cavil though the dumplings ate like grapeshot and the meat had left pools of grease in the syrupy gravy.

I had done no more than to make a start when Cavanah flung open the door and swaggered in, accompanied by some half-dozen or so of his fellows, all drunk as a Scottish parliament. One of them slapped the landlord's wife upon the fundament as he passed her, whereupon she forgot her spoon and betook herself back into the stronghold of her kitchen, fixing her husband with a withering glance the while, though what she expected that he should do is beyond my comprehension. Very likely it was beyond his as well, for he stared after her helplessly until Cavanah pounded on the counter before him with the flat of his hand, making such a noise that he gathered up his scattered wits and went about his business.

Cavanah and his companions took possession of a table that lay handy by and bawled for rum, and for rum again, but though their voices were so loud as to extinguish all other conversation, there need have been no trouble if only they had been content merely to drink and to bait the landlord. This was common practice, and in truth one of them was good enough at this rough brand of humor that folk began to nudge their neighbors and smile at his sallies.

Some men find elevation in ardent spirits, while others are simply rendered disputatious. The sergeant being of the less agreeable sort, he did not join in the raillery, but sat silent and brooding until at last he hove himself to his feet and began a long discourse on the subject of Lieutenant Mowatt and his iniquities. He went from table to table, alternately shouting in people's faces about how it was a miscarriage of God's justice that Thompson had been prevented from hanging Mowatt out of hand as soon as he had been taken, and calling the Englishman names a carter would not have laid tongue to. Poor Wheeler Riggs was sitting at a table but a little removed from mine, and when Cavanah left off from Mowatt and started in on Major Freeman, he could not abide it. He stood up and shouted back.

"The major's saved the town," Wheeler told him. "You got no right to talk about him like that." He had started to go on about how Mr. Freeman had got Mowatt to send ashore the prisoners that Hogg had taken when the Brunswicker rounded on him and sent him crash-

ing against the wall. Wheeler's eyes fluttered and rolled up into his
head, and he slid down the wall to the floor.

Cavanah's friends were on their feet in an instant, so that if anyone
had thought to go to Riggs's aid they did not. Cavanah pulled himself drunkenly upright and glared at us. "Anybody else?" he chal-
lenged. "I say your damned milksop of a major's playin' the Tories'
game for 'em! Him and Preble both! Well, there's an accounting
coming, you can bet on it. We gave Mowatt his parole like they was
cryin' for, but they'd best hope that he keeps it. If he don't, by God,
we'll have our fun with him instead!" He drew up one side of his
mouth in a smile and gave a last look from side to side as if daring
someone to move or to speak. When no one did, he turned his back
on us contemptuously and went back to join the rest of his party,
kicking chairs out of his path. One of the men put his arm around
Cavanah's shoulders and handed him a gray pottery mug. He took
a long drink from it, the rum streaming down both sides of his chin,
and threw the empty mug to the floor. Someone said something to him
and he laughed. The Brunswickers all sat down then, and Cavanah
called to the barman for more rum.

It took a minute or two before any of the Falmouth men moved.
Finally two who sat closest picked Wheeler Riggs up under his arms
and lifted him to his feet. His face was very pale, and there was blood
around his nose and mouth. He shook his head muzzily as they left
with him.

I could hear the chairs scraping on the floor as I picked at what was
left of my meal. Shadows flickered across my table as people filed
silently out the door. I watched them go until it came to me that everyone else had left, save for the barman and the Brunswickers. I looked
at the food on my plate. It was cold and unappealing. Suddenly I felt
very conspicuous. I got up and made my way to the door. As it closed
behind me, I heard Cavanah and his friends call for the landlord to
bring another round.

30

As bad as the night had been, the morning that followed was worse. Colonel Phinney had caused word of Mowatt's capture to be spread abroad during the hours of darkness, with the result that his men and others to the number of six hundred came into Falmouth early Wednesday, as they thought to see the Englishman hanged in Market Square. Many had walked as far as twenty miles to see him dance in a Tyburn tippet, and they were exceedingly exasperated to learn that the intended victim had been discharged. The countrymen demanded that he render himself up to them agreeable to the terms of his parole, and when he would not they took and made prisoners of General Preble and Major Freeman in his stead. Them they kept in close confinement, giving them no dinner and allowing not even their children to speak with them.

Meanwhile, the men went about our streets under arms, insulting or detaining the people they met and quartering themselves upon whomsoever they chose. The old woman who cooked for us came late for work, clucking indignantly about her treatment at their hands and full of how they had broken down the door of Captain Coulson's fine house and were using it as a barrack. When Elizabeth heard this, she would not suffer us to leave the house for fear of their coming, and fell fainting when my master would have gone to the quayside to see how the *Industry* fared. I helped him to make her comfortable and then went on the errand myself.

The few soldiers I met seemed to think me beneath their regard and I was able to reach the waterfront without incident. From their talk I learned that the town was under military government. The officers of the companies present had resolved themselves into a board of war to consider an attack upon Captain Mowatt's ship. After some hesitation and argument they had admitted our own officers upon an equal footing, though in sooth the townsmen were of little account, and the vote was passed by a considerable margin. The board then formed itself into a committee to discover in what manner the attack should be made, but I have never been able to learn that they accomplished anything save to call before themselves men who were suspected of being Tories, to question them, to draw promises from them, and especially to extract from them money and provisions.

Of the accused some came willingly and some under guard, but I have it from those who were there that they acquitted themselves as well as could be expected, so that the Liberty party rather lost than gained in comparison. The Reverend Mr. Wiswell, it is said, surrendered himself without even a summons, and seemed rather impatient until he was to appear, saying unto all that would listen that he was ready to die at any time, as he knew that he was in a good cause: the cause of the Church of England.

Old Mr. Wyer had a file of men sent after him and was brought before the committee with a pistol at his breast. He was mightily angry about the interferences from out of town, for he had said as much before on divers occasions, and they got little satisfaction out of his presence. They asked him whether he had not said that our militia should have been called out to rescue Captain Mowatt from the hands of the Brunswickers, and he replied in the affirmative. Someone then required of him whether he did not think that it had been an imprudent thing to say, whereupon he is said to have glared about him like a captured eagle and answered yes again. When asked if he were still of the same mind, he told them no, not as matters were circumstanced, which did not wholly satisfy the men from the country, so that they asked him again, whether he would say anything against the body of men then in town, and he said he would not. I imagine that the committee found him an uncomfortable opponent, for they soon agreed to dismiss him, as not being worth their time and trouble. To this Mr. Wyer made a low bow and said gravely that he thanked them all for their civility, and prepared to take his leave. One Captain Stewart, smarting that the old man should have come off the better in the engagement, called out to the crowd before the door, to make way for him, and told them that the committee was of a mind that he was not worthy of their attention.

Jeremiah Pote was fetched before the board without any resistance, even though he had made formidable preparations to defend himself. I can only assume that he gave himself up because such a course seemed better calculated to enlist the sympathies of his fellow citizens. He was fined, for the benefit of the troops then in the town, about fifty pounds in cash and provisions, and was forced to give a bond of a further two thousand pounds, to appear before the Provincial Congress and there give an account of himself. This done, the board adjourned until the afternoon.

Thus far had affairs gone when I went forth on my errand. No one had offered to board the *Industry* in our absence, and Grizzell pronounced himself well pleased not to have to do with such contentious folk as I had seen and heard. From the ship I was to have gone to Pagan's direct, so as to quiet Elizabeth's fears upon her brother's score, but in the meantime I wanted to see Sarah, and shaped my course for Freeman's house instead.

This proved to be a mistake on two accounts, the first being that the major's house and the street before it were so full of people that I could scarce pass by, and I left more worried than I had come. The second was that in making my way from thence to Pagan's I fell in with Jack Tukey, who had joined a party of Gorhamites led by one Calvin Lombard. Some of them had made free of Coulson's house, and the lot were well raised with liquor, having found a barrel three parts full of good New England rum in the captain's cellar. What they had not drunk on the spot they had drained off into jugs which passed from hand to hand. I saw that Jack had slung his musket over his shoulder on a bit of rope so that when his turn came he might drink the easier.

Such stalwart companions as these could do no other than get Jack into trouble, and it seemed to me that it would be a good job to part him from them. With this in mind I fell into step and trooped along down King Street with the rest.

The company struggled on, and I with them, until we came to the seaward end of Goodwin's wharf, which, though it was shorter in length than the one named for the brigadier, was closer to the *Canceaux*. Apparently not even Lombard had given any thought to what they might accomplish in coming here, and I took advantage of their hesitation to urge Jack's return to the house on Jones Lane. He soon made it clear that he wanted none of my advice while there was yet rum to be had, and I made up my mind to leave him until I had been to Pagan's at the least.

To this point nothing of moment had occurred, the men for the most part milling about aimlessly while some few cut capers on the dock, shaking their fists and hurling imprecations across the water at the men on the *Canceaux*'s deck. There was, however, a boat on the shore nearby which belonged to Captain Coulson, and as I turned to go Lombard dispatched a party to secure it and take it back up the hill out of Mowatt's reach. The Gorhamites pushed past me, whooping and yelping.

In an instant the *Canceaux*'s people had seen what the countrymen were about and raised the alarm. One of the midshipmen on board ordered them to stop, saying that the boat was now king's property. The men on shore took no notice, though he shouted until his voice cracked, he being still a beardless boy. They took the boat upon their shoulders and began to carry it away.

Another shout came from the *Canceaux*, and though I could not make out the words the tone of command was unmistakable. I looked and saw that Mowatt himself was now come on deck. The lace on his hat and his single epaulet flashed bravely in the sun as though they were real gold and not mere pinchbeck. He came to the ship's rail and raised his speaking-trumpet to his mouth.

"Hold!" he bellowed. "In the king's name, bring ye back that boat. Hold, ye rebels, or I shall fire!"

"Why don't ye then?" Lombard replied. So well did he mimic Mowatt's voice that the men around him laughed. Some of them stooped and threw loose cobbles or bits of garbage which left unsightly stains on the yellow-ochred side of the ship. I looked and saw that the men with the boat had scaled the bank. In another minute they would be safe behind the walls of Fort Loyall.

Mowatt turned to one of the officers at his side. I did not need to hear to know what he had said, for there was a flurry all down the length of the *Canceaux*'s bulwarks. Men were moving behind the guns. I could see the muzzles swing around as the crews hauled on the train-tackles, and the gunners swinging lengths of slow-match in the air to make sure they were fairly straight. Other men with cutlasses clustered in the waist.

The crowd began to thin around me, and suddenly it seemed as though all the *Canceaux*'s cannon were directed at my person. Lombard and his men were running away: all of them save Jack. I watched as he unslung his musket and went down on one knee to steady his aim. I called him seven kinds of fool and crouched behind a hogshead for cover.

Close upon the crack of the shot there was a thump as the ball went home. Jack stood wreathed in powder-smoke, fumbling in his pouch for another cartridge. There was a shot or two from the *Canceaux*. I huddled lower and listened to the angry whine of the British bullets. When they had passed, I raised my head and shouted for Jack to run. He shook his head and poured a fresh charge down the barrel of his musket.

"There's time yet aplenty," he said, plying his rammer as deliberately as if he had been shooting at a mark. He cocked the piece and raised it with wavering aim. "Would you have the lobsters think so ill of us?"

"The devil with what they think! Come or he lets go his great guns!" The thought of what their iron balls would do to us wrenched at my stomach, but I had to look. The smoke had cleared and I could see Mowatt's cutter pulling strong for the wharf. "Shoot!" I told him. "For God's sake, shoot!"

Courage is not to be despised whatever its source, but Jack's was mostly of the Dutch variety, and his shot went wide. The men in the cutter gave a great shout and drove their vessel against the pilings below. I ran forward and took Jack by the sleeve. "In God's name," I said, "run!" We took to our heels.

It was a near thing. At first my thought was only to put as much distance between myself and the British as I might, but away up on the hill I could see that Lombard, or someone, had a body of men under arms and forming up into line, and so I bore off onto Fore Street rather than chance being caught between two fires. Jack ran with me, neither daring to stop to draw breath until we had come as far as Moose Alley. Here we leaned gasping against the wall of a small two-storied house. Jack grinned at me weakly and ran his sleeve across his brow.

Inwardly I cursed Jack, and then myself as well, for being fool enough to be caught up in his adventure. My heart was pounding madly, and for some minutes I could only stand there listening to it. Then I slowly realized that my heart was all that I heard. In our rear all was silent; the sounds of battle there had died. This struck me as a curious circumstance, and possibly worth the investigating, but I

had learned more caution than to do so with Jack for my companion.
A hasty glance showed Fore Street to be deserted. I urged Jack onward
and followed him to where the *Industry* lay.

The idea of sleeping snug in her forecastle was a tempting one. At
length I bethought me of the captain, who was waiting for word that
all was well. If he had heard the shooting he would be the more concerned. I knew, too, that I should go back and stop at Pagan's, but I
did not care to risk falling into Mowatt's hands after I had been seen
with Lombard and his men. In the end I decided to leave Jack on
board with Grizzell and made the best of my way home. By happy
chance Elizabeth's brother was come there before me, so that I escaped
censure for failing that charge. I took small pleasure in the fact, however; the news that he bore gave me the same sick feeling I had known
at the sight of Mowatt's cannon.

"Thompson's lost it," Pagan exulted. "Thompson and Phinney and
these rakehells from the country. They were finished as soon as they
laid hands on Preble and Freeman. It's all over, Will, all but the hang-
ings, and if you don't want to swing along with the rest, now's the
time to say so.

"Your Thompsons aren't the real leaders, Will. Even their precious
Hancock hasn't brains enough to make a hog-reeve. It takes brains and
money both to run this liberty thing, and 'twas men like Preble who've
supplied it from the start. How long d'ye think they'll keep doing it
now? Now that it's clear that it's not just Tories those men from the
country are after, but every man with a home of his own and a guinea
in his pocket? Don't try to tell me any different, Will; I had to listen
to them half the morning. Most of 'em would just as soon fire the town
themselves once they've got all they can from it. It's the truth! Go
out and ask them! They hate us all, Will, and the sooner you realize
it, the better.

"It's out in the open now, and I say thank God for that! They've
tipped their hands, and there'll be lean days ahead for the Liberty Boys
now folk can see the kind of liberty they have in mind. Liberty Boys!
In six months there won't be one of 'em who's not been hanged or
kenneled!"

My master looked at Pagan long and thoughtfully. After a time he
asked him if he would not stay and take some refreshment, but the
merchant shook his head.

"I think I should get home," he said. "There's no telling where this will end. The soldiers have taken the bit in their teeth for fair, and their so-called officers can't do a thing with 'em. They've plundered Mr. Tyng's already; taken his gold-laced hat and all his plate. I mean to be home if they come for mine. Give my best to Elizabeth."

I let Mr. Pagan out and returned to where my master stood staring blankly out the window. I watched him narrowly, wishing that I could plumb his feelings. Which way would he turn? I could not say.

We remained there until a knock at the door roused the captain from his contemplation. I went out into the hall to see who it might be. I opened the door and found Joseph McLellan and two or three others. I took them into the parlor.

They looked at each other uneasily when the captain asked if they would join him in a glass of wine, hemming and shuffling their feet until at last McLellan took it upon himself to speak for them. "Thank you kindly, Will," he said. "It's been a thirsty day." Ross nodded and I poured from the decanter. McLellan waited until he had his glass before speaking further, and then put the sherry down scarcely tasted.

"You may have guessed that we've not come on a social call," he began. My master's eyebrows went up ever so slightly at this, and McLellan hastened to explain. "It's not like that at all, Will: we're here for the town, not for Thompson. We need a favor, and we're hoping you'll help. If you can't we'll leave, and there's an end to it. Fair enough?"

Ross told him to go on. I stood at the edge of the group polishing the remaining glasses and trying to look unconcerned, but McLellan's next words startled me so that I dropped and broke the one I was holding, earning myself a look of reproof from the captain.

"You'll have heard that the Gorhamites fired on the *Canceaux*," Joseph said. "Mowatt wants the man who did it, and he wants the rest of them out of town." I had told my master nothing of what had befallen at the waterfront, and listened intently while McLellan told the tale. I was relieved to note that no name save that of Lombard had been mentioned in connection with the incident, though how I was to stop Jack from boasting of his exploit was more than I could tell.

My master ran his fingers along his jawbone as he listened. "The man's a fool," he said when McLellan had done, "but we can't give him up to be hanged. What do you want me to do?"

It seemed to me that McLellan looked relieved. "We're to go on board the *Canceaux* and wait on Captain Mowatt," he told him. "We'll be speaking for the town only; Thompson says he won't even talk with Mowatt, now he's broken parole."

One of McLellan's companions gave a derisive laugh. "I'd 'a' broke parole too, so be someone wanted to hang me," he said. The others looked at him in disapproval. He shrugged and drank down the last of his wine.

Joseph turned back to Ross. "What we thought, Will, was that Mowatt might be more likely to listen if we had you along with us. We're naught but names to him: names he mayn't be any too fond of at that. I just met him the once myself. You he'd remember."

The captain rubbed his jaw again. "I'll go," he said. "I've a wife and property in Falmouth the same as you do. But it seems to me that you're missing a bet. There's others in this town who can talk loud enough that Mowatt would have to hear 'em."

"Freeman's in jail," McLellan's outspoken friend reminded him. "Thompson's the only one louder nor the major."

Ross shook his head. "That's not what I meant," he said. He looked at each of the men in turn. "I say we send a delegation of Tories."

There was a moment's silence while the shaft sunk home. McLellan glanced at the others for a comment, but no one spoke until the talkative one coughed and muttered that he'd send the devil and his imps if only it would accomplish their purpose. Joseph took this for assent and turned back to the captain. "Who'd you have in mind, Will? Pagan?"

My master nodded. "Robert was here just a few minutes ago," he said. "He'll help if I ask him, and he can get the others to go along. The Potes, maybe; maybe the Oxnards. They might even talk Mowatt into leaving if you promised to deal fairly with 'em. His being here hasn't helped them any more than it has the rest of us: just keeps the country people riled."

"That's the truth," McLellan admitted. "If he went, they might go home. I wouldn't be sorry to see that."

"None of us would." The captain looked at his visitors once more. "It wasn't long ago," he told them, "Falmouth folk stuck together. Seems to me it's time we worked that way again."

31

M Y master came to be much praised for his suggestion, though
it is hard for me to say how much real effect it had. Certainly
some of those in Falmouth who favored the cause of government
remained in communication with Captain Mowatt throughout the time
that the Brunswickers were in town. Further, it is nowise clear that the
Englishman ever meant to carry out his threat. If Colonel Thompson
had given him ample cause, then it was equally true that the lieutenant
had been handsomely treated by others. Preble and Freeman, for
example, he might number among his enemies, and yet their defense
of him had been gentlemanly done. It would have been the act of a
blackguard to repay them with fire and the sword.

Mowatt would know, too, that the loyalists who suffered could be
expected to make the strongest of representations against him in such
an unhappy event. Hindsight argues that he would not take strong
action without explicit instructions from his admiral. The life of a
half-pay lieutenant is probably not worth the living.

That afternoon, however, the threat seemed sufficiently real, and
Ross went off directly with McLellan and the rest to find Mr. Pagan.
For the space of several hours I was left in the house with Elizabeth
and the cook. I found this less than pleasant. The old woman had
seemingly been born a shrew, where my master's wife was by way of
achieving the same result by constant application. She had me both
upstairs and down packing and repacking the things she simply could
not live without if she were driven from her home, and hiding that
which we could not carry off, some of which I made shift to conceal
beneath a loose stone in the kitchen hearth. Still, I could not please her,
and as my own concerns had put me in something of a liverish mood,
I fear we did not pass the time at all agreeably.

The captain returned toward the shank of the evening with McLellan
on the one side and Elizabeth's brother on the other. Clearly they had,
as the saying goes, strong drink taken, and they looked well pleased

with themselves. Elizabeth took one glance and withdrew upstairs to her chamber in a huff. Ross watched her in fuddled consternation. When he turned to the cook, the old woman gave a snort and took herself off as well. A moment later I heard the back door slam. My master cocked his head owlishly and then just shrugged.

"To the parlor," he said. "Pyrrhus, pour the port. You'd best break out a fresh bottle or two while you're about it. We've earned a drink this night, by heaven."

I could smell spirits on his breath, and my thought was that whatever they may have earned, they had likely been paid in full already. Ross laughed and clapped me jovially upon the shoulder. "Best make that rum," he told me. "You look enough like your friend Colonel Thompson to turn good port into vinegar. Cheer up, man; 'tis no night for long faces! Freeman and Brigadier are released from jail, and we've talked Mowatt off his high horse."

"Don't be forgetting the wee matter of that boat he bought of Captain Coulson," Mr. Pagan reminded him. "That's still to be settled."

Ross waved the objection aside. "That's easily mended. Lombard's not like to haul it off to Gorham, after all."

"Will's right," McLellan put in. "If Mowatt's willing to forget about being shot at, he won't raise hell about a boat. Worse comes to worst, the committee'll just pay him and get the damned thing back later on. Ain't nobody going to disagree with that: nobody but Thompson, anyway."

"I suppose that's true enough," Pagan conceded. "Major Freeman won't. He was as glad to be shut of this whole thing as any man."

"There you are, then. Right, Will?"

"Right. It's more than just that, though: we've shown 'em all what Falmouth folk can do once we stop working at cross purposes." Ross led the way into the front room, and when I had poured he took his glass and raised it high. "Here's to a swift end of our troubles," he said, "and a return to business as usual."

Business as usual held few charms for such as I, but I do not doubt that the majority of the residents of Falmouth agreed with my master and his friends. Early the next morning the inhabitants met and voted their disapprobation of Colonel Thompson, noting in their resolve that they lacked the means to resist him. This seemed to satisfy Mowatt as far as it went, but later in the day he heard that the country people designed to bring cannon into town for use against him. He sent on shore to tell the assembly that the moment another shot was fired, he would have no choice but to consider that the town was in a state of armed rebellion, and to fire upon us in return. Thus the meeting ended on a sober note.

This day being one of the fasts ordained by the Continental Congress, the bells were rung to call the people to church at the end of all this business. Deacon Codman came back to the house with the captain and escorted him and his lady to hear Mr. Deane's sermon. I followed along behind and found a seat in the balcony. Afterward folk made much of my master's role in saving the town, which seemed to go a long way toward reconciling Elizabeth with his behavior the previous evening, and they had so many invitations that I was sent off to make half-holiday on my own. Being at my leisure, I had occasion to observe that the fast was adhered to with great strictness by most of the people of the town.

In contrast the men from the country took no notice of the day, unless indeed they were more anxious to obtain provision than otherwise. Seemingly the solemnity of the day was not to their taste. Perhaps a hundred of them paraded in the streets around noon and hauled Captain Coulson's boat into Captain Moses Pearson's back lot, down almost to Clay Cove. What they hoped this would accomplish escaped me, as if anything it was more easy of access there than formerly, and they succeeded only in annoying the inhabitants with their unseemly mirth. In the meantime the council of their officers had met and sent around to Deacon Titcomb for one hundred pounds of bread. He answered that he had no bread beyond what he wanted for himself, but he undertook that, if the men would stop and go out of town immediately, he would find them the quantity they required. Colonel Phinney promised to do his utmost to persuade them to depart, and therefore the bread was delivered, although in fact it was not in great plenty in the town at that time.

On Friday the country people began at last to disperse, and by six in the evening only the Gorham company, which left that same night, and Thompson's men, who were supposed to do likewise, still remained. The captain and I were about the town during a goodly portion of the day, so that we saw a number of the detachments as they marched away along the Back Street and so on down the Neck. The spruce twigs they had sported two days before were gone, and the fifes and drums mostly packed away. The unshaven men plodded through the mud with muskets muzzle-first over their shoulders like so many hunters turning homeward after an unsuccessful chase. I owed them, I think, no goodwill, neither I nor any man else in Falmouth, but the fact was that their departure depressed me extremely. It seemed to me that the revolution on which my hopes depended was crumbling at its foundations, and I found myself wondering whether I should not hear any day that the army that had gathered outside Boston were gone off with its tail between its legs as well.

As I have said, it had been noised about the town that Colonel Thompson and his men were to depart for Brunswick once night had fallen, which rumor was given added credence by the fact that they had seized another of Mowatt's boats during the afternoon. The *Canceaux* fired at several vessels to bring them to, and then released them, by which the colonel understood that Mowatt had divined his intention of returning by water, and went instead on Saturday morning by a different and safer route. Later we learned that Mowatt had lain in wait for him all Friday night to the eastward of town, having armed his cutter with a swivel gun for the adventure.

The Reverend Wiswell went on board the *Canceaux* again on Saturday, notwithstanding that the town was not clear of outsiders, and on the morning of the Sabbath sent to his warders that he should not preach in the church again, but would hold his services on the ship, to which they might come if they chose. I did not hear that any went save George Lyde, the customs man, but his people were all in a toss. Some said that he was gone for good, and would try to get himself settled at Portsmouth or in Boston, while others said no, for he had left his family on shore. A few spoke against him, saying that his action tended to widen, rather than to heal, the breach between the two parties in the town, as was Wiswell's ghostly duty.

At first light on Monday the town was roused to wakefulness by two guns fired within the harbor. At first we feared the worst, and Ross sent me to packing while he and Elizabeth dressed, but when there were no more we went down to the waterfront to see what boded. Apparently the shots were no more than signals of a sort from Mowatt to his convoy. When we got to the wharf, we found that the *Canceaux*, the *Sphinx* tender which had come on April 24, and

Coulson's ship and Bristol sloop had unmoored and got under way. It must have been that the wind would not serve, however, for sometime later they came to an anchor in the roads beyond Hog Island, and abided there the better part of the day.

That same forenoon the weather broke, becoming warm, as befit the middle of May, where before the spring had been cold and rainy. The coincidence did not go all unmarked. Old wives nodded sagely and gabbled of omens, while more practical folk took heart from the sun and the promise of a good growing season to follow.

Next to her own flowers, the fruit trees were Sarah's especial delight. There were then five or six large orchards upon the Neck, besides which most of the houses would have a tree or so planted in the yard for the making of pies and sauces. Because of the wet the cherries and plums had bloomed but indifferent well. This it was too late to mend, but the apple trees, which were by far the most numerous, came into flower as though determined to make up for the loss. Sarah loved to walk among them, and we spent hours there without talking; though my thoughts were of other things, I remember them still. While the trees were yet in full blossom, there were places where their gentle perfume was stronger even than the sea-tang, and when at last the petals began to fall the lanes were drifted over as with snow. All the days were fine and hot, and filled with the sound of bees.

For a fortnight at least this soporific scene endured with little news from other parts to disturb it, none of it reliable. I was in agony of waiting, and would snap at Sarah's well-meant efforts to soothe me, but most of the people seemed glad enough of the lack. Talk was rather of crops and voyages than of war. There was a vessel come in from the southward that had long been looked for, and the cargo of breadstuffs she carried caused more interest than any of her master's rumors. It was as though folk had decided that they had need of bread, but that what happened in other parts was of no import in Falmouth.

Our daily lives began to fall once again into familiar patterns. There was no regular customs, but William McLellan, Joseph's brother, assumed the duties of the office. My master accordingly began to put together a cargo for a merchant of Mr. Pagan's acquaintance in the Jerseys who would trade grain for lumber and fish, and no one raised voice against him for dealing with a Tory.

None of this was particularly encouraging to a man who looked to the revolt for his freedom. I feared lest Falmouth become a mean back-water, and my fear made me increasingly impatient and disagreeable. All this Sarah bore patiently until one day near the end of the month. We had been sitting together on a rude bench under the apple trees which had become a trysting place for us, when finally my ill humor became more than she could bear.

"Go off with you then, if you can't bide here," she told me. "Lord knows you're not worth having around. Why don't you go to Virginia? I hear the governor is to raise a regiment of slaves to fight the Liberty Boys there, and will free them as will enlist. Go there, or just run off. It's better than eating away at yourself and me the way you've been doing these weeks past. I can't stand to watch you much longer."

I looked at her and scowled. "Virginia! And how am I to get there? I can't walk that far."

"No," she agreed. "That's so. But you can go by ship. There's a brig in the harbor just now: Captain Blancher's. She's bound for New York with spars and such for the shipyards there. I've spoke to him already, and he'll take you for a price if you'll get aboard so he doesn't have to see you."

"For a price? And where did you suppose I'd get the money?"

"From me," she said, and pressed coins wrapped in a bit of cloth into my hand.

"Say you'll go," she urged. "Promise me. You can send for me or not, once you're clean away, but go." She brushed my face with her lips, and then she was gone.

I sat there until the sun began to go down, and in the end I took the money and hid it in a hole in the garden. There was no time on the day following, but the very next I took it and went down to the waterfront to seek Blancher out.

The brig was an old one, dirty and foul-smelling, but I made up my mind that I would go if Blancher would have me. I would not have to suffer her for long. As I approached, a man came out of the after companion. He wore a coat of blue broadcloth and a large cocked hat set far back on his head, from which I concluded that he must be Captain Blancher. I put my hand in my pocket to reassure myself that I did indeed have hard money to buy passage and started forward. As I did, Blancher chanced to turn his head in my direction. His eyes slid past me without any sign of interest, but for some reason I slunk back into the shadows.

Blancher took a step or two and spat a long amber stream of tobacco juice into the water. A final trickle found its way through the un-razored stubble to the point of his chin; he wiped it away carelessly with a sleeve. Profanely he told a seaman who was working amid the deck cargo that he was going ashore for a time.

He passed close enough to where I stood that I could smell the reek of him above that of the harbor. When he had gone, I found that my hand was clenched tight about the coins. Blancher in the flesh was an unlovely creature, so much so that I had no desire to sail with him, to New York or anywhere else. I had no reason to believe that he would not take my money and sail without me as the shipowner of Surinam had done to Candide. I would have no recourse if he did. Worse: Blancher might take me south only to sell me into bondage. Perhaps it were better to wait a more trusty captain, a better-settled plan, or yet news that might tell me which way I might best shape my course.

Blancher went his way without me, and a day or so after he sailed I gave the money back into Sarah's keeping. The cause of this was what I had heard from the convention held of delegates from the several towns within the county, which met on the Neck at the last of May. It seems that there had been a petition sent off sometime before to the General Court that the regiment, so-called, of Colonel Phinney, be stationed within the borders of the towns wherein it had been raised for the comfort and defense of the people hereabout. The Court had sent for answer that four hundred of the men at the least were wanted in the camp in Cambridge. This word came to us by the hand of Mr. Dawes, being the same man who had ridden upon the Lexington alarm with Paul Revere. Dawes was a high Whig and risen in prominence since the affair, though nothing like so much as Revere himself. He found in Falmouth rather a lukewarm welcome, and several times was heard to say that he was dismayed at our lack of martial spirit. In the end he had got the men he had been sent to secure, but as they were the same who had lately given the town so sore a turn, it may be that the generality of people voted to send them in order that the trouble-makers might all be out of the neighborhood.

Mr. Dawes also brought news of the affair upon Noddle's Island in Boston Roads, where the army killed some hundred or so of the British and drove off all the sheep and cattle they had pastured there, and notice that Crown Point was taken by Colonel Allen and a Colonel Arnold from Connecticut. Where this Crown Point might be I did not then know, nor Ticonderoga either, which Dawes said was also fallen; only that they were posts of some importance, situate on the borders of Canada to our north and westward, and a longish way from Falmouth.

Everything, it seemed to me, happened a longish way from Falmouth. Doubtless it was safer this way, though I found it as hard as ever to wait upon the deeds of others while my future hung in the balance. Yet until affairs took a definite turn there was no telling which way I should go, and in the meantime, there was Sarah, patient and long-suffering. She walked silently beside me up and down the orchard lanes while I pondered. Of course I might have the chance to cut and run when I was in New Jersey; there was that, but in the end I decided for diverse reasons to let things bide as they were until the autumn, when the apples which had lately bloomed would be ripe and red.

32

Not long after, we sailed for the Jerseys. The captain disposed of our cargo to good advantage and purchased flour from Mr. Pagan's friend. In some fashion he contrived to lade near four hundred barrels on board, though scarce a foot remained anywhere for the working of the vessel. Ross therefore laid our course well offshore, longer but with few changes of tack, and we ran with a following wind clear to Georges Bank before it became needful to put the helm over and make our westing.

At dawn on the first day of July, Jack descried the top of Munjoy's Hill on our northerly horizon, distant about five leagues. This news put my master in great good humor, for we had been absent just on a month and now were come safe home, hindering no man and with none offering to hinder us during the whole of that time. While he was shaving, Ross told me that this proved his case, that so long as men of goodwill kept to their business, there were few quarrels so great as not to be readily compounded.

I went on deck again, where Grizzell stood at the helm and Jack tended sheet and spoke of the quantities of rum he would drink upon our arrival. I went forward so to be spared the listening and watched the outer islands slide past on either side.

As the schooner rounded the point at Purpooduck I saw a shore boat pulling hard on a course to cross our own. When I sang out, the captain came on deck to look, and told us to slacken sail that he might speak it more easily when we should be near enough to do so. Through the glass I could see that the craft pulled four oars, with another man in the stern sheets. When we had closed to within long pistol shot, Ross recognized this last as Joseph McLellan's brother William, and hove to.

Just then McLellan put hand to mouth and hailed us. "What schooner's that? Ross, is that you?"

My master answered back that it was.

"Wait, then," McLellan told him. "I'll come aboard."

I could not think what all this might betoken, but in a stroke or two of its oars the boat was at our side. Seamanlike, McLellan clambered over the rail without waiting for me to hand him up and told the others to wait. I followed in his wake to the quarterdeck.

"I've been looking for you to arrive these three days past, Captain," he said. "It was feared you might have gone astray, although from appearances, your friends need have had no concern. I trust that you've made a prosperous voyage? How long at sea?"

"Ten days," Ross replied. "I'd soon it wasn't eleven."

"You'll not have heard, then," McLellan said. He let the jibe pass. "How laden?"

"Flour. In barrels. Not have heard? Heard what?"

"Nothing else? No powder nor arms? No . . . letters?"

"No. Now damn it, Will McLellan, are you going to tell me what's afoot or no? I don't remember you as one to waste a man's time."

McLellan lowered his voice, but not so far that I could not hear him. "Joe asked me to keep a weather eye for you, for friendship's sake," he said. "Things aren't the same hereabouts these days as when you left. After what's happened, he figured you should be warned, or you might have put your foot in it for fair. We didn't know but what you'd be carrying something for your wife's brother or the Potes that folk wouldn't take kindly to: only that you'd gone off to the Jerseys, and to friends of theirs at that.

"The troubles started again the week after you'd left. That beggar Coulson was back, God rot him, with the *Senegal* man-of-war out of Boston. He come for his family, him and the sheriff, and for his cargo of masts he had in the Presumpscot. We let them take their people, we did, but he never got them sticks. He lost another boat and eight of his men before he give up and went back, and lucky for him that he did. If he'd been here when the news came about the battle in Charlestown, he'd have lost a lot more than his boats."

McLellan's eyes lit up at the recollection. "You should have been here, Will," he said. "It was just a few days after word come that there had been a fight down to Machias, and a king's ship took. Folks have been in a state ever since. There's two companies been raised in town to go after the Regulars, Brackett's and Bradish's, and every one of 'em loaded for bear! Then that Blancher feller come back to town last week. He'd been took off Cape Cod and carried into Boston, so he'd seen the whole thing from Copp's Hill himself."

At the mention of the name I forgot myself and broke in. "Blancher?" I asked. "Captain Blancher? The one who sailed for the southward the week before we left?"

McLellan looked at me coldly. "The same," he said, but in such a tone that I hastened to excuse myself, while Ross added that we were making more leeway than he liked, and that he was for getting under way again. This we did, taking McLellan's men on board and towing his boat from our stern. The extra hands made for light work, so that I was able to listen to enough of what passed between my master and Joseph's brother to satisfy my curiosity.

McLellan said that the armies had fought on a point of land called Bunker Hill, where the Province troops had built an earthen redoubt. The Regulars had come against it three times with superior numbers, but the militia held firm, and were only driven out when they had expended their powder and ball. For this reason it was accounted a victory by the Liberty party even though the field had been lost. Of the redcoats at least five hundred were said to have been slain, and an equal number wounded, against betwixt forty and seventy of our own men dead, a figure which included a colonel from someplace in New Hampshire and Dr. Joseph Warren, by all accounts the noblest of the Whigs and the president of the Congress in Watertown. His loss, McLellan affirmed, was a grievous one, and the more lamentable because he left four motherless children. "But you know, Ross," he continued, "it's fortunate for you that you were not situated to learn the news at closer hand. Captain Blancher has lost his vessel and his cargo both, but then he came away again. His men were all pressed on board the men-of-war."

When I heard this my head flew around like one of Mr. Congreve's rockets, and I broke out all over in cold sweats. I had come only too close to sharing their fate, and my escape seemed to me so clearly Providential that I blessed M. Arouet and his hero.

The flour we had brought was in such demand that we could hardly land it fast enough, and the next few days are but ill defined in my memory. Sarah was affectingly relieved to see me returned, but she had to content herself with that until the cargo had all been brought ashore. Ours was the first vessel in from the southward in some time, the captain and Mr. Pagan doing a brisk bit of business, for Falmouth was far from self-sufficient in foodstuffs. A fortnight later there were three vessels in with corn from Maryland, and three from the West Indies, so that goods of all kinds were plenty. In the meantime, Captains Brackett and Bradish had marched for Cambridge with their companies, and Captain Dunn from Cape Elizabeth beside, all to join Colonel Phinney, who was gone before. There was another company under a man named Strout which was formed for service in the county and served all year until it stood down in November.

Samuel Freeman was returned to the Congress in Watertown soon afterward, which was almost the only civic business of the summer. When court met they could do nothing, owing to the absence of both Sheriff Tyng and Mr. Freeman, who was the crier. Old Mr. Freeman was plentifully occupied with building whaleboats on the Province account, having taken the brigadier for a partner.

The news we had from other places was various. The people in Boston were said to be in great want both of firewood and provisions. General Gage looked to the navy to supply them, and Admiral Graves had sent cruisers with orders to take any vessel they encountered and bring it there. In addition, he had sent a ship to dismantle the fort at

Penobscot and a convoy of eight sail to gather wood to the eastward. We had word later that the people at Bagaduce had voted to supply him, and there was some talk that a Captain Pendleton had a thousand cords ready cut and waiting transport. The vessel at Penobscot came away safely with the arms and all the powder, but some of the others were less fortunate, being captured and taken into the Province service together with a schooner and tender sent to chastise Machias.

On the heels of these small successes Brigadier Preble had occasion to go to headquarters in Cambridge on some matter, which started tongues to clacking from York to the Passamaquoddy country that he was to raise a force for the purpose of invading Nova Scotia. A party of twenty men that passed through Falmouth from the eastward on their way to join their regiment told us in all seriousness that he was to have upwards of two thousand men for the enterprise. Of these, nine hundred were supposed already to have been raised and quartered in Falmouth. There was a store of powder and arms besides, it was said. At the King's Head one night someone asked them where they thought we had hidden these soldiers away, there being fewer than any of us liked in the neighborhood since Brackett and Bradish had gone and no more than a quarter of a pound of powder to a man. The new-comers just shrugged and said that it was common talk up and down the coast. We all laughed at their simplicity, little thinking that any sensible man would credit so mad a rumor.

In the main the summer passed away without Falmouth's being further touched by troubles either from without or within. For a time there was talk, some of it heated, when it was learned that an obscure Virginia colonel had been sent by the Continental Congress to take command of the troops assembled around Boston. New Englanders had been accustomed to choose their own officers when they went to fight, and everyone had expected that "Old Put," General Israel Putnam, or mayhap Colonel Hancock would be chosen. Finally a letter came for Mr. Freeman from his son in Watertown which he made public in order to end the argument. This Colonel Washington, he said, was a likely enough man, polite if a trifle stern. Beyond that, he seemed a good disciplinarian, which, as we knew from our own experience, was all to the good, and so long as the men were disposed to follow him, he could find no objections. Thus the controversy was largely laid to rest.

This relative calm did not mean that there was no pressure brought to bear by the Liberty party upon those whom they viewed as their errant fellow citizens. From this coercion our own household was fortunate enough to be exempted, for the captain had managed to retain his ties on both sides without alienating either. Mr. Pagan was not so favored. He began finding it difficult to buy food and other necessaries except at ruinous prices, so that we were obliged to help him from our own stocks. Others among his acquaintances were forced to sign statements which promised good conduct in future, or retracted earlier opinions, in order to obtain relief. Even so, I believe that we in Falmouth were less bothered than folk in most towns in either Maine or the rest of Massachusetts by anything touching upon the war.

"Them redcoat rascals can't do nothin'," a man home from Cambridge for the harvest exulted at the King's Head one night in early September. "Our George has 'em bottled up in Boston tighter nor a spinster's never-mind. They eats rats mostly, them as eats, and drinks their fat king's health in ditch-water."

Even the royal navy seemed powerless to do us hurt. Occasionally we might read that a ship had been taken by one of Admiral Graves's cruisers, but it was common knowledge in the streets and in the taverns that General Washington was after fitting out a fleet of his own to feed upon English transports, so that we daily looked to receive news that they had put to sea. In any event our coastwise trade was little discommoded by the admiral's efforts. It being the hurricane season in the Indies, the *Industry* found herself much employed in this service and never sighted a hostile sail. This was as well for her crew, for often we were about such business as would not have borne close examination, as once when we put into Newburyport on the Merrimack River to load ironmongery and oakum the Committee of Supply had sent for the building of Mr. Freeman's whaleboats.

In Newburyport we had an experience the significance of which escaped me for a time, but became amply clear later. Three men came on board as we lay at the wharf and asked to see the captain, saying that they were from the Marine Committee. When my master came on deck, the eldest of them told him that they were considering the *Industry* for use in a matter of importance to the colonies. Ross made answer that she was already so engaged and produced our papers. Fortunately these included a pass countersigned by the committee with which Mr. Freeman had furnished us and which these gentlemen consented at last to honor.

"Where there's smoke there be fire," old Grizzell said out of the side of his mouth as the three left us to continue their rounds of the harbor. "Mark my words, they'll be for Halifax." This seemed so plain that none of us doubted the verity of what he had said. The navy yard lay there all undefended, as rich a prize as could be found; the captain related that Mr. Pagan had told him Governor Legge was in a very panic lest an armament from New England should suddenly descend upon him. What guns he had lay on the ground unmounted, so that if a fleet had suddenly hove in sight scarce a shot would have been fired for the honor of England's flag.

Back in Falmouth we told of what we had seen and what we suspected, and for several weeks we waited for the news that Halifax was taken. In the end we learned that the enterprise which had been launched from Newburyport was an attack upon the city of Quebec by way of the river Kennebec and the back country of our own Province, led by the same Arnold who had been at Crown Point and was now a general and a great favorite of Washington's. The ships which might have intercepted him on the way Admiral Graves had sent to cruise off Halifax instead. This news we had in Falmouth at the last of September together with a great frost, and we cheered ourselves with the knowledge that if we had been deceived, the British had been no less so, and in imagining Graves's discomfiture.

Still, there had been no decisive battle, no grand sign to tell me which way I should turn, and though the apples were ripe and mellow I put off making my decision from day to day hoping that news would come, or the weather, which was cold and rainy and altogether unfit for traveling (a favorite excuse), should mend. New England weather being what it is, mend is the one thing that it did not do, not more than a day or so at a time, and I was still in Falmouth into the month of October, when we heard of how a British transport gave itself into the keeping of the Liberty Boys at Piscataqua. Portsmouth was by now entirely in American hands, Governor Wentworth and his family having left that place with the *Scarborough* frigate sometime before.

Joseph McLellan brought my master the news, laughing easily as he did when something greatly pleased him, and in truth it was a humorous story. It seems the English captain was off his reckoning and stopped to ask a fisherman the way to Boston. "There, your honor," the fisherman says, pointing straight-faced toward the spires of Portsmouth. "There be Boston." The captain thanked him and sailed in under the guns to anchor.

"There'll be empty bellies for Gage and his friends this winter," McLellan crowed. "The *Prince George* had nineteen hundred barrels of Philadelphia flour on board when she dropped her hook. Why, he'll have to leave off putting powder to his hair so to make bread from it instead. I hear the redcoat officers are eating their horses already. They'll be on cats and dogs ere New Year's!"

Elizabeth sniffed at that, and said she found Mr. McLellan's sentiments inappropriate for any man who called himself a Christian.

"Your pardon, ma'am," was his rejoinder, "but, whatever 'tis like here in Falmouth, it's war up Boston way, and war's not like to be Christian. Not the way a man's Christian in his parlor. The folks in Boston, they're the enemy. They can stay and starve, or they can go home to King George and leave us be. It's their choice, after all."

Ross took Elizabeth's hand and said that he thought that she meant that we should have a care for the women and children who were besieged along with the men. McLellan nodded. "It's a fact," he admitted. "Still, I can't think of any way to starve the men and feed the rest of 'em. It all comes down to stay or go. In the meantime we got 'em trapped like red-coated rats."

"But even rats will fight, Mr. McLellan," Elizabeth put in with a fierce little toss of her head. McLellan smiled and tipped Ross a wink.

"Why, that's so," he said. "I only wish they would. My father used to tell me about how Wolfe never would have beat Montcalm if he'd set tight inside Quebec. It was coming out to fight that beat him. If Gage'd fight we could beat him. We know it, and after Bunker Hill, I'd say that he knows it, too. We've got to make him come out somehow, Christian or no, if ever we're to beat him in proper fashion. Until he does it's bound to get a little unpleasant."

A few days later we had some measure of how unpleasant it had become, for word came from Watertown that there were near two score of transports and armed vessels that had set out from Boston to gather supplies and firewood. One of these, the Marblehead schooner *Hannah*, which General Washington had fitted out to cruise upon the Continental account, came near to taking off Nantasket before she herself was chased into Beverly harbor. Some said the foragers included a sixty-four-gun ship and three frigates, which would have been one tenth the force the British had in all of America and the Indies and like to cracking filberts with a ten-pound hammer: the crews of such great vessels would eat in a day more food than could be got from any town along our coasts. It rained very heavy all the day that we heard this and for two days after, when the sun came out from behind the clouds as hot, almost, as in the month of August. I wiped the sweat from my face and waited for news that Gage was come out and was beaten at last.

The end of the week brought us strong northwesterly gales and an excited fisherman who put in to tell how he had seen six great ships off the outer islands. Nervous folk averred that this was the fleet that had been talked of earlier, but on Sunday we heard from Townsend on Booth Bay that they were Lieutenant Mowatt and some transports. He had taken a few sheep and burned a shed or two, but no more than that; the committee met and decided to send a few men to guard the cattle and hay on our own islands early the next morning, but none doubted that in the end some accommodation could be reached. We had that day small breezes and a drizzling rain, and the most memorable occurrence seemed to be the fact that Mr. Deane was unwell, so that old Parson Smith came down from his son's house in Windham to preach all day and administer both sacraments. In the English church there was a Reverend Bailey come from out of town to preach for a time in room of Mr. Wiswell, who, Elizabeth's brother said, sufficed very well.

Monday dawned fresh and clear, the captain rising at his accustomed hour and going about his business and I with him. At nine of the clock we were in Mr. Pagan's counting-room when we heard talk in the street that six ships had been seen in the offing, and seemed by their motions to be approaching the harbor, though the wind was very nearly dead foul for them to do so. About eleven we could see them from the upper windows within Cape Elizabeth and spreading all their canvas in an effort to reach the harbor. Three o'clock saw them at anchor in Hog Island Roads, perhaps a league distant still.

Mr. Pagan saw no need to be alarmed at Mowatt's arrival, and reminded my master that he had cause to remember Falmouth folk more kindly than he did those to the eastward. "He's done no great harm as it is," I heard him say. "Probably the few buildings were fired by accident, or because someone resisted. They are hasty folk at Booth Bay, and need will brook no denial. Mowatt's his orders to victual the fleet for Boston: we've beasts enough to spare him a few after all. He's a friend, and if we treat him properly I've no doubt he'll pay us well."

With this sensible advice the captain voiced agreement, adding that since we lacked the means for effective resistance in any case, only madmen would seek to provoke the English.

"Well, then," Pagan said, rubbing his hands together and casting about him for his inventory book, "let's be glad that the pestiferous Colonel Thompson is gone back to wherever it is the devil keeps him, and see what there is we can sell to yon Mr. Mowatt."

With this he took his ledger and led the way to the storeroom. A few minutes later we heard the report of a gun, and then another, muted by distance and the walls around us but nonetheless distinct. Outside, people began shouting. One of the clerks ran out to see what was the matter. He came back with the news that a small schooner had slipped past the English fleet by rounding the far side of Hog Island,, and that the *Canceaux* had fired to bring her to. "She wouldn't stop for him," the youth concluded, "so they've lowered a boat, and given chase."

From upstairs we could see that there was little chance that the barge would catch her prey. Even as we watched, there was a wreath of smoke from the longboat's bow: musketry, or a swivel gun, and the British craft turned back. A ragged cheer spread from the docks back up the street as people realized that the schooner was safe.

The newcomer proved to be the *Arrow* out of Townsend, with news from that place of Mowatt's late exactions, and of the arrival in Booth Bay of the schooner *Britannia*, of and for Newburyport, with great store of powder and of arms she had brought from the West Indies. The *Arrow* herself was of trifling burden, but very fast, and was manned with an unusually large crew so that they were able to work her up to the town by her sweeps in a matter of but a few hours. Seeing her chased and fired upon had so inflamed the susceptible members of the crowd that some of them manned a boat lying at the end of Preble's wharf and went to help, while the others hurled threats of vengeance and epithets at the English fleet full a league distant. In the evening the committee met and seconded these, but took no more hostile action than to relieve the guards upon the cattle and to observe the actions of those they now denominated the enemy.

My master attended the public part of the meeting and came home nonetheless convinced that a passive attitude was the safest of possible courses for the town, but warned me to be ready for an early rising, when we would go down to the *Industry* and shift her anchorage up-river. "Just to be sure," was how he put it, and the events which followed revealed the sagacity of his impulse.

The morning of the seventeenth was one of outward peace and inward agitation. All of us went about our affairs with one eye on the task at hand and the other on the harbor until the hour of eleven, when it became known that the *Canceaux* could be seen to be warping herself close under Hog Island Ledge. It could only be that she was preparing to get under way; with the wind in the quarter in which it lay, she would have from there the best chance of making good a course for the town if such were Mowatt's intention. At two in the afternoon Mowatt fired a gun; at half-past, another, when the whole of the fleet weighed and came to sail in line astern. They sailed directly up before the town and anchored as for battle, the *Canceaux*, a large ship with ports for as many as twenty guns, two more armed vessels, and two others. I think it was now nearly five o'clock.

The town was not much longer kept in ignorance of what Mowatt's intentions might be, for as soon as he came to an anchor and handed his sails, the *Canceaux*'s barge was brought around and manned, in which the lieutenant dispatched one of his officers to bring a letter to the people on the shore. This officer landed at Preble's wharf, where near every man in town was come to receive him. A score or more of the Cadets and others appeared in uniform and under arms, constituting themselves a sort of guard of honor, and escorted the messenger to the town house. This they endeavored to do with proper ceremony and decorum as they conceived it to be, but the close press rendered this impossible in the narrow part of the street, and the whole show was much impaired by children, drunkards, stray dogs, and a few whose sole concern was to be able to flourish their fists beneath the man's nose so as to boast about the deed afterward. All this the young man bore patiently, though from the close vantage of Mr. Pagan's window I could see that it made no good impression upon him.

At length he was gone from sight, and we all of us went back down the stairs to wait the issue in more comfortable surroundings. I do not think even then that Mr. Pagan apprehended any harm at Mowatt's hands, he appeared so calm, with never a sign of lapse in his speech as so often occurred when he was excited. The captain's show was less successful: or perhaps I merely knew him better and so was able to sense his agitation. For myself, my hands were shaking as I poured from Mr. Pagan's crystal decanter, so that I wished I might have a glass along with the others.

A half an hour at the least was past when we had the first intimation of what was to be. At first the street was all confusion and tumult, but when the officer was at last closeted with the committee this was replaced with a profound silence. From time to time there was a voice rang out from the direction of the town house, so that I think that a man had been stationed in the window to relay information to those who could not gain admittance, but it was too far for us to make out his words. Finally there was a space longer and somehow ominous, when at last a galvanic start ran through the crowd and of a sudden they were all pushing and running and trying to talk at once.

From the snatches of what could be heard, Captain Ross was able to learn that Mowatt was under instructions to burn the town, and that no more than two hours had been allowed for the removal of all the people. Elizabeth forthwith turned pale and sank back into her seat, but when Ross would have taken her up and made his way to the house on Jones Lane, Mr. Pagan counseled him to be calm and wait until the streets were somewhat cleared. Thus we sat and watched through the windows as though it were a set-piece of the last moments in Pompeii. I cannot exaggerate the affecting nature of the scene, in comparison with which all that had happened in the early alarms was as nothing. In the next moments we saw women with babes at the breast or helpless in their arms, running precipitately through the crowd with the light of reason gone from their eyes. The useless objects that the people had caught up in their flight left me at odds between compassion and laughter: here an old broom, there a pail in the one hand and in the other a handful of glasses, and one man with a greasy old blanket bundled into his arms who left behind him his terrified wife and several small children.

Ross held Elizabeth's hand the while and urged upon her a mouthful of her brother's smuggled French brandy. Presently her color began to return, and my master rose to leave. "We'll be going now, Robert," he announced. "Two hours seems to be all Mowatt's friendship is worth, and we can't afford to waste any of it. You'd best hurry along as well. Save what you can, and stop up by the house on your way. You'll be all right, I hope?"

Pagan nodded without turning. "Yes, fine. What I'd be bringing will all fit in one bag. There's no sense in trying to move the rest anyway. But I'm thinking this is all bluff, to get the committeemen to let Mowatt have what he needs cheaply. Look: here comes Brigadier Preble, Mr. Parsons, and Dr. Coffin. They're not running, at least! By the looks of it, they're coming here, too! Wait a minute and see what they've got to say, why don't you?"

Ross stayed only long enough to confirm that Mowatt had indeed threatened the town with imminent destruction, but that he would speak to an embassy of three men from the town on board his ship first. Preble said that he was come to see if Pagan would be the third with him and the doctor, and Pagan answered that he would.

"You see?" he said, kissing Elizabeth lightly on one cheek. "I'm sure we'll find that 'tis all bluster, just as I told you. I'll send word by my clerk directly I'm back, and by nightfal we'll be laughing at all this."

We went back to Jones Lane and began to pack the things of greatest value and least bulk, together with a few changes of clothes and of linen for the captain and his lady. This took us the better part of an hour. At the end of that time there came a knock at the front door. Elizabeth straightened up with a look of relief and bid me go and answer it. "Do hurry," she said. "I'm sure that must be Robert."

I ran to the door and opened it to find Joseph McLellan standing on the front step. "I can't stay," he told me. "I just stopped by to let your master know that we'll have wagons coming in from Gorham tonight. He's welcome to one if he wants it."

Ross came up the hall behind me and greeted his friend. "I was just making the offer of a cart for your things," McLellan said.

"Will it come to that?"

"Hard telling. I'd have to say it doesn't look good. Preble came back with Mowatt's last word, or so he says. He'll hold off the burning till sunrise if we give him eight stand of small arms. They're talking it over in the courtroom still. Which reminds me: Elizabeth's brother's there, and he says to tell her he's all right, but that he'll be a while yet before he can come. I guess that's all, but the wagons'll be here around midnight. My brother's gone to fetch 'em, and I'll have one of our boys drive yours down when they get here." Ross shook his hand and thanked him, and then he was gone.

It was well into the evening before Elizabeth's brother arrived, with a valise in his hand and his account books under his arm. Over a glass of wine and a biscuit he told Ross and Elizabeth that Mowatt had extended the deadline until nine o'clock next morning. "I've never seen a man so affected," Pagan said. "He told us that his orders left him no choice but to proceed, and even shed tears when I pressed him. I thought then that there was a chance that he might relent, and spoke of the bonds of friendship and affection between him and many of the people. He told us that his orders permitted him no discretion, but that he would take it upon himself to delay their execution if the committee would agree to further sureties."

"Then there's still a chance that he won't go through with it?" Ross prompted. Pagan took a swallow of wine and shook his head.

"I think not. Mowatt engaged to make representations on our behalf to the admiral if the town would surrender their cannon and musketry and send hostages to Boston, but he could make no promises beyond that, and of course the committee would not agree. Some of the hotheads say they'll fight first, though God knows what with; they never did get the cannon mounted. They won't do anything yet, but I know there have been riders sent to the inland towns for men, and they might attempt something later on. Something with boats: there are enough of them about, I should think. Mowatt warned us he'll attack at once if they do, so Preble's set patrols in the streets to stop any disturbance." He drained his glass and handed it back to me. "Come along," he said. "I'll lend a hand. With luck we can have the furniture out of the house by the time the wagon gets here."

It was already after midnight when we had done. Elizabeth wrapped herself in a coverlet and sat in one of the parlor chairs to wait, but Pagan said that she might as well come down to his house and get some sleep. "Nothing is likely to happen until morning," he reminded her, "and there's nothing that a woman can do here." Ross concurred, and went with them to see her settled, leaving me to await the arrival of the wagon. There were a number of conveyances that passed in the time he was gone, but all save one was laden and going out of town.

My master's face, when he returned, showed his disappointment that McLellan's wagon had not arrived. He rubbed the back of his neck and looked up the hill. "Run up to McLellan's and see what's become of it," he told me. "I'll stay here. If it's not coming, we'll carry what we can into the field across the way."

I made the best of my way to McLellan's, though Middle Street was populous with fugitives, some of them people who had run into the country at the first alarm and were now returned to carry away a few of their belongings. Near the hay scales, where Middle Street joins the road out of town, a wagon had broken down so that it more than half-blocked the way, and only one cart could pass at a time.

McLellan's house and yard were bright-lit and abustle when I arrived. A large wain was drawn up before the door, nearly loaded, with Joseph's brother William standing on the seat. He was shouting orders and advice at two of his Gorham blacks who were trying to load a tall chest into a wagon bed, his instructions doubtless all well meant but serving, I think, more to complicate the evolution than to aid it. When I asked him about the wagon, he seemed puzzled.

"Ain't it there yet?" he asked, and then, in a loud voice, "Easy there, Plato! By God, that thing ain't made of iron, and it's worth more'n you are!" He turned back to me. "Where the hell can it be? I sent Prince around with it an hour ago at least." He pushed his hat back and scratched his head. "Hold on a minute. We're most done here, and when we are I'll come with you and see what's become of it."

To speed matters along, I lent Plato and the other a hand. A few minutes later they were on their way to Hugh McLellan's farm and William was free to help me find the missing wagon.

Our search took us along Back Street as far as Meetinghouse Lane. We went the length of the lane and then down Jones Lane. My master was waiting by a small fire he had kindled to warm him, and said that he had not seen either Prince or wagon. At Fore Street we turned right, past Captain Thomas's house, intending to go back to McLellan's by way of Love Lane.

While we were passing Deacon Cotton's tanyard, McLellan suddenly stopped and pointed up the road. "Look at that, by God!" he exclaimed. "There's that damned wagon now." I looked, and there it was, drawn up at the side of the road next to a body of men clustered around a bonfire. McLellan ran on ahead and clambered into the wagon. There was no sign of Prince, and for a moment he stood there in the wagon bed with his face illumined by the firelight. As I approached a figure broke away from the crowd, and I could see a large keg had been broached and set by the side of the road.

"Massa Willum!" the figure said in Prince McLellan's voice. "Massa Willum! Oh, for God sake come here! Rum 'nough, Massa Willum, rum 'nough. Sugar and 'lasses 'nough to put in him, too. Oh, Massa Willum, glorious times these be, glorious times these be!"

❦❦❦ 33 ❧❧❧

THE first hint of dawn was lightening the eastern horizon when we finished loading the wagon and started Prince on his way. Fortunately the three hours of labor had restored to him both his dignity and his sobriety, and it seemed not unlikely that he would make the journey with little difficulty. There was no time for rest, however, for Mr. Pagan had sent word that he had got a gundalow from the Potes and, the tide being up, had brought it in to the wharf to load with what West India goods he might in the time that was left. Accordingly we went down and worked as long as we dared and then sent the vessel around the Neck, close inshore so as not to be intercepted by Mowatt's boats. With it went another owned by the silversmith, Paul Little. By this time it was somewhat after nine o'clock. My master told Mr. Pagan that it was time that he took Elizabeth to safety, but that he would leave me with him to help close up the house, which he did. A few minutes later Colonel Waite came by, telling everyone that it was time to go, and we locked the door and left.

Mr. Pagan said that it was best we went directly up the hill to meet Back Street and Sanford's Corner. I followed him up King Street, and when we had gone past the old windmill and were coming to the head of Lime Street, I saw the *Canceaux* hoist a flag and fire the first gun.

The ball was aimed high, to terrify rather than to kill, and passed between me and the Old Jerusalem meetinghouse. Doubtless it ended its flight in the Back Bay, harming only the fishes, but at the report, several dozens of the people around about me fell upon their faces and screamed that they had taken mortal wounds, and some few that they were already killed. It took a goodly amount of earnest remonstrance to convince them that they had taken no hurt and should rise and seek shelter, but in the end they did, when Mr. Pagan and I took to our heels as well.

The whole fleet now commenced a smart fire that continued into the afternoon, shells, bombs, and carcasses of all sorts raining down upon the houses and shops from the distillery at Jordan's Point westward as far as Fish Street. Mr. Pagan and I hurried down through the Back Fields, flinching a bit with the report of each gun, around behind the old church to Main Street, where we rejoined my master and his wife on the high ground near Joshua Brackett's.

A little after ten, fire broke out in the southern part of the town, and again on King Street, in a house that belonged to old Captain Hoole, but these burned down without harming any others because the day was fair and calm. I have heard that a shell landed in the churchyard, and a man pushed it aside with the muzzle of his gun lest the old meetinghouse should take fire. The captain seemed disposed to think the *Industry* safe enough where she lay near to Tate's Landing, and we stayed the day to watch the destruction of the town. The king's ships made no essay to interfere with her, or with the gundalows in Back Cove, but the rest of the shipping lying before the town they destroyed, to the number of thirteen sail, save only two large sloops new-come from the West Indies, which they preserved as prizes.

Around noon I should think that we had the more part of two thousand people standing there on the height of land. Most were people of the town, but there were also hundreds of men who had come in from the country upon the alarm. Being armed only with musketry, they were of little enough assistance, and in later years folks have spoken slightingly of them, saying that they were no more than low rascals come in hopes of carrying away a share of whatever escaped the flames. Some have claimed that they lost more to reivers than to fire, but I think that this is untrue; at least, I saw none of it. It may be that the owners themselves forgot where they had disposed their property in the confusion. Many valuable objects ended in unlikely places, as a pair of fine portraits that spent the night in a field.

In the afternoon a bomb opened the front of the English church, so that it took fire and burned like a torch, but there was still no wind to make it spread. Mowatt then sent his lieutenant ashore with a score or two of seamen and marines, their instructions being to fire what remained. Seeing an enemy at hand with whom they might come to grips, the militia moved forward into the town to engage them. After a sharp skirmish our people were forced to retire, but it may be that this demonstration was all that prevented the English from enlarging the zone of destruction. I do not think that many on either side were wounded in the fray, though people say that an English officer was killed at the door to Moses Pearson's, and a deserter gave himself up to Lieutenant Libby and was sent to Washington in Cambridge.

Near three hundred dwellings, or three parts in four of the whole of the town, had been burned when Mowatt signaled the cease-fire at sundown. Some of the militia went down again to take popping shots at the shipping, which were seldom answered and probably did no execution. Presently the fleet weighed and stood on down the harbor to Hog Island Roads. There was little wind yet, but as evening came on it began to rain, gradually at first and then in the night quite hard, so that those who were left without shelter suffered considerably from the cold and wet, and we lost many of our people in the weeks that followed to quinsies, pleurisies, and fever. Still, these were less than they might have been, because those whose homes had survived, among which were my master and his wife, took in the others for a time without thought of pay. There were those in Falmouth still who clung to the king's cause and blamed the misfortune upon what they called "the blustering Sons of Liberty," and some, like Elizabeth's brother, who became in after years refugees to Canada, but by and large they were few. Those who had hoped that the war might pass us by and leave them to do business as usual had found that their hopes were fraudulent and became as hearty for the cause of liberty as any. We did not know then that every port along the coast had not been served as Falmouth had, for Mowatt had said that his orders extended even to New York; in the end we learned that only Falmouth was destroyed, which was a joy and a sorrow both. Amid the melancholy remains of the most eligible and thriving city in North America we faced the gloomy and distressing prospect of approaching winter and the specter of bitter war. As one among the "hewers of wood and drawers of water," I had to work harder and make do with less than ever before, even though clement Providence had spared my master from loss. Still, I found that I had a growing sense that I was not alone, and I wonder even now if it were not then, before the issue was tried upon the fields of Saratoga and Yorktown, that the Revolution was fought and won in the hearts and minds of the people, among whom I conceived myself to be included.

III

THE MAN

34

I turned my daybook to a fresh page and with a clerkly flourish wrote the date: January 8, 1791. There I stopped, staring bleakly at the inscription while the ink dried unheeded on the nib of my pen. Could it really be that I was forty?

It had been Sarah's idea at the first, to reckon my age from this day and so to commemorate my independence. That had come in 1784. Though in point of law I was already free some time before I broke with the captain, I had found that Pyrrhus Ross, freedman, fared much as had Pyrrhus Ross the slave. No doubt he thought me content. There was room and board and steady work but little else, and when Sarah, who had since replaced the hateful old woman in the kitchen, spoke to Elizabeth about our being paid our worth, she got no more than an incredulous look and a reminder that the silver wanted polishing. Within the hour we had packed and were gone for her father's house, on a day so cold the harbor was frozen to the islands, Sarah six months with child, and I with a change of clothes and no more. Sarah, bless her, laughed.

"I was just thinking," she told me, "how you've always missed having a birthday. Now you've got one, if you will."

"Why, that's so!" I agreed, thinking to cheer her in my turn. "Rather an elderly infant I make; perhaps I shall follow the European mode and call this my name-day instead."

Sarah stopped and looked up at me. "Then you should have a new name to go with it," she said firmly. "A proper one, this time, and not someone's cast-off." I realized that she was right. To keep the name of Ross would remind folk of a connection that no longer existed, one I did not care to recall. Nor was I inclined to share Fitzgore with Frederick.

"Fair enough," I said. "What shall it be? They say it's important a woman's name should sound well with her husband's, but few wives have the opportunity to choose both man and name. Come along: we can think as we walk. A name! It should mean something, but Freeman, I fear, will not do."

Sarah laughed once more. "No," she said, "not in Falmouth. Though it would be funny to see the major's face when he heard."

"Then I shan't be a Smith, either. Would you be Sarah Blackmore instead?" She hesitated, and then shook her head. "Cook, perhaps? I was cook on board the schooner when I came."

Sarah made a face. "Too common."

"Something finer, then. Foreign, even. Lafayette? Sarah Lafayette? No?" I shifted my bundle to the other hand, which brought my well-thumbed book to mind. "Candide? No; I don't like that myself. But Pyrrhus Voltaire sounds not amiss. How about Voltaire?"

"Sarah Voltaire?"

"What's wrong with that? I like it."

"I don't know. It doesn't sound like me."

"But you've only just heard it." I glanced at her face and saw that it was no use. "You'll have to help, then. I'm running out of ideas. Othello? Not Africanus, surely. Nor anything else from the classics: no sense in changing one slave-name for another." I kicked at the snow in frustration.

"Oh, Pyrrhus!" Sarah chided. "You've read books enough; I venture you'll think of something."

"That's it!" I exclaimed. "That's it exactly! Venture! I was bought on a venture, and now I venture into freedom. Does it suit your ear?"

"Indeed it does. Sarah Venture. Mistress Venture. I think it sounds grand. Pyrrhus Venture, Esquire." She paused and made as though to drop me a curtsy, though her condition rendered the movement an awkward one. A shy glance downward. "Venture and Son?"

"Yes." I held out my hand to help her across an uneven spot in the snow, shamed to be so aware of her growing ungainliness. To cover my feelings I smiled. "Venture and Son."

Venture and Son: hyson tea, Hollands gin, Swedish iron. Chandlery and cheap crockery from Liverpool, headed up in barrels filled with straw. A bit of anything that would sell at a profit bartered for what the country produced in return. Pot and pearl ash, flaxseed bound for Ireland, fish. With a small house on one of the lanes off King Street and a frame store just east of Clay Cove, near to where Mr. Pagan had kept, I was by way of becoming a prominent man among the persons of color in the town: the shadow of what was called a "regular-bred merchant."

It had not come at once. When I left Ross, the greater part of the old settlement upon Falmouth Neck lay in ashes and ruin, scorched chimneys standing amid the rubble. A few of the great houses and the Old Jerusalem had survived, but these too showed the scars of ill treatment and neglect, mirroring Falmouth's fortunes in eight years of war. The town was like an orchard after a great storm. Some old familiar names had fallen root and branch while others like Codman and Tate were blasted and crippled but still alive. Some few hoary giants, Preble, Deering, Freeman, enjoyed what Homer called "a green old age, unconscious of decay," but in the main it was the saplings to whom the new age belonged. These were the young and ambitious, small traders and shipowners who, like Ross, had lost little or nothing to Mowatt's guns and the hazards which followed. Men who would take risks if calculation showed them worthy of the candle. They stayed and took root in the ashes of Falmouth while others went to Boston, and in the end it was those who stayed who prospered.

At first I took such work as the rising crop of merchants had to offer. By turns I was a stevedore, a clerk, a teamster; once I carried brick for the masons who built Peleg Wadsworth's fine new house near Brackett's in the west end of town, begun in 1785 and two years in the finishing. The first of its sort in Falmouth, it seemed to me a sort of promise that better times were at hand.

And so they were. On the fourth day of July, 1786, as if to follow my example, Falmouth had changed its name to Portland. I took this for an omen and, with the help of a loan from Sarah's father, invested in a small share of a cargo for the British sugar islands. It was one of few which got through in defiance of Lord Sheffield's restrictions, and paid handsomely. The profit I used to buy my store, a structure cheaply built in wartime and now no longer grand enough to suit its erstwhile owner.

It was the location that first caught my eye. Though the seat of trade was shifting slowly westward, Clay Cove was a busy place. Faber and Dunn kept on the cove itself, and here also came cargoes consigned to prosperous merchants in King Street: John Butler, who through repeated misfortunes eventually lost his reason; Abraham Osgood from London; Thomas Cumming; Stephen Codman. The air was thick with the mingled smells of molasses and of rum and it throbbed with the hoisting songs of the wharfmen. From my window I might look out upon the brigs and sloops tied up at Tyng's wharf, which Mowatt had spared, and to the row of new-built stores and warehouses along Fore Street on the opposite shore. One of the largest bore the name of William Ross and Company.

I had met Ross on Middle Street only that morning, I alone and he with Elizabeth, bundled against the cold. For an instant he seemed about to speak, but then Elizabeth took his arm and said somewhat to him so that he swept on past me with only a nod. I turned to watch them go and it seemed to me that Elizabeth looked back quickly from the corner of her eye, but of that I was never sure. In any event the captain and I would have had little enough to say.

He had done well since we had parted ways, as well perhaps as his friends William and Joseph McLellan. Like them he now owned his pew in the Second Parish meetinghouse where Mr. Kellogg preached, as true a badge of his rising station as his counting-house and the fine new brig moored before it, for the young nabobs of Portland all favored Kellogg's ardent, lively style over that of Smith or of Deane. Off Sabbath-day their combinations and associations were on much the same lines. Our circles never touched save by way of business, so many casks of this for thus many bushels of that, and no more.

There were footsteps on the stairs without, and with a guilty start I dipped my pen into the ink and commenced again to write. When the door opened I looked up to see, not Bob Waters or young Plato Darling, who were my apprentices, but my friend Jack Grove, seabag carelessly balanced on his shoulder and a smile splitting his plum-black face. I rose to take him by the hand.

"My God, Jack," I said, "you've made a speedy passage. I wouldn't have looked for you for a week at least."

Jack laughed. "Fastest time from Brest I ever see. That Captain Caldron sure a driver: no wonder he call that sloop the *Race Horse*. Sometimes I think he must wear spurs."

"It seems to agree with you," I told him. "You're looking well enough."

"Not so bad," he agreed. "And you? You taking on a little ballast from the look of it."

I pulled my waistcoat down over my middle. "You had to notice that. Sarah says it makes me look successful."

"She's right. A good belly is always in style."

"That's what I keep telling myself. Perhaps I should listen to you, since it's your line. Folk say you're the best cook this side of Boston. But say, what was Caldron carrying to be in such a hurry? Not wine, surely."

"No," Jack said. "Few more days in the cask don't matter. We had a passenger: rich one, very impatient. Pay us extra for a fast run."

"American?"

"No, he French all right. Call himself St. Cyr. Young's me, almost, and, Lordy! how he do go on. Talk more than a preacher on Sunday. Talk to me, talk to the captain. Even talk to Spanish John; and how he understand that dago I don't know. You like him, though. He remind me of you. Real smart, got big plans. Say he off to San' Domingo to help the black folks. Want to hear about how we live in America, whether we all free, what we do. I ran out of stories 'fore we get halfway. Anyhow, I tell him 'bout you and he get real excited. You his favorite story."

"What did you tell him?"

"Only the truth. Tell him you was a slave, and now you got your own place. You richer than half the white folks in town already. He like that, call you a 'natural man,' some such nonsense. I say, of course you natural, and he laugh like the devil. Then he run get some book and read at me. He a little crazy like that. I think he rather read than eat."

I looked down at my stomach ruefully. "I'm afraid that's not one of my problems these days," I said. "But I think you've made more of me than there is."

Jack snorted. "Where your old master be without you? You keep his books for years, you teach him everything you learn in the old days in the islands. After he lose his schooner at Bagaduce, when nobody hereabouts got money, you figure a way he can get started again. Now look at him. No, you the smartest man I ever see, and helpfullest."

"You're too warm by half, Jack, and you know it. Ross would have done well enough in any case. For all our differences, he was always an able man. You have to give him that."

"Maybe so; but I tell you this, Pyrrhus: I got no use for him. You ask me, he treat you bad at the end. And I tell you this, too: you won't find me on any vessel flies his flag. No, sir. I picks my berths and I picks my owners."

"Well," I conceded, "that's your choice. But don't judge him on my account. It's in the past, for all of me."

Jack shook his head. "I think you got too big a heart. Me, I don't forgive so easy. But I don't want to talk about Ross. I want to tell you about the Frenchman. I like him even if he sound a little crazy. You like him, too."

"From what you say I think I would. I hope I have a chance to meet him before he goes on to Santo Domingo."

"You will," Jack said. "I forgot to tell you; he been waiting outside all along."

❦❧❦❧ 35 ❦❧❦❧

A T first I did not know quite what to make of Jean Baptiste St. Cyr. He was an obvious sprig of the nobility, scarcely more than a boy, dressed as he would say *à la mode* in trousers rather than breeches and a bottle-green coat with many-caped shoulders, his face barely reddened by the winter wind off the bay and otherwise looking like a plate from the *Gentleman's Magazine*. Seemingly he belonged to that elegant breed on whom the rain refuses to fall and who do not sweat if ever they should choose to labor. I found myself prepared to dislike him for that and it may have showed. He hesitated for a moment as he reached the landing before he doffed his high-

crowned castor and stepped forward with a radiant smile that instantly
won me over.

He started to introduce himself in rapid French I could just follow,
then stopped in embarrassment and began again in English. "You must
excuse me, Citizen Venture," he said. "I am, as you see, overwhelmed:
our excellent Jack has told me so much about you. I have looked
forward to making your acquaintance already these many weeks."

"*De rien, monsieur, de rien. Enchanté.*" I spoke in French to put
him at his ease and found to my surprise that the polite phrases I had
not used in years still came easily to my lips.

St. Cyr smiled again, with visible relief. "May I compliment you on
your French? For some time now I have been compelled to listen to
Captain Caldron's, and while he is an exceptional navigator I fear he
is no linguist: at times it makes me tremble just to think where he
may have learned it. Yours, however! Citizen Jack has told me you
were born in the Indies. One of the French islands? Or were you
schooled in my country?"

"Neither, monsieur: I spent my childhood in Saint Kitts. But I was
so fortunate as to have a tutor, or likely I should speak as your good
captain does." We all three laughed at that, and I looked around for
my small liquor chest. "But I've forgotten my manners again, it seems.
Woud you care for a glass of brandy to welcome you to Portland?
Jack?"

St. Cyr accepted, but Jack shook his head. "I think I leave you two
to parly-voo," he said. "Best I get home and stow my gear. I stay
'round here long enough, even Spanish John goin' to start soundin'
good."

"Be sure to come by the house this evening," I told him as he swung
his seabag up from the floor and made to leave. "Sarah will want to
see you, of course, and today is my day, so we'll be having a party."
Jack grinned an acknowledgment and went out through the front
room. I turned to St. Cyr. "Doubtless you will have plans already," I
said, "but if not, we would be honored if you would come as well."

"But of course I shall! I have no plans, none whatsoever. After all,
I have only just landed. And it will be my honor to attend."

We sipped at our brandy. "I understand you're bound for the Indies
yourself," I prompted, after what seemed like a mannerly interval.

"Ah, *oui*. Saint Domingue, to be precise. You might say it is the realization of a lifelong ambition, to be of some use in an important cause."

"And what cause is that?"

"That of my friends who have gone before me to prepare the way. The cause of true republicanism, Citizen Venture: of Equality, of Liberty, and Justice. The natural rights of man, which we have so recently secured in my own country, the same for which General Lafayette fought under your President Washington." He looked at me earnestly. "Do you know what life is like for people of color on that island, which could so easily be a paradise?"

"In a general way."

"Of course. Forgive me; I have a way of forgetting myself. Jack has told me you were yourself a slave until but a few years ago. So few of the people to whom I have spoken have had that experience."

I assured him that I had taken no offense and urged that he continue.

"Well, then. I attended school with the sons of mulatto gentlemen from Saint Domingue: Haiti, as they call it. No man could wish for truer friends, I assure you. But their stories of the richness of the island and of their treatment at the hands of arrogant wastrels of planters! *Ces sont affreux!* Horrid! Why, in one case a white woman who was annoyed with her maid set the woman on fire! Yes, and when the poor servant died, all the authorities required was that the woman pay a fine. I think that in a civilized country not even animals would be so mistreated."

"I agree," I said. "But may this not be an exaggeration? Stories have a way of growing when recounted."

"No, Citizen. It is only too true. I heard it from Vincent Ogé himself. With his own eyes he has witnessed this, and worse. The people of color, the mulattoes and the blacks, they make the country thrive, and the white planters set them at odds and live off their sweat. But the time comes soon when all will be set to rights. Ogé and my other friends have sailed already, as I said. Now I follow them with supplies, if only what I have thus far gathered. The good God, he will aid the right."

"You chart a dangerous course."

"That is true. But it was dangerous for your Washington, dangerous for Lafayette to join him. And if I should fall in the fight I would be honored, as would any one of *Les Amis des Noirs.*"

"Friends of the Blacks?"

"*Oui*, Citizen Venture. We are a brotherhood, from Citizen Brissot and General Lafayette down to the least of us, who are willing to make any sacrifice to extend the rights of man from France herself to all parts of the Republic. Some of us will die, but that has always been so. My family, though once accounted of the nobility, has had a tradition of opposing unjust authority. My own father died in the Bastille. Therefore I have chosen to devote my life and what little fortune I have to the cause of human dignity.

"Saint Domingue is in a sad case. Perhaps it is true that we of the brotherhood go to our deaths. What man does not? Someone must make a start, don't you see, for there is much to be done, and so little time.

"You must understand that the situation there is worse by far than it was in your own colonies. Everything is faction! At the top are the governor-general and the intendant, ever striving after the upper hand. The Assembly is a mockery which consists wholly of corruptionists and officers of the regime. The colonists themselves, white or mulatto, have no more voice than do the slaves.

"Despite this many contrive to become wealthy men. Even some of mixed blood — as a class they control perhaps a tenth of the land and some fifty thousand slaves. Thus, both the blacks and the whites have cause to hate and fear them. My friends are the sons of such men. They will lose by it, but still they hope to bring this enormity to an end, to provide instead a new system wherein all men share alike the rights and obligations of citizens. Surely an island of such beauty has room for all." St. Cyr ceased his rhapsodizing and looked at me. "But you are frowning!" he said in dismay.

"Not at what you have said," I told him. "It is what you did not say. You are talking revolution, and such a thing can easily get out of hand. But beyond that, there are practical considerations: arms, medical supplies, food . . ."

"*Exactement!* Ah, Citizen, I knew that you would understand! But then you have been through it all yourself. You know the hazards. Do not trouble to deny it; Jack has told me again and again. Of your bravery and wisdom I know well, and selfishly I hoped to enlist your aid. Will you assist me? The advice of a soldier of the great General Washington would be a priceless boon."

I was constrained to smile. "I don't know what kind of nonsense Jack has been telling you, monsieur. I was never actually in the army. Indeed, we saw little fighting down this way."

"But the British attacked and burned your town. You were there, *n'est-ce pas*? And afterward you helped with the fortifications, and with the grand expedition against Castine? It is no fault of yours it came to nothing. Though your modesty becomes you, to me it speaks more eloquently than even our good friend Jack. You need say no more. I am of France; I understand. Ah, but those were glorious times, Citizen; glorious times."

"I have a friend who once said the same thing. You and he must have a talk one day. As for your request, I suppose I'll say yes in the end. What is it you need most?"

"Nearly everything, I am afraid. Muskets, ammunition, cannon if there are any to be had. In France I was able to secure only small arms, and few indeed of those. Uniforms and accoutrements. Drugs. Rations. As a former soldier you will know these things. Most important, I require a vessel and a captain upon whom I may rely, to take me to Saint Domingue. Captain Caldron unfortunately will not chance it."

"I will do what I can. You'll want salt fish and spirits, I should think. Those we have in plenty. Flour and drugs you had best buy in Boston. We have no regular market for them here, and prices are ungodly high. I know it sounds strange, but Portland vessels carry them to Boston, land them there, and then we merchants buy what we can sell and pay the freight back. No reason you should. Put in there on your way south. I can give you letters to men with whom I do business, or, if you prefer, there are others in Portland whose names would be more impressive. I will arrange the introductions.

"Buying arms will be the only real problem. They have always been scarce: you may know that the colonies were forced to rely on France during the late war. Of course our present needs are less. I will see what can be had."

"A thousand thanks. And the matter of a ship?"

"I have one in mind. A brig; not sharp-built like Caldron's sloop, but fast enough. I'll sound out her captain myself. I don't suppose I need to remind you to keep this under your hat?"

"Under my hat? Oh, you mean to say that I should be discreet. Of course not. The authorities might feel themselves obliged to interfere if my purpose became common knowledge. I have only been so open because I was certain from what Jack had told me that you would approve."

"Approve? I'm not sure that's the word. Sympathize, perhaps."

"Sympathize, then, if you will have it so. But I tell you, Citizen, that your help will not be forgotten. When all is settled you will be our agent in America. Or come with me, and my friends will make a place for you in their government."

"A fine figure I should cut, trailing behind Monsieur Ogé and his army at my age! My marching days are well past. It's a young man's job, monsieur, and a young man's dream, but it is safe with me." St. Cyr nodded his acquiescence. I suggested that he call for his letters at any time the next day which he found convenient, and then repeated my invitation for the evening.

"But of course I shall come," he said. "How should I not? And now I have kept you too long from your work. If you would be so kind as to direct me to a good inn, I will take my leave." I brought him out by my front door and watched as he strode away, saluting each man he passed, full of youth and naive republican zeal.

Sarah was both delighted and distressed at the thought of guesting a high-born Frenchman. In plain truth if St. Cyr had not been of such an egalitarian turn of mind I would have been as flustered as she. I assured her that everything would be fine and after a light supper we went upstairs to dress.

Shortly after seven there came a knock at the door. My son Benjamin — then nearing the age of seven — raced to be first to answer. His glad shout may have been heard as far as the harbor.

"Uncle Jack! Uncle Jack! Look, Mother, see who's come! Where have you been, Uncle Jack? Did you bring me a present? Did you fight any pirates?"

Jack swung Ben up in his arms and kissed Sarah lightly on the cheek. "One thing at a time, Ben," he said. "No pirates from here to Ushant and back. Anyhow, I don't fight them no more: just tell 'em you my friend and they leave Jack be. Scare the liver clean out of 'em. And, yes, I bring you something, but you got to wait your turn. Ladies first, you know. You want to see what I got for your mother?"

"Yes, Uncle Jack," said Ben dutifully. "Mother first. Let's see."

Jack set Ben on his feet and winked mysteriously. He held out his hands, showing the back of the left one and the palm of the right, and then his left palm and the back of his right hand. He passed the right over the left, and there in the pale hollow was a tiny box. He proffered it to Sarah.

Sarah took it and opened it. Inside was an Italian cameo brooch. "Jack!" Sarah gasped. "It's beautiful." She held it out for me to see; truly it was of the finest quality. "Wherever did you get it?"

Jack shrugged. "Plenty things like that for sale in Brest these days."

By now Ben was all but hopping with suppressed excitement. Jack looked down and smiled. "Well," he said. "What's all this? We got something here for young Ben, I think, but where I put it? Let's see. Nothing up the sleeves. Nothing in the pockets. No, nothing in the hat, either. Where it get to? Why, maybe it just too big to bring inside. Maybe Jack left it on the doorstep instead." Ben gave out a whoop and ran for the door.

Sarah reached out and kissed Jack once more. "You'll spoil us all," she warned him.

"It ain't nothing. I ain't got a real family. Who I buy things for, unless I buy 'em for you? I look might' silly with that brooch pinned on me."

Ben came back inside, wide-eyed with wonderment. In his arms was a large brass telescope bound in leather. Jack grinned down at him. "What you think?" he asked.

"Is it really mine, Uncle Jack? Mother, Father, look! See what Uncle Jack brought me!"

"That there the best Glasgow looker made," Jack told us. "Won it from a Manxman over to Brest. Powerful upset he was at losin' it, till I tell him Cap'n Ben Venture need him a glass to look for pirates with. But maybe that not what you wanted. You want some 'lasses candy instead?"

Ben hugged the glass close to his chest. "No, Uncle Jack. No candy. Candy is for little boys. I'm a big boy now."

"You surely are," Jack said, running his hand over Ben's head. "Bigger every time I see you. You make a topman pretty soon, way you growin', then you and your old mate Jack go hunt pirates together. Right now your mother gettin' that look in her eye again. I bet it time for your watch below. You run along and sling your hammock like a sailor-man, hear?"

"Aye, aye, Uncle Jack. But I still wish I could stay up with you."

"I got no truck with mutiny, but don't you worry, shipmate: old Jack, he on watch. You turn in now and in the mornin' I come by and show you how to use that looker. Maybe we go up the hill and see can we find them pirates." He glanced at us for permission and Sarah laughed and said that Ben could if he went right to bed.

"Can Uncle Jack come with me?" Ben wanted to know. "He always tells me a story." Sarah agreed, at which Jack looked as pleased as Ben, and the three of them trooped up the stairs together, my son holding Jack's hand and hanging upon every word of a rather fanciful account of his late voyage.

Of course Ben's admiration was no more than natural. At his age he was bound to prefer the romantic figure Jack cut to the drudging, deskbound merchant I must seem. I told myself that I had had my share of adventures, and that in time Ben would come to appreciate my accomplishments in the trading line as well. Still, I must own I was not quite satisfied. Was there another course to follow?

Here my thoughts were interrupted by the sound of someone at the door, and with renewed cheerfulness I went to answer. The new arrivals proved to be not the looked-for Frenchman, but James Boaz and his wife, good friends nonetheless and the more welcome because James was a fiddler of some note. He established himself in one corner of the parlor and immediately began to rosin up his bow. Sarah came down when she heard the first strains of his music, and Jack after, in time to admit Prince McLellan and the Shepards, Joseph and Lewis. Close behind came Bill Newall and Rolen Moore, and then Caesar Dean, so that with all these, and wives and sweethearts besides, the house was tolerably full. Bob Craig made his appearance amid a chorus of welcomes and was thrust forward through the crowd to stand next to James Boaz, who greeted him with a dignified nod and struck up the air to "The Crafty Farmer." Bob sang the words in a voice that was deep and mellow.

Bob Craig was then a very young man, tall and lean, and made his living, as did so many of the black folk who had flocked to Portland since the war, working on the docks. He was of no uncommon strength but much in demand all the same; shipmasters accounted him the equal of two men in the handling of cargo because when he sang the gangs did more work. Thus, like Jack Grove he could pick his jobs and name his wages, and for some years now has not laid hand to rope, but "calls the mourners," as they say, from a plank athwart the hatch and keeps time on the rail with a pair of belaying pins, dressed as fine as that fellow Brummell and never soiling a ruffle.

Billy Hans, younger then, too, but already in decline, came in toward the end of Bob's song. I think he was the only white man in Portland that I might call a friend. Ross certainly was not, nor any of the others with whom I had occasion to do business, and Jack Tukey and old Grizzell both were dead, Jack killed in a skirmish with the British near Trask's Rock at Bagaduce, and Grizzell carried off by the epidemic fever that took Bryce McLellan and so many others in the first long winter of the war.

Billy was a hero once, though not the sort the public relishes, a drunkard and a loafer, yet a true and honest man. Some tales he would embroider, especially if it were a joke on himself, and turn a night's carouse into an epic, but on the subject of the war he was painfully exact. It was the one great moment of his life. If Billy never amounted to much afterward, I for one am inclined to forgive him. At least he never sought to excuse himself, nor to trade upon his service, as many did who deserved less.

Billy propped himself against the sideboard in the dining room, whence he could watch the festivities and still be handy to the punch-bowl, a palsied relict clothed in faded regimentals. He had been a lieutenant in the Continental Line and always resurrected his uniform for what he termed "occasions of state," though of the silver epaulet he once wore only a few cotton threads remained. "Sold for a bottle of kill-devil rum," he told me once, "nor I don't want to forget it. A sorry sort it takes to drink away what come so hard." I had wanted St. Cyr to meet Billy. Seeing him reminded me that the Frenchman had not yet arrived.

As the evening was well along I took the next opportunity to ask Jack Grove if he knew where St. Cyr might be.

"St. Cyr?" he repeated. "I wasn't sure he was supposed to come. He was in Ross's dooryard when I come along by: figured must be you had sent him." While I was digesting this piece of news, a laughing young lady took Jack by the arm and drew him back into the parlor to partner her in a dance. I was left there in the hall alone to deal with my disappointment as best I might.

36

Ross and St. Cyr! It was but too easy to picture their meeting, the Frenchman shaking the captain's hand and bowing low over Elizabeth's in his damnable disarming fashion. The image made me sick with the same helpless anger I had felt in the barracoons of Antigua.

I had been put off my guard, flattered by his egalitarian manner into exposing a piece of a vulnerable secret self. Very well; I was now become disabused. It did not matter whether the boy believed that he believed, or merely pretended. He had made his choice. Nor could I blame him. A connection with Ross had all the advantages: he was, after all, one of those who passed for gentry in the town. I was not. And if he himself lacked something of polish, through him St. Cyr would meet the cultured men among us. Doubtless he would be the darling of the people of fashion for as long as it suited him to stay. My house, my guests, would seem rude and provincial by comparison.

Brought to the fore something of my own dissatisfactions: thoughts I largely had left unvoiced, even to myself. Here in Portland I had comforts proportionate to my bodily wants, and my black companions were good-hearted folk. Yet between myself and them there was a bar as well as a bond, for scarce one had read so much as the *New England Primer*. Sarah had made such effort as she was able in order to please me, but she had not succeeded in mending the defects in her education far enough to discourse upon such topics as might Elizabeth, say, or young St. Cyr, or some other person of liberal upbringing. With these in many ways I held myself to have a great deal in common, although it appeared unlikely that I would ever be admitted into their homes, save perhaps in some servile capacity. In Portland, I told myself wryly, men were created equal only insofar as they were useful.

Small wonder if I should sound bitter, for ofttimes my money would find welcome where I did not.

There was the affair of the library, if an example were needed. Most of the books had been scattered and lost during the war, and the few volumes that remained in broken sets were of little use. In 1784 two dozen men were admitted to the society, paying two dollars each in money or in books, and others on the same terms in following years. Still the collection languished. Knowing me for a lettered man, some of the members with whom I had commerce spoke to me of the sorry state in which it lay — privately, but in such a way that it seemed to me that they spoke for the society. I dared to presume that the door might be opened and made a substantial gift of books from my own shelves in this expectation: Raynal's *History of the Indies* in six volumes, Belknap's *New Hampshire*, and some poetical works besides. So far from an invitation to join the society, all I received was a stiff and somewhat hasty note from Samuel Freeman. I frowned at the memory.

The utopian vista the Frenchman had limned had been bright enough, but it was practice that told, and here he had failed. Let St. Cyr and all his race play me false: surely my own would not. And if they would not accord us freely our rightful place in their world, did it not then rest with us to find our own without them?

I found myself pacing the hall, pounding my right fist into the opposing palm. The dancers paid me no heed; Billy was too deep in communion with the punchbowl to notice. Alternately I damned St. Cyr for deceiving me and upbraided myself for believing in him.

I was well into the rhythm of it when I heard a rap upon the outer door. Impatiently I threw it open, as by reflex. There on the doorstep, hat in hand, stood young St. Cyr.

For a long moment I stared at him without the slightest comprehension. He seemed to be waiting for me to say something, but for the life of me I could not think what it could be. At last it was he who spoke.

"*Mes excuses*, Citizen Venture," he said, putting the hand holding the hat to his breast and bowing his head slightly. "I am late, I know, but I trust not too late to be forgiven. May I not come in?"

Dumbly I stepped aside to make room. "Rather an awkward thing occurred as I was preparing to come here," the Frenchman explained. "A gentleman with whom, as I understand, you are acquainted, Captain Ross, sent a note to my room at Marston's tavern inviting me to spend the evening with him and his wife. Apparently he had learned of my arrival through my good Captain Caldron. Of course I could not accept, but it was so clearly well intentioned that I felt compelled to give my reasons in person. Alas! It took longer than I had expected, but here am I to make such amends as I may."

I recollected myself and assured him that none were necessary. Still, he made a very pretty apology to Sarah when I presented her to him. Each of the others he greeted in their turn with a warmth that could not be other than genuine. By the time he led Sarah out for the next dance my good humor was completely restored and the success of the evening assured.

Seemingly he had a natural gift for putting folk at their ease. With the ladies he exchanged pleasantries and discussed the latest in fashion, contriving at the time to avoid giving offense to the men. Of these a few were not particularly forthcoming at the first, although Jack, of course, was already a firm friend and I was glad enough for the news from France, yet I think that by the end of the evening he had found with each guest some topic of common interest.

He seemed more than commonly taken with two of his new acquaintances. Prince McLellan was the first, who after his liquid disgrace on the day of the bombardment had left the county without a word. Everyone had assumed at the time that he had run off to escape punishment, but along about the first of the year there came a letter addressed to William McLellan. It had been written at Prince's request by an officer aboard a Marblehead privateer, and said that Master Bill ought not to worry, that Prince was gone to get the British, and that he would return to his chores just as soon as they was got. Prince had included a part of his pay and prize money in the letter; some he said he needed for his use but the rest was for his master.

Prince was a powerful man, reputed the strongest in the Province. He used his strength to good advantage and became a gun captain and an exemplary sailor, earning the praise of Captain Manley, with whom he finished the war on board the frigate *Hague*. Prince also received a document proclaiming him a free man, but when he returned to Falmouth he told McLellan that it meant nothing; he had had to take it with his discharge from the Continental service. McLellan was so impressed with his loyalty that he told him no, that Prince had won his freedom fairly, and made him a gift of a parcel of land in Gorham. I had heard it before, but it was a good story.

Prince's tales St. Cyr found engaging, but it was Billy Hans who fairly captivated him. Billy was somewhat loath to brag, and at first he would tell only of the card game at the Catamount Tavern wherein "One-Eyed Tom" Chittenden had relieved him of his epaulet. Without seeming to try, St. Cyr shaped the conversation so that ere long he heard the whole story of Billy's rise and fall.

If Vermont had been Hans's undoing, and he liked to claim it was, Bennington and Fay's kill-devil rum and "that thundering ass, Ethan Allen," he had had his moments of glory during the war. Billy told how he had joined Captain Smith's company of Voss's First Massachusetts Regiment early in 1777, serving at Stillwater, Saratoga, Valley Forge, Monmouth, and, last, at the siege of Yorktown. Twice wounded, he had served with courage and vision through the worst of the war; from time to time as he spoke I saw not the man who was but the man who had been, and I believe that St. Cyr did as well.

"We was like a kicked dog, we was," Billy told him. "Then we got our teeth dug in. Just hung tight and couldn't do no more, but the gen'ral wouldn't let us let go, neither. Nothin' very romantic, not as you'd say, but he had grit. He was a real man, was the gen'ral. Made his share of mistakes, but he was there with you. Not like us, but we give him our best. He stayed, and so we did, too."

"But what of my countryman, the Marquis de Lafayette? Perhaps you saw him?"

"Saw him! I knew him! Called me Mr. Hans, he did: him a gen'ral and all! He was a caution himself, you know. That pretty uniform, an' them feathers in his hat! A green boy when he came over if ever there was one. You'd 'a' took him for one o' them popinjay tailors 'r such, like so many of 'em were. But he was tough as nails underneath, and bold as sin.

"Saw him! I guess I did! He dropped flat beside me at Brandywine Creek and I had to catch him a horse. He might have won the war down to Monmouth save for that catamite Charles Lee. Oh, he was a fine one, Lafayette. He was a French caution."

Thus Billy refought the war for St. Cyr. I drifted in and out, refilling their glasses and helping them to the collation that Sarah had prepared. At the end of the evening, St. Cyr waited while the rest of the guests made their farewells and then clasped me impulsively to his bosom.

"Citizen Venture," he exclaimed, "how can I thank you? My first

day in America! I have enjoyed it more than I can say, and it is
entirely on your account." He turned to Sarah and kissed her hand,
thanking her for a delightful entertainment, and then took mine in
both of his. "My friend," he said, "we have had less time to talk than
I would have liked. I hope I shall hear of your exploits on another
occasion. In any case, I pray you will do me the honor of accepting
this small token of my heartfelt gratitude and esteem." He reached
into his pocket and pressed something into my hand, and then
was gone.

37

S T. CYR'S gift was a round silver box filled with fine rappee snuff.
Doubtless it had been his own. Sarah snatched it up with an
exclamation of delight at the workmanship and turned away teasingly.
It was an unfortunate gesture. I took the box back and thrust it deep
into my pocket. After she had gone to bed, I brought it out again
and turned it over in my hands while I sat before the fire.

The box was about the size of a Spanish dollar and as thick as a
finger. Around the edge of the hinged lid were the words *Les Amis
des Noirs*, and in the center there was a raised design, two clenched
fists breaking the chain that shackled them together. A brave sort of
boast, that: precisely the simple idealism that a boy would find
irresistible. Wars preyed upon such as St. Cyr, but from bitter experience I knew that it was not they who ended winners.

Our Revolution, which he so admired, had been a case in point, what
with the swaggering Bobadills and Copper Captains like Colonel
Thompson, who haled neighbors out of bed on imagined charges, who
pilfered and profiteered from state supplies and then pleaded poverty
when the General Court sought taxes for the relief of the shivering
soldiers in the field. Shipowners had been just as bad. Privateers enough
had sailed to harry unarmed transports, but not one could be found to

lead an attack at Bagaduce though the fate of the Province hung in the balance.

Summer soldiers, Tom Paine called them; frogs inflated into bulls, now, grown fat upon forfeits and indemnities. After Mowatt they'd managed to keep Falmouth a backwater because it suited their purposes. They claimed to have fought like lions. So, indeed, they had: fought among themselves for the property of Tories and those who could be made to seem so.

That at least I had seen coming. Ross had been one of the lucky ones, for his house and vessel both had escaped destruction, but Pagan's was gone, together with what had been the heart of the town. Elizabeth was in a state, helping her brother to pack — he was bound north to Halifax, and she was strong for going with him. Finally Ross had been able to listen no longer. He and I went walking among the cellar holes and blackened chimneys, past the house of Sheriff Tyng, miraculously spared, and on down to the remains of Preble's wharf.

Ross kicked a bit of charred wood over the edge into the dirty water. "Now what, Pyrrhus?" he asked. "Now what? Where do you begin again? Half the town gone, winter's coming, and Elizabeth wants me to take the *Industry* to Halifax. I try to tell her there's no coming back if I do, but she don't listen. Halifax, by God! It'll be damned near as bad there as here. Every Tory in the Province will be in Halifax."

"You're right there, Captain," I told him. "What you've got to do is step back a bit, and look it over. There's nothing to be gained in Halifax, not that I can see. Here you've a house and your vessel, and Elizabeth's safe even if she is upset. It seems to me that those that go will get their property seized. Whether that sticks or not remains to be seen, but for now that's the way of it. Stay, and Elizabeth might get to keep what's left of her brother's."

"You couldn't get half a joe for that today," Ross said bitterly.

"Not today, no. But it stands to reason that the town'll be rebuilt someday. You told me yourself how it was burned out before. When this is over, that land will be worth money. Mowatt only burned the wharves and the houses. The harbor's still deep. Whoever wins will be back. If it's the colonies, why, you'll have saved some of Pagan's fortune: that should be reason enough for Elizabeth to stay. If the English win, her brother can do the same for you. You've nothing to lose by staying and everything to gain."

"You're right, of course, Pyrrhus. It's a good thing, too; I couldn't have stood living in Halifax, not after what that bastard Mowatt's done. It sticks in my throat like these damned ashes. Why, you can't even draw breath without tasting them! I don't know what I'd have done with a cabin full of Tories all blaming it on the rest of us."

"It seems to me that it doesn't matter whose fault it was, if you don't mind my saying so: it's happened, and there's an end to it. Hate's an expensive commodity. A luxury for the rich, you might say. I know your books as well as you do, Captain, and you can't afford it. Nobody hereabouts can. But you can buy a deal of other goods. There's the town meeting this afternoon. Likely there's been talk about you and Elizabeth's brother. If so, now's the time to undo it. Put yourself forward, Captain. Speak your mind about Mowatt. This is your opportunity to make a name for yourself. Don't miss the chance."

Ross did not miss it. That afternoon he was elected commander of the port, riding upon the same crest that made his friend Joseph McLellan county treasurer and elevated others of the sapling squires into like positions of responsibility. Old Preble and Freeman were sent back to be Falmouth's representatives in Massachusetts, traveling southward with Will McLellan and forty hogsheads of fish, which were to be traded for supplies to carry the town through the winter.

The winter was a hard one, filled with sickness and with many privations, but by spring solid progress had been made. There were forts and batteries upon the Neck and at Spring Point and Portland Point besides, sufficient to give an alarm and some measure of protection should the British return, and we had careened Tobias Oakman's old sloop with an eye to setting her to cruise against the supply-ships of the ministerial army. She had been got up by Joseph McLellan, who offered my master a share in the vessel if he could provide the guns with which to arm it. He told them there were none to be had. I called him out of the room upon a pretext and asked him if there were really nothing to be done.

"You, too? Where am I going to get cannon?"

"They don't need many," I pointed out. "Just enough for a show of force. Surely you can spare something."

Ross squinted at the ceiling. "Well," he said, "there are those two rusty old relics from Windham; they're no real use here. I'll write Joseph an order for them if he wants it."

"Good," I said. "We've little enough to fear for the time being.

The British have enough on their plates now they've evacuated Boston. By the time they are ready to make trouble again, Mr. Freeman should be back with Falmouth's share of the guns from Dorchester, the ones General Knox brought from Fort Ticonderoga. This is an opportunity you shouldn't miss."

"That may be," Ross answered. "But I will buy my share in the privateer, if Joseph will take my money." He went back out into the front room to give McLellan the news.

The captain's investment proved a profitable one. McLellan sold the sloop, all found, to the bridagier, on the eve of her first voyage. My master made a profit of five hundred pounds. But in the long run the *Retrieve*, as she came to be known, was not a lucky vessel. In October she was taken by the British frigate *Milford*, and though by then she carried ten new guns sent by the General Court in Boston, not a shot was fired in her defense.

The lesson I learned from the *Retrieve* was a simple one. I saw to it that Ross never backed any enterprise on his own, but shared the risk with others. Even then he got in early and then pulled out at the right time. For us the right time was just before sailing. There were plenty of men anxious to assume the risk in hope of greater profits.

Sometimes profit came with very little risk indeed, as when the British cartel-ship *Nancy* went on the rocks at Cape Elizabeth. The *Nancy* was under flag of truce, bound from Halifax to Boston with some fifty prisoners from the defeat at Bagaduce. Falmouth had taken losses there and feeling still ran high, so that when word came that she had grounded and bilged, half the town turned out to pick her clean. They even burned the hull for the scrap metal it contained.

It took some time to arrange for a horse and cart, and by the time that Ross and I arrived on the scene the first-comers had got the best of the salvage. Some was gone already, God only knew where; I managed to turn an honest profit on the hire of the rig by hauling a portion of the McLellans' findings back to Falmouth, and Ross followed later with a set of charts and the captain's shoebuckles, which were of silver and London-made. No one in the town thought any less of their fellows for having profited from the affair, nor was there any effort to conceal what had been taken. Folk allowed it was rare good sport and a right clever bargain as well. The owner, one Prescott, was of a different mind. He complained to Governor Hancock in

Boston, and, as the names of the men involved were perfectly well known, in the end the governor was obliged to issue a warrant for their arrest. Yet I do not think that he found the crime especially heinous, for the warrant was served through the ordinary channels, which meant that it went to the very men who had done the deed. In effect Hancock ordered them to arrest themselves. Of course they did not, and the affair became a standing joke to everyone save poor Prescott and the *Nancy*'s erstwhile captain, who was discharged.

We pulled through it all in double harness, my master and I, straining for every shilling, buying and selling whatever we could do so to advantage. By 1783, we had succeeded well enough that Ross had begun to sign himself "merchant" rather than "mariner," though he would never be as much at ease in the countingroom as he was on a quarterdeck. Elizabeth proved much more adaptable to changed circumstances. She made her own contributions: through the captain's friends we had secured for her the remains of her brother's holdings and even succeeded in collecting upon some of his outstanding accounts, yet for these things to come to pass it was necessary that she take her place in the new-risen society. In private Elizabeth was wont to look down upon the people with whom she was forced to associate. In public view she was ever bright and gracious. Elizabeth took Joseph McLellan's country wife, Mary, firmly in hand and she set about to make her over, which earned her partisans enough. More came when she championed the idea of finding a new minister more lively and congenial than old Parson Smith or the Reverend Deane. Where once she had been a dedicated partisan of the High Church she was now heard to speak slightingly of Anglican Popery. And she was careful to be heard. Elizabeth was born to the trade, as much a regular-bred merchant as her brother, and she used the tools that came to her hand with instinctive skill. Mary McLellan was one of these; I had been another. I leaned back and stared into the fire. The flames were the color of sunlight on her hair. . . .

I awoke from a troubled sleep to find the fire burning low. My mouth held the foul taste of Yankee hypocrisy and too much rum. Water would not wash it away, nor was I in the mood for sleep. I went to my secretary, sat down, and began to write out a list of the things a man bound for Haiti would need.

At the first light of dawn I shaved and made a Frenchman's break-

fast of coffee and bread and then, without waiting for Sarah and Ben
to rise, I went off to my store. There were a few routine matters that
needed attention: I could trust my apprentices to deal with those.
When they had been given their instructions, I was free to act for
St. Cyr.

I made my way along Fore Street. It was the custom among our men
of business to gather on the street or, in inclement weather, in the
coffeehouses and taverns during the early hours to exchange intelligences and prices from foreign ports and to discuss and debate the
news of the day. Sometimes words would lead to blows; though my
fellows were Federalists almost to a man, they often disagreed on
specific issues, when a chance remark would touch upon some smoldering resentment and fan it into flames. Tempers at least were not much
improved from pre-Revolution days. There were canings as well as
more subtle reprisals. Not long since, Tom Waite, the editor of the
Cumberland Gazette, had given offense to Joseph McLellan, who then
went about and bought up all of editor Waite's bills of hand and
demanded present payment. Of course Waite could not pay, even as
McLellan could not have paid had positions been reversed. Joseph stood
upon the letter of the law and had Waite jailed. The printer was bailed
out by his friends and gleefully made note in the *Gazette* that he was
again at liberty to say or "to PRINT WHAT HE PLEASES."

At times indeed, it did not seem to matter what the *Gazette* printed
or did not print. And so on this day I found that word of mouth was
gone before me, and every man knew my errand.

"Doin' the Frenchman's shopping, are you?" demanded Daniel
Tucker, a shipowner who before the war had been making knee-
buckles for Paul Little. "Well enough, well enough: only I'd make
damn' sure his credit's sound, if I was you. Just friendly advice, you
understand. I just cleared from Cape François myself, and it's looking
to be quite a kettle. Bad troublt brewing, and no mistake. I'd 'a'
steered clear myself, save that the market's gone mad there. Always
money to be made where there's trouble, by God! But be sure you
get paid in gold and not in promises. Promises don't spend worth a
damn."

I had gone all the way to Fish Street before I got more for my pains
than this; foodstuffs were scarce and therefore dear. Young James
Deering, watching a shallop tie up at his father's breastwork, allowed

that the firm of Deering and Son had a quantity of salt provision that might be available for a price. He led the way into his office and gave me a chair.

I had expected to waste a certain amount of time on preliminaries. Deering surprised me by coming directly to the point. The figure he quoted was fair, and, I gathered, firm. I agreed to it and made to leave, when I noticed upon his desk a copy of the last volume of Gibbon. I took the liberty of applauding his taste.

"I wish my father agreed with you," he said wistfully. "He calls it throwing good money after bad print. I suppose he's right in a way: I can't say I've read to any purpose like Henry Knox did. Rome one day, a romance the next. It adds up. But we can afford it."

Deering looked across the desk consideringly. "This is very pleasant," he observed, "but it occurs to me that we might perhaps do another stroke of business before the day gets much older. Is your principal in the market for anything other than eatables?"

As casually as possible I asked him what he might mean.

"I might mean almost anything," he retorted mildly. "There are the most unbelievable rumors on the street. Quite extraordinary, and considering the complicated diplomatic situation, potentially embarrassing. But I was thinking that your Frenchman might be interested in a consignment of iron."

"Iron?"

"Just so. My father has had four ton of it in storage with Will Tate these ten years past: eleven it soon will be. He would part with it on advantageous terms, and from what I hear good iron will be much in demand where your friend is bound. Mention it to him, if you will. He can examine the goods at Tate's warehouse by the old Stroudwater landing. Tell Mr. Tate that I sent you about the Dutch iron. Be certain to ask in just those words: Dutch iron."

I furrowed my brow. Dutch iron? I knew of no mines in Holland, nor of any reason why St. Cyr should wish to buy iron if there were. Then I realized what Deering meant. "Cannon, by God!" I said. "You have cannon for sale?"

"Dutch iron," Deering repeated firmly. Then he smiled to take the sting from his reproof. "Six little sparrow-guns we got from the Nova-Scotiaman that went aground on the Cape. Dad put 'em by at Tate's when it looked like there'd be trouble and Will listed 'em as

Dutch iron because we paid him in Hollands gin. Never sold 'em for a privateer for fear someone might ask where they came from when she went to be licensed. Since the war we never had an offer. They're for sale if you want to buy 'em."

James Deering's cannon were the only stroke of luck we met with in Portland. As I had expected, it was necessary that St. Cyr buy the bulk of his wants in Boston. He shipped on board the sloop *Anarchiad*, Captain Thurlo, on January 11, the day after the new lighthouse was finished at Portland Point. I had engaged Captain Mussey's brig to follow him within the fortnight, bringing the salt cod and the cannon and whatever else I might be fortunate enough to find. St. Cyr would arrange credit in Boston against which I was to draw.

I found that I missed the Frenchman as soon as he was gone, and to fill up the space I took to visiting young Deering daily on the pretext of business. Instead, we talked of books and of places I had seen; Deering had a taste for travel but had stayed at home from a sense of duty toward his parents. I told him what St. Cyr had told me about Saint Domingue and its promise. He listened attentively and countered with what he knew of the Spanish half of the island. Had Sarah shown but a fraction of his interest I might have been content with talk.

At dinner on the fifteenth of the month it came to a head. I mentioned in a casual way that I was riding down past Black Point to see if a doctor's widow would sell her late husband's large stock of medicaments. I would be leaving early and was likely to be home late.

"It's that French boy, isn't it?" It wasn't actually a question. "I've hardly seen you all week. What about your own business?"

"The market's far from brisk," I told her. I was a bit surprised that the words came out so quick and sharp, but I blundered on. "The 'prentices are handling things well enough. Besides, St. Cyr's commissions are more than fair." I cast about for something to end the argument. "Look," I said, "when I'm done I'll buy you a Boston dress."

"I don't want no Boston dress, Pyrrhus Venture. I don't want nothing that comes from that French boy. He's trouble and you know it. Everybody in Portland knows it. They know what he's going to do. They know you been working for him, too.

"You want to know what I want? I'll tell you what I want. I want you to forget that you ever met that John St. Cyr and mind your business like before."

"Trade is my business," I reminded her stiffly. "Ben and the house are yours."

"What happens to Ben and the house if you go off on some fool's errand with St. Cyr? What happens to me?"

"What on earth do you mean? I'm filling an order, for God's sake! That's all I'm doing."

"That's all?" Sarah's voice cracked as she said the words. She had to pause for a moment before she could go on.

"Maybe you believe that, Pyrrhus Venture," she said. "Maybe you do. But I been with you long enough to know different. I ain't seen you so stirred up since the war.

"You got a comfortable life here. You got a house and you got your store. You got Ben and me. What you want to throw it away for? Yes, throw it away! That's what you're fixing to do, isn't it? That French boy's got you so damned worked up you can't see it. Well, I can. You're going to go with him, aren't you? Off to that damned island!"

"And what if I do? That's not such a bad idea at that. In fact the prospects are excellent." They were. If Ogé were successful, there were no limits to what his friends and supporters might hope for. I would be accepted; more than that: revered as a hero of the new republic. It was all very dazzling, and very different from things as they were.

When I came to myself again, Sarah was watching me with an expression of infinite sadness. "I was right," she said. "Wasn't I?"

I nodded, and Sarah buried her face in her napkin. When I reached out to comfort her, she shrugged my hand off her shoulder.

"There's no place for a black man in Portland," I told her as gently as I could. "It won't be like that there. And once Ogé has my guns, the fighting won't last long. You'll see." I waited for some response, but Sarah was silent. After a time I got up and left.

38

A DECENT regard for truth compels me to admit that inwardly I had welcomed Sarah's outburst, for it gave me leave to feel more the misunderstood husband and less the villain. Thus she had brought down upon herself the frustrations of my years in Portland. Sarah had had everything she needed. I had striven to repay the debt of her devotion, and all that time I had resented her unthinking adaptation to life there so strongly that I could not begin to explain my own discontent. I had told myself that Sarah would hardly have fathomed it if I had. Not Sarah. When the argument was over, we reverted to form and did not speak of it more.

Indeed, we spoke even less than had become usual. I had begun to liquidate holdings and had little time for speech in any event. I wanted cash. I called in debts where they could be quickly met and sold them or accepted less for prompt payment. There were goods in store to dispose of, and also the time of my two apprentices. Of course word got around, and it became difficult to get fair value; for a time it seemed that my own paper would be called in faster than I could meet the demands. St. Cyr would have backed me, I know, but I was surprised when young Deering came forward.

Deering claimed it was strictly business: he said that he wanted to make sure that our transactions went through unimpeded and without anyone's taking too close a look at the merchandise. Of course it was more than that, and I told him so.

Deering waved my thanks aside. "You're good for it, aren't you? Most of it I bought at a discount in any case. But look: what are you going to do with your house and your store? There's no way you can sell them for what they are worth. Not while people think you're about to be broken."

"They weren't far wrong," I said. "But what can I do?"

"Let them to me until they can be sold. No, I don't want to buy them, but I'll act for you. The market will pick up in the spring and all this will have blown over."

I knew that I was fortunate to have Deering for my agent, and agreed instantly, though I told him I would have no rent from him for six months at the least. In the end he accepted. He was to sell my property on the Neck and my back-country lands as well, and forward the proceeds to me at Cape François unless I should write directing him otherwise. It was the best arrangement I could have made under the circumstances.

This success buoyed my spirits, but I was glad enough of Sarah's silent acquiescence and for the presence of Jack Grove, who kept Ben from underfoot. I was too busy to mark what they did and nearly too busy to care, so long as Jack kept my son's mind from dwelling on the loss of his playfellows. Someday he would come to see that it was partly on his account that we were leaving; as yet he was too young.

"Father me no fathers," Fitzgore had told me, and I had begun life without even a name. By a narrow margin I had not seen my son born nameless: Sarah would have endured it for my sake, though I could not. Still, it was a slender patrimony. It was not enough. I wanted to leave Ben more at my death than a name and a collection of dog-eared ledgers. If, as it seemed, folk would not have me do what I wished for him in this town of Portland, I would go somewhere else. But one does not explain all that to a boy scarcely out of petticoats.

I had sent word of my decision to St. Cyr in Boston by the mate of a coaster; the mail coach ran but twice a week in winter when it ran at all, and was slow at best. It was driven as often as not by the old post-rider, Joseph Barnard. He had begun the service four years earlier as an experiment, leaving Motley's tavern on the back street across from Joseph McLellan's and taking the better part of three days to reach Portsmouth, where he met the coach from Boston. On the return trip Barnard counted himself fortunate to reach Kennebunk at the end of the first day and Broad's Tavern near Stroudwater on the second, arriving back on the Neck before noon on the third. Thus I only had St. Cyr's note announcing his arrival safe at Boston on the twentieth of the month, nine days after he had left me, and I did not look for an answer to my own at all, since the first mail by which it might come would get to Portland two days after I planned to be gone.

Still, the best news is that which comes, as the poet Pope says Fame does, all unlooked for, and on the morning of the twenty-fourth Captain Thurlo of the *Anarchiad* presented himself at my door with a letter from St. Cyr, warmly written and cheering beyond all measure. I could not linger over it as I would have liked to do, having many things to see to and little time in which to get them done.

At slack water in the afternoon I went aboard the *Neptune* brig to see Captain Mussey. I was relieved to find that preparations for taking the guns on board were complete. He had got out a good part of the rock and coarse shingle in the bottom of her hold and hove her on her side as if to repair a plank that had started. Now he put her on an even keel and warped her right up the Fore River, as close to Tate's Landing as could be without taking the ground. He anchored and we waited for night to fall.

Darkness came. I was on deck, for thoughts of all that might yet go awry made me too restless for the limited comfort of my cabin.

A sound came to me across the water and I turned to peer out into the night. Was there something there? No. Yes! There was a boat approaching, blacker against the surrounding black of the water. I heard the rattle of an oar against thole pins, saw the white splash of an incautious stroke.

"Boat ahoy," I hailed, and received in return the call "Haiti." It was Prince McLellan, then, using the signal we had agreed upon. I could relax a little.

The boat was nearly full of men. I counted a dozen, just enough for the task at hand. With Mussey's crew, each man would have to lift and carry eighty pounds.

It was time. We joined the others in the boat, perching uncomfortably upon the heavy timber bracing as Ross and I had done in the harbor at Antigua years before. I told the men at the oars to give way and we set off up the river.

There were lights at Tate's. When the boat was almost even with them, I bade the rowers rest on their oars and searched the yard for signs of trouble. I did not fully trust Will Tate, though I could think of no motive he might have for betraying me to the sheriff, nor of how he might do so without at the same time implicating himself. He would be chary of that; Portland already regarded him with an ill savor for having killed his mother in 1770 with a trip gun set for thieves and for living openly with his housekeeper after the death of his wife. His was a strange family; one brother was a farmer and shipmaster who had fought for the colonies, another had been a Tory and the captain of the vessel that brought Lord Cornwallis to America, and the last was become an admiral in the service of Catherine of Russia. Their father, English George, was long retired and lived a quiet life. He had been born in 1700, so people said, which would make him ninety, older by two years even than Parson Smith. Before the war he had been a man of wealth and power by reason of his monopoly of the mast trade. He was nearly turned out of Falmouth as were others connected with the crown, staying on only because of his age and evident neutrality, but the business he had passed along to his son Will was sadly diminished. For his part William Tate seemed to have no other thought than to restore the family to its lost prominence. I judged him to be almost totally mercenary, and while this may have been the origin of my uneasiness it was probably my best guarantee of good faith. I was paying him well for the nocturnal transfer.

Bob Craig was at my elbow. He asked in a hoarse whisper if aught was amiss, and I could only answer no and give the word to begin rowing. In a few strokes the boat was at the pier.

Will Tate came out of the warehouse with a lantern. His teeth flashed disconcertingly in the lamplight.

"Well, you're here, be you? I thought for a bit we wasn't to have the pleasure of your company, but as you're come, let's get on with it. Deering sent the invoice for the iron" — there was an ironic lift to his voice that underlined the word — "so now all that's left is to pay the storage and you can load away."

"Storage?" I said. "If you'll check your records, Mr. Tate, I think you'll find that storage was paid in advance."

Tate squinted at me appraisingly. I met his gaze with all the firmness I could muster.

"You're right, you're right," he admitted. "Now that I think on it, it was. No harm done, I don't suppose. If you'll just follow me I'll show your men the way and then leave you to your work."

The guns were mounted on their carriages for storage, but it would be better not to put them in the boat thus. I set a few of the men to hauling the guns out onto the wharf and driving out the wedges from the cap-squares which held barrel and mount together. The rest began making cat's-cradles of stout hemp rope. These would be knotted together under the long iron tubes, with the many long tails sticking out on either side. With a man on each line we could lift the guns and lower them carefully into the boat.

It was a difficult process, made more so by the darkness and the state of the tide. Once the ebb came we might use the edge of the dock as a purchase to let the gun down gently. Now the water was high, so that the awkward burden had to be raised to clear the gunwales of the boat, and half of us were working while trying to stand in the bobbing craft. It had to be done because I could not tell how long it might take to get the guns aboard and safely out of sight. For that reason I did not dare to waste a minute of the night. The slightest slip could send twelve hundred pounds of iron through the bottom of the boat, sinking it instantly, almost certainly crippling one or more of the men, and ruining everything.

Bob Craig started in singing when the men turned to on the first of the cannon. His voice carried alarmingly in the still cold night. I had visions of Colonel Waite riding up with pistol drawn, and hastily told him to belay that nonsense and bear a hand. I tailed on to one of the lines in order to set an example and to take the edge from what I had said.

With this much of the loading well disposed I went along in the boat to view the arrangements on board the *Neptune*. Captain Mussey had rigged a tackle from the main yard that made light of the work. Really, I need not have concerned myself. Handling weight is a great part of the mariner's art, as any man who has shipped before the mast can tell. In a matter of minutes the gun, so ponderous and troublesome ashore, was swayed up and lowered handsomely into the hold.

The rest was here labor. We worked through the night, alternately sweating and shivering. We got the guns aboard and then the carriages, and covered them over with barrels of salt beef and cases of bottled spirits I had bought from Tate. When we were done, the guns were hid from view. In the fore part of the hold we packed all solid with the *Neptune*'s water casks and provisions, leaving the remaining space for what I had in store at Clay Cove and for Mussey's own Boston-bound cargo. No casual inspection could reveal the contraband cannon.

When we had done, Captain Mussey sent up topmasts and stood down the river with the last of the ebb. Low water came at four in the morning. At the first light of dawn I went ashore with Prince and the others, to get an hour or two of sleep.

Sarah was awake when I came into our chamber. She arose as soon as I lay down and went away without a word. I could hear her in the kitchen below while I readied myself for bed. There was a clashing of pots as she began to prepare breakfast, and the clink of crockery. Just as I passed into sleep the noises ceased, and there was a low sound of someone weeping.

Some time later I got up, dressed myself, and went downstairs. I went to my place at table and waited while Sarah brought me coffee and bread and some beans she had kept warm on the hearth. She had nothing to say. When I had eaten I told her that the night had gone well.

"I expect we shall have the rest of the cargo on board today," I said. "I will send some men up this afternoon for the household things."

Sarah received this wordlessly. I took this for assent and went on. "There will be room in the cabin for only two chests," I reminded her. "Be sure to pack some lighter dresses in the bottom of yours. I expect you will want them and you may not be able to get to the rest of the baggage until we reach Cape François. Ben and I will have to make do. By the bye," I said, "I haven't seen him this morning. I had thought to take him down to watch the loading."

"Oh," said Sarah distractedly, "he has gone somewhere with Jack. To say farewell to his friends, I believe." She busied herself with her work and seemed disinclined to pursue the conversation. At length I rose and went out.

The muskets St. Cyr had brought from France had already gone into the *Neptune*'s hold. They were packed twenty-four stand to a case and the cases labeled as tools and agricultural implements. On top of them had gone other crates and barrels, squeezed tight so that none would shift once the brig was at sea and so arranged that considerable labor would be required to come at them.

The disposition of the weight was important because it determined how the ship would handle. Down too much by the head, she would refuse to about smartly. Lading too deeply astern was just as bad. Mussey was down in the hold supervising the stowage for himself to make doubly sure it was done to his satisfaction, with his mate Robert Wakely on deck to mind how things were swayed down to him.

I looked to the wharf and saw a man approaching. He cut a fine businesslike figure, and even at that distance it was easy to recognize him as Nathaniel Fosdick, the collector of customs. When Mussey heard, he spat out a curse and clambered out on deck to receive him.

Fosdick was widely known for a high-toned Federalist and an ambitious man. He had held the office then three years, having been appointed to succeed Thomas Child in January of 1788. Child had lived near Nathaniel Deering, and as soon as Deering had had news of his neighbor's death, he sent young James up Fish Street to bring word to Fosdick, with a hint that he had best act quickly. I have heard that Fosdick was saddled and on the road for Boston within the hour, though it was late at night and a heavy snow was falling. The other competitors for the office did not leave until the next morning and arrived too late. The commission was already in Fosdick's pocket. He held the office for another eleven years, until Jefferson removed him to make a place for Isaac Ilsley in 1802.

Mussey greeted him with an easy "Good morning," and Fosdick looked pained. "None of that, now," he warned. "I'm here on official business. I've a report that you're carrying contraband, to wit, arms for a foreign power inimical to this country."

"Arms, Nat?" Mussey asked. "There's no arms. Come on down to my cabin and look at our papers."

"I intend to. First, I want to tell you something. I think I know what's going on here. I don't care a whoop about France or any other place except this one. I've got my job to do, and when somebody makes a complaint, why, I investigate it. If you've got arms on board, you can't sail. Why not make it easy on all of us? Tell me now, unload the damned guns, and I'll see you're away on the next tide. There's no need for this to go any further unless you want it to."

He fixed a challenging stare upon us. I wondered how much he knew for fact and how much was mere supposition. Abruptly Mussey laughed. "If you want to waste your time," he said, "I guess that's your business. But let's go below and straighten this out, shall we? Then we can both get back to work."

Mussey's cabin was larger but little better furnished than Ross's had been. Fosdick sat at the table and Mussey produced the ship's books and the cargo manifests. The collector perused them carefully.

"What's this business about 'Dutch iron'?" he said when he got to the line where Mussey had entered the weight of the cannon.

My heart sank, but Mussey answered without a quaver. "Just ballast," he said. Fosdick raised one eyebrow. "I needed all the hold space I could get for this cargo," Mussey explained. "Iron's heavier than rocks, and I figured Venture, here, could sell it when we got to the islands. Deering had it for sale and we bought."

Fosdick rubbed his jaw meditatively. "Ballast, eh. Be hard to get at, then. But Dutch iron? Dutch?"

Mussey smiled. "I never heard of it before last week either, Nat. But just you wait here." He went out and up the companion. I tried to look nonchalant while I waited with Fosdick.

In a moment Mussey was back. He was carrying a box about eighteen inches square and not quite so deep. I recognized it instantly.

"I can't show you the iron, Nat," Mussey said, "but this came from the same place." He set the case down on the deck with a thump and prised up the lid to reveal a dozen bottles of gin. Fosdick reached down and took one. Mussey winked at me over the collector's head. "Go ahead, Nat," he argued, producing a glass, "open her up and tell me what you think."

Fosdick poured himself a stiff tot and sampled it, rolling it around in his mouth like a true connoisseur. I watched him tensely. At last he smiled. "Damme for a Frenchman," he said. "That's Dutch, by God!" He drained the glass and held it out to be refilled. "Well, Mussey, it seems I was wrong. You and Venture have got your clearance."

He drank again. "Dutch iron," he mused. "We live and learn. I'll take a bottle or two of this, ah, evidence with me when I go, in case the sheriff hasn't heard of it either."

39

AT Portland Point the *Neptune* left behind the protected reaches of Hussey Sound and dipped its bow to the rollers of the broad Atlantic. Abaft the beam to starboard stood the lighthouse which the new national government had recently completed at a cost of fifteen hundred dollars. Sarah I had left in the cabin with Benjamin, who remained sullen and withdrawn despite the excitement of leaving port. I had expected to share this vista with my son and was disappointed and rather annoyed that I did not; directly I had seen how things were I had come on deck alone. I was not about to miss the sight myself. The *Gazette* had reported that the stonework was seventy-two feet high exclusive of the lantern, which was fifteen, and the whole was accounted somewhat of a marvel in the neighborhood, but it did not move me as I had thought that it might.

Mussey was retracing the course that had brought me to Falmouth Neck so long before. Pond Cove opened to view, and then Broad Cove, with Cape Elizabeth fine on the bow. The land had not changed greatly in the intervening years, and small boats and canoes still plied the narrows between Spurwink and Richmond's Island. Belike some of them were paddled, as before, by Jordans, for some at least of that numerous brood remained upon their ancestral acres, but none of the craft passed close enough for me to see their occupants.

The islands of the bay disappeared beneath the horizon astern, and the Cape likewise. Because the wind showed a tendency to veer to the eastward, Captain Mussey put the helm over and stood out to sea. This he did as a precaution, to avoid the lee shore, but it deprived me of a last look at Mount Agamenticus, which had been the first sight I had had of the land I was now leaving, as I thought, forever.

Two days' sailing brought us to Boston even so. The *Neptune* came to in six fathoms, riding easily at her anchor, and shortly after, Sarah, Benjamin, and I were in a boat which put us ashore near to Faneuil Hall.

St. Cyr's lodgings were across town from the wharf where we had landed. We walked, and I was glad to see my son taking notice of the bustle of the place, though it would have pleased me more if he had not held so tight to his mother's skirt. It seemed to me that he showed a want of manly spirit, and I promised myself that if he continued thus it should not be my fault. Still, it was good to see that his insularity was not unbreachable.

St. Cyr was enthralled with Boston, which he revered as the cradle of republican virtue. Of course, there were few in the city who would bar their doors to a handsome and wellborn foreign visitor, and it also seemed that St. Cyr had brought with him introductions he had been too polite to mention. John Hancock he had met, cured by age and infirmity of many of his earlier excesses, and Samuel Adams, seedy as ever but still a power to be reckoned with, and divers others. His only particular disappointment in this regard was his failure to make acquaintance of Paul Revere. He had been to Revere's silversmith shop in Anne Street, where he had found one of his sons, but the man himself had been absent from Boston that day on some business having to do with his foundry in the north end of town. St. Cyr assured me that this was worth seeing even though Revere had not yet begun to cast the bells for which he has since become justly famed.

"He has done well, there among the shipyards," St. Cyr informed us. "Already he makes castings for the ships, stoves and firebacks, anvils and forge hammers. It is quite amazing, the way he does everything: a silversmith, an engraver, a citizen, and a soldier, and now a foundryman as well. But then, his father was a Frenchman!"

St. Cyr wanted me to come with him again before we departed to see if Revere had returned. I declined and said that there was a bookseller in Cornhill I wanted to visit instead. "Do you go anyway if you want to," I urged him. "I have met the man some years ago."

"You have? But that is wonderful! You were comrades in arms, perhaps?"

"Comrades may not be the right word," I temporized. "It was at Bagaduce, and I saw very little of him. He was a colonel of artillery at the time, and I was there with Captain Ross." As an afterthought I added, "It's not worth mentioning if you speak with him."

St. Cyr took this last for modest self-deprecation, which is what I had intended. "Very well," he agreed with a smile. "Then perhaps you will tell me."

"Perhaps," I said. "There may be time during the voyage."

"I shall remind you, my friend," he said, and then he left.

St. Cyr and Revere never did meet, and I forgot about the matter entirely for a time in the haste and confusion of the next days. The *Neptune* had tied up to discharge at Hitchbourne's wharf, and all of Captain Mussey's goods were gone ashore, so that it was time to load the things St. Cyr had bought. This we wished to accomplish as rapidly as might be done, for the little news we had from Haiti was disquieting. Dissensions among the white colonials had become increasingly bitter; Cape François, where we were to meet Vincent Ogé, was the stronghold of the privileged orders.

"They have allied with the faction of the governor," St. Cyr explained. "That is very bad for the people of color, for the governor wishes to maintain the authority of the National Assembly against that of the colony. It is in the colonial assembly that the people of color have their sole chance of being heard. A resort to arms is the only course left if the governor's party is successful. We must make haste, Citizen: without such aid as ours the rising must inevitably fail."

When St. Cyr declared his determination to put out on the next day, Mussey wagged his head doubtfully. "It won't serve," he warned us. "Hurry all you like, we'll not clear Nantasket Roads with the wind in this quarter." So it proved. At St. Cyr's instance we spent the fore-noon beating fruitlessly back and forth in hopes of weathering the long spit north of Hingham. Finally even he was forced to admit that Mussey's prediction had been accurate. We anchored the brig and settled in to wait for a change.

All the while we lay there he was as nervous as a cat. I thought of encouraging him to go ashore and hire a horse to take him to see the family seat of the vice-president in Quincy. Adams himself was most probably in Philadelphia, which had been designated the capital in place of New York the year before, but I was at my wits' end with his pacing. In a careless moment I said that he might just as well learn to relax; the Penobscot fleet had been embayed in this same roadstead for six days before it was able to sail.

St. Cyr pounced on my remark as if the cat I had thought him had seen a mouse. "Penobscot? You mean the one bound to the place with the barbarous name, Bagaduce? Castine is so much easier, both for the tongue and for the ear. But come, Citizen: you promised to tell me the story of that campaign if we had the time, and now it seems we have nothing but time. How was it that you met the great Revere?"

"I never really met him," I said. "Not to speak to, I mean. I saw him, though, and I heard him. Enough to know all I wanted about him. You'll have to judge for yourself.

"It was in the summer of seventy-nine," I recalled. "The British had come down from Halifax with two regiments to build a fort and a base for their ships at Bagaduce. We had word of them at Falmouth in the middle of June, and sent it forward to the General Court in Boston, praying them to raise the militia and a sufficient naval force to deal with the invaders."

"Where were you then?" St. Cyr asked. "Here, in Boston?"

"No, at Falmouth. Ross was commander of the port, if you re-member. He found a shallop to take the messenger up to Boston and sent him on his way. The crew didn't want to go. They said that the British would be in Falmouth next, to finish what they'd started. Nor did it help when we heard that Henry Mowatt was in command of the king's ships in the river."

Indeed it had not. The people had come close to panic, and great numbers of them removed back into the country from which they had but recently returned.

Those who did not flee vacillated between anger and apprehension. When it became known that the General Court was resolved to mount an expedition, there was a deal of controversy as to whether this was likely to bring retribution upon us.

The word went out, in any event, to raise a regiment in the county of Cumberland, and another in Lincoln, each of six hundred men. Colonel Mitchell had command of the local troops, to which Falmouth contributed one company and Cape Elizabeth another. Joseph McLellan was made commissary of supplies; he came to Ross to arrange transport.

"The committee's depending on you," McLellan told my master. "There's no sense going unless we get there right smart, before the lobsters are ready for us. You can hire shipping or impress it, just so you get enough."

Ross looked doubtful. "The owners aren't going to like that," he offered. "I know I wouldn't. On whose authority? And what do I do if someone says no?"

McLellan took a paper from his coat pocket. "Here's your commission," he said. "Orders come direct from the Board of War. Anybody makes trouble, you tell me, and I'll tell the colonel. He'll straighten 'em out proper. But look, the court's insuring everything, and they'll pay the seamen and officers the same rate as in the state navy, so it may not be that bad. My brother Will says you can have his *Centurion* sloop, soon's he gets her unloaded, and he'll sail her himself."

"That's good," Ross said. He folded his commission and put it away. "I'll take the *Industry* too, of course. Otherwise folk would wonder. If I can keep the vessels in port now from going off on their own, there'll be no lack."

"You can close the port if you want, Will. The committee will back you up."

"Well enough. But how are you for provisions? Prices have been ungodly high all season. Seems to me that this will only make things worse."

"Molasses is up to sixteen dollars a gallon already," McLellan conceded. "And coffee at four dollars the pound. Sugar's at three, and this morning that thief Nichols told me he had to have seventy-four dollars a bushel for wheat meal." He gave Ross a wolfish grin. "Nichols don't know I'm authorized to seize whatever I can't afford to buy."

Peter Warren raised the Falmouth company with Daniel Mussey, a cousin of the sea captain, as first lieutenant. There were near sixty of them, with Will Moody as drummerboy and William Harper for a fifer, all of them friends and neighbors, Storers and Waites and Larrabees, Tukeys and Bracketts. Joseph McLellan's son Hugh was a corporal, and Deacon Codman's son signed on for a private. Poor Wheeler Riggs was another, who was killed at Castine when a ball from a British cannon struck a tree behind the place where he was hid and bounced back and killed him.

Two armed brigs and a number of merchantmen came into the bay on July 13, to sail in convoy with our vessels to the rendezvous at Townsend. Joshua Jordan brought his company of fifty-three men from Cape Elizabeth to the Neck three days later and embarked on one of the transports which Captain Ross had provided. The Falmouth men were marched on board *Centurion*. Our own *Industry* was loaded deep with provisions and was to take field artillery and a boat on deck when we got to the rendezvous. Dispatches from Boston ordered all vessels for this service to carry at least four of a crew, so my master engaged two brothers named Young and a likely youth by the name of Sprague who lacked his front teeth and could not go for a soldier because he could not bite the cartridge.

Between the time we had heard of Mowatt's descent upon the Penobscot and the day we sailed, July 18, a whole month had slipped by. There had been some concern on this account, that the redcoats would be entrenched and prepared for our assault, but in the end that was allayed by the fine martial appearance of the troops and the brave show of the fleet. At last the order came to up and anchor and make sail. Every vessel that could, fired a gun, and we sailed out with flags flying.

The brief passage had a holiday air. On board the *Industry* we bowled along merrily, trading jests with the smiling men on the other transports and skylarking in the rigging. Everywhere I looked it had been the same.

Ross had given us the news just prior to sailing. "The others have been told," he said, "and I guess it's time for you to know. The lobsters are in a kettle at Bagaduce. We're going to put the lid on and boil the bejesus out of 'em! When we get to Townsend we'll be joining a fleet: the biggest that's ever been seen in these waters! Nineteen armed vessels, headed by the *Warren*, as fine a frigate as any in Fat George's navy! Thousands of men and hundreds of guns! What do you say to that? Give a cheer, there, lads!"

Our cheers had joined with the others as the remaining ships' companies had been told. We had cheered and joked all the way to Townsend, and there the cheering stopped.

The anchorage was nearly empty. We looked in vain for the fleet we expected and saw only two sloops, one with American colors over English, and a cluster of smaller craft. On the shores were a few straggling lines of tents.

On shore it was worse, if that were possible. Ross took me when he went to report with his friend Joseph, and we learned that of the twelve hundred men that were to be raised in the counties of Cumberland and of Lincoln, fewer than nine hundred had yet reported. More: the best men were already in the army, so that in some cases towns had been able to send only old men and boys scarcely fit for service. One officer swore that he had seen a company comprised of invalids and halfwits. " 'Tis all you can do," he said with a great oath, "just keeping them clear of fire and water!"

We lay at Townsend for two eternal days before the *Warren* and the rest of the armada arrived. By then our sanguine mood had long since leaked away, and there were mutterings that the expedition should be given over as a thoroughly bad job. The two Youngs had gone ashore the second night we were there, which would, as I recall, have been the twentieth of the month, and said that many of the men were of a mind to go home whether they got leave or no.

The next day the fleet came in, and it was a thing to behold. There was the frigate, with a company of marines on her deck and the fifes and drums playing, and nine more ships, five brigs, and other vessels. Commodore Saltonstall came on shore with General Lovell and General Wadsworth to review the troops and to hold a council of war. Everything was as military as the people could make it. From a distance it looked well enough, and was quite inspiriting. On the ships we nodded knowingly and told ourselves that we were just the fellows to kick Mowatt and the rest of the redcoats clear back to Halifax.

For some reason we remained at Townsend all that day, and the next day, and the day after that, though it must have been evident to those who were in command that the delays made it imperative to move upon the enemy as quickly as we could. Early on the morning of the twenty-fourth we got orders to get under way. The wind was then fair, but by nine o'clock it died away, so that we spent the balance of the forenoon becalmed. Around midday the wind came up again from the southwest, and we proceeded in a body to the Penobscot.

At four in the afternoon the *Warren* fired a gun, and the fleet came to anchor in the lee of the Fox Islands, Castine bearing north by a little east about nine miles. When everything on board the schooner was secured, Captain Ross sent me into the upper rigging with his glass. From the masthead I could see the earthworks on the heights and the three English sloops-of-war anchored across the mouth of the Bagaduce River.

All that night there was a flurry of boats going from ship to ship to councils and to tell off the men for the next day. We on the *Industry* received orders to launch the boat we had on deck in preparation for an assault. Some of Captain Warren's men came to fetch it late in the evening.

Morning brought a light fair breeze that freshened as the day wore on. We ran before it boldly in order for battle.

The fleet was in three grand divisions. The frigate *Warren* was in the van. The sight of her at the head of forty sail of vessels, all with ensigns snapping and the foam curling white at their bows, brought a catch to my throat. I do not think I would have felt more pride had the ships been mine own.

We were in the *Warren*'s division, with six of the privateers and a number of the other merchant vessels, including the ordnance brig, *Samuel*. She carried gunners' stores and Colonel Revere's artillerymen, a hundred or so trained matrosses from Castle William at Boston.

The frigate was a vessel of more than twice the force of any the English had, but when the commodore arrived at the harbor entrance he seemed to lose his resolve. He sheered off out of range and waited for the ships of the third division to come up with us. The transports and their escort, the three brigs from Massachusetts, carried on past according to the plan. They anchored in the lee of the peninsula a few cables north.

They passed the signal then for the captains of the armed vessels to repair on board the *Warren*, although what there was for them to talk about was more than I could see. Here we were, and yonder stood the enemy. It seemed clear enough. Ross was of a like mind.

"There's but three of their ships to all of ours," he marveled. "And a fort not half-finished. We come all this way to get the British; by God, let's get 'em."

Around two in the afternoon the commodore must have come to the same conclusion. We saw the captains go down over the *Warren*'s side and into their boats, and Captain Ross leaped up from where he sitting and shouted to us to look lively because things were starting to happen.

The attacking force was comprised of nine of the stoutest privateers. They detached themselves from the fleet and put about on a course to close with the king's ships in the harbor.

I saw smoke blossom along their bulwarks as the privateers tried ranging shots at the enemy. Waterspouts showed where the balls landed. The firing was random and irregular. Ross watched through his long glass and cursed the poor shooting.

The first three of our vessels were nearly opposite the British sloops and still Mowatt's men held their fire. Then, just as the privateers altered course to pass in line, the king's ships let go their broadsides. All the guns went off together so that the smoke was in one solid bank instead of separate puffs like that of our own ships. Even without the glass I thought I could see splinters fly from the privateers' sides as the shot struck home. Three or four seconds later the sound came to us like thunder.

Perhaps in that initial volley one of the privateers had lost her helmsman, for two of the ships came close to fouling one another; they could not have escaped collision by more than a few inches. There was a lot of confusion as the rest came up and hove to. The British guns crashed out again, and the smoke drifted down on our ships. They began to reply, and at times all that was visible were masts and rigging standing clear above a rolling shoal of smoke. The guns were firing at their own speed now instead of by broadsides, as the more experienced crews outstripped the others, but there were so many engaged that the roar was virtually continuous and uncomfortably loud.

Of course, it was not only the sound that the men would have to endure, but the shot and the splinters and their mates falling around them. There was sand on the decks to soak up the blood that poured from the wounds torn in bodies that weren't quite human any more because nine pounds of iron traveling at a thousand feet per second had taken off the head or smashed the chest. I only knew about such things in the haziest way as yet, though I was to come into more intimate contact with them before my days had passed.

The men did endure those things for a space of some two hours, when, the wind coming on rather fresh, the privateers bore up and joined the main body. There was a cheer from the fort when they saw our ships standing down out of range. It came uncertainly at first, and then full-throated. Shortly it was answered by three from Mowatt's ships. There were more cheers later; Ross took up his glass and saw a party of men dressed in scarlet and gold lace upon the shore, by which we decided that the general and his staff must have come down to mock us.

The next morning the fleet pounded the bluffs at Dyce's Head for two hours to deceive the British into thinking that a landing was imminent. Later, two hundred marines went ashore on Bang's Island and took the battery of four-pounders the enemy had erected. They were supported by two armed brigs and a sloop. By evening they had shifted the guns so as to be able to fire on the anchorage where Mowatt's ships lay. There was a brief engagement, but not enough in all conscience, the sloops firing on the marines and on the troops who were being ferried ashore to reinforce them, and our men shooting back with the captured cannon. In the end the ships were forced to withdraw far back into the harbor under the guns of the fort. Before they did, however, one of the sloops hit the boat in which Major Littlefield was riding and sank it, so that he and two others of our men were drowned. The largest part of his detachment of one hundred and fifty men from the southward were already on the shore. They found that the enemy troops who had manned the battery had fled so quickly that they left their tents and all their baggage behind them, and the men plundered it in retaliation for the major's death. There is no telling what they got, for Wells folk are tight-lipped and close, at least those I ever met, and all that I heard of was a British flag which was captured and given to the general for a trophy. In the evening the transports landed entrenching tools and four guns, two of them eighteen-pounders, on the island to make another battery.

We were under orders to land the fieldpiece we had on board, but our boat had not got back in time and so we did not get it to the shore until morning. When at last we arrived at the site of the battery, we found Captain Hacker of the Continental sloop *Providence* in command.

Ross reported to Hacker that we had brought him his six-pounder. "Damn your six-pounder, sir," Hacker said. "Where is Colonel Revere?" Before my master had a chance to answer, Hacker apologized for his asperity, explaining that Revere had been supposed to come on shore early in the morning to lay out the new battery and had not been seen. "Everything is to hang on Revere, they tell me: don't do anything without Revere, but where is Revere?"

"Indeed," St. Cyr interposed. "And where was Colonel Revere?"

"I have no idea," I told him. "All I know is that he is said to have spent very little time on shore during the first week of the siege. But as yet I had not seen him: I did not lay eyes on Revere until the council of war that evening."

❧❧❧ 40 ❧❧❧

WE had rain that night and when I rose the next morning Captain Mussey informed me that the wind had come around and was continuing to do so; he expected that we would be on our way again by the middle of the forenoon watch.

He proved to be an accurate prophet. With a southwesterly breeze the brig cleared Nantasket handily. Mussey took the wind on her starboard quarter and set his course for the open ocean. St. Cyr and I remained in the great cabin after we had eaten our breakfast, and I picked up the thread of my narrative where I had left it.

"The *Warren* was cleared for action," I told him. "I went aboard with Ross in my character as his manservant and no one made to stop me. Below, all the bulkheads separating the cabins had been struck down into the hold in preparation for battle. There were canvas curtains to give some privacy for the commodore's sleeping accommodations and for the officers of the army, but that was all. They must have brought the council table and chairs up especially. Wadsworth and Lovell sat there, and the two colonels commanding divisions, Mitchell and McCobb, and Commodore Saltonstall. There was another place as well, which was empty. There might have been forty officers gathered there abaft the capstans, and more coming. Ross wormed his way forward and found a seat on one of the twelve-pounders. I stood next to him with my head cocked to clear the deck planking."

"And where was Colonel Revere?" St. Cyr wanted to know.

Revere had been very nearly the last to arrive. He had got one of the officers by the arm, and was talking to him with great earnestness. At first I did not know who he was, and I remember thinking that his full, almost voluptuous face looked not a little like a rendering I had once seen of Lord North, who was the king's minister. General Wadsworth pulled his watch from his pocket and looked at it every bit like a schoolmaster reproving a tardy scholar. Revere took no note of him that I could see, but sat down in the chair with an air of vast satisfaction.

When General Lovell brought the council to order, he had Commodore Saltonstall read a letter signed by over thirty masters and commanders of the fleet, which urged that he should lead an immediate attack upon the harbor.

As soon as Saltonstall had finished, General Lovell said that he was in agreement; their orders from the Board of War stated that they were to captivate, kill, or destroy the whole enemy force, and that to his way of thinking the *Warren* had been lent for just such service. Saltonstall pressed his lips together sour while he listened. He seemed no better pleased when General Lovell introduced Colonel Brewer. Brewer, the general said, had been in the English fort but a few days previous, and come out again with intelligences of great import.

Brewer came forward and told the council that when he had been ashore the fort was less than half finished. The curtain walls had been no less than four feet high, and two of the bastions hardly begun. No gun platforms had been laid in them, and he doubted that guns could be mounted before the week was out. There was only one small battery close down by the water that could fire on the harbor.

"Now is the time for an attack," Brewer urged. "General McLean has set the inhabitants of the town to felling trees and to working on the walls. Today a man might leap ditch and wall with a musket in each hand. This day week it will only be reduced by a regular siege."

"And just how, sir," Saltonstall inquired, "would you recommend that this attack be mounted?"

Brewer's answer came back immediately. "Go in with your ships, Commodore," he urged. "Only go in with your ships; the enemy's vessels and his battery may be silenced, and in half an hour you will have everything."

"You seem to be damned knowing about this matter," Saltonstall said bitterly. "I am not going to risk my ship in that damned hole."

"Colonel Brewer is right, sir," one of the privateersmen said. "Nothing the British have can stand up to your ship if she is resolutely handled."

"And I will have your ship turned into a provision vessel if you make another such suggestion out of turn, Captain Salter." Saltonstall looked down the length of the table. "I am as anxious as anyone to promote the success of this enterprise," he said smoothly. "However, it is my duty to point out to you that I was sent to support this attack, not to make it for you. The *Warren* is the only ship of force in this fleet. She must be held in reserve in case the British send a frigate from Halifax. It would be irresponsible of me to expose her to fire from the battery on shore when a landing could sweep it away. You must make the assault first; carry the battery, and I will answer for the enemy's ships. Mowatt must either come out then or be taken where he lies."

"Damned good business for you, that," someone muttered. The voice came from among a knot of militia officers gathered off to one side. "We do the fighting, and you collect the prize money." There was a murmur of agreement.

"I'll have none of that," Lovell snapped. He glowered at the standing men. "That kind of talk gets us nowhere. Commodore, your pardon. Now, sirs: General Wadsworth, you've said nothing thus far. What is your opinion?"

"I agree with Colonel Brewer, General. We must attack."

The two division commanders nodded. Lovell looked to Revere.

"I don't know," he said. "It sounds risky."

"Risky?" Wadsworth put in. "Of course it's risky. But it's better than waiting here until the British scrape together reinforcements enough to come after us. I say we should go in now."

"Easy enough for you to say," Saltonstall told him. "You aren't responsible for this ship."

"I will lead the assault myself, Commodore, if General Lovell will give the order. With your ship or without it. May I count upon the navy for covering fire at the least?" Saltonstall answered with a bow so exaggerated that it was the same as sneering.

Lovell seized upon the chance to bring the discussion to a head. "Then we are in agreement, I believe. Has anyone else any matter to lay before this council? If not, I shall ask you to record your votes."

Lieutenant David Porter, the first of the *General Putnam*, spoke for the officers who had signed the letter. He was against delay and in favor of any plan that promised speedy action. Porter ended by saying that he would defer to the better judgment of those placed over him and then sat down. Saltonstall gave qualified assent; General Wadsworth and Colonel Brewer had nothing to add to their earlier pronouncements. Colonel Revere was still unsure.

"I would not go so far as to urge you to go in, when there remains a chance that the enemy must come out and fight on our ground," he said. "But neither would I cheat General Wadsworth of his chance for glory. You may do as you will for all of me."

Lovell told him that he required a specific answer, and Revere shrugged. "I don't see why," he replied peevishly. "It isn't my men who will be at hazard. But since you seemed determined you may count me with the rest."

Despite his reservations, the initial assault went quite smoothly. General Wadsworth's men were in their boats long before the dawn. A little before dawn they gave three cheers and pulled for shore.

The western side of the peninsula was rocky and steep and the men had to pull themselves up by the trees and bushes that grew between the boulders. On board the ships we could see nothing at first but the muzzle-flashes of the guns. When the British fired, their volleys lit up the whole cliffside, and I did not see how any man could climb so long as they held their ground. There was a battery of cannon on the heights as well, which fired grape down upon our men and did great execution; when the ships sought to silence it, they were forced to fire high in order to miss Wadsworth's troops. Their balls fell into the woods between the battery and the fort and thus did no damage to either.

Yet somehow the landing succeeded. Captain Warren's company from Falmouth was the first to reach the high ground, and they swept the English from the field.

As soon as it was light enough to see, the battery we had built on Bang's Island opened on the king's ships with a brisk and well-directed fire that continued through the day. In the middle of the morning the frigate *Warren* with three other ships made as if to enter the harbor, but at the last moment they hauled their wind and stayed outside the mouth. For half an hour they traded shots at long range with Mowatt's sloops. At last they bore up and sailed away. *Warren* passed close aboard our vessel on her way to an inlet between Bagaduce Head and the point opposite. She looked hard-used; all on her deck was confusion, and I was certain that I saw blood trickling from her scuppers. We heard afterward that she had had her mainmast pierced by shot in two places, her forestay was gone, and her bowsprit gammoning shot away. All this day and the next she spent licking her wounds.

It may be that the beating he had received broke the commodore's spirit. Truth to tell, I think we all were dismayed by the harsh reality of wounds and sudden death. General Wadsworth led some minor skirmishes, but most of the officers seemed content to wrangle and to point their fingers at one another in the nightly councils, with the result that little was done. Saltonstall was a morose and formal sort of man, which made him hard to know and easy to blame. Worse for him, he was from Connecticut, where the rest of the officers were Massachusetts almost to a man. The army was reduced to a third of its former strength by battle losses, sickness, and desertion. Some of the privateer captains warned that their men would only stay for a few more days, a week; perhaps a fortnight. General Lovell sent one of the chaplains express to Boston for reinforcements. Even then I wondered whether he ever truly believed that they would come in time.

Ross and McLellan did not. My master's work on the harbor defenses at Falmouth had given him an eye for ground, and he had an idea that it would be well to plant a battery on the point at Stockton where it could cover a retreat. We went to his friend to see if he would lay the plan before the generals. Joseph listened and shook his head. "Wadsworth would be in favor of it," he told the captain, "and that means Revere would not. They've taken a dislike to each other, as you may have heard. Besides, the general already has a like proposal. He wanted to fortify the narrows at Buckstown. We could hold off the entire British navy there, he said, and he's right. Have you ever seen how the river curves when you get past the island? They'd have to come at us one at a time against the current, and any cripples would drift back on the rest of the line. The place is a gift from God, but Lovell said no. He said he didn't want to injure morale by implying the possibility of failure."

"And just what are our chances?"

McLellan's mouth set in a grim line. "The prisoners we have all say that Mowatt expects a fleet from Halifax or New York. If we take the fort before it gets here we may be able to drive them off. If not we'd be caught between two fires."

General Wadsworth did his best to see that we were not. He seemed to be everywhere, tireless. Wadsworth it was who sustained the army, leading sallies and raids and then hacking doggedly at the inertia that crippled the endless councils.

Revere continued to oppose him. In council one night Wadsworth spoke for a plan to cut off the fort from the mainland by landing three hundred men in its rear. General Lovell was inclined to favor it, and there seemed a good chance it would pass. Then Colonel Revere reminded Lovell of the risks involved. He argued that our numbers were insufficient for such a division of forces, and Lovell reluctantly agreed.

General Lovell must have found his position supremely difficult. He was trapped between an active subordinate and several reluctant ones, between the knowledge that action meant losses and the possibility of defeat, and inaction, disaster. Lovell could not bring himself to order a full assault until Saltonstall removed the threat of the enemy's three ships, which could flank our column, and Saltonstall refused to go in after the ships until the fort had been reduced.

"What advantage would it be to go and take the enemy's shipping?" he asked. "They must come out directly the fort is ours."

Another week went by. Finally Saltonstall replied to one of Lovell's requests with an offer to go into the harbor if the army would storm the fort at the same time, whereupon the general called his officers together yet again. They deliberated for some time and then reported that the plan could not be carried through with any prospect of success. There was a grand council of land and sea officers the next day on board the *Hazard* with no more result. The patience of many began to grow thin, and they cried that if we did not attack the fort we should withdraw. That night it began to rain.

The last council I was at I can remember clearly. There had been intelligences received from Boston of a British fleet off Sandy Hook, and many of the privateersmen were strong for abandoning Bagaduce to the enemy. Lovell refused.

"I cannot give my vote for leaving so important a station," he told the assembly. "If a superior fleet does arrive I can but retreat to some convenient place up-river and await reinforcements. As yet the information is not substantiated. I would not give up that which we obtained at so much loss, as it is the only high ground without the fort. Let us wait and see, and in the meantime it may be that there is yet something which we can do."

In the end they came back to a plan that had been discarded earlier. The council passed it over the protests of Colonel Revere and Colonel McCobb from Georgetown in the county of Lincoln, quite simply because it was the only choice left. But it was a queer half-hearted decision that inspired no confidence. That very night orders came to remove most of the guns which had been landed back on board the transports.

The next morning, being the thirteenth day of August and a Friday into the bargain, General Lovell marched four hundred men around by the rear of the fort. The hour of the attack was set for noon, with *Warren* and the largest of the armed ships to force the harbor at the same moment. The British had shown themselves to be unusually vigilant. That very week a strong detachment led by Major Brown of North Yarmouth had been ambushed and driven back into the camp in confusion. I think that it had come to the point where many of the men scarcely cared what happened, so long as it brought a change from the heat and waiting.

On board the *Industry* we were red-eyed and irritable. We had worked through the night: our field gun had run away from us down a hill in the darkness, so damaging the carriage that we had been obliged to draft men to carry the barrel to the boat. There was a light breeze from seaward, tantalizing with its promise of relief, but here and gone again, and very little shade. We lay and panted like dogs.

At noon I heard the pipes shrill from the armed ships and watched the men race aloft to set their sails. The canvas spread and billowed. Slowly the ships gathered steerage and paid off, forming into line. The *General Putnam* was first, a fine ship of three hundred and fifty tons or thereabout mounting twenty nine-pounders, followed by the frigate *Warren* and three other vessels, all with doubled crews.

They were headed for the harbor mouth when I heard the alarm gun. The sound volleyed and echoed from the islands to the shore and back again. My master raised his head from his arms, as he had been dozing, and blinked dull-wittedly. Then he saw the *Putnam* and the *Warren* come into the wind and let go their anchors, with the other ships a few seconds behind.

"Into the rigging!" he told me. I snatched the glass from the becket and ran up the weather shrouds. The brigantine *Active* was running before the wind with all sail set. Even as I watched she let go sheets and left them flying.

"That's the signal for the approach of a fleet," the captain explained. "God send it's ours!"

Of course there was a chance that the ships might be the reinforcement which General Lovell had requested, but with the issue in doubt there could be no question of launching the attack. Saltonstall sent word on shore, and the general brought his men back into the camp.

Again we waited, through the afternoon, with the wind light and fluky. The captain of the *Active* had set his men to wetting down her sails so as to catch every breath. Even so, it was hours before she was hull-up from our deck, and later still that she came within hail. We could get no word from her. She continued on her course and rounded-to a cable's length from the commodore. We watched as she lowered a boat. An officer went over the side and into the stern sheets. The oars dipped and flashed. The officer went on board and left us no wiser than we had been.

The ships were English.

Six of them, fat and menacing, stood off and on in the bay beyond the islands. Ross had us keep them under observation by turns, and I think that every other master in the fleet did the same. They seemed even bigger than they probably were, magnified by a trick of the gathering fog.

"That's the reason they haven't come for us," Ross decided. "The fog. They know they've got us in a sack, and they don't want to risk the Penobscot in the fog with night coming on. I can't say I blame them either, the bastards. They've got us in a proper spot."

"But can't we use the fog to cover our escape? We could run down past them in the night."

Ross shook his head. "They'll be expecting that. If we all went, some of us would probably get through. But there is a chance: General Wadsworth's plan. The fleet mounts guns enough to hold these ships here until the transports can get away up-river. We'll have one tide to help us. Once we're past Buckstown we can build those batteries and stand them off until their bottoms rot away."

But the night slipped away in idleness and indecision. At three A.M. Lovell ordered the troops to reembark and at five the retreat began. We got under way as soon as the signal was given, hoping that we might get above the ledges at the narrows before the set of the ebb. As we passed the *Warren,* we saw General Lovell in his barge, still pleading with the commodore to make a fight of it at the mouth of the river. While I watched, Saltonstall gave the word to weigh anchor. He put the frigate before the wind and sailed after us. General Lovell was left standing in the stern sheets of his boat, shouting first at Saltonstall to stand, and then at his men to row the faster.

A number of the transports had passed Fort Point before the lightness of the wind and our small spread of canvas compelled us to come to anchor. The men-of-war spread stuns'ls and hoisted our boats to aid them. They ran past us with curses and threats to fire into us if we should get in their way. Meanwhile General Wadsworth had gone ashore at the point to see that the hospital there was loaded back on board, and we went off up the river in his cutter to lay out a site for a battery.

One of the transports was run up on the west shore of the river and the crew was taking her sails and cordage ashore to hide it in the woods. The general hailed the rest of us as he went by, and told us not to do the same. "They can't come up with us on this tide, boys," he shouted. "You're bound to get a breeze soon! Save the ships! We'll need 'em when Colonel Foster comes! Only a few miles and you'll be safe! I'll be back in a couple of hours to show the way!"

Unfortunately the English ships carried the sea-breeze with them until they were at last forced to anchor only a little way below the eddy where we lay. We were out of range of their guns and apparently their admiral did not dare to send his boats into our midst. Two of the armed ships which tried to escape around the back side of Long Island were taken, and this, I think, with the threat of the armada that only wanted a fair wind to come among us, penetrated to the hearts of many of our fellows. They ran their vessels aground, stripped them, and set them afire. Their crews and troops they carried scattered into the woods.

One of the Youngs suggested that we should do the same, but Ross had cut him short with a blistering oath. Thereafter I did not turn my back on them, nor let them get between my master and myself. Probably I need not have worried. They whispered back and forth, but they were a long way from being brave enough to face the captain when General Wadsworth returned.

Wadsworth came storming up the side of the *Industry*, exceeding wroth with the destruction of the other transports. "What, sir," he said to Ross, "aren't you going to run ashore? If you don't hurry there won't be a foot of space left."

"There was some talk about it," Ross said, smiling at the two brothers. "We decided not. There's a deal of provision on board we thought might be wanted up-river."

"That's the thing!" Wadsworth replied. "There's a bit of a breeze coming and the tide's due to turn. Get some sail on this bread-barge and let's see if we can't get her past the ledges and out of harm's way."

With a hoarse shout that was almost a cheer we turned to and hoisted every sail that would draw. Ross set a course across the river and down to gather momentum and then went about on an upstream reach. We jibed, and jibed again, and so came even with the place where we had been anchored. As the river narrowed we made less headway. Finally we found that we could not make legs long enough to make up for the ground we lost in turning.

"If we could get one or two of those boats to take us in tow we might still save her," Ross suggested to the general. Wadsworth nodded and the Captain put over his helm to approach a good-sized cutter that was pulling upstream.

I took over the tiller and Ross went to the rail. "Ahoy the boat!" he hailed. "Can you give us a hand?"

The answer was short and profane. I could see the captain take a firm grip on his temper and try again. The man in the stern sheets made a rude gesture.

General Wadsworth joined my master. "This is General Wadsworth," he bellowed. "I order you to assist this vessel."

"And I am Colonel Revere," the man in the boat replied. "I am sorry, General, but you have no right to command this boat. I am using it, as you can see."

"Using it, sir! And just how are you using it, save to leave the field?"

"I am transporting my baggage to a place of safety," said Revere. "What I have in these chests is of considerable value and should not be left for the enemy."

Wadsworth shook his head, as though he could not believe what he was hearing. "But this schooner has a considerable value, for which the state must answer."

"Then let the state take care of it," Revere shot back. "Who will take care of me if I lose my own property in saving the state's?"

"My God, sir! Did you come on this expedition to take care of your baggage, or to serve your state?"

"I came, General, to expel the British; since this is beyond our power, the expedition is at an end, and I must consider myself. And now I have tarried long enough. Good day to you, General Wadsworth!" He told the oarsmen to give way, and they pulled slowly away from us.

"Damn your eyes, Revere!" the General shouted after him. "Once this army is collected I will see that you answer for this if it is my last act on earth!"

41

B RISTLING with impotent anger, Wadsworth had watched Revere until the boat had dwindled to the size of a water bug.

"The *Samuel*'s steward said there were spoons in those chests, sir," I told him.

"Spoons! Then he'd best save himself with one long handle, for I'll see him sup with the devil!" He turned to Ross. "Run her ashore, Captain," he said softly. "It's over."

My master found a spot above the old fort where the bottom was soft and laid the *Industry* so close to the shore that her bowsprit lodged among the trees. The general went to see if he could get men to unload our provisions and to defend the schooner from the enemy through the night, but the troops had either run away or would not obey his orders. The Youngs drifted off into the dusk. Ross worked with Sprague and me to save what we could. It was little enough: a few bags of bread, a keg of small beer, a bit of meat, an anker of rum. Before the captain set fire to the schooner I made one last trip and brought away his navigating instruments and a change of clothes wrapped in the blankets from his berth.

We burned the *Industry* at ten in the evening. Sprague had found friends among the departing troops and my master let him go since that was what he wished. We stood and watched the flames reach hungrily from the hatches toward the tarry rigging. When the shrouds caught, the fire raced upward, and in an instant the whole intricate tracery of sheets and halyards was a web of flame. The sails were brailed up tight and burned more slowly.

Ross took it all in impassively. Five thousand pounds, and a dead loss if the chronically insolvent General Court should fail to make good on its assurances.

All of the fleet that had not ascended the river was destroyed. Some of the other transports were no more than smoldering hulks, or a few charred ribs jutting from the mud where the ebb had uncovered them. A few still blazed brightly. And there were armed ships as well. The state brigantine *Active* lay near Brigadiers Island. She had been taken from the British in the spring but they would not have her back. *Defense*, a new brig mounting sixteen six-pounders, was half-scuttled and burning in a cove. As the heat reached her cannon they went off in a last scattering volley.

Flame showed now on board the ship *Sky Rocket* as well. It flickered about her waist, moving toward the hatch. I saw a boat rowing swiftly away from her and then I understood. Five minutes later the *Sky Rocket* exploded.

Ross and I retired to a house on a height of land overlooking the river. We met General Wadsworth there, with perhaps a score of others, and stayed the night. In the morning he gave orders to collect the troops so that he could see what might be done.

At eight o'clock he called the officers together. Colonel McCobb reported that he had but forty men under orders of all his regiment. Colonel Tyler said that he had been told that General Lovell had given word that each man must shift for himself. Major Brown, I think it was, came forward and said that although he did not believe that further resistance was within our power, nor even that the few men remaining could be held, he at least would not desert his post if General Wadsworth gave orders that it must be held. There was an embarrassed silence after he sat down, punctuated by the clearing of throats and shuffling of feet. Then Lieutenant Colonel Howard, from Lincoln County, cut a sidelong glance at Samuel McCobb and said that he guessed that he'd stay too. Colonel McCobb stood up, and Major Hill from Biddeford, and Captain Ross, and then we were all standing, and someone began to cheer. General Wadsworth rose and put his hands in the air for silence, but we did not stop for a long time. When we did the general addressed us. He spoke haltingly, and his eyes had an odd wet look to them.

"Had all the officers behaved thus," he said, "we should not have come to this pass. I will not forget. General Lovell, however, remains in overall command. Regardless of what we may have heard of his intentions, it seems to me that we must join him as quickly as we may."

The best information was that Lovell had embarked with Captain Williams on board the state brig *Hazard* to go to the head of tide. One of the captains who knew the river said that he probably would have anchored at the mouth of Kenduskeag Stream below the falls. Accordingly the general bade Colonel McCobb assemble his men, and the rest to muster what men they could find and all the supplies and arms that we could carry, in readiness for the march. Men were told off for the few boats that remained. One he sent ahead to seek out General Lovell and to apply to him for orders. The rest we began to load with provisions from the piles on shore.

We had scarcely more than begun when we saw the boat which had been sent up-river returning to the landing-place. All the men stopped work to watch it, so that the beach seemed a sort of hazy waterfront tableau. As soon as the keel touched bottom, one of the boatmen leaped ashore and ran up the hill, shouting, "General Wadsworth! Dispatch for General Wadsworth!" We put down whatever we were doing and followed him.

General Wadsworth met the courier on the doorstep of the house. His face fell as he read the message, but he gravely thanked the man who had brought it and then turned to the anxious faces that surrounded him. His voice was flat and without emotion.

"General Lovell has sent word that the expedition is disbanded," he announced. "The boat I sent met his above the narrows at Buckstown. The commodore has burned the *Warren* near Oak Point, and the army will make its way cross-country to Fort Western."

Wadsworth folded the letter and put it into his pocket-book. "This command will depart for Camden in one hour," he said. "Destroy the boats and any state property that you cannot take with you." He turned and went back into the house.

We set out for Camden in the rain. From there we went to Thomaston, and so on down the coast.

I grimaced at the memory of gray drizzling days that flowed one into the other, seemingly without beginning or end. "We might have been in the tropics from the weather," I told St. Cyr. "It rained morning and afternoon, and when the sun broke through it did not stay long enough to dry us, but only increased our discomfort. The trails were churned into mud so that walking was an effort. By the time Ross and I reached home we had lost our shoes, and our wet breeches had chafed the tender parts of our bodies until they bled."

It had not been a happy homecoming. "Elizabeth railed at us for not sending word that we were well. She had heard that a captain named Ross had broken his leg on the day the British fleet had come, and said that she had not slept since from worry. Then there was the trouble with Colonel Jackson's regiment, which had been sent from the south to reinforce the expedition. He had learned of our defeat near Piscataqua, and had marched his men from Kittery to protect Falmouth. They took to greeting the companies straggling in from the Penobscot with catcalls and jeers. Ross and I went out to meet Joseph McLellan, who had gone by the Kennebec with General Lovell, and when my master heard them he turned on the man who had spoken first, a big man with the look of a blacksmith about him, and thrashed him senseless. Afterward we heard no more, and the two regiments camped apart to prevent further incidents."

"And Colonel Revere?" St. Cyr prompted.

I shook my head. "He was never brought to account: at least not the way that General Wadsworth had planned."

"How do you mean?"

"Wadsworth had friends, but so did Revere. Governor Hancock was one. And there was the matter of the losses the state had sustained. The General Court reckoned them at seven million dollars. Hancock wanted Congress to assume the debt, and in order to do that he needed the blame to fall on Saltonstall's shoulders. Revere got off with a light reprimand."

St. Cyr said that he did not see how that was possible.

"How so?"

"Why, with your captain's testimony to corroborate General Wadsworth's . . ."

"Captain Ross never testified. Nor did the other officers in Saltonstall's squadron. The court heard General Wadsworth, of course, and other militia officers, the captains of the state vessels, and some of the privateersmen. My master never said a word."

St. Cyr looked at me in disbelief. "Not a word? But Revere had caused him to lose his ship."

"That's just it. Ross had lost the *Industry*. That was why he took me to Boston, to speak before the court and press his claim for the loss. We left Falmouth the week after the frigate *Boston* came into the bay with a prize. That gave folks a turn! They thought it was Mowatt come to finish the job. The committee mustered both regiments, Mitchell's and Jackson's, and they got all mixed up with the people trying to get off the Neck before the shooting began. The same thing happened the next day with the *Deane*.

"Ross and I left as soon as we heard the court had been appointed. Then we sat in Boston for two weeks. The day before Ross was called, a man came and said there was a gentleman from the Marine Committee who wanted to see him. The captain assumed it was about his settlement, and so we went.

"The gentleman was my master's brother, who had worked his way into Hancock's favor. George told him there would be difficulties with his claim if he were to testify: questions about the *Industry*'s value and condition. The payment could be held up for months, even years.

"It was not a threat, he said. Merely what he called a bit of brotherly advice. Did my master want to save Saltonstall? Of course not. Saltonstall deserved some of the blame at least. He had lacked the resolution that might have bound the self-willed and independent privateersmen into a cohesive fighting force, the strength of character to hazard his own command and risk the censure of Congress. Wadsworth would come off with honor in any event. It was in everyone's interest that he should, and so the captain's testimony was unneeded. All he could do was ruin Revere. A man worn out in his country's service, George called him. Revere would not serve again in the field, he said. His friends would see to that, but they would not stand idly by and see his reputation destroyed to no purpose, and my master would do well to think on it.

"Ross did think, and in the end he went to Wadsworth for advice. By then it was clear how the wind set. The general excused Revere. So many poltroons were going unpunished, he said, that one more or less made no difference. That decided it. Ross did not speak, and the next day we went home.

"Saltonstall took all the blame. He was dismissed from the navy and went privateering on his own account. And Congress was left to foot the bill, so the captain got his money. He never had another word from his brother. Revere went back to his spoons and buckles, and there, I think, it lies."

Young St. Cyr freely admitted that he found the outcome of my story disappointing; yet he was not glad to see it come to an end. Neither, I confess, was I. I had spread the narrative out over a period of several days, until it became a part of shipboard routine. The cold air and leaden skies meant that we kept mostly to the cabin; talk served to occupy our minds and to speed the idle hours. In this we were left to our own devices. Sarah was increasingly remote and unresponsive. She sat and did needlework, answering in clipped monosyllables barely within the bounds of politeness. Ben kept to himself, though I sometimes saw him coming out of the forecastle. He had nothing to say to St. Cyr or to me, and little interest in anything we had to say.

We talked for a time of Haiti, but there were too many uncertainties for it to be a comfortable topic. We had been too long without news to do much planning. St. Cyr searched his memory for things Ogé had said or done which he had not already recounted. We spent a day thus, and another on his own history. From his life we turned back to mine. St. Cyr held that it was my turn, and insisted that I begin again, with my childhood at Fitzgore's, my education, and how I had come to be a slave.

Morning or evening was all one to us in the twilight below-decks. I started after breakfast on the sixth day out of Nantasket, nor did I mark anything outside of my story until Captain Mussey came into the great cabin for his dinner.

"Damned dirty weather we're having," he said, slamming the door behind him. He was dressed in oilskins, and streaming water. I noticed then for the first time the lively motion of the brig, and the heavy beat of rain on the planking overhead.

I went to fetch Sarah and Benjamin. When I returned with them, the cook was setting the table. Captain Mussey turned as we entered. "I was just telling Mongseer we've made a tolerable passage," he said. "Tomorrow, God willing, we should be in the latitude of the Bermudas. At that, ten days would see us at Cape François, though I see small hope of arriving so soon. There's a storm making, or I'm no seaman. Say a fortnight instead, then, and I'm betting the missus won't be sorry to set foot on land again from the look on her." He inquired politely enough how Sarah was keeping, and she responded with a thin smile. The cook came back in with the steaming tureen, and Captain Mussey bade us take our seats and eat hearty. He leaned forward solicitously.

"Pea soup again, missus, but thick and hot. Likely you're tired of it already: I could eat it every day, myself. Come to think on it, I guess I do. But take a bit anyhow, do. It'll warm your innards and stick by you proper. 'Sides, there's no telling when you'll have dinner hot again if the weather comes on the way it is."

"That is right," St. Cyr put in. "But a few minutes ago your husband was telling me how he and his captain subsisted for two days on cold boiled pork and peas. Is that not so, Citizen?"

I swallowed a spoonful of soup and nodded. "It was our first voyage, when we lost that man Bibber over the side. I hope that it won't get so rough as it was then, my dear, but you really must try to eat. Eat when you can; it's the first thing a good sailor learns."

Sarah looked up from her plate with eyes that snapped. "I'm not a good sailor," she said. "I don't ever want to be a good sailor. I want to be what I thought I was, a woman with a home and a husband." She flung down her napkin and left.

Benjamin stared at me accusingly and made as if to follow. I ordered him to stay where he was and went after her.

I found Sarah on her berth in our cabin. She was lying with her face buried in the pillow. Frustrated and angry, I asked her what was wrong.

"Everything's wrong," she replied in a voice muffled by the bedding. She sat up and looked at me. I saw that she had been crying. "This ship is wrong. It smells bad, and the ceiling in here leaks. Everything is musty and damp. It's cold and uncomfortable and it's going in the wrong direction. I don't want to go to Santo Domingo, Pyrrhus. I want to go home."

"Saint Domingue," I corrected. "Or Haiti. From what St. Cyr says, we probably won't use the colonial names once the island is free. As far is home is concerned, Haiti will be our home."

"No, it won't. It never will. It's going to be just as bad as this cabin, only it will be hot instead of cold. And there will be rats and bugs and fever, and people trying to kill you. I thought that once I'd worried you through one war that was enough. Not for you, it wasn't! You weren't happy. We were safe in Portland, and you went and found some place where you could get shot at, and where I could worry all over again."

"Now Sarah," I began, "that's hardly fair."

"Fair? What's fair? You've dragged Ben and me out of our nice house in Falmouth into this leaky old tub in the middle of a hurricane, for God's sake! Is that your idea of fair, Pyrrhus Venture? Is it?"

"You're exaggerating. To begin with, it's not a hurricane."

"Oh," she said. "Excuse me. I suppose that's sunshine leaking through up there. Is this your idea of a nice afternoon for a sail?"

"Of course not. It's a little rough, and it is raining, but the wind's no more than half a gale. And I'm sorry if you're uncomfortable. You might feel better if you ate something." I paused a moment in hopes that she would agree to come back to the table. Sarah said nothing.

"I know I told you when I opened the store that I was done with all this. I meant it, really I did. But this is something different. Something I had to do. I told you before that I didn't feel as though I was a part of Portland. I will be a part of what we have in Haiti, though. I will because I will have helped to make it. I will belong."

"You belong with us," Sarah said. "With Ben and me. And we belong in Portland. You helped make that, too."

"I know I did. Only others didn't seem to believe it. They treated us differently. You know they did."

"They'll treat us different in Haiti, too. My God, Pyrrhus, I don't even speak the language!"

"You'll learn," I assured her. "Ben will learn even quicker. And you needn't worry. I won't be fighting. I'll be in the cabinet. I'll be at home. We'll be happy and safe, and you and Ben will be proud of me, because I'll be doing important things for our people."

Sarah looked at me plaintively. "You're my people," she said. "You and Ben." She lay down and turned to face the wall.

"You'll see things differently once we're there," I told her gently. "It'll make you a great lady: the wife of a cabinet minister. You'll see." There was no answer, and after a time I left. As I closed the door I heard what might have been the sound of weeping.

42

BENJAMIN left the table when I returned and went to join his mother in our cabin. Or so I thought, yet when I went in the evening to call Sarah and him for supper he was not there. I found him at length in the empty forecastle. He had fallen asleep in one of the berths. I woke him and asked him what he was doing there.

"I was waiting for Mr. Dubbin," he said stubbornly. "Mr. Dubbin said I could come whenever I want."

Dubbin had iron-gray hair and a brass ring in one ear, and possessed great skill at knots and rope-tricks. He was Benjamin's favorite of all the crew.

"Not without permission you can't," I told him. "From now on you must ask before you go. Your mother was worried about you. With this weather you shouldn't go anywhere alone, and Captain Mussey says it's getting worse. That means your Mr. Dubbin won't have time for little boys. He'll be on deck until the storm blows itself out."

The gale grew more intense while we sat at supper. We were running to the southeast under reefed topsails, and at the end of the meal Captain Mussey announced that he was minded to take a second reef. "I might heave to," he conceded. " 'Twould be more comfortable for all of us, I suppose, but you're anxious to get where you're going, and that would mean lost time and a long beat to windward later. I think that I can run out from under this storm if I can keep on through the night."

St. Cyr answered that for his part he did not mind a little discomfort, but that he would leave it up to Sarah. My wife said nothing. Captain Mussey looked at me with eyebrows raised. I shrugged and said that we would rely upon his judgment.

"That being so," he said, "perhaps you will excuse me. Good night, missus. I trust you and the younker'll sleep well enough if you take care to put the bunk-boards in." He pulled on his oilskins and went on deck.

Sarah and Benjamin took advantage of his departure to leave as well. St. Cyr tipped a little more wine into his glass and braced himself securely into his chair.

The brig heeled madly, and I felt pleased that it was not I who was going aloft on such a night. Mussey was turning into the wind to spill the air from the sails, making them more manageable, but reefing in a blow is no simple task, and darkness compounds the difficulty. Bent over the yard, dangling in the air with only a slender footrope beneath, you claw at the stiff canvas with fingers made clumsy with cold and pray that you will not fall.

Sometimes you do.

The scream did not reach us, but there was a heavy blow to the planking above my head, followed by the rush of footsteps.

By the time they brought the injured man below, St. Cyr and I had the cabin table cleared and ready to receive him. Two of his hands carried him in, pale-faced and bloody. It was Dubbin.

"Put him down there," Mussey told them, "and then get back on deck. Mr. St. Cyr, Mr. Venture, keep an eye on him while I get my medical box." He squeezed past us to his sleeping cabin right aft.

Dubbin groaned.

Behind me Benjamin gave a shriek and darted forward to the sailor's side. He was dressed for sleep; when he heard the commotion, he had slipped out to see what was amiss. Sarah followed after him in a dressing gown thrown hastily over her night-rail.

Mussey returned, and Benjamin ran to him. "Make Mr. Dubbin well again," the boy pleaded. "Mr. Dubbin will get well, won't he?" It gave me pain that my son should turn to another for comfort before me, but something prevented me from offering reassurances, and there was no time for my sorrow.

"He'll get well if you leave us alone," I told him curtly, and motioned to Sarah to take him away.

Captain Mussey examined Dubbin quickly and expertly. "He was born to be hanged," he said when he had done. "His nose is broken, and some of his ribs: three or four, I can't be certain. Bear a hand, there, gents, while I strap him up. Handsomely, now." He stripped Dubbin's torso and passed the bandages around him as deftly as any shore physician, and then proceeded to set his nose. "He'll keep until morning now," he told us at last. "We'll put him in my bed. I'll be short-handed without him, and I won't be needing it as long as the storm lasts."

"Will he live?" I asked. "Benjamin will want to know."

Mussey shrugged. "Jack's the luck of the devil," he said. "Any normal man would have split his brain-pan, but he's of a thick-skulled race, and suffered no more than a good bump. No, he'll live, will Jack, though we'll have to wait until he's come to before we know if the fall has addled his wits." He stepped back from the berth, where Jack was trussed tightly so that he could not move however the brig should toss, and pronounced himself satisfied. "Jack'll keep until morning now if you gentlemen will be kind enough to look in on him."

In the morning Dubbin was sensible but weak. The cook came in long enough to feed him a few mouthfuls of soup made from the carcass of the last of the chickens, and to attend to his personal needs. Captain Mussey came for a few minutes when he was done, to see how his patient was faring. He proclaimed himself satisfied with Dubbin's progress, yet cautioned us to keep him tied in except when absolutely necessary, for the storm showed no sign of abating. If anything, it seemed to be getting worse. The sea had taken on a wicked cross-chop that had the *Neptune* pitching and rolling in corkscrew spirals. Even after a week at sea I found it difficult to walk around without hand-holds; Sarah gave up trying and took herself back to her bed.

St. Cyr and I lingered as usual in the great cabin, but about midway through the forenoon watch the cook interrupted us. "Cap'n's compliments," he said in the formal fashion of the royal navy, "an' would Mr. Venture please come on deck." Puzzled, I donned my outer garments and followed him.

Captain Mussey was aft at the tiller. I made my way to join him. With the wind and spray sweeping the deck the footing was worse than it had been below. Mussey had to shout to make himself audible.

"I want to take another reef," he told me. "I'm short one man. I need you to mind the helm so that I can help. Can you do it?" I said that I thought I could, though it had been years since I had stood a trick, and I had never handled anything but sloops and schooners. "It's just for a minute," Mussey urged. "You'll have no trouble. Unless you'd rather go aloft?" He smiled broadly to show that he meant it as a joke.

I took the tiller and tried to get the feel of how the *Neptune* steered. "I can't tell much in this," I shouted back. "I guess I can manage if you hurry."

Mussey nodded and called all hands to take in sail. He knew his brig's every whim, and with him at my side there was no trick in my bringing her around. "Hold her at that," Mussey bellowed, and began the laborious climb to the topsail yard.

There was a brief lull in the force of the gale which made the work go quickly. First the fore staysail was done, then the fore topsail, the largest and most difficult. The men were coming down off the yards; only one of them was still inching along the footrope to the security of the main top, and Mussey was halfway down the shrouds to the deck, when I heard a soft shout aloft and saw a man with his arm outstretched and pointing.

The black squall hit with insane force, the winds twisting and tearing in totally unpredictable directions. They plucked the sailor from the yard and spun him into oblivion. The next gust lay us on our beam ends, and I thought we were gone. One rope's end caught me across the cheek so hard that I nearly let go of the tiller. I noted with an odd sense of detachment that a halyard had parted. Then the rain closed in like a curtain.

I have relived the next moments over and over again for a quarter of a century, and even though there was nothing I could have done I know I shall never be rid of them. I saw in brief snatches between the volleys of raindrops how the slings parted and the lift lines let go, and the main yard came arrowing down through the deck planking, right above the cabin where Sarah and Benjamin would be lying in their berths. I heard someone shout their names, and I realized that the voice was my own.

The squall passed us by, and we were still afloat. Afloat, but with the brig half-crippled in the middle of an Atlantic gale. Yet after the madness we had just survived, the return of the mere gale seemed like a sort of haven. Mussey was on the deck again, shouting orders. I turned the tiller over to him and ran to the main companion.

The door to our cabin was jammed. St. Cyr was there before me, trying to force it open, but even with the two of us it would not give so much as an inch. Sarah was crying for help and screaming Benjamin's name. I braced my back against the opposite wall and kicked out against the door with both feet. The panel split and I wrenched it away.

The interior of the cabin was a shambles. The heavy main yard had torn a jagged hole in the decking overhead and plunged through the single thwartship's bunk in which Benjamin slept. Rain and sea water were still pouring in through the hole. It was only after an endless, heartstopping moment that I realized that there was no blood, no tiny body impaled among the bedclothes. Perhaps he had crawled in with Sarah. I fought my way through the wreckage to see.

A broken plank from above had smashed the empty upper berth down upon her. With St. Cyr to help I prised it off.

One of the oaken beams that supported the berth had struck Sarah just below the small of her back. It was a small beam, but it had come down with crushing force and pinned her helplessly against the thin mattress. She screamed when it came away, and fainted before I could ask what had become of our son.

But Benjamin would have to wait; clearly Sarah could not be allowed to remain where she was any longer, for a chill added to her injuries would be fatal. As gently as we could, St. Cyr and I brought her into his cabin. When he left to fetch Captain Mussey, I cut away her sodden garments and pulled the covers up to her chin.

St. Cyr returned with Mussey's medical gear and his promise to come as soon as the wreckage aloft was secured. "He says that when they are finished he will give me a man to help look for your son," the Frenchman told me. "I am sure we will find him. It may be that he took fright during the squall and is hiding. Unless you have further need of me I will go and begin." I do not recall what I said in return, but I heard him close the door. I sat chafing Sarah's wrist and waited for Captain Mussey.

When St. Cyr returned, Mussey was still in with Sarah. St. Cyr was wearing a smile. "Benjamin is safe and well," he announced. "And your good lady?"

I shook my head miserably to indicate that I did not know. St. Cyr frowned, but then he brightened. "Your son is asleep in the forecastle, in the berth of his friend Citizen Dubbin. He must have slipped in and slept through everything. I thought it best not to wake him." I nodded in absent agreement.

The cabin door opened and Mussey joined us. His brow furrowed with concern. "You'd better get in there," he said. "She's starting to wake up, and it would be best if you were with her when she comes around."

I asked him the extent of her injuries.

"Ask a real doctor," he snapped. "I told you I'm no quacksalver."

He caught himself, and made an effort to speak reasonably. "I don't know. There's too much swelling to tell for sure. It's like I said: breaks and sprains and a touch of colic I can manage. Back injuries are, well, they're damned tricky."

"What are you trying to say?"

"Nothing," Mussey said. "I'm not saying nothing. I just think she should have a real doctor look at her. I'll come around for Charleston; we can be there in about four days."

Sarah's voice came to us through the cabin door. "Pyrrhus?" she said. "Pyrrhus?" And then with a rising note of panic: "Pyrrhus! I can't move my legs!"

43

THE good doctors of Charleston, for all of their diplomas from Edinburgh and from Leyden, could tell me no more about Sarah's affliction than Captain Mussey had, but they said it at greater length. In the end Sarah simply refused to submit to their proddings and poulticings, insisting that rest and fresh air and good simple food would help her better than any number of doctors, however skilled.

At another time I should have enjoyed a stay in this agreeable city, which might have been lifted entire from the islands of my youth. There were the same gardens, the porticos and piazzas, the tiled roofs and jalousied doors and windows, the brick and the stucco washed in cool pastels. Seeing it for the first time, as it seemed to rise from the water before me couched in green and crowned by the spire of Saint Michael's church, I had the eerie feeling that time had turned back upon itself like the Great Worm of myth, and that I might meet a younger Pyrrhus dreaming at the quayside.

I installed my family in lodgings kept by a man named Booth in a lane between Broad Street and Tradd. The Sign of the Rose, as he called it, was a three-storied affair of the sort known thereabout as a double-house, slightly down-at-heels, and built end-on to a street amid walled gardens of honeysuckle and jasmine. They were still in bud, with the promise of later beauty. Booth was a descendant of one of the original proprietors of the colony, one of the caciques who, with the landgraves and barons, formed the philosopher John Locke's defense against a widespread democracy. He explained that the resemblance between Charleston and the port cities of the Indies, which to me had been so unsettling, was due to the fact that most of the original residents had been planters from Barbados who wished to continue to live in the West Indian style.

For Sarah's convenience we took rooms on the ground floor. St. Cyr took the room immediately above ours while he waited for Captain Mussey to repair the *Neptune*'s quarterdeck, ship a new main yard, rereeve the rigging, and sign on two new hands to replace Dubbin and the one who had been lost in the storm, whose name I never knew.

It took about a week to ready the brig for sea. Mussey stopped in to inquire after Sarah's progress several times when he was ashore and his other errands permitted, and so I was not surprised when St. Cyr came in one afternoon and explained that he would be going on to Cape François without me. The young Frenchman was disconsolate, but at the same time deeply sensible of the need for him to continue with the arms and supplies for Ogé's army.

We walked out onto the faded, paint-peeling piazza. Even in February the weather was not unlike that of a particularly fine spring day in Portland, and Sarah was sitting in the warm sun in a chair our landlord had placed in the garden. St. Cyr waved to her with a courteous little half-bow, but she affected not to notice. He let the slight pass and turned to me.

"This needn't change your plans completely," he urged. "Directly your good wife has recovered from her injuries, come and join me in Saint Domingue. Your welcome there is assured. I will see to it personally."

"And who can say how long that may be? It could be months before Sarah is well enough to travel."

"No matter. Vincent Ogé knows of your efforts. Even if I were not at his side to remind him, he is not the sort of man who forgets. There will be a place for you in the new order. And do not feel as though you have forfeited your right to claim it simply because you are delayed and will not be with him from the first days. You have earned a seat in his government already, and you will have the opportunity to earn new honors in the times to come. This matter of guns and fighting is only the beginning. The real work will begin after the peace is signed."

The bells of Saint Michael's, the pride of the city since its construction and the more so since their return from wartime captivity in England, began to chime the hour. From where we stood it was just possible to glimpse the graceful octagonal spire with its clock-faces and gilt wind vane. "You see?" St. Cyr said. "That is to tell me that it is time that I was leaving. The new age is about to be born!"

St. Cyr sailed with the *Neptune* and her precious cargo on the evening tide; but it was a death-knell, not the joyous peal of new birth, that the bells of Charleston had sounded. Within a month of my young friend's departure Vincent Ogé was dead, and many of his followers with him.

The news that reached me was fragmentary and infrequent, but with a tragic inevitability that I could not ignore. There was nothing to be done, of course; Sarah was too unwell to travel and I would not have left her in any event. Beyond that was the fact that the freshest reports were already weeks old when they appeared in the pages of the *Gazette*.

Still, the need to know was consuming. St. Cyr had had time enough to join Ogé and be sacrificed along with the others, although he had evidently been too late for the arms in the *Neptune*'s holds to have altered the balance of power. April was trending into May before I felt that I had a picture of how it might have been.

I had pieced the story together from printed accounts, from the rumors which circulated over rum and arrack punches at Kerr's tavern, where the masters of King and of Meeting Street gathered at the end of the day, by listening wherever men came together, and by asking questions of shipmen newly arrived from the Indies. Although I spent as much time within Sarah's call as possible, I had need to be abroad on my own affairs and on a few commissions from young Deering, which I had undertaken to defray our expenses. These few hours I used to full advantage.

My chiefest concern was for St. Cyr, but of him there was no word. Indeed, the only names that were mentioned were those of Ogé and his lieutenant, a mulatto named Chavanne. Relying on promises of aid which never arrived, Ogé and Chavanne had raised their banner in the very citadel of the colonial overlords, Cape François itself. Only a handful of men had succeeded in joining them, and this pitiful band of martyrs was easily defeated by the well-armed troops at the governor's disposal.

The rigor with which Ogé was punished elicited sympathy even in slave-holding Charleston, where servile insurrection among the Gullah folk was the recurrent nightmare of the planter class. I could well understand how this might be, for I had sensed a watchfulness behind the surface gaiety of the Gullah, a barrier between myself and the people with whom I had spoken that went beyond their strange patois and which left me, even me, feeling alien and guilty at the same time.

The final confirmation of Ogé's fate came in a newspaper from Jamaica which our landlord had from the new upstairs tenant, the mate of a pilot schooner.

The morning was a fair one, bearing the promise of a fine hot day to come. I had brought Sarah out into the garden to sit until the sun got high, when I would carry her to the shade of the piazza. Mr. Booth came out, looking rather more harried than usual. He gave us both good day, and then asked if it would be convenient for me to join him in the hall. After I had seen to Sarah's comfort I followed him inside, wondering at his unwonted secretiveness.

Booth took the newspaper from the hall table and thrust it into my hands. "I feared to tell you in front of your wife," he began. "A shock like this in her present state of health, and all. But they butchered the poor man proper, they did! Worse than the planters did with that wretch Cato, down Stono way, when I was a lad. Broken on the wheel he was, and all for the crime of asserting the natural rights of man! Oh, but those Frenchmen are devils, sir: proper devils, and no mistake."

It was only with the greatest of difficulty that I calmed him sufficiently to ask to whom this had been done. "To whom? Who but that poor wretch Ogé? God save me: I see what you mean! No, not our friend Monsieur St. Cyr! But you can read for yourself."

I took the paper to the door where the light was better and read the report in all its grim detail. Ogé and Chavanne had been executed on March 12: their limbs broken in several places, they were left upon the wheel until death relieved their sufferings. Afterward their heads were cut off and displayed on posts along the highway.

Heartless it was, as when runaway slaves had been burned in iron cages in the Place d'Armes. The governor's methods had ever been brutally direct. Make an example of the leaders, and the herd will become docile and return to their labors. Such a man would not hesitate to put St. Cyr to death in the same barbarous fashion, but he would make much of it if he did. Liberals were a threat to his dominion, and the messy death of one of their number might take the romance out of intervening in the domestic affairs of Saint Domingue.

No, the governor would not miss the opportunity to trumpet St. Cyr's death to the very heavens. That he had not could mean but one thing: St. Cyr was still alive. He would be in hiding, certainly, moving from place to place to stay ahead of the pursuit, and meeting at every opportunity with the lesser leaders of the movement: the whites who supported the liberals in the National Assembly, who were trying to extend political rights to people of color. Trying to find common ground, trying to keep them from dissolving into factions like those of the colonial aristocracy.

It would be difficult. St. Cyr was rich; he was French; he was white. Without Ogé to vouch for him he would have a great burden of distrust to overcome. For that matter, so might I. I was, after all, from abroad. I had been born on another island, had lived in another country, spoke French in the manner of their masters. I would have to help them to understand that these things were of no account. That I was black as they were, that I had been a slave; that I was bone of their bone and flesh of their flesh; that I had, finally, embraced Haiti and her people as my own, and that they could do no less.

They would be my people. We would share the land of Haiti as we had shared a dream for her future. The governor might kill our leaders, but he could not kill our dream. That dream needed me now, the dream of one island, one people; hazy the way the future is always a trifle hazy, but clear at the same time.

A sharp clash of voices recalled me into the present as Booth's quadroon cook argued with a Gullah fishwife over the price of a basket of shrimps. I looked out of the dark hallway and saw Sarah. Sarah, sitting where I had left her, with Bess, Booth's tortoise-shell cat, sprawled across her lap, uncomplaining but perhaps a little too hot from the brightness of the sun and the sharp inky look of the shadows. Sarah needed me, too, and regardless of Haiti's golden future hanging in the balance I would have to see to her first. Surely in a few more weeks she would be well. Then I could show her that she had been wrong, that her little dream could be a part of my greater one. One island, one people. A place where I truly belonged at last. As I walked out to her, I heard from the alley behind the kitchen the rich, haunting tones of Gullah laughter.

I tended Sarah with devoted optimism through the month of May, while Charleston filled up with planters and their families from the low country, come to escape the rigors of the fever season. For them there were the usual round of balls, concerts and cotillions, the torchlit boatrides, the games of ombre and of something called golf, which is played upon a lawn. It was a recent import from England, but already sufficiently popular in the city that two clubs devoted to the sport had been formed. The entertainments were many and lavish, so that Charleston seemed to be, as was its boast, the first city of the continent and perhaps another London, albeit smaller and with streets of hard-packed sand. My landlord beamed when I made this comparison, for though Charleston had suffered extremely during the British occupation, it was a point of local pride to be the most English of the cities on this side of the Atlantic. Still, he said wistfully, this season was not a patch on the last, when President Washington had come to town, and stayed at Thomas Heyward's house on Church Street. The gentry had outdone themselves to make him welcome, and at one ball all the ladies had worn bandeaux bearing his portrait.

So May became June, and June simmered over into July. With increasing impatience I conned over the news from abroad; how the French National Assembly had decreed that men of mixed blood who had been born of free parents should be admitted into the colonial assemblies, and of how this had excited the fears of the white aristocrats. The governor had gone so far as to issue a proclamation suspending the operation of the law. That suited me well enough, for it had not extended the franchise beyond a small minority, and his intransigent behavior could only hasten the day when the present system would be replaced by a government of all the people. I was anxious for that day to come: anxious to have my judgment confirmed, to find St. Cyr, to resume the work which we had begun and which he must even then have been carrying forward.

Only Sarah's infirmity held me back. Her constitution was improved since our arrival in Charleston, and she had recovered some feeling in her lower limbs, but no movement. More and more I chafed at the restriction. A carpenter I had met, a Hessian who had chosen to take his discharge in the colonies, had introduced me to a German doctor who suggested a course of mineral baths as a restorative, and I pressed Sarah to submit to them. There was another who prescribed manipulations of the spine, and yet another, an itinerant, who possessed a certificate proclaiming him to be a disciple of Dr. Mesmer's and to have studied under him in Paris. None of these quite suited Sarah, whose refrain of rest and fresh air at length became so frustrating that it often led to words. Young Benjamin was another subject upon which we disagreed. I know that I had neglected him during Sarah's convalescence, but of late he had become sullen and rebellious.

Benjamin's favorite resorts were situated on the far side of the city along the waterfront. I had brought him there myself once or twice early in our stay, though because of the dangers I had forbidden his going unattended. Latterly it seemed I simply did not have the time. I should have realized that my son was as much in need of my understanding and companionship as Sarah was, but I did not, and on looking back there were whole days when I addressed no word to him save to say that he should be quiet so not to disturb his mother's rest. In after years I came to regret all the things I left unsaid.

Still, there was little for an active lad to do about the boardinghouse, and no boys of Ben's age and station with whom he could play. He began to defy my prohibition and went down to the docks at every opportunity. If he were not somewhere about the house or the yard I came to know that he would be on Gadsden's Wharf, or Indian Wharf, or on the piers near the Merchant's Exchange at the end of Broad Street. Every time I was forced to seek him out I took him in tow and issued new and stricter injunctions, which Benjamin received with stony indifference.

Once, and only once, I succumbed to the temptation to use force. Ben took his stripes silently, but the experience left me feeling sick and ashamed. I watched him walk stiffly out of the room, the track of a tear wet on his cheek, and cast the switch away with revulsion.

Later I went to seek Ben out, in order to explain myself and to apologize for my actions. When I could not find him in our rooms, in the gardens, nor yet in the kitchen where he sometimes wheedled treats from the cook, the anger rose in me again and I headed for the docks.

I cast about in my son's usual haunts without success. At the last of the wharves but one, I was delayed while a chanting crew unloaded a gleaming varnished chariot, ordered from a London carriage-maker complete with its own coachman, who stood by swearing at the long-shoremen in harsh Cockney accents. In truth, it was a tricky piece of work to sway the rig up and over and onto the pier unscratched, and I had to admire the skill of the foreman in keeping control of his men despite the coachman's stentorian bellows. Presently I realized that I was enjoying myself. Watching the workers had allowed me to forget my own problems for a time. I breathed deep and leisurely to savor the cool tang of the air off the water, and looked about. There was plenty of activity to capture and hold the eye. At the end of the quay an outbound brigantine was taking on cargo for foreign parts: rice in bags, and indigo, and baled cotton. There were hawkers and crimps and seamen off the ships, smartly dressed or outlandishly rigged out according to their taste and custom. It was a boy's Eden, a kaleidoscopic place that made me feel more than a little boyish myself. At the sea-ward end of the wharf Ben was sitting on a bollard. I walked down and stood beside him.

"You made me miss the gold," he said in a flat, accusing tone.

I considered that for a time, and because I did not know what else to say I asked him what gold he meant.

"The gold from that ship," he said, pointing at the French merchant-man. "Chests full of it. The prince sent it. From Porto. And men with fine coats and beautiful ladies in gowns. I missed them all."

"I'm sorry," I told him, even though it sounded then as if someone had been peddling him stories of the pirate Teach. Ben did not reply. After a while I asked him who had told him about it, just to get him talking again.

"A man," he said. "One of my friends."

"That's a French ship," I pointed out.

Ben eyed me warily. "So?"

"Did your friend say why a French ship is carrying gold from Portugal?"

"I never said Portugal."

"Oporto, then," I said lightly. "Surely they haven't moved it."

Benjamin shrugged and settled himself to watch the ship once more. "I don't know," he said. "All that he said was that it came from the Porto prince."

It took a moment or two for that to sink in. When it did, I seized Ben by the shoulders and swung him around. "Port-au-Prince! Did he say Port-au-Prince?"

My son squirmed uncomfortably in my grasp. "You're hurting me," he said. I let him go and repeated the question. "I don't know," Ben admitted. "It was something like that."

"Then they're from Saint Domingue! That's what comes of neglecting your lessons, Ben. But come on; I want to speak with the captain, and you may as well start learning about your new home right now."

Unfortunately the lesson was not such as I had expected. I gave a Gullah fisherman a piece of money to row us out to the ship in his skiff, but the captain was gone ashore. The two seamen he had left on anchor-watch were surly louts who spoke only to warn us to keep our distance. I told the boatman to go closer. "I have business with your captain," I told them.

One of the men produced a pistol and leveled it in my direction. "You will have business with the coroner if you do not shy off," he said. "Begone!"

He appeared ready to carry out his threat, and I bade the fisherman return us to the wharf. "We might have learned something if you had got the words right," I told Ben. "If you had told me this morning I would have stayed with you and we might have met the people from that ship when they came on shore. They could be anywhere by now. There's naught to do but wait for the captain to come back."

"My friend knows where they went," Ben said.

"What friend is that?"

"Old Tom Perry. He told me about the gold. He knows. He's the one that took 'em."

It was the work of fifteen minutes to find Tom Perry, an aging barrow-man with a long white beard well stained with the juice of tobacco. He was unusual in many ways, not the least of which was the fact that under untold layers of ancient grime his skin was apparently white. He had a high, cracked voice and he squinted in a way that led me to believe that he was nearly blind, but there was little that escaped him.

"Oh, aye," he said, when I explained what it was that I wanted. "Aye, Tom can tell ye where they be, that can old Tom."

"I'd be glad if you would," I said, and gave him a coin.

Perry took it in his palm and brought it close under his nose. "That ye will," he said with a laugh, and thrust the coin deep into his pocket. "And Tom will, but mark 'ee, Tom's his doubts whether they'll be as glad to see ye. Nay, nay, that's enow: you'll find the most on 'em down to Shepheard's, ye will. But mark 'ee, now, Tom ne'er told ye!"

I went to Shepheard's, with Kerr's and Dillon's one of the most fashionable of Charleston's taverns, and inquired after the gentlemen from the French islands. The girl seemed a little doubtful, but I re-assured her with another shilling, and she said that there were four, three with families. She took my card and said that we should wait in the hall while she ascertained whether any of them would receive me. In the darkness at the back I found a pair of chairs flanking a small trestle table. I motioned to Benjamin to take a seat and we waited there for her return.

Before many minutes had elapsed she was back. In the manner of a superior servant she said that she had spoken to three of their guests, and that none of them wished to see me, and if I had no further business I might take myself off.

Benjamin and I had already begun to leave when I heard a stream of curses, half-French, half-English, from one of the private dining rooms off the hall. I opened the door and stepped inside.

An old man, gorgeously dressed, stood before a long table set for dinner. A pretty yellow wench cowered nearby. "Out, *crevettine*," the old man was saying. "Out, and take this dried-up *bouse de vache* with you!" The serving-maid fled in confusion. The man turned. "Nearly twenty years I've waited for a decent bit of beef, and they send me something looks like it was scraped off a shoe! Reminds me of the time I —" He stopped, seeming to notice me for the first time. "Now, what do you want?" he asked. Before I could answer he looked at me again and his face broke into a grin. "I'm a Dutchman!" he exclaimed. "Pyrrhus Ross!"

"Pyrrhus Venture these days, Lemuel," I said. "The captain and I parted ways. But where on earth did you drop from? We thought you were long dead in some French jail."

"I near was," said Lemuel Titcomb. "There's a story to that." Before he could begin, the hall door burst open and the innkeeper came inside. Behind him were two husky black men and the housemaid I had left in the hall. The taverner began to apologize for my bothering his distinguished guest, but Titcomb cut him off with a word. "This man is an old and valued friend," he said, the French intonation heavy and obvious where it had been nearly absent from his speech when we were alone. "We do not wish to be disturbed." The man wiped his hands on his apron and bowed his way out, closing the door behind him. Outside I could hear him berating the maid as they went back down the hall.

"Only way to treat 'em," Titcomb observed with relish. "I always figured it'd be nice to be rich. I was right. But you look's though you haven't done too bad for yourself, neither. This'll be your boy, no doubt. The very spit of you, he is." He looked around for his chair. "Sit," he said, and then followed his own advice. He dipped two cups from a bowl of rum punch on the table and passed one to me. "This's liable to be thirsty business," he said. "We may as well get started.

"It's a funny thing," he began, having drained his cup. "After last month I never thought I'd be glad to see a black face again. No, don't rush me. Everything in its time.

"When we was taken off the *Pretty Polly*, all them years ago, I figured it was up for me for certain. You and the captain went off one way, and Frost and me with the Froggies. We was at sea, must've been two weeks more, chained down in their damned orlop when we wasn't working for 'em, and then they put in to harbor. Guess they thought that the ones that had you would have took the *Polly* in and sold her: greased the right palms and such. That evening, the Frog cap'n comes back all excited, unlocks our irons all polite-like, though he don't speak a word of civilized talk, and gets us berths on a lugger bound for Jacmel.

"We was puzzled at first, but that glad to be shut of him that we didn't ask questions. Later we got to know the mate of the lugger, Jerseyman, he was, so we could talk. He said that you had got away with the sloop and all the evidence, so there wasn't any grease, not for the judge nor anybody. Seems the captain was afraid they'd think he'd kept it all, and thought it was best just to get us out of there. 'Course he turned a profit on us anyway, just like happened with you. The lugger was short two hands, and the Frog turned crimp and sold us.

"My friend the mate gave us our chance at Jacmel, and we took it. There was an Indiaman in the harbor there, bound for somewhere south of China. Frost signed on, and that's the last I seen or heard of him.

"Me, I wanted to go home. I took a job with a mule train to get out of town before the master of that lugger found me, overland to Leogane and Port-au-Prince. That's where things began to go wrong." He stopped for another cup of punch.

"How wrong?" I inquired. "And why didn't you come home sooner?"

"I'm coming to that," he said. "There was this woman, you see. Ran a nice little place just back from the harbor in Port-au-Prince: comfortable sort of tavern downstairs, with a few rooms on the second floor. I stayed there when I got to town because there wasn't a Maine vessel in the harbor, not unless you count a little horse-trough of a schooner from York County. Anyway, she took a shine to me, right off. Pretty little thing she was, too, with just a touch of color, and hard-working besides. Only her husband was a drinker and a gambler, mind, and didn't appreciate what she was trying to do. So we used to sit up nights and talk, she being alone a lot, and one thing just naturally led to another." He grinned. "Still does, even at my age: why, one night on the voyage up here, why . . ." He looked down at Benjamin, who was taking everything in, and stopped himself.

"Anyhow, there she was, working her fingers to the bone, and he spending it as fast as it came in. It made a sad story, especially the way she told it, no matter I couldn't understand one word in three. I knew what she meant.

"The long and short is, she gave me a job. I was tending bar and doing a little handiwork by day, and at night I was improving my mind and learning the language." He coughed delicately. I nodded to encourage him to go on.

"She began putting by a little money," he said. "Trouble was, her husband wanted more'n what he was getting. When she told him he had all there was, he took to beatin' her. Finally I couldn't stand no more.

"He come in one night, drunk's a lord, and began to slap her around. I was on the veranda outside their room at the time." He looked squarely at Ben. "Fixing the railing, I was," he said. "Didn't have time to get to it during the day. Anyway, he turned his back an' I let him have it with a piece of the rail.

"Marie thought I'd killed him," Titcomb said. He shook his head. "Kind of thought I had myself. But he was still breathing, and I found he had a pocket full of money. It looked to me like he had hit it big, got drunk, and went home to celebrate by knocking Marie around.

"I took the money, all but a fistful of small stuff, and told Marie to get her savings and an old dress. Then I took her husband and sort of dragged him down the stairs to the kitchen.

"I propped him up in a chair with a half-full bottle of that cheap wine he drank, and went out to the coop for a chicken. I brought it in and cut its throat. The blood got all over everything. Marie came down and near got sick from it. I took her old dress and soaked it so it was good and bloody, and then I built a nice fire in the oven and threw it on. Marie got the idea, and got the ribs and a shank-bone from some veal she had put by to stew. Charred a bit, we figured they'd be good enough. Then we took the money and left." Titcomb smiled triumphantly. "When her old man woke up, he must've thought he'd killed her and burned the body, just like I'd planned. Leastways, he never looked for us that we ever knew."

He took another drink. "We headed north, to a place called Gonaives, and bought a little wine shop." He held out his arms so that we could appreciate his clothing. "Did well, we did, too," he said. Then his smile faded and his shoulders drooped, so that he seemed to shrink into himself. "We was happy as hell. Even talked me out of coming home for the war, Marie did. Then this damned revolution came and spoiled it all."

"Spoiled?" I asked. "How, spoiled?"

"Killed her. They killed Marie, for God's sake, when she never harmed a one of 'em in all her life. And her with a touch of color herself. But that didn't matter. The blacks went crazy, Pyrrhus: pure crazy. They killed everyone they could lay hands on. Men, women, little children. Whites or coloreds. They didn't care. Voodoo. Don't make fit tellin'. I only just escaped myself with my clothes and the money Marie and I had put by."

"It wasn't supposed to be that way," I said helplessly. Titcomb looked at me sharply, and I recollected myself. "When did all this happen?" I asked. "Who were the leaders?"

"It started around the third week of August. Things had been getting worse for months, of course, but we never thought it would go this far. Thought that the mulattoes might get the vote, but most of them was folks. Like Marie. Lots of 'em been to school, same's you.

Some of 'em rich, owned plantations and slaves just like the white planters.

"Didn't hold with it when the governor killed the law about them voting, but I didn't think it was worth killing for. Hell, they wouldn't let me vote neither, and I never lost no sleep over it. There was three of them started it. Boukmann, Biassou, and somebody called Jean-François. They started up on the Great Road through the Plaine du Nord. They got those drums going, and the maroons, the wild men, came down from the hills and killed everybody and burned the plantations to the ground. They say there's a thousand plantations were burned before we left. God knows what it's like now." He stopped to moisten his throat.

Benjamin's young voice broke the silence. "We almost went there, too," he blurted out. Titcomb looked from him to me, and then looked down at Ben with a kindly old-man's smile and patted him on the head.

"Did you, now, Sonny? Did you? Well, you just thank your lucky stars your daddy had sense enough not to go."

❦❦❦ 44 ❦❦❦

THE familiar islands of Casco Bay had closed around astern of the *Charleston Packet* with oppressive finality, signaling an end to my questing. From where I stood they had hemmed in my horizon as straitly as the locks and bars of a prison. There was no longer any escape, no place of refuge. There was only Portland. Portland, Ben, and Sarah. Of course Sarah had responded rather better to the change of prospect than I. Soon after our return she gained a painful mobility with the aid of crutches, so that she moved ungainly through my close-pent world, at once my fellow prisoner and my jailer.

Sarah never addressed to me a word of blame, but neither did she proffer forgiveness. I would not broach the topic on my own. She did not even complain, save to rate herself for her incapacities. Sarah did not ask for help, but I took it upon myself to do what I might to ease her life. I found a house with rooms enough on the ground floor and let the upstairs to lodgers with the understanding that the woman would cook and clean for us.

This one purchase took all my ready money. Still, there was credit to be had, and since young Deering had not found a buyer for my property on Clay Cove, I resumed my affairs almost as though I had never been away. This was ordered as I would have had it in more ways than one. My friends pressed for no explanations, and my connection with Saint Domingue was not widely known. Thus there was no need for me to talk about that unhappy island, nor indeed to recall it to mind, not even at Christmas, when Captain Clapp's account of the burning of Port-au-Prince made Haiti the common talk of all the town. Samuel Stone, of the schooner *Active*, and William McLellan, whose vessel was greatly injured in a gale on the homeward passage, were likewise witness to the massacre. I avoided their company and did not even ask for word of my friend St. Cyr. There was no doubt in my mind as to the nature of his end, and I had no stomach for their tales, or to hear of the fleet of fifty-three vessels that carried refugees to exile in Baltimore. I have no more desire to hear such things today. Even now Haiti's troubles are not at an end, and the news from thence is little changed.

As it happened, the Creoles merely anticipated events in the mother country, and that by scarcely more than a year. In 1792 the French Revolution took an ugly turn, and before the winter was out the king and queen had been done to death, and France was at war with England. Until that time, the people of Portland had been much in sympathy with the republican aspirations of the French, and had widely adopted their fashions in dress and speech. Portland Federalists celebrated Washington's birthday with a supper at Citizen Motley's, with Citizen Fosdick presiding, and Citizen Weeks directed the artillery salute.

To many the commencement of the Terror came as a personal affront. There were bitter arguments in the streets and the coffee-houses over the misdeeds of the Jacobins. With a few exceptions the nabobs were staunch Federalists, siding with their former enemies, the English, and against the Frenchmen they had latterly deemed friends. So profound was the change that even some of the banished Tories were forgiven, so that they were able to return to their homes. Sheriff

Tyng was one. He took up a quiet existence on a small farm in Gorham, being too wise to take part in any new controversy. Like Tyng and many of our neighbors, I held myself aloof and looked no further than my own four walls. War between England and France meant death and suffering for millions abroad, but whatever else it brought, it would be good for business.

Good, that is, so long as we in America remained neutral and so able to traffic freely with both sides. The merchants of Portland responded with huzzahs when Washington proclaimed a policy of neutrality in the spring of 1793, and built three large wharves in anticipation of an expanded trade.

And the trade came. At first the French were content to let us go our way, though we were bound by the treaty of 1778 to come to their aid in time of war, for our military power was negligible. We were far more useful to them as neutrals, carrying the produce of their colonies home to needy Europe. When the English countered with the Orders in Council, which called for the detention of vessels carrying French goods and the forced sale of their cargos, the Paris government sent Genêt to draw us into the war with his intrigues. The French seized our vessels to lend force to his arguments.

None of this had import or interest for me save in how it might affect the rates of insurance or taxes. I was not among the eighty thousand Minutemen Congress called up to enforce our neutrality. This service was so popular that some of our people offered money to obtain a place in the Portland company once it was fully enrolled. My whole attention was given to weightier matters.

War meant that our commonest exports were in great demand, and a dollar shrewdly laid out in Portland would yield eightfold in the islands. I brought Ben into the counting-room to copy out the invoices, so as to learn how it was done. We shipped Maine lumber, boxes and barrels and even frames for houses knocked down ready for assembly, barrels of beets and potatoes and parsnips, onions, fish dried and pickled, meat and corn, soap and candles, with some on nearly every vessel that set sail for the southward and never too much on any one. When a return cargo arrived, Ben had to cope with hogsheads of molasses and brown sugar, tierces, barrels and boxes, puncheons of rum, cotton and oranges and coffee. Sometimes there would be white or brown sugar from Havana, shipped in long boxes sealed with clay, or raw Muscavado from Matanzas, where it is made by draining the liquid from hogsheads of molasses which has been allowed to crystallize. Refined sugar in loaves and cones was a rare luxury, but it passed through our hands on occasion. More common were staples like cotton, rice, and indigo, bought in Charleston and traded for manufactured goods from the mills of Liverpool. Meanwhile the nation damned John Jay for writing the treaty which made prosperity possible.

During the summer of 1795, not long after the death of the venerable Reverend Smith, a deranged sailor jumped overboard from a vessel moored in Clay Cove. The poor soul sank directly to the bottom. A passing samaritan pulled him out and attempted to revive him by rolling the body upon a barrel, which aid he administered so energetically as to put a swift end to the few sparks of life which remained.

The captain came on shore just in time to receive the final pronouncement, which he took calmly enough because, as he observed, the departed had never been of much account to seamen. "If he had," he said, "he'd have jumped six hours ago, and give me time to find another to fill his berth. Not George, the lubber: he couldn't tell ebb from flood, and now we'll miss the tide."

I told the captain that he need not be delayed by the death of lubber George. There was a likely lad I knew who would ship with him for five dollars a month and found; if he said the word I could have the boy here in the quarter of an hour.

"Done," the captain said, and I sent Ben off to Madam Shepard's.

The boys were back in a trice. The shipman took young Shepard aside and soon returned to say that he would sign him. "Five dollars and found, with a month's advance for the boy, less your fee."

The Spanish dollars clinked musically in my palm. Until then I had thought of refusing, of reminding the captain that I had a small interest in his cargo which would bring profit enough. Why not? the weight of the silver countered. The lad was happy; I had got him half a dollar a month more than was current. And the captain was content. Wind and tide would not have waited. I put the coins into my pocket and waved to the boy as he went on board.

Ben watched enviously until I was forced to remind him that he had other work still undone.

From that day I placed cooks, cabin boys, and foremast hands, especially those lately arrived in town, and began to contract for colored labor in the port. It was a profitable sideline. Blacks came to me because I was one of them, only rich enough to live like a merchant; the whites, because I was a man of business and knew their needs.

The following summer I came back from an errand across the new bridge at Back Cove and found my people all in a toss. Plato Darling was then my senior clerk. I took him aside and rated him soundly.

"I took you back when you had served your apprenticeship to be an example," I told him. "Is this your idea of how my store should be run?"

Plato explained that it was Ben who had caused the disturbance. "A schooner come into the harbor this morning after you left and sent a man ashore with a list of things they needed. You know how Ben likes to go on board the ships when he can. He beg and beg, and finally I let him take the stuff off in the boat. He come back all excited. He says the schooner called the *Ranger*, all black crew, bound down east for gypsum rock."

"That's hardly unusual. There's quarries and lime-burners half the length of the coast."

The youth shook his head impatiently. "I don't mean that," he said. "I mean they all was black. Even the captain."

"The captain?"

"Yes, sir. Man named Paul Cuffe, from Westport on Buzzards Bay. Trades to the southward mostly, so Ben said."

"And where is he now?"

"Gone. He sailed when the tide turned. We were hoping he'd stay and maybe come ashore for you to meet him, but he only put in because his beef was bad. Once he had what he needed he left. Shame you weren't here, but I guess Ben'll tell you everything. He ain't stopped talking about him since he come back."

I sent Plato off with a warning to keep better order in future, and to see that Ben minded his work. "Tell him I am raising him for a merchant, and not a seaman," I said. "The sooner he comes to understand that, the better it will be for the both of you."

Though Benjamin remained a concern to me, I soon forgot about the incident in the press of events which followed.

James Deering stopped by with the news that the corrupt French Directory had refused to receive our envoy Pinckney, the man who had arranged the treaty with Spain in 1795. "They think they can insult us because we have no navy," he told me. "And have you heard the latest? They've started taking our vessels again. Worse than before: your old master Ross has lost his brig *Elizabeth* to a Frenchman in the Mona Passage, and her captain writes that he is awaiting trial in Martinico with six others from New England alone."

"How did Ross take the news?"

"Well enough. His paper sank a little until folk saw that he was standing behind the notes, and then it was all right. I'm not ashamed to say I sold off some of mine as it was. He's been sailing too close to the wind for my tastes, keeping up with his friends the McLellans. He's been building a brig or schooner every year now since ninety-one, or was it ninety-two?"

"I can't recall," I admitted. "It's none of my affair. But he has been doing well. The whole crowd has. And as for building ships, I only wish that Congress had done as well. If the frigates they laid down two years ago were in the water today we wouldn't be having this trouble."

"Be a year at least before they're launched," Deering said bitterly. "Hackett's yard in Portsmouth has stopped work entirely to build the thirty-two for the Dey of Algiers. There are two schooners and a brig on the stocks in Philadelphia that they'll be handing over to the pirates as well. Rushing to get them finished, so the Dey can use them to capture our merchantmen next time he gets the notion, when we haven't so much as a two-oared wherry to show the flag! No wonder the French think they can do as they please!"

The French did as they pleased all that year and into the next. By the time the first of our frigates was launched in the summer of 1797, they had taken over three hundred American vessels. In an effort to avert war, President Adams, then newly come into that office, sent Pinckney back to them as one of three commissioners, the others being John Marshall of Virginia, and Elbridge Gerry, since governor of Massachusetts, and for two years vice-president under Mr. Madison. They sailed late in summer and must have arrived in Paris in the fall.

None of this caused the nabobs to take a reef in their plans. Captain Ross laid the keel for a new *Elizabeth* even bigger than the first, and Joseph McLellan built a replacement for the captured *Ça Ira*. A dozen or more houses went up in different parts of the town, including Thomas Webster's fine brick one at the foot of Free Street, and the proprietors of the toll bridge at Back Cove laid out Washington Avenue between Congress Street and the bridge and lined it with Lombardy poplars in hopes of attracting people to build on their land. There were new shops and stores, and an addition to the pothouse as well, because working for the nabobs gave the mechanics and craftsmen a thirst. Much of this building was financed by subscription, or by new crops of notes and bills of hand. Already there was talk of founding a bank in Portland to print paper money for our use, but for the time being bills issued by Ross, the McLellans, or John Taber were held to be as good as any printed in some Boston bank, and near as good as coin.

Jeremiah Pote was put in jail that winter, for murdering his wife with a shovel during a fit of intoxication. It was supposed that he killed her from jealousy, and for a while this led to more speculation and argument than even the French troubles. Poor Pote was bound over until the summer assizes, and was eventually convicted and sentenced to be hanged in August. His health had broken during his long incarceration, however, and he was reprieved until September, and finally died of his illness before he could be hanged.

Meanwhile the commissioners Adams had sent were ashore in France. After their initial meeting with Talleyrand's emissaries they sent coded dispatches to Washington, bearing the insulting news that the French demanded bribes amounting to millions of dollars which must be paid before negotiations could begin.

These demands were not at first made public. Likely Adams foresaw the inevitable consequences, and wanted to give his men a chance to place themselves out of reach before war was declared. Yet he must have felt that time pressed. Late in March he urged Congress to expand our forts and arsenals, and issued an order permitting merchant vessels to be armed in order that they might protect themselves against pirates.

Portland is a seafaring town, and so these measures met with general accord. Certain ardent Republicans argued that the arming of merchantmen without the assent of Congress was illegal, and might result in the crews of such vessels being treated as pirates themselves if they chanced to be taken. The most vocal were the members of the Jacobin society which had been founded here in 1794. They trusted government so little that they elected a new chairman every time they met. Young Joseph McLellan was one, and so were Major Bradish, Samuel Dunn, and John Baker, the saddler from Middle Street. The Jacobins met for supper one night a month in a house on Free Street, and the next week Mr. Waite's new *Eastern Herald* was sure to print a full account of their doings, with arguments against war with France, which they called our wayward friend, and in favor of more restrictive policies toward England. James Deering was friendly with a number of the members, so that he was privy to much of what did not find its way into the paper. He told me that they had had a communication from a Republican in the Congress that accused the President of with-holding the dispatches on purpose, to seduce the people into going to war with the French. The Jeffersonians believed, Deering said, that the truth would force the Federalists to settle our differences with France in a peaceful fashion. Instead it precipitated us into the conflict.

The XYZ papers, with Pinckney's bold reply, came express to the Columbian tavern, as Marston's had by then become known, about two weeks into the month of April. Close upon the rider's heels came further news, that the frigates *Constitution, United States,* and *Constellation* were to be equipped and made ready for sea with all convenient speed.

Of course Benjamin was of an age that the prospect of war was enchanting, and even Sarah was caught up in the excitement. Her eyes flashed at the mere suggestion that it would have been expedient to pay the French rather than to fight them. She would thump the floor with her crutch and argue until sometimes I conceded her point out of sheer exhaustion.

Still I tried to make her see that it was an illogical one. "The French are already on a war footing," I told her. "They have dozens of frigates to our three, and ships of the line as well. Even the English have not been able to defeat them once for all, but can only attempt to blockade them in their ports. We stand to lose much more than we may gain. And even while we argue about defense and tribute, we are giving twenty-six barrels of silver dollars to the Dey at Algiers, with four stout vessels which he will only use to enforce further extortions."

My difficulties with Ben doubled the day that Edward Preble was made first lieutenant on the *Constitution.* Preble was the late brigadier's third son by his second marriage, a man of great force of will, and known and respected throughout the town. As a young man during the Revolution he was taken by the English and imprisoned on the *Jersey* prison ship, where old Sheriff Tyng had found him and nursed him through a dangerous fever; later he served as first lieutenant on board the Massachusetts ship *Winthrop* and earned a reputation for coolness and daring. Since the war he had become a merchant captain of some note. He was also a close friend of James Deering's, and this is where the trouble largely lay.

At the time he was commissioned, Preble was absent from Portland on a voyage to the Antilles. Benjamin went to Deering and besought him to use his influence with the lieutenant on his return to obtain an appointment on board the *Constitution*. Fortunately, like a good friend, James asked first whether the project had my consent and Sarah's. When he learned that we had not been consulted, he refused outright to discuss the matter until it had received the parental blessing.

He respected Ben's confidence, however, and so the first I heard of it was when my son came to me in my office a day or two later. I told him that it was the maddest thing that I could imagine.

"Beyond that," I added, "I had understood that her captain was already appointed. But perhaps you had decided to settle for a lieutenancy instead."

Ben gave me a smoldering look, not unlike one of his mother's. "I will take whatever Mr. Preble sees fit to give me, so long as I get my chance," he said.

I asked him what chance he meant. "A chance you'll never give me," he said. "A chance to better myself."

"To better yourself! Have you any idea of what it's like on a frigate? You'd be lucky to ship as an ordinary seaman."

"Maybe so," he admitted. "But I won't be that way for long. I can read and write and cipher. There'll be vacancies. A warrant. Master's mate, maybe; maybe even midshipman."

"Midshipman!" I exclaimed. "Now I know you've taken leave of your senses. Take a look at yourself, Ben. People like us don't get to be officers."

"Captain Cuffe's an officer."

"Captain Cuffe?" It took a minute to place the name. "That's different. They called your mother's father captain, too, because he owned his own fishing boat. But nobody ever saluted him. And on a frigate he'd have been just another seaman. He never sailed out of sight of land in that boat of his because he couldn't navigate. Calling yourself captain doesn't make you one."

"Captain Cuffe could navigate," Ben said stubbornly. "You can yourself, a little, only you won't teach me."

"You never asked. And I haven't taught you because you don't need to know. There's a lot of things you need to learn, if you really want to better yourself, as you say, and navigation isn't one of them. If you want more than you've got, then pay more attention to your clerking. You're a clerk, Ben."

"Yes," he snapped. "And if you have your way, a clerk's all I will ever be."

"That's not so. Look around. Who do you think this is for? You're going to have to run this place some day. You won't be able to if you spend your youth mucking out the heads on the *Constitution*. You want to better yourself? You'd be lucky if you ended up a cook, or maybe the gunroom steward. That's as close to a warrant as you'll ever see in the navy, Ben." He looked unconvinced. "Besides," I said, "your mother would never agree. She needs you." I wanted to tell him that I needed him, too, but before I could there was a knock at the door. Plato Darling came in to tell me that James Deering was come to see me, and asked whether he should show him in. I said yes, and told Benjamin to stay.

"What do you think of this young puppy?" I asked Deering. "He says he wants to join the navy and be a gentleman like Mr. Preble." I laughed at the idea, and Ben scowled.

"I told him he'd have to work it out with you first," Deering said. "But right now it doesn't look like Preble will be able to accept his commission in any case. His vessel's been taken by the French off Havana. He's a prisoner in Guadeloupe."

"You see?" I told Ben. "That's what you're headed for if you go haring off to sea. Or worse. You've never seen what happens when a man gets hit by a cannonball."

"They won't be shooting at me," Ben said bitterly. "Why should they? I'll just be mucking out the heads, remember? Your servant, Mr. Deering. I have my clerking to do."

It may be that Preble's capture so soon after the announcement of his lieutenancy was a fortunate thing for his career. Overnight he became one of the most popular men in the town, a thing which his own thorny nature had rendered unlikely. When at last he was released by the French admiralty courts, he was given a leave of absence from the *Constitution* to come home and deal with his personal affairs. This occupied him through the months of November and December, so that he was unable to accompany the frigate on its cruise. Instead he was given an independent command, the schooner *Pickering*, of fourteen guns and ninety men. Preble took her on a cruise to the Indies in February, and succeeded so well that he received his promotion to captain in June. Less than a year after his return from Guadeloupe he was ordered to Newburyport to take over the thirty-two-gun frigate *Essex*, which the citizens of Massachusetts had built by subscription and presented to the national government. Even the Quakers, so John Taber said, found this war acceptable.

Certainly it was going well. On several occasions American ships had captured French cruisers, including the *Insurgent*, which was taken into our own navy. The navy's successes meant prosperity at home, because with the French at bay our merchantmen sailed and returned unmolested. Henry Titcomb, the deacon's youngest son, had two brick stores built at Union and Middle streets the previous year, and Captain John Mussey had made enough from his several enterprises to commence a block of stores at the corner of Temple Street. James Deering's row at Fore and Exchange was nearly complete. The McLellans were deeply involved in the Portland Bank, which they had established in a dwelling house on Middle Street. Joseph installed his son Major Hugh McLelland as its first president, and he brought in his friend Captain Ross as a prominent shareholder.

Through investments like this my former master was by way of becoming one of the most important men in Portland. Sarah said that Elizabeth was doing her part to foster that impression: acquaintances told her that Portland dressmakers were seemingly no longer good enough for the captain's lady, who now must needs have her clothes sent down to her from Boston. Portland remained a small town when it came to gossip.

At the same time it was the sixth merchant port in the United States by tonnage, and lived by and for Exchange Street and Clay Cove. Yet in many ways the merchants' Portland was even smaller than that of the ladies. I could not avoid hearing that Ross had been a founder of the Marine Society and a charter member of the Second Fire Society. I heard — never mind how — when he joined the Freemasons' lodge. It was my business to know the vessels that flew his house flag, and those that did not but which he had shares in, his land speculations with the McLellans in Maine and in the back country of New Hampshire and Vermont, and his investment in Ilsley's distillery. In the same way all the men of affairs in the town knew well before it appeared in the *Gazette* and the *Herald* that Ross had been appointed naval agent for the district. The day that I heard the news I was waiting in Salmon Chase's hall when Ross came out of the office. I rose and offered him my congratulations.

The captain seemed genuinely pleased. "Thank you," he said. "It is an honor, certainly, but I think I shall have to be satisfied with that. The opportunities to act under my commission seem limited."

"Limited?"

"Yes; the ships Congress ordered are bought or built, and it is unlikely that a prize would be sent in the far north. They say Captain Preble is for the Pacific, so Portland is not to profit from that connection. Just as well he is fitting out where he is, though. Every apprentice in the city would have been clamoring to sign on with him."

"I know," I admitted wryly. "My son Ben would be gone in a minute if I would let him."

"No different than a hundred others. Perhaps you should let him go: it might be good for his career. You never can tell what will happen. This appointment of mine, for instance. The new secretary of the navy, Stoddert, is from Maryland. Cabot I knew, but not him, and I'm sure he never heard my name until he was nominated. Mr. Adams suggested me, he said. So I owe this post to that dinner we shared at Deacon Codman's, twenty-five years ago."

"I remember."

"You see? You never can tell."

I smiled. "Then if Captain Preble asks Benjamin to dinner I shall let him go."

Ross shook his head. "You don't change," he said. "We see each other so seldom. The price of success, I suppose." He tugged at his gloves and put on his hat. "I'm off to Ingraham's. He's putting that new street through on the west end. Then I must see old Taber. I've plans for a new ship. Three hundred tons this time, bigger than anything the McLellans have got. Beats the *Joseph* by more than thirty tons."

"Have you a name for it yet?"

"*William*, I think; I've got an *Elizabeth* already. I'd call it *William Penn* if it would help pry that Quaker loose from some of his money. He promised last summer to take a third share. Now he's talking poor. As if it mattered: he'll just run off another batch of bills, same as Major Hugh's bank."

Taber's bills built Ross his ship; though he named it *Washington* instead. The melancholy tidings of the general's death reached Portland in January. The day before my birthday the city mourned his passing with a military ceremony, colors cased and drums muffled, the militia smartly turned out and the veterans marching in their regimentals. Billy Hans was there, sober for once and crying unashamed. He stood at the roadside in his coat of creased and rusty blue until a scapegrace apprentice saw fit to make light of him for his tears; an old comrade passing by recognized Billy and took him into the ranks after giving the young rascal a taste of his cane. This was too much for the old campaigner. When I saw him later in the day he was drunk and in the hands of Sheriff John Waite, on the way to the jail. He remembered the one to the end of his days and conveniently forgot the other, so that I guess it all came right in a way.

That was the year that Ben reached the age of sixteen. Of a sudden he was very nearly a man grown, but as remote from me as ever. Preble was gone by way of the Cape of Good Hope to Batavia; he was to return in the fall with a convoy of American merchantmen. On occasion we would hear that thus and so vessel had spoke him, which fact duly appeared in the newspapers along with other intelligences having to do with the war. My son read and reread them until I told him that it seemed that he spent more of his time over his papers than he did at the books which were his charge.

When I complained of this to James Deering, he merely laughed. "Our Mary is worse than Ben," he assured me. "We call my sister 'The Grenadier' because she's as unbending as a ramrod. She won't admit it, but since she became engaged to Captain Preble she searches every newspaper from first page to last for word of the *Essex*. Three days a week you can't even talk to her until the mail boat's in from Boston. I don't know what she expects; he wrote last from Table Mountain, and the chances are that he'll be home before another letter comes.

"Strange about the pair of them. I didn't think she would ever wed. She's been the retiring sort all her life, so far as society is concerned, even if she was rather a Tartar to the rest of us. And Preble! Damn my eyes if he didn't surprise me! A fire-eater when it comes to boarding a man-of-war in the midst of battle, and yet he wrote to me and not to Mary last December. Of course I'm the head of the family since my father died, but I learned long ago not to tell Mary what to do or how to do it. I suppose Edward will have to learn that on his own."

"When do you expect him back?"

"Your guess is as good as mine. Five months to get there; a month's stay in harbor to refit; five months back. Christmas, I should think, with a wedding in the new year. I'll give Mary a send-off to remember: spare no expense, by God! It'll be worth it to have a quiet household. She's to be friend Preble's problem from then on."

"Perhaps not," I reminded him. "If the war continues, she could easily elect to stay at home."

"Don't say that! It would be just like her. Sensible, she'd call it. But I'm looking for news of peace at any time. The French must know that they can't keep on as they have been, not with our thirty-sixes beating their ships of the line like Truxton did to *Vengeance*."

"*Vengeance* was rated as a heavy frigate."

"Frigate or liner, she mounted fifty-odd guns, and *Constellation* fought her to a standstill. The new commissioners have been in Paris since March. They must have heard the news by now, and they won't let the Frogs forget. We'll have peace before the year is out."

Deering's judgment proved sound. In September Adams's envoys agreed to a peace plan under which the United States assumed the responsibility for twenty million dollars in damage claims against the French in return for an abrogation of the 1778 treaty and an end to hostilities. Unfortunately for the Federalists, while the new treaty was ultimately ratified by the Senate, when added to certain abuses dating from the middle years of the administration, it rendered their party sufficiently unpopular that Jefferson was able to defeat them in the autumn election.

Though Jefferson favored economies and fostered the construction of tiny gunboats instead of seaworthy frigates and seventy-fours, it was the Federalists themselves who ordered the reduction of the wartime navy. The Federalists feared that Jefferson would turn the weapon they had forged against their friends in England.

Only nine of our captains were selected for retention when the new president was inaugurated in March of 1801. One of these was Edward Preble, married at last to Mary Deering after a delay occasioned by his health, which had broken during his arduous voyage to the East Indies.

This season commenced the erection of Captain Ross's great house on State Street.

Stephen and Hugh McLellan may be said to have started the fashion with their mansions on High Street. This was then the west side of town, and the land was part of the old Brackett grant which Major Hugh and his partners Robert Boyd and Matthew Cobb, who became so rich he is called "King," bought up and divided. Hugh built a lavish new house overlooking Bryce McLellan's old homestead, Union Wharf, and the harbor. Stephen's was built on a lot across the street, and was only just being finished by the housewright John Kimball.

Few homes even in Boston or Salem may be said to be superior in design or finish to these. Major Hugh's sits on a sort of mound, with an ornate portico at the front. It has a balustrade and fence with carved urns, and a masonry wall around the garden. Matthew Cobb built one just as fine at the head of High Street, and Eben Storer lower down, though his old house had stood only ten years. It was a question of fashion.

So High Street had a fair start on State Street, which Mr. Ingraham had just laid out and fenced. In order that he and Captain Ross should not lose by their investment they found a young architect newly come to Portland and began their own houses upon the land which they had bought.

Mr. Ingraham's house, like Cobb's, was of wood, and sufficiently elegant. Captain Ross, however, determined to build his with brick, like Hugh McLellan's, which was painted with yellow ochre and had a name for being the handsomest house in town. Scarce had he broke ground before the word came by way of Gibraltar that the *William* had been taken near Malta by a vessel belonging to the Bashaw of Tripoli. Of a sudden we were at war again.

The first two years of the war Edward Preble remained mostly in Portland unwell, but in 1803 he was appointed to the command of the *Constitution* and our squadron in the Mediterranean. He took with him from our town as acting lieutenant young Henry Wadsworth, the general's son.

Ben had already heard the news. "I can't spare you," I warned him. "It's out of the question. James Deering says it's only a matter of time before the French are at England's throat again. That will mean more work for us. So don't bother to ask."

"I won't," Ben said.

"Good. Now, how's that new boy working out, the one that's been helping you and Plato? Well enough?" Ben shrugged, which gesture I took to mean that he found him satisfactory. "That's fine, then, because I mean to move you downstairs." Ben said nothing. I picked up my pen and made a notation on an invoice from Carolina.

"It's high time you learned what it's like to work with your back instead of your mind," I told him briskly. "Your mother thinks not, but a little sweat won't harm you. You may as well start this afternoon." I went on down the page ticking off items. Hard labor would be good for Ben; it would serve to keep his thoughts off other things.

I reached the end of the listing before I became aware that Benjamin was not yet gone. When I looked up at him over my spectacles, he turned and went out.

The summer was near spent before Preble had the *Constitution* in condition to cross the Atlantic. I kept one eye on my son all through June and into July, whenever word would come that Preble had hove the frigate down and recoppered her bottom, that he had shipped her guns, or that he was recruiting seamen for her crew in Providence and New York. Ben never said another word about going, and in time I came to believe that my plan had succeeded. On the first day of August he slipped away.

45

A T Sarah's insistence I took her to see General Wadsworth, who was Portland's representative to the Congress, so that she might plead her case to him in person.

"You're going to have to be more explicit, Mistress Venture," the General said when she had told him her suspicions of what Ben had done. "Pray, just what is it that you would have me do?"

"Do, sir? Why, I want you to help me get my son off Captain Preble's ship."

The hero of Bagaduce had gained in girth since he had put his uniform aside. He folded his hands comfortably across his middle and smiled. "I'm afraid you overestimate a congressman's importance. I can't order the commodore to do anything. Oh, I can make a request, and I will, if that is your desire; yet the fact that we are neighbors will carry more weight with Preble than will my office. You could do as much yourselves. Still, it doesn't seem at all clear to me that Benjamin is in the *Constitution*'s company."

Sarah darted a glance in my direction. "Where Benjamin went has never been in question."

Wadsworth raised his eyebrows at me but that was all. "Quite," he said. "Quite. Well, assuming that your son is in fact on board, we still face some difficulties. For example, he might have enlisted under a false name. It is done sometimes, but in the present case I think it is unlikely. He is more apt to have used his identity to gain admittance than to have concealed it. Very well; I put it to you that we find him. Then what?"

"Then we make him come home. Whatever else have we been talking about?"

"Shall I send the sheriff to hale him kicking from the fo'c'sle? My dear lady, we have no legal right to interfere."

Sarah's head jibed around and she eyed the man in blank amazement. "No right? General Wadsworth, we are Ben's parents."

"Just so. I had not fancied otherwise." Wadsworth favored Sarah with a kindly smile and raised one hand to forestall the outburst that was coming. "I can appreciate your feelings," he assured her. "Benjamin is how old? Nineteen? Just the age of my Henry, then, and older than Alexander, both embarked upon the same expedition. Believe me when I say that I experience the same trepidations for my sons that you feel for yours. Against them we may reckon the knowledge that each is acting a man's part, and that they are enlisted in an honorable service.

"For the rest, I will do as you ask. I will write to Captain Preble and tell him what you have told me. I caution you, however, that the matter is entirely in his hands. You are asking that he discharge an able member of his crew on the eve of departing for a foreign station. Likely he believes that he has not men enough already; no captain I ever met was satisfied on that score, and so his sympathies will naturally lie with your son. After all, it is not as though Benjamin were a runaway apprentice, or a servant. No, I misdoubt that yours is a bootless errand,

and were you to bring your Benjamin home, he must infallibly run away again at the first opportunity. In my mind at least it were better to let him go, and then trust in the Lord God of battles to watch over him and bring him safe home."

Now Sarah was but ill pleased with the general's advice, though it seemed to me that it was sound. Benjamin was endowed with a full measure of his mother's stubbornness, and if we brought him home now I knew it would be as Wadsworth had said. Captain Preble was as able an officer as any who held Congress's commission; if so be that Ben was determined to try his fortunes in the navy, he could hope for no better commander. One thing more: Preble was known for a stern and humorless taskmaster, and so it might well be that a cruise with him would leave my son more kindly disposed to our own mild yoke.

Such was the rhumb line my reason drew, off-course, perhaps, but constant in its obliquity. After I had deposited Sarah at home I went on to my store, whence I sent one of the boys to General Wadsworth to say that his kind assistance would not be required.

The true cost of this secret decision none save myself can ever reckon. Not for ten years and more did I confess it to my wife Sarah, so that even after the *Constitution* had sailed a fortnight later she kept hoping for the sound of Benjamin's feet in the hall. Her expectant look whenever she heard someone in the lane outside, and, afterward, her air of sweet resignation, came near to penetrating the resolve in which I had armored my own feelings. I longed to pillow my head upon her bosom and open my heart unto her; but in the end pride and force of habit carried the day, and I suffered my fears in an isolation as sublime and as absolute as that of any bey.

The *Constitution*, together with the schooner *Vixen* of Preble's squadron, was reported at Gibraltar after four weeks' passage. For near a month following his arrival, so we read in the newspapers during October and November, the commodore was employed in chastising the Emperor of Morocco, which petty monarch had been encouraged to emulate the ruler of Tripoli by reason of the small success enjoyed by our forces under Commodore Rodgers and his predecessor the unfortunate Morris. Tidings of how Preble had secured assurances of peaceful intent from the Emperor came on board Rodgers's own frigate, *John Adams*, when it returned home.

The ancients denominated Gibraltar's rock one of the Pillars of

Hercules, and took it for the uttermost limit of the world. So now it might almost have been in good earnest, for once he had passed beyond it into the Mediterranean, news of Preble's doings became ever more rare and belated. Distance, and the winter crossing of the Atlantic, and renewed war between England and that rascally speculator in land and lives who called himself Emperor of the French, conspired to keep us unenlightened for weeks at a time.

The sketchy intelligences that reached us only served to awaken Sarah's liveliest apprehensions. Rumors of warlike preparations in Tunis and among the Algerines appeared sandwiched in between the closing arguments on the Louisiana question and notices of the opening, by Bonaparte and his Spanish minions, of their West India possessions to American shipping. This transparent attempt to weaken our new ties with England would have seemed contemptible had the potential for profit been less enormous. The diehard Francophiles seized upon it and made it a major topic of speculation throughout the season.

The loss of the *Philadelphia* frigate to the corsairs all but drove such lesser subjects from the field. Winter was well advanced when word came that the proud forty-four had run on an uncharted rock in Tripoli harbor late in October, and so been taken despite all that poor Bainbridge and his men could devise. With Tripolitan gunboats on his quarter where no gun of his could bear, he had thrown the ship's armament over the side, choked her pumps, and drilled holes in her bottom before at last hauling down his flag.

Captain Bainbridge was a month in the hands of the infidels ere Preble knew that aught had gone awry. The commodore's published reports were not overly critical, but in his letters home Preble admitted to being distressed beyond description by the incident. James Deering said that he seemed almost obsessed with the desire to bring the bashaw to his knees.

"The old pirate will have small joy of his little victory," my friend predicted. "Edward will find a way to singe his mustachios. His last to Mary talks of little else."

Sarah looked thoughtful. "Wouldn't it be more prudent for him to wait before doing anything? Until more ships could be sent to him, I mean. He has only the one frigate now: surely that isn't enough to take against the forts and the bashaw's whole navy."

"Lord bless you, Sarah," he laughed. "You don't know Edward Preble if you think that he'd sit still while someone else pulls his chestnuts from out the fire. Why, when he was a boy, his father hired a man to dress up like the Grand Turk and pretend that he was come to town to make off with willful little boys, so to teach him a lesson. He hid himself in the next room, you see, and was to come to the boy's rescue, but when the Turk would have come in by the window, Edward snatched up a brand from the hearth and thrust it into his face; the man was so surprised that he ran away, nor ever came back to be paid. No, Ed Preble's not the one to count his foes. He never has been."

"Oh, dear," Sarah said. "I do wish that Benjamin had picked a more careful captain."

Deering laughed. "Careful? What's careful got to do with fighting, if you don't mind my asking? Preble's careful enough when careful's the thing to be, if you take my meaning, but caution won't get the *Philadelphia* back from the Musselmen. And there's another reason that he won't wait for help, even if it's coming. He's too low on the navy list. Anyone that they send would be senior to him, and he'd never allow himself to be superseded while the work's left undone. He'll try something on his own first, and trust to luck to see him through."

Sarah nodded, a little wistfully, I thought. "That's what Madam Wadsworth said when she came to see me yesterday. She had a letter she let me read, from young Henry. He's extremely proud of his commodore, and anxious to distinguish himself."

Deering asked if we had heard from Benjamn. Sarah gave him a wintry little smile. "No," she said. "Our son, I fear, is just as proud as his commander. He durstn't write to us first, and doubtless none of our letters has reached him yet. But Madam Wadsworth's been very kind. She always shares her letters, and she's asked Henry to send word of Ben himself, you see, if there's some reason he can't write to us."

There was an awkward little tremor in Sarah's voice, and though she met Deering's gaze bravely enough, I could see her lips start to quiver. Evidently James noticed it as well, for he suddenly recollected an engagement uptown, and beat as hasty a retreat as the counterfeit Turk's.

Preble accomplished the destruction of the *Philadelphia* by manning out a prize vessel and sending her in under the guns of harbor forts in the character of a distressed merchantman. This was in February; in May he went to Naples, where he arranged the loan of a number of gunboats from the King of Sicily's navy. Not long after he returned to Tripoli and made one last attempt to persuade the bashaw to end the war.

Preble had been authorized to pay as much as forty thousand dollars as baksheesh for the Grand Vizier, such being the custom in that place, and ten thousand more upon the resettlement of our consul. But he confided in a letter to his wife that he did not expect that those terms, nor indeed any reasonable ones, would be acceptable to the bashaw. If they were not, he went on, he would endeavor to beat and distress "his savage highness" until he was minded to make peace.

By the same post we had word of our son from Henry Wadsworth. Ben had been transferred in a draft from the *Constitution* to a gunboat commanded by a lieutenant named Somers.

Sarah contrived to find this at once reassuring and distressing. "Lieutenant Wadsworth says Ben is well and that our men are well treated," she told me. "Still, I can't say that I like the idea of his being with foreigners. The letter said that there were too few sailors in the fleet to man all of the gunboats and so half of Ben's fellows are Neapolitans." I answered that from what I'd seen seamen were about the same wherever they might hail from, and that likely these were no worse than our own. Sarah's disapproving expression did not change. "You may say so," she observed primly. "I just don't think it's right. They are foreigners, after all, and you know as well as I that they don't live the way we do. They eat tomatoes and the Lord only knows what other outlandish things. I wouldn't want Ben getting sick from eating their food. And I'm certain those little boats can't be near as safe nor so comfortable as Commodore Preble's nice big frigate."

"He'll be as safe with Mr. Somers as with Captain Preble," I said as reasonably as I knew how. "Look at the *Philadelphia*." Still she looked unconvinced. "Really, Sarah," I said, "you can't worry all the time, just because Ben might get his feet wet. I won't have it." Sarah sniffed and said that only a heartless and unnatural parent could speak so when his only child was half a world away.

"Unnatural?" I cried. "And what do you call a son who runs off without a word just when he's most wanted? The ungrateful whelp! He didn't think of you then; no, nor does he yet. Not a word in all these weeks. It wouldn't have cost him to have written. Well, I don't propose to sit about while you worry yourself into a early grave. I won't have it, I say." With that I rose and went out, slamming the door behind me.

Thereafter Sarah and I avoided the use of Benjamin's name, and did not discuss the progress of the war. That was the summer that they painted the First Parish church, and in September they shipped a new bell which they had had cast in England. I think it was about a fortnight after the bell was hung that word came of the first attack on the harbor at Tripoli: how our fleet had bombarded the city for a space of more than two hours, and captured three of the bashaw's vessels at the cost of one man killed and a dozen wounded. Jack Grove came in with a newspaper from Boston which said that the *Constitution* had been struck several times by the enemy's shot. One ball, a thirty-two-pounder, came in through an after gunport while Preble was wearing ship and glanced off one of the quarterdeck carronades, missing him by inches. Jack excitedly pointed out a description of Stephen Decatur's fight with the Tripolitan captain, and the treacherous shooting of his younger brother by some coward among the pirates. I affected to show what I thought would appear as a polite interest and gave him his paper back, but I did not fail to mark that Lieutenant Somers's boat had been in the thick of the fighting.

Of course Sarah must have heard this as well. It turned out that she knew more than I; at the time I did not ask, though I saw that she grew thinner and was begun to turn gray. One morning after the leaves had started to fall I was summoned home from my counting-room by the frightened daughter of the woman who helped Sarah about the house. My wife had swooned, she said; another child had been sent to fetch the younger Dr. Coffin, if he would come, but that was about the limit of what she could tell me.

I arrived to find Sarah conscious and sitting up in bed. The woman from upstairs had some salts of ammonia which she was waving back and forth under Sarah's nostrils. Sarah coughed and pushed her hand away.

"Lieutenant Somers and Henry Wadsworth have been killed," she said. "In September at Tripoli. Their boat exploded. Madam Wadsworth says there were no survivors."

I sat down heavily in a straight chair that someone thrust at me. I looked up at the woman with the vial of salts. She was eyeing me speculatively. "Ben?" I managed to ask.

The woman looked to my wife. "There were no survivors," Sarah repeated. "Benjamin is dead. My baby is dead."

But Ben was not dead. The vessel which had blown up was a ketch which Preble had taken from the Tripolitans and renamed *Intrepid*. She had had a crew of three officers and thirteen men on board when she was lost, all volunteers, and our son had not been among them. The casualty list was published surrounded with wide black borders; I read it over twice before I began to believe that the name of Benjamin Venture was not there, and even then I awaited the Boston mails with trepidation for some weeks to come.

Commodore Preble was superseded by Samuel Barron not long after the attack in which Somers and Wadsworth were lost, and he returned home in the spring to find himself a national hero. I met him once at Deering's; he told me that he thought that Ben had stayed on with the *Constitution* after the gunboats had been returned to Naples in October. When the treaty was signed, I began to look for him to return, but the weeks went by and there was no word. Later I heard that Ben had transferred to one of the schooners when the frigate paid off, and that he had taken his discharge in New York. They said that he had taken ship for Baltimore, but all my letters in care of merchants there went unclaimed. I had hoped that that somehow I might recall him to his filial duty, and bring him back for Sarah's sake, but at last I was forced to accept that Benjamin would come home when he was ready and not before.

✤✤✤ 46 ✤✤✤

CAPTAIN Ross hosted a grand reception in Commodore Preble's honor that season in his mansion on State Street. I chanced to walk by after darkness had fallen. From within I could hear music and laughter, and light from hundreds of candles reflected off the polished silver and cascades of crystal. That one evening furnished grist for the gossip mills of Portland for a month and more.

Ross had designed from the first that his great house should be talked of. This he achieved in baronial fashion. Sections of the house were torn out and rebuilt several times to reflect developments elsewhere in town, or some new whim of Elizabeth's. This happened so many times that at the end I doubt if the captain himself could say how much it had cost. The curious jog to the moldings on the portico, which has always troubled my eye, may be laid to one of these changes. No expense, folk said, had been spared. There was crown glass in the windows and the reeded pilasters, sprigs and shells and the stairways had been crafted by the most-approved ships' carvers in the town.

The French wallpaper was widely admired, but their other imports drew less applause. One of my neighbors, a joiner who worked for the Radfords at the Sign of the Mahogany Bureau on Union Street, explained why.

"Portland ain't good enough for 'em," he grumbled. "They got to send to the Seymours, up to Boston, or to Philadelphia, or to England. Ain't we got men enough right here in town? 'Course we do: there's Ben Ilsley if they don't like our work, and the Haskells, and Joseph Very, and Joseph Lindsey, John Haggett, and Sam Ward, all on the same street. They could take their pick, and not one of us but could use the custom." I asked him whether it might be a question of taste; that perhaps our people had lagged behind the latest mode.

"Hell," he said, "you should know better'n that. They got to have a drawing or something to order from in the first place. Sheraton's book, most likely. We got one right in the shop, and if what you want ain't in it, if you can describe it we can build it. No; I'll tell you what it is: it's meanness, pure and simple. They'd best learn to spend their money here to home, 'stead of sending it off some place else. If they don't, time'll come when there ain't any, and they'll go down with the rest of us."

In April the house of John Taber and Son gave notice that they could no longer meet their obligations. A new issue of Taber's bills failed to find acceptance, and the old Quaker was reduced to dunning those who owed him money in an effort to satisfy his creditors. When he went to Samuel Hussey, Hussey paid him in his own old notes.

Taber objected. "Friend Hussey," he said, "thee knows that those bills are good for nothing."

"I understand so," Hussey replied. "Thee, Friend, should have made them better."

Taber's collapse was felt throughout the town. It may be that

Joseph McLellan held a quantity of the worthless bills and that this brought about the decline in his own fortunes which began about this time. Certainly McLellan had close ties to Captain Ross, and Ross was said to have had as much of Taber's paper as anyone.

We had the news of the British blockade of the continent of Europe not long after. By coincidence there was a great eclipse of the sun almost the same day. Thus, said the philosopher, the world was made, so that certain signs come before certain events.

I had a notion, however, that there was opportunity in the midst of troubles, and had a scheme for stepping into the vacancy left by the firm of McLellan and Brown. They were suffering from Joseph's failing fortunes, but they had done well with a shipment of black and white beaver hats and some thousands of dollars in textiles, goods formerly brought from Europe by way of Boston. The jobbers there exacted high prices for the things our own vessels brought thither, but Portland was become large enough that this procedure was no longer essential.

I went to Deering's first, but James told me that he was too deeply involved with other matters to be able to take on a new enterprise.

"It's a good idea," I urged.

"I know that," he said. "I'm just not in a position to do it." He thought for a moment. "Ross could be your man. I'm not sure how much cash he can raise after this Taber thing, but he still has his ships. There's one in port right now, come to think of it. From what I hear he hasn't much on the fire right now, either. You could be doing him quite a turn."

"I don't owe him anything," I objected.

"Who said you did? You need a partner. He needs a good stroke now to keep him from going under."

"Is it that tight?"

Deering shrugged. "Who can say? I know he was deeply involved with Taber, and that some of his other affairs have not gone well. He should be ready to deal."

"You're right," I told him. "But it will have to be on my terms." Having made the decision, I was impatient to put it into execution. I left Deering's and went directly to my former master's place of business.

The chief clerk there informed me brusquely that Ross was not in.

Something caught his eye, and he turned away. "You there," he shouted. "You, boy, what's-your-name! Yes, you, Whittle! If I catch you staring out the window one more time today I'll see you on the other side of it for good!" Quite obviously, he had forgotten about me entirely, so that when I spoke again he did not hear me properly.

"When will the captain be back? Not today, certainly." He scrutinized me rudely. "Look," he said, "what's your business with Captain Ross? You can tell me, you know; I'm in charge here when he's out."

I informed him that I had a proposal to make, but that it was for his master only. "Suit yourself, then," he said. "Likely he's gone home, but he'll be back in the morning. You can come back then."

I left there in no very good humor, but without any clear intent. At the corner I brought myself up short. I turned round and with firm, decisive steps I walked back past Ross's store to the foot of State Street and on up the hill to the captain's house.

I knocked at the big front door. At first the woman who answered was dumb with surprise but she recovered swiftly enough. " 'Ere, now," she scolded. "No servants 'ere. Kitchen's round back." She shook her head disapprovingly, as though I were a particularly dull child, and she started to close the door.

Elizabeth's voice came from somewhere within. The maid turned to answer, and as she did I saw Elizabeth herself. I stepped up onto the threshold and said that I was come to see Captain Ross on a matter of business. Elizabeth waved her servant aside.

"My husband is not yet returned," she said, "but I expect him presently. Do come in; we shall wait for him together."

She led me through the drawing room, which was done up in the highest style with mahogany furnishings and candelabra of crystal and blue Bristol glass. Although it was not dark enough that they were needed, she paused to light the candles in a pair of ornate girandole mirrors on either side of the door at the far end of the room. Her movements were practiced and graceful, and as she reached upward I found myself becoming acutely conscious of her classic form. For an instant I saw the reflection of her eyes in the convex glass. Without a word she put the tinderbox aside and continued on into the next room.

One wall of the chamber was lined with books. There were a gaming table and chairs and one of the English forte-pianos that were just replacing harpsichords in fashionable circles. Elizabeth laid her hand upon it fleetingly as she walked by and sat down before a delicate English secretary with turned legs and a high top. She smiled graciously and indicated a nearby loveseat expensively upholstered in striped satin.

Elizabeth was still a remarkably handsome woman. She wore a dress cut in the French manner. The color matched that of her eyes, and set off her creamy skin and the golden tones of her hair. I shifted uncomfortably on the stiff little sofa. Elizabeth's lips curved slightly in a long slow smile.

Hastily I got up and crossed the room to where her portrait hung above the carved mantel. Elizabeth laughed delightedly. She reached out and patted the satin cushion I had vacated.

"Come back here and sit down," she demanded, and weakly I obeyed. Elizabeth smiled again, very much the great lady. "Now, then, Pyrrhus," she said, "you must tell me how we can help you. William and I are always pleased to assist an old friend. What did you have in mind? Not a loan, I hope: that could be a problem just now. Still, I'm sure that my husband could find you a posting as a clerk, or make room for you in one of his enterprises."

Her bland self-assuredness chafed me. "Actually," I told her, "I had come to give the captain a chance to invest in one of mine." That brought Elizabeth up short. I could not resist a smile of my own. "People say he's not done well of late," I said. "I thought I might help."

"You thought you might help?" Elizabeth's laugh had a brittle sound, like breaking glass. "Look around you," she said imperiously. "Go on, look. Does it look like we need help? Least of all from you! What makes you so special?"

"I don't know," I said. "Maybe nothing. But when I worked for the captain, he used to value my opinion."

"Well," she told me, "he doesn't need it now. He always was too free with you. People used to talk sometimes. I won't have it said that my husband takes advice from some jumped-up nigger cook. You hear me? I won't!"

There was a long silence. I got slowly to my feet and bowed to Elizabeth. "I believe I understand," I said. "I shan't trouble you again." I walked back through the elegant drawing room to the hallway, where, frozen in time, the wallpaper image of Captain Cook dazzled the polychromed islanders with a few worthless handfuls of beads.

Lacking a partner, I was unable to purchase textiles enough to achieve the stroke that I had planned. I went ahead with a smaller quantity on my own. These found a ready market, and the cash that they brought in saw me through the bad times that followed. Still, I have come to regret the lost opportunity, and the hubris that led me to bait Elizabeth as I did.

Captain Ross survived Taber's fall, and through the winter he seemed to do so well that I began to doubt what Deering had told me about his position. In the spring Ross appeared as an important backer of Captain Moody's observatory, which was built by subscription upon the summit of Munjoy's Hill to provide an early sight of approaching vessels.

There was a sort of carnival spirit to Portland that season despite the ominous events of the preceding year and the increasingly worrisome news from abroad. Even the Reverend Mr. Kellogg, the popular minister to the Second Parish, was so caught up in speculations that he had begun casting about for an assistant. A painter was come to town with a sixty-foot panorama of Preble's bombardment of Tripoli, and at times it seemed like all of the city were lined up to pay their twenty-five cents to view it. Preble's death in August, from a stomach disorder brought on by overwork, called forth another prideful spectacle, which Ross and the other nabobs gathered to plan. The commodore's funeral procession, marching through the streets four abreast, took more than an hour to pass.

While this was going on, British cruisers had begun to dog our coasts, so close that their topsails could be seen from the observatory. They were guarding against vessels bound to or from French ports in Europe and the Indies. H.M.S. *Leopard*'s attack upon our frigate *Chesapeake* in June was yet unavenged, and the British searched even fishermen and coasters with a view toward impressment. Many of Portland's shipping houses had men taken, and Captain Ross lost his fine new brig *Commodore Preble*, which was sent down to Halifax prize court and her master and crew left to get home as best they might.

From ill-advised economy the Republicans had sold off most of our smaller warships and neglected the rest, so that when Jefferson complained to the English they paid him little mind. All along the coast folk clamored for him to take some action. The nabobs were loudest of all.

Jefferson's answer was the Embargo, which passed into law late in December.

The Federalists in the Congress made certain that word of the act reached us before it became effective. Near every vessel fit to take out of sight of land was hurriedly fitted up, and crews worked night and day to get cargoes aboard and under hatches. As quickly as one was ready they warped it out and brought another. Some that did not sail in time hoisted anchor in defiance of law, but the British made this a hazardous occupation. They knew the government would be unlikely to make many difficulties about men impressed off a smuggler. Heavy bonds were laid on coastwise travel, and gunboats and revenue cutters were sent to enforce their collection. Trade slowed to a trickle and died.

Eleven of Portland's great mercantile houses failed within a month that winter. The McLellans were broken. Old Joseph owed money to his sons and to Reverend Kellogg, who was his son-in-law, and all of them owed banks in Portland and in Boston. The banks called in their notes, and Kellogg, so folk say, threatened to sue McLellan so that he could pay his debts. The ailing Joseph was forced to sell his house, and one by one the rest of the McLellans tottered and fell. Lemuel Weeks went down, and Captain Tucker, Woodbury Storer, and Joseph Ingraham. Grass grew green on the wharves.

For some months Ross managed to stave off the disaster that had overtaken his friends. The candles burned as brightly as ever in the windows of his great house, and for a time it looked as though he might come through the crisis unscathed. The candles gave the impression that all was well, yet even while they burned they were consuming the substance of the captain's fortune.

But a month or so before the Embargo was succeeded by the Non-Intercourse Act the firm of William Ross and Company announced that it was forced to suspend payment on its debts. The office and warehouses were sold, as were the few vessels which still hoisted the house flag. His back-country land was auctioned off together with his shares in the Portland Bank and the wharves and Henry Ilsley's distillery. The sale raised cash enough to satisfy Ross's creditors, and his mansion and his household goods were saved.

Elizabeth took to her bed before the auction, it was said from mortification. The talk was that it was only a matter of time before the bedding was sold from beneath her. Stephen McLellan had lately been forced to surrender his house to some Boston merchants for the sum of two thousand dollars. They had turned it into a boardinghouse, so that Stephen was now a tenant in his own parlor. It seemed certain Ross and Elizabeth would soon meet a like fate.

The captain came to my counting-room one fall afternoon after I had sent my people home. He let himself in the front door, and at first I thought it was one of the clerks come back for something he had forgot. I heard his footsteps outside the office, and looked up, and there he was.

I was amazed at his careworn appearance. Ross seemed to have got twenty years older almost overnight. I started from my seat in surprise, but he waved me back.

Ross took a chair, somewhat gingerly I thought, and let himself down into it as though his joints troubled him. I waited silently while he examined the room. I had nothing to be ashamed of; the furniture was substantial and well made though the mahogany grain was paint and not veneer. Ross smiled absently. "You've done well," he said at last. "Well." Then he looked me directly in the eyes and announced that he was come to bid me goodbye.

Nothing could have shocked me more. "Goodbye?" I blurted. "Where are you going? Surely not to the Ohio country!" Joseph McLellan's grandson was considering such a move, and folk said that if he went then Joseph and Joseph, Jr., might be going with him.

Ross laughed. It was a dry old man's laugh, but it brought back echoes of better times.

"No," he said. "Not Ohio. I can't see myself that far from tide-water. No, I'm going to sea again, and things being what they are, I thought I should stop here and thank you before I go."

"Thank me?" I repeated.

Ross nodded. "Elizabeth's not been well these six months," he told me. "Not since the sale. She's a proud woman, as both of us have reason to know, and the shock of it was too much for her constitution. I thought for a time that I might lose her. She's some better now, but one night when she was poorly she told me how you came to help and she sent you packing."

"I didn't exactly make it easy for her," I admitted. "Besides, it was strictly business."

The captain shrugged. "Elizabeth wouldn't have cared. What she worries about is appearances. I could have gone with her brother after the war. Still could, save for Elizabeth. She says she won't be run out of Portland; if she leaves, she wants it to be when she's rich enough to buy the town if she'd fancied it."

"You were damned near rich enough to do just that before the Tabers went down," I told him.

He laughed again. "You think so? That's how Elizabeth wanted it. There never was a day I wasn't on the edge of ruin, not for ten years now. It was all paper, using one loan to pay off another as the notes came due. The house took all my ready money and everything I could drain off from my business. You want to know something? It never has been finished, only the parts that people see. The changes Elizabeth made after it was begun, and her damned furniture, and her parties and the dresses she wore at 'em, I never could afford to finish off the upstairs. Elizabeth didn't care: she said that it didn't matter so long as people saw what she wanted 'em to see. She figured that if they thought we were rich they wouldn't look too close. By and by, if I was lucky, I'd be as rich as folk thought. Maybe she was right, too. Maybe if it hadn't been for the war in Europe and the Embargo people would have gone right on thinking that Taber's bills was money, and I'd be rich now instead of broke."

"I've got a little hard money," I offered. "You could buy a share in that brig Deacon Jewett's fit out to go to Guadeloupe for coffee. He might ship you for captain if you bought a plank or two, and you could pay me back out of what you made."

"You should know better than try to help me," Ross chided gently. "It never works. But I'll thank you for the offer even though I don't need it. Elizabeth's brother has sent me enough money to take a schooner to Carolina for cotton. They say it will sell for a dollar a pound in Europe." He shook his head. "Forty years later, and I'm just about where I started." He rose and clapped his beaver atop his head. "Well, that's said. I'm off on the morning tide."

I knew I did not want him to go, but could think of no way to stay him. "What course have you planned?" I asked hurriedly.

"To Charleston first, of course," the captain replied. "Then to Falmouth and England, to join the fall convoy for the Baltic." He held out his hand. "Goodbye, old friend," he said.

I took the proffered hand and assured him that we should meet again.

But in this I proved no true prophet. Jewett's brig *Rapid* arrived in the Indies too late to buy coffee of the French. Instead they shipped cotton and sailed to join the same convoy Ross had mentioned. When the *Rapid* returned a year later, after a series of adventures in Memel and Riga, the captain's schooner was long overdue. Jewett said that Ross had never entered at Falmouth and to the best of his knowledge he was not among the seven hundred sail in the convoy. Elizabeth kept to her great house after that and denied all callers until she died in June 1811.

47

A T Elizabeth's death the *President* and *Little Belt* had but lately given notice that eventual war with Britain was certain, and so when her brother Robert came to settle the estate, he stayed only long enough to sign over to her creditors the title to the great house on State Street. He hired workmen to crate up the contents and ship them on to his home at Saint Andrews in New Brunswick. Pagan took himself off next morning on a cramped little coaster bound for Eastport. He had no longer any ties here, and as a colonel of militia he could not afford to be in any enemy country when war came.

It did not come until the summer of 1812, and then the Federalists called it "Mr. Madison's War" and blamed the partisans of Jefferson and the West. The Portland Rifle Company and the Mechanic Blues paraded in full dress, and privateers were manned and fitted out, but few men of consequence were eager to fight, and those who were willing would as lief had fought Napoleon as England. The trade in English manufactures was too important to interrupt. In fact, our soldiers were dressed in English woolens, and slept under English blankets.

The authorities let it be known that British goods consigned to American merchants would not be molested by the regular navy. The privateers were not a party to this understanding, and cargoes were ferried across the St. John River at night, or shipped in vessels disguised as Swedish neutrals in order to deceive them. England needed American gold for the European war, and so occasionally British men-of-war sailed to protect American smugglers from their countrymen.

This comfortable arrangement pertained for a twelvemonth at the least. The war seemed very far away, though our navy had lost the fine frigate *Chesapeake* to the *Shannon* no farther off than Boston Light.

Not many weeks later a fisherman from Pemaquid came to Portland with news of a British armed brig and a "Swedish" trader off Seguin. The government brig *Enterprise* was then in our harbor, and word soon spread along the waterfront that her commander was of a mind to fight. There was no keeping my people at their work then, and I let them go even though it was Saturday and not nearly late enough for me to close my doors.

Seguin lighthouse is just within view of the observatory upon Munjoy's Hill, and the next morning a crowd gathered at an early hour to discover what Captain Moody could learn of the expected battle. At half-past eight he reported that smoke might be seen, as of cannon. Several hours passed, when the crowd, apprehending that the Englishman had escaped, began to disperse. I was on the point of going home to dinner when Captain Moody announced that he saw smoke once more, and a cheer went up notwithstanding it was the Sabbath. The smoke continued thick until near four o'clock, but of course it was Monday before we knew the issue.

Captain Moody kept a watch until the two vessels came in. They tied up at Union wharf, where all who wished were allowed to go on board the captured brig *Boxer*. The triumph was marred by the announcement that both captains had died of wounds suffered in the battle. Later, they were interred together in the cemetery on the hill.

From that time the British admiral in Halifax was uncooperative. Our coastwise trade with Canada was made more hazardous, and when any of our people were taken they were transported across the sea to the infamous prison at Dartmoor. In 1814 he dispatched the *Bulwark* seventy-four to burn the shipping at Saco, and sent a fleet to take possession of Eastport. A score of vessels with four thousand men then went on to despoil Bangor and Hampden. A small force of militia hurriedly brought together to protect the crippled corvette

Adams was routed. The ship's officers, a Captain Morris and Lieutenant Alexander Wadsworth, brother to him who fell at Tripoli, destroyed the *Adams* to prevent her capture and brought their men overland to Portland.

None of this stopped the stealthy traffic between Maine and the Maritimes, and late that season a man from Freeport came to me with a parcel he had got from a merchant in New Brunswick.

"Didn't give no name," he said, "nor did I ask for one. Just said to put it in your hands, was I comin' this way, and I said I would. Good day to ye."

I own I had no idea what the thing might be. It was securely done up in several layers of paper and tied with string. I found my penknife and cut it open.

Inside I found a book, a slender volume bound in morocco. It was Voltaire's *Candide*. When I opened it, a slip of paper fell out and landed facedown on the floor.

I bent down and picked it up. The note was headed with Saint Andrews and the date. There was only one line. It read, "You were to have this," and was signed with the letters R.P.

I recognized the binding then.

I called for my coat and cane, forgetting that the boy was at work on the new battery at Fish Point with the rest of my people. I fetched them myself and went out, locking the door behind.

Alone I toiled up Munjoy's Hill to the eastern burying-ground. Elizabeth lay there beneath a stone carved with urn and willows. A few feet away was another on which the captain's name was graven, though his bones must wait their resurrection somewhere between Georges Bank and the Azores.

The slates were gray and cheerless, and the afternoon no better, hinting at the winter which was to come. I sat down upon the stump of an old pine which had stood until struck by lightning in a great storm some five years before, and took *Candide* from my pocket.

It must have been that Pagan was so affected by his sister's death that he was unable to examine her things until some time later. Likely he had found some note from Ross among her papers. Or perhaps it had been she. In a curious way it did not seem to matter. They were both at peace now; I was sure of that, and as I held the book I could feel an inner harmony such as I had not known in many years.

From my seat there among the dead I could see the topsails of the

Bulwark looming above the islands. She was the flagship of Commodore Milne's blockading squadron which was become bold of late, and sided daily up to the lighthouse when the tide was making. There was a guard of eight men at Portland Head to give warning, Fort Preble and the lime-washed blockhouse upon House Island called Fort Scammel, and the two works at Jordan's Point, but the committeemen were not satisfied. They had laid out a battery for a half-dozen forty-two pounders at the eastern extreme of the Neck. Near the whole of the populace had turned out to work on it, rich men and ministers shouldering their tools and marching through the town with the rest. The new fort was not of sight beneath the brow of the hill, but I could hear the ring of hammers as carpenters built platforms for the cannon. This time Portland would be defended.

The knowledge was reassuring, for I had no wish to witness a repetition of the panics of the last war. Or was that all? Was Portland merely a place where I had come to work and then to garner the fruits of my labors? I gripped my little book more tightly and smiled. Was that so very little, after all? Throughout all his misadventures, Candide had found nothing more satisfying than to be allowed to tend his garden.

I got to my feet and started down the hill. I felt that I had experienced a revelation of sorts and I was eager to share it with someone. Sarah, I thought. Sarah would understand.

With that first awakening came another. I came to realize how deeply I had been hurt by Ben's departure. I had hardened my heart against him rather than acknowledge the pain, bolstering my pretended indifference with the idea that I should have word through the Navy Office in our capital if my son were taken ill or wounded. I was still wrestling with it all when I had word that Washington had been taken by a British army, and the public buildings put to the torch. There was every chance that Ben might die without my knowing, and now no way for me to reach him.

I suppose that I might have made inquiries as I had when Ben was newly returned from abroad, but the mails had been deranged by the presence of the enemy on our coast. Governor Strong had given orders that the whole of the militia should be called up, with seven thousand men for the defense of Portland. All the specie in the banks, and valuable stocks of goods, were removed to the country. Ten thousand dollars' worth was reserved for public use. The troops were all encamped about the Neck by the middle of September. Redoubts were thrown up with guns mounted on likely eminences and sentinels placed all along the shore. An old man who had been a captain in the Revolution mustered a company of sixty exempted men to assist with the guard, and I took my turn among the rest.

The troops that came were no worse than any other men, though through idleness and rum they caused a certain amount of mischief. They were held for about two weeks and then sent home. The town repaired what damage they had wrought and returned to its usual pursuits. Three months later the war came to an end.

In many respects the peace was an unsatisfactory one, not the least to the Federalists, who were caught unprepared and lost what few offices they had. The treaty left unresolved the issues for which the war had been fought. To me it mattered not a jot. What I wanted was peace, and word of Ben.

The summer of 1815 was a hectic one, as merchants raced to regain markets lost during the war. The Russian trade was open once more and George Tate's son was an admiral in Kronstadt. There was China and the Indies. In every port it was the same. Ships too slow to put to sea in wartime, hulks laid up since the Embargo with barrels on their mastheads, were fitted out as quickly as the men-of-war paid off. An emotional reunion, perhaps, on a run ashore, and the men were off once again. Months went by, and the sailors came and went, yet Benjamin was not among them.

Lacking Sarah's comfort, my faith had certainly failed me at the news of the murders at Dartmoor, where our men were imprisoned for months after the war had ended. We had no names at first, but the grisly things I had heard preyed upon my mind; how the prisoners were starved and beaten, and finally how they had been fired upon by order of the inhuman Captain Shortland, for the crime of asking for bread instead of hard biscuit with their rations.

Dozens of Americans were killed or wounded, and in my dreams they all wore the face of my son. At last there came a night when I could not sleep at all, but lay awake with my imaginings while the moon rose and set.

All this time I had spared Sarah the worst of the reports. Now she stirred beside me and touched my arm, asking what was amiss that I had not slept. "Nothing," I said, and she drew back. Impulsively I reached out and seized her hand in the darkness.

"It is Benjamin, my dear," I told her. Haltingly I began to pour out all of my fears for him, and from these I passed on to my regrets. I told her how sorry I was that I had not been more approachable. "I fear I was no father to him," I said. "We just never got on. Perhaps we might if I had been more like Jack Groves, but somehow I never knew quite what to say. A poor father," I repeated, "and not much of a husband." Sarah silenced me with a finger laid across my lips. We embraced then, and I found rest.

Sarah and I waited together. In the waning weeks of the year we heard from a Quaker merchant who fancied he remembered Ben as mate of a vessel from New Bedford; he had taken the liberty of writing to a friend in Newport who would make inquiries.

The letter came late in January of 1816. Billy Hans fetched it around as he often did. He laid it on the desk before me and went to help himself to something for the easing of his rheumatics. When he had done, he put the decanter down and came and stood over me. His breath smelled of the rich aroma of Admiral rum. "There she is," he prompted. "Bain't you goin' to open her?"

"No," I said at last. "Not here; not without Sarah." She was now become my full partner in life, and I would no longer seek to distrain her of either joy or sorrow.

We broke the seal together, Sarah and I.

I unfolded the letter and gave it to her to read. She began well enough, but then her voice faltered and she indicated that I should continue. I skipped over the conventional salutation to the place where Ben's name first appeared.

"I am sorry to report," the Quaker had written, "that your son is no longer resident in these parts, having embarked last month for Freetown on the coast of Guinea with his wife's father, Captain Paul Cuffe." It took me a moment to recover from the surprise of hearing that Ben had married. I found that I still thought of him as the boy he had been when he left home. I cleared my throat and went on.

"The girl's name is Phoebe," I read. "They were wed soon after your son returned from the western lakes, and the neighbors say that Cuffe had no idea that Benjamin had family living, or he would have insisted upon your permission to the union. He is a member of the

Society, and held in good repute; Phoebe is said to be a mild and dutiful child. I make no doubt but what you shall hear from him yourself directly upon his return."

I sat holding the letter. After a time Sarah put her hand on mine. I covered it with my other one.

Two months, I thought. Less; six weeks. I had even seen the notices of Cuffe's departure. The newspapers had been full of his plan to transport people of color from America back to Africa. The English had tried it twice in the last century with indifferent success and had been forced to import an army of Jamaican maroons to keep order. The scheme was no longer to my taste. I had taken notice primarily because I recalled Cuffe's name from the time he had come to Portland years before.

The changes I had gone through and my recollection of Benjamin's bitterness had never led me to believe that he would do such a thing. It seemed the very height of folly. Perhaps it was precisely because I had once been that sort of fool that Ben was forced to go. We had never got on well, that son of mine and I; now I realized that it had been our similarities and not our differences that had come between us. That and my pride, my need to appear strong and unerring. Ben was following the course I had charted and stubbornly followed until I had nearly brought about the deaths of the two people I most loved. He would not be aware of the fact any more than I had been until a few moments earlier, but he would follow it with the same destructive single-mindedness as I very nearly had done. Unless someone showed him the truth of it: likely he would never come back, never understand or forgive, but I had to tell him what I had learned since he had left.

Of course there was no question of taking Sarah. Her health would not have withstood the voyage, let alone the stress of the equatorial climate. The idea of separation and the risks it would entail were difficult for me. Still, they would have to be borne. I swallowed hard and searched for the words to explain.

"I must go to Africa," I began, groaning inwardly at how clumsy it sounded. Sarah's fingers tightened on mine.

"I know you must, dear," she said.

It is a two months' crossing from New England to the factories of the African coast. Most of our traders were already set forth so as to be gone again before the rains which may start as early as the end of May. It was already March when I put to sea with a captain from Piscataqua who was bound to the Coromantees to trade cheap cloth and rum for gold dust and elephants' teeth. I had some small store of goods I had purchased as gifts and the like; for a fee the captain agreed to touch at Freetown on his way.

Of the passage itself the less the better. The weather was cold even for March and more than commonly windy, so that I spent the better part of my days in the cabin with the smell of mildew and bilgewater. The damp clung to my bedclothes and penetrated my joints, making them stiff and painful.

After fifty-four days of this it was no small relief to hear that the lookout had raised the cape. Later I came on deck to watch it rise from the sea: Lion Mountain, the Serra Lyoa of the Portuguese, who were the earliest Europeans on this coast. It was the first of Africa that I saw, as it was often the last for the shivering wretches who despite the best efforts of the king of England's navy were still stolen away in great numbers by the panyarers and slavers.

We ran north and east with the land to starboard. The wind brought me its scent, febrile and heavy with the odors of growth and decay. Land birds wheeled overhead. I saw branches still in leaf bobbing in the swells, southward-bound in the current. Gradually the water itself took on the color of African clay carried to the sea by the rivers down which slaves had traveled in chains since the days of Henry the Navigator.

That same alluvial silt, too finely divided to be visible should I dip a tumblerful from the ocean, was the substance of Africa, no less than the solid mountain on my right hand. It would fetch up on some foreign shore, a barren and inhospitable one belike. Not all the fleets of the world could bring it back. Particle by particle it would collect, this one from Africa, its fellow from some other place. In time there would be soil enough for a few blades of grass; perhaps, with tending, a garden.

After noon the next day we had worked around into the harbor and lay waiting for the shore boat to come and give me leave to land. My possessions were all on deck to be examined and the duty paid. I used the time to look about.

Freetown stands on the site of the settlement named Granville Town which the Temne chiefs destroyed in its infancy near thirty years ago. The shore is rocky, beat upon by an ugly surf, and in consequence the governor had built a fine wharf to reduce the hazards attendant upon going ashore. The estuary has a good bottom and serves as the base for the British squadron charged with suppressing the slave trade. The freed slaves, known as recaptives, they send ashore. They live in Freetown or in clusters of grass huts under the eaves of the forest. On the west side of town are the dwellings of the Kroo boatmen and laborers.

The ground rises back of the harbor and provides a good view of the city. I saw more thatched roofs than shingled ones, but the best houses have dormers and verandas and are lime-washed against the heat. The streets are well laid out and sufficiently straight. Gangs of black men wrestled great blocks of granite into place on the main street where it came down to the water. Nearby I saw foundations for warehouses and a large three-story building of gray stone which seemed but newly completed. It was grand and impressive, but I was surprised that in all this town there was no church nor meetinghouse, no public buildings at all save this one.

The harbor official came aboard then to ask his questions. He must have come to an understanding with my Piscataqua captain, for when he had done my few things were lowered into his boat. No sooner had I begun to climb down after them than I heard the order given to hoist anchor and set sail for Accra.

The governor's man waas no more disposed to waste time, for he set his pullaway boys to rowing before I was fairly settled on my sea chest. There was no apology. The man sat stonily in the stern sheets without the slightest evidence of interest. Beyond him the brig braced her yards up sharp for the beat back out into the open Atlantic. I looked over my shoulder at Freetown and the gray granite structure which stood over it.

"Government House?" I asked the tidewaiter. His eyes flickered at me and then away.

"Jail," he said.

At setting foot on shore I was met with an overwhelming Babel of native dialects: Foulah, I fancy; Kroo; Ibo; each one equally incomprehensible, mingled with what I took to be Arabic of a sort and with all the tongues of Europe and the Indies. The tidewaiter had slipped away. I stood hesitating on the quay with my goods piled all around me. There was no American vessel in the anchorage. Captain Cuffe, then, was already returned home, unless indeed he had sailed the *Traveller* to the watering place or to one of the factories up-river. Some clerk of the governor's should be able to tell me that, and direct me to the place where the colonists Cuffe had brought might be found.

First I had to get to the governor's. The curious were already starting to pry at my chests. I would need two men at the least with barrows, and possibly a guide, one who spoke English. Surely there was someone in the crowd who did. I took out my pocket handkerchief and mopped my brow. The heat and confusion were more than I had expected.

"Master wish?" said a voice. I saw a grinning youth, very black, harlequined out in a purple coat, fawn-colored nankeen breeches, and a pair of thread stockings filled with holes. He was tall and rather stout. I should have called him well-limbed save that his legs were short in proportion to his body and somewhat crooked withal. "Master wish?" he repeated patiently.

"Don't call me Master," I told him: "My name is Mr. Venture. What is your name?"

"However Master wish. I am Jemmy, son old King Jemmy."

"Well, Jemmy, I am looking for my son, Ben Venture, from America. I need someone to take me and my things to Government House. Do you know where that is?"

"Sure, Jemmy know plenty too much. You give dash, Jemmy fix."

Jemmy held out his hand. I put a coin into his sweaty palm, and then, because he seemed to expect it, another one. Jemmy flashed a smile and put them into his pocket.

He picked three men from the crowd to carry my things. "Now we go," he said. "This way."

It turned out that the governor lived in a rented house at the foot of Water Street, just a few rods up from the quay. Jemmy halted our caravan before it. "Governor House," he said proudly. I gave him a disgusted look. He smiled back. "Governor House," he repeated. I told him to wait.

The governor's secretary received me cordially. Governor Mac-Carthy was at the King's Yard, he told me, where the recaptives were landed. He was overseeing construction of the new stores. He was a very busy man. Doubtless I had seen the gangs working on the stairs up from the wharf, the breakwaters, and the Commissariat.

I explained my errand. His face grew long when he heard Ben's name. "We have many sorts of people here," he told me. "Creoles, maroons, Nova Scotia blacks who fought for the king in your revolution, white whores shipped here from London. Ministers and lay preachers: entirely too many of them for my taste. Church of England, Baptists, Methodists. Mostly well intentioned, but they don't always get on."

"What are you trying to say?"

"His Excellency is a very active man, a practical man. He is trying to make Freetown self-sufficient. He has little enough to work with and too much to do, just keeping things going from day to day. Keeping people fed, keeping them from each other's throats. The recaptives sometimes find it hard to understand that being free does not mean that they are free to take what they want. As a result, the governor does not always have time to devote to the niceties. Your son found this difficult to accept. He objected because the recaptives could not be treated as full equals. He did not approve of native children being brought into white homes where they might be raised as Christians. He called it slavery because they were expected to work for their keep. He made enemies among the missionaries by telling them this. Perhaps in the grand sense he was not wrong, but he had no patience, no sense of priorities. He would not compromise. When he saw how things were he left."

"Left?"

"Yes: he went up-river to live. It was soon after the *Traveller* sailed for America, about six weeks ago, I should say. He said he was going to found a Province of Freedom of his own. I wish him luck. None of the others who came with Captain Cuffe would go with him. I'm afraid they seemed glad to see him go."

"He took his wife with him?"

"Yes. A few of the recaptives, one or two locals. Porters from the village. The usual. I believe there was a child: his son. That would be your grandson. If you intend to join them, I should lose no time. This place becomes very nearly an island once the rains come. You'll need porters of your own, a guide. Perhaps I can help."

"Thank you," I said. "I already have one, I think. A fellow by the name of Jemmy." My mind was not really on our conversation. A grandson!

"Jemmy," the secretary said. "Yes, well, I suppose that he will do. He has brass enough, certainly, and I seem to recall that he was the one your son hired. He claims to be related to the local royal family, for what that's worth: I don't pretend to understand how they reckon those things. Sons of mother's brothers on the mother's side, or some silly such. Good luck, then. Feel free to call back if there's anything else you need."

I went outside to Jemmy. He was sitting in the shade of the house, and sprang to his feet when he saw me. He spoke harshly to the porters, who rose and stood beside their burdens.

"Mister wish now to go to Ben-Venture house?"

"Yes," I said. "Why didn't you tell me that you knew where my son had gone? You could have saved us time if you had."

Jemmy shrugged. "I got plenty too much time. You not say, go Ben-Venture house. You give plenty dash, Jemmy fix."

"How far is it? Will we need supplies? More porters?"

"Far. Seven, ten, oh, plenty too many day. Jemmy fix. Jemmy fix for Ben-Venture, too. Jemmy know damn-all. You give plenty dash, Jemmy go see Gree-Gree man, fix all, sure." Jemmy held out his hand eagerly.

"No," I said. "We'll go to your Gree-Gree man together."

Jemmy led me across a stream and through a thick wood to the distance of perhaps half a mile, where we came upon the Negro town. In different places among the houses I saw rags stuck on poles. At the foot of each was some object, a rusty cutlass, a copper basin green with verdigris, a bottle containing reddish liquid. Jemmy signified that I should not meddle with them lest I offend the people: they were Gree-Grees, set there to protect the town from devils.

The author of these charms was wizened and fifthy. Jemmy called him forth from his hut and treated him with great deference, for old age is respected, and I think that the Gree-Gree man was the most ancient human I have yet beheld. He reached within his hut for two little carven stools and seated himself on one of them. He indicated that the other was for me. Jemmy squatted upon his hams. The old man said something in a quavering voice.

"This very great wizard," Jemmy told me. "Know plenty too much. He say you come for find something."

I nodded. "Tell him what we need," I said. "Tell him that I wish to start tomorrow."

The old man spoke again before Jemmy had begun to translate what I had told him. "Gree-Gree man say he help you. First you give dash, then he help." Jemmy bent forward. "This very good. You give plenty dash, old man help. Plenty no trouble if old man say go. He take money, black sand for gun, rum, maybe calico. He talk to spirits, make medicine. Tell future. Plenty good. Man from village not go else."

The price for a divination was set in what the natives call bars, Spanish milled dollars being one dollar the bar, so many yards of Manchester cotton, thus much rum. I gave the old man what he asked. He took the trade goods into his hut and emerged again with a skin bag. The hair had come off it in patches. The wizard sat down again and spilled the contents of the bag upon the ground. There were beads and musketballs, cowries, nuts like horse chestnuts called cola, knuckle-bones, and three small dried pieces of anatomy about which I did not care to speculate. As he studied the arrangement his face grew grave. Jemmy asked him what was wrong. The old man spoke, and Jemmy translated.

"Gree-Gree man say spirits not happy. Plenty too much trouble. You need fetish. He make. He say, you give dash for fetish?" I told him yes. This sort of dodge was only to be expected. Jemmy smiled broadly and relayed my answer. The old man paused thoughtfully before continuing. I saw him steal a surreptitious glance out of the corner of his eye.

"Gree-Gree man say you hire three guard, nine porter. He say you come back tomorrow for fetish, he have for you here. You give dash, he pay men. Then three day later you go."

I thought for a moment. "Twelve men is too many," I said. "And I don't wish to wait. I mean to go tomorrow. Tell him that."

Jemmy spoke with the diviner. The old man's answer was shrill. "He say, must be so," Jemmy insisted. "He say he see you give plenty dash, hire twelve man, go in three day."

"Jemmy," I said. "I am a sort of Gree-Gree man myself. You tell him that. You tell him that I have read the signs, and that I think he has made a mistake." Jemmy did. The old man eyed me suspiciously and made to sweep his magic bones and bits back into the bag.

"Tell him to stop," I said. "Tell him that if he looks again he will see me pay for six porters and two guards. Tell him he will see me give him plenty dash to start tomorrow. Tell him that if he looks he will also see that if he does not accept I will go down to the camp of the Kroomen, to their diviner, and hire men there, and also a different guide. Tell him to look, and ask him if that is not what he sees."

Jemmy translated. The old man stared doubtfully at his little pile of magics. At last he grunted, and Jemmy sat back on his heels in evident relief. "We go tomorrow," he said.

Jemmy found me a place in Freetown to rest for the night. Next morning we presented ourselves at the Gree-Gree man's palaver house and found that he had provided all that I had asked. There were also a number of canoes to set us across the Bunch River, and so out of his territory. "Gree-Gree man not want people know how you bamboozle him," Jemmy decided.

A relay of canoes from the next village brought us to the mouth of the Rokel River, across from Bance Island. "Ben-Venture live up river," Jemmy told me. "We walk now, ten, twelve day. Canoe not go because this Borgne-Fesse country."

"What," I asked, "is Borgne-Fesse?"

"Not what. Who. Borgne-Fesse very big man, rich too much, got too much woman. Also very bad. He read book, learn to be rogue so well as white man. He take money from trader, take plenty musket, go up river. Trader suppose he work for him, buy slave, buy ivory, send to trader at Bance Island. Then trader rich. Borgne-Fesse buy slave, give slave musket, then got him army. Not send to Bance Island. Got him place like king, ten, twelve, oh, many day up-river from Ben-Venture. Trader not go up, he not come down."

Lacking canoes for river travel, Jemmy advised that we should strike inland. That way we would avoid the worst of the mangrove swamps, which he assured me were very bad. This seemed to be a reasonable suggestion, and we set out on the course he proposed.

The first day was, indeed, very bad, but then we passed from the mangroves into a hardwood forest of what is called African teak. In Freetown I had heard that there was a scheme afoot to cut these trees for use in shipbuilding, and that at least two saw mills had lately arrived for that purpose. Thus the new governor thought to find employment for the people and a source of money to replace the trade in slaves. We were long in the forest. I asked Jemmy how much farther it continued, and always it was the same. Another day, two. After that we would be in the grassland, and then we would make better time. With each day that went by my doubts became more mature.

I was nearly ready to call Jemmy to account when the trees began to thin out. At last we stood on the edge of a marshy savanna. It reminded me of the wetlands near Black Point south of Portland, on a larger scale. "Three day to cross," Jemmy said. "Then one day more through forest on other side. Ben-Venture house there."

Despite the fact that we were evidently nearing our goal, I noticed that night that Jemmy was acting unsettled and nervous. When I asked him what was wrong, I got evasive answers. It made me wonder once more whether I had been wise in my choice, or if the governor's clerk had not been trying to warn me, and I resolved to sleep lightly thereafter.

It was well that I did. Two nights later we made our camp on the further edge of the grassland hard against the forest. An hour before dawn I woke and found Jemmy rummaging about in my baggage. He had a bundle in his hand and a cutlass belted around his waist. One of the muskets the guards had brought leaned against a tree just out of his reach. I rolled over quietly and pressed the muzzle of my pistol against his left temple. Jemmy froze. I could see his eyes go wide with fear.

"I hope," I told him, "that you have a very good explanation for what you are doing." I clicked the hammer back to full cock. At the sound he collapsed, whimpering.

"Not kill Jemmy," he pleaded. "Men not go on, you kill Jemmy. All Borgne-Fesse fault anyway. Borgne-Fesse he very bad man, too much wicked. Also not like Jemmy. Bastard he say Jemmy no come he country no more. I think, Mister, he plenty close find Ben-Venture, he not get lost now. I think I go now, Borgne-Fesse not find. That way no trouble."

I assured him that there would be plenty of trouble if he did not live up to his part of our bargain. "The only reason I do not kill you now is to give you the chance to fulfill your promises. If you lead me to my son's house, I will pay you as I said I would. This foolishness will be forgotten. If you are afraid of Borgne-Fesse, remember that you yourself said that he lives many days from this place. I and my pistol are here. Who do you fear most?" Jemmy rolled his eyes at the ugly little muzzle and swallowed uncomfortably, but in the end he agreed to go on. I had given him little choice.

When we got the caravan under way, I had Jemmy's wrists bound as a precaution, and I positioned myself close behind him with my pistol in easy reach. The morning passed, and when we had walked some miles without incident Jemmy began to seem more assured. We forded a stream. There was a trail on the far side. Jemmy let out a shout. "Ya-hoo!" he hooted. "This way. Very close now."

The trail led up a gentle rise. At the top was an opening in the forest, five or six acres in extent at the least. The trail ran down the middle to a cluster of thatched huts. "Ya-hoo! Ya-hoo!" Jemmy said again. "That him Ben-Venture house! Jemmy find! Jemmy no bamboozle Mister! Ya-hoo!" He plunged ahead down the path with the rest of us running behind.

The huts were ranged in a circle. Mostly they were built after the native fashion, but one of them was larger. It was shaped like houses at home and had a proper door and curtained openings for windows. Poor Ben, I thought. Already you have discovered that you cannot be perfectly equal in all things if you wish to set an example.

We were in the midst of the houses when I realized that we had seen none of the inhabitants. Jemmy must have had the same thought. He stopped directly in front of Ben's house and looked back at me uneasily. The guards fingered their firelocks. For a long breathless moment we stood, straining our eyes and ears.

Like jungle beasts they were there: ragged men with guns and spears. They came from the huts in twos and threes. More sprang from the tall grass that surrounded the little court. I looked back and saw a solid rank of them form across the path. We were trapped.

The door of Ben's house opened and four robed Moors emerged. The lined themselves on either side of the opening. I glimpsed a tall shadowed figure within. "Borgne-Fesse!" Jemmy hissed. He ran forward two steps and prostrated himself.

Borgne-Fesse limped as he came forward into the sunlight. He wore a shirt of fine white linen with white trousers and a vast three-cornered hat, extravagantly looped and laced. His skin was a shade lighter than that of any of his companions, and his features less broad. He prodded at Jemmy with his callused foot. "The last time you are here," he said, "I tell you, don't come back. True?" He prodded Jemmy again, and I heard a muffled assent. Borgne-Fesse nodded. He seemed pleased. "I say then that if ever Jemmy come back here, he shall die. Also true?" Jemmy said nothing. Borgne-Fesse kicked at him disinterestedly. "True?" he said again. I heard Jemmy agree in quavering tones. Borgne-Fesse looked at the men ranged about him. "Borgne-Fesse don't lie," he said. It was a death sentence. Before I realized what was happening he snatched an ornate flintlock dag from the belt of the nearest of his retainers and fired it into the back of Jemmy's head.

Incontinently one of my guards threw his firelock to his shoulder and pulled the trigger. The cheap Birmingham trade gun, foul with rust, flashed and exploded. He dropped the wreck and went to his knees, blood from his ruined face streaming between his fingers. From reflex I began to reach for my own weapon, but I stopped when I saw the muskets of Borgne-Fesse's men leveled at my breast. Even if I should get my hand on the grip, I had not drawn the charge nor changed the priming since we had crossed the stream. It was less than an even chance that the pistol would fire. While I hesitated, Borgne-Fesse took a swift step crabwise and relieved me of the gun. He stepped back again. One of his lieutenants had disarmed my remaining guard. He drew a long curved sword and stood over the wounded one. He looked to his master for permission. Borgne-Fesse considered briefly and gave a curt nod. The lieutenant swung his sword. There was a meaty sound and the guard's head rolled on the ground at my feet.

I gagged; recovered. At last I found my tongue. "What have you done with my son?" I demanded. Borgne-Fesse regarded me with bland curiosity.

"Which of these was your son?" he inquired. "Not that one: nobody claim Jemmy. I know him already many years. Guard? He is better so. He dies anyway."

"No," I said. "He was not my son. My son owns this house which you have taken. My son is called Benjamin Venture. I have come from America to see him."

Borgne-Fesse's expression softened. "Benjamin Venture?" he repeated. "I don't kill Benjamin Venture. I think you come with me." He took me by the arm and led me lurchingly through Ben's house, and out the back door. At the edge of a bit of plowed ground I saw three mounds of raw earth. Rude crosses had been erected on them. Already a few tentative vines and creepers were taking root in the soil, reclaiming it for the jungle. One of them twined around the markers. As I looked upon the graves, I felt a sudden constriction in my throat. I could not breathe. Then the sun grew dark and I felt myself falling.

I slid into a long fevered dream peopled with all those who had been closest to me through the years of my life. Sarah was there, dressed in black, and old Fitzgore, but mostly there was Ben: Ben lying dead in the foreign land because I had failed him yet again, Ben as I imagined him grown to manhood. Ben as a boy on the wharf at Charleston, Ben crying in his cradle. He went on crying for a long time, and I can remember the desperate feeling it gave me to know that I would not reach him in time.

I struggled, but there was someone holding me down. I heard Borgne-Fesse speaking. That was impossible. Borgne-Fesse in Portland? I had to get to Ben. Borgne-Fesse said, "Hurry, now, you leave. He wakes up. Go quickly. I call you if I want you." I heard departing footsteps. When I opened my eyes, Borgne-Fesse and I were alone in my son's house.

The slaver smiled. "How is it with you?" he asked. "You are dead already two days. Sometimes I think you don't come back, but see! Here you are. That is good, I think: not to die easy. Me, I don't die easy, too. That is how I get my name. Now I think I am entirely too bad to die. The devil, he thinks I take his job. How about that? Here, you drink some water, then we talk."

He raised me up gently and I drank, supported by his arm. When I had done he settled back one-sidedly in his chair. I looked and saw that he was propped up on the left with a pillow. Borgne-Fesse saw my confusion and laughed. "Yes," he said. "Once, when I am young, I turn my back on a man I think is my friend. It is mistake. Still, I am too quick for him: he cut me with his sword, but I turn in time and I kill him. French doctor saves my life, but even he cannot put back what is gone. So now I am Borgne-Fesse. Is good name, I think. I have already many others, but this one I like best.

"Now you know about Borgne-Fesse, as much as anybody. I say I know all about you, too. You are very talkative corpse. I listen all day, all night, all next day. I know you come long way to talk with son. I know why. So now son is dead, wife of son is also dead. What you do now? You tell Borgne-Fesse, perhaps he decide to help."

"Do?" I asked bitterly. "What is there for me to do but to go home? And why would you help me? You killed Jemmy for bringing me here. Were you some sort of friend of Benjamin's?"

Borgne-Fesse laughed. "Friend?" he said. "No, I am not his friend. Your son think I am the devil. He says I am not Christian, I sell my brother. I say to Ben, who buy him? If white Christian don't buy, Borgne-Fesse don't sell. Then he say I am bad man, got too many wife. What he want? I say. Let six wife starve? I am rich, make wife very happy. Clearly, is good. Besides, I got bad luck; all wife barren. Nobody else want. Anyway, I need new one for children. Is very Christian, like king in England. I read in book, also maybe in Bible. So I say, got four Muslim wife, three country wife, maybe now I take one Christian wife, is good. Ben he say I am very bad man, not Christian.

"Freetown full of Christian, argue all the time. This one say that one wrong, that one say, no. Do what I say or you will go to bad place when you die. Jemmy, he Christian. Where you think he go?"

"What about Jemmy?" I said. "Did you kill him because he brought me here?"

"No. I kill Jemmy because he is thief, bamboozle everybody. He want to be king, rich like me, so he sell my land to Ben. He cheat you, too. Take twelve days to get here from Freetown. I send you back in seven. By river is less.

"Jemmy bring Ben here maybe two month gone. I come, I meet Ben, I say I let him stay because he is good man. Also I got plenty room. Mostly I stay up-country at fort, don't come down without good reason. Send slaves overland to Spaniard. So I go away, but I steal one of your son's people so mine don't think I get soft when I let him stay."

I shook my head. "No wonder he thought you were the devil."

"Sure. Look, I tell you something. Ben, he was plenty good man, but he one fool. See governor at Freetown. He very good man. He say to native, we build city in your country. He say to slave, you free man. He tell settler, this your city, be brother to slave, be brother with native. He give them food, he tell them what to do. He don't ask them what they want. Same as before. White man talk, black man do.

"Ben don't like this. He also don't like it when colonist from Nova

Scotia treat recaptive bad. Ben too good man. He say Freetown not free. So he go to Ibos off slaver, say come with me, I treat you like brother. He bring them here, work hard all day like slave, give them food he buy, tools he buy. He don't give them guns, no powder, no rum. Don't need guns, he says. Country people know we don't steal slaves, don't bother us. They don't because I say no. But Ben say I am bad man because I trade guns for slaves, rum for slaves. Sometimes just take. But one day long time ago I am stuck in mud at river. I start to sink. People from village pull me out. They don't like me, but they pull me out. Otherwise no powder, no guns, no rum. Still, Ben say I am bad. But Ben get sick, wife get sick, baby get sick. Ibo take all he got, go away in forest. I am bad man, I hear he get sick, I come to help, only I am too late."

"So was I," I told him. "I was too late all along."

Borgne-Fesse looked at me long and carefully. "Is too late, as you say. But how if not? What you do then? Is long trip from America. Once I go so far as Cairo. I think maybe is further to America. You just want son to say he forgives you, maybe?"

"No," I said. "What good would that have done? Perhaps it would have made me feel better, a little, but no, I think I would not have come this far for that.

"I came because I wanted him to know what I wasted a lifetime in learning. I hoped that I might spare him some of the mistakes I made. That was part of the problem. I never admitted to myself that I might have been wrong. Instead I kept looking for a place where things were different. It never occurred to me that what needed to be different was me." I frowned. "My wife nearly died because I tried to take her to a place like Freetown. Ben was just a boy.

"And I shut them out of my life because I was not all that I wanted to be. That I blamed on the time, and the place, and the people. I didn't explain, and I never asked Sarah or Ben what they wanted. I just did it, because it was for their own good. Benjamin grew up hating me for it. Maybe that's the reason that he couldn't get along with the governor." I paused and rubbed my hand over my eyes, down my face. I needed a shave.

"When I heard that Ben was come here to Africa, it was like living through the bad time all over again. It's over now. I've failed, and it's over."

"How, over?" Borgne-Fesse asked me. "You are not dead. I think maybe you don't die for a long time."

"No," I said. "But Ben is, and his wife and son. When I heard he had a son, I thought that, maybe, this was a chance for me to undo some of what I had done."

Borgne-Fesse laughed. "You think you do better this time, is easy to find boy. Not so long ago I think maybe I adopt boy myself. Is cheaper than new wife. Also I got Dinka soothsayer who tell me all wife barren until I make pilgrimage to Mecca." He rose and limped to the door. He said something in a language I did not understand. Then he turned back to me with a smile. "I tell them, go and fetch boy," he said. "He is orphan; parents die from fever. Boy almost die, too, but I am lucky. I get here just in time." A bare-breasted woman came into the room. Propped on one hip she carried a small child. "I think you like this boy," Borgne-Fesse told me. "His father was a very good man."

By the time I was fit enough to travel the rains were nearly upon us. Already there had been intermittent showers, some where the rain came sheeting down for as long as half an hour. Borgne-Fesse decided that I must go to Freetown by canoe if I was to go at all. He made all the arrangements. When I offered to pay him, he refused to accept the money.

"Jemmy pay," he said. I looked at him in dismay.

"You robbed a dead man?" I asked.

Borgne-Fesse shrugged. "Why not? He don't spend it anyhow. I get money, get land back, get all the things you bring from America for dash. All you get is small boy and canoe ride. My people think I bamboozle you plenty. Is good. Also, men from Freetown join me. Also good. You take grandson to America, nobody think Borgne-Fesse get soft. That very good."

I shook his hand and stepped gingerly into the canoe. In front of me my grandson slept in the arms of his nurse. The steersman barked a command, and we set off down the river.

Five days later we crossed the estuary to Freetown. There were heavy clouds up-country, and the river was dark and swollen. Its color came from the African soil washed down by the rains, down from the highlands, past the King's Yard, past the wharf, past the anchored ships and so out into the wide world beyond. That was the way of it. Somewhere, someday, each atom of clay must come to rest once more. Was it chance, or something higher, that chose its destination? I could not say. Some, perhaps, would be whirled away again by wind and weather. The world would be no better for their passing. Some would stay, bound together by the green growing things they supported and nourished, until at last they themselves became a part of the substance of the new land.

Such was my hope for my grandson. So it remains. The oarsmen drove the canoe around the breakwater, and the dugout rocked in the chop at the harbor mouth. The change in motion woke Ben's son from his sleep. He began to cry, and I reached out and took him from the native woman. I held him up so that he could see past the cape to the open ocean.

"Look there, William Benjamin Venture," I said. "On the other side of that ocean is our home."